PRAISE FOR
## Baseball's Great Experiment:
## Jackie Robinson and His Legacy

"A rich, intelligent, cultured history. Fascinating."
—*New York Times*

"Tygiel merits great praise for his valuable and comprehensive book. Tygiel's intelligence, insight, and exemplary yet equitable candor command one's attention: not a facet of civil rights issues passes without his incisive commentary. His book is the definitive statement."
—*Library Journal*

"Not merely is this book long overdue, it turns out to be a book that was well worth the wait. It is comprehensive, perceptive, balanced—and into the bargain it is eminently readable, written in plain prose that is generously sprinkled with anecdotes."
—*Washington Post*

"The best baseball book of the decade."
—*Journal of Sport History*

"This is a remarkable book, comprehensive and fascinating."
—*Chicago Sun-Times*

JULES TYGIEL is a leading authority on Jackie Robinson. He is the author of the acclaimed *Baseball's Greatest Experiment: Jackie Robinson and His Legacy*. He lives in San Francisco, where he is professor of history at San Francisco State University.

# The
# Jackie Robinson
# Reader

Perspectives on an American Hero,
with contributions by Roger Kahn,
Red Barber, Wendell Smith, Malcolm X,
Arthur Mann, and more

## EDITED BY JULES TYGIEL

A PLUME BOOK

PLUME
Published by the Penguin Group
Penguin Putnam Inc., 375 Hudson Street, New York, New York 10014, U.S.A.
Penguin Books Ltd, 27 Wrights Lane, London W8 5TZ, England
Penguin Books Australia Ltd, Ringwood, Victoria, Australia
Penguin Books Canada Ltd, 10 Alcorn Avenue, Toronto, Ontario, Canada M4V 3B2
Penguin Books (N.Z.) Ltd, 182–190 Wairau Road, Auckland 10, New Zealand

Penguin Books Ltd, Registered Offices:
Harmondsworth, Middlesex, England

Published by Plume, an imprint of Dutton Signet,
a member of Penguin Putnam Inc.
Previously published in a Dutton edition.

First Plume Printing, March, 1998
10   9   8   7   6   5   4   3   2   1

For permissions to reprint the material herein, please turn to page 280.

 REGISTERED TRADEMARK—MARCA REGISTRADA

The Library of Congress catalogued the Dutton edition as follows:

The Jackie Robinson reader: perspectives on an American hero with contri-
    butions by Roger Kahn . . . [et al.]; edited by Jules Tygiel.
    p.    cm.
    ISBN 0-525-94096-0 (hc.)
           0-452-27582-2 (pbk.)
    1. Robinson, Jackie, 1919–1972. 2. Baseball players—United States—
Biography. 3. Afro-American baseball players—Biography. I. Robinson,
Jackie, 1919–1972. II. Tygiel, Jules.
GV865.R6J33 1997
769.357'092—dc20
[B]
                                                              96-34800
                                                              CIP

Original hardcover design by Jesse Cohen
Printed in the United States of America

BOOKS ARE AVAILABLE AT QUANTITY DISCOUNTS WHEN USED TO PROMOTE PRODUCTS OR
SERVICES. FOR INFORMATION PLEASE WRITE TO PREMIUM MARKETING DIVISION, PENGUIN
PUTNAM INC., 375 HUDSON STREET, NEW YORK, NY 10014.

# CONTENTS

# ACKNOWLEDGMENTS

Ironically, although Jackie Robinson ranks among the most celebrated figures in twentieth century America, he still awaits his Boswell. Robinson himself participated in two autobiographical efforts: *Jackie Robinson: My Own Story*, written with Wendell Smith in 1948 and *I Never Had It Made*, co-authored with Alfred Duckett in 1972. Several other books deal primarily with Robinson's baseball years. Arthur Mann's *The Jackie Robinson Story* (1951) gives a good account of his early career. *Wait Till Next Year* (1960) written by Carl Rowan with Jackie Robinson's cooperation is an excellent biography of Robinson through the 1950s. (Unfortunately Rowan would not allow an excerpt to be included in this volume.) My own book, *Baseball's Great Experiment: Jackie Robinson and His Legacy* (1983), although often described as a Robinson biography, is really a social history of the integration of baseball, which looks primarily at Robinson's baseball years as part of a larger story. In *Jackie Robinson: A Life Remembered* (1987), sportswriter Maury Allen collects reminiscences about Robinson. A recent attempt to deal with Robinson's life in its entirety, David Falkner's *Great Time Coming: The Life of Jackie Robinson, from Baseball to Birmingham* (1995) is deeply flawed. Princeton University professor Arnold Rampersad is currently working on an authorized biography of Robinson.

In *The Jackie Robinson Reader* I have attempted to craft an alternative biography of the Brooklyn Dodger star, exploring the outstanding events and issues of his life through a broad variety of writings about him. The selections include Robinson's own biographical and newspaper writings, articles from both the black and white press and periodicals of the 1940s and 1950s, two previously unpublished documents relating to his breakthrough, reminiscences by other participants in the events described, and recent scholarly works. I have tried, wherever possible, to eliminate unnecessary repetition from these sources. The introductory sections alert the readers to any errors that appear in the individual articles.

Many people assisted me in compiling this collection. Rachel Robinson graciously allowed me to reproduce many of her husband's writings. Peter Williams suggested Milton Gross's wonderful description of the last game of the 1951 regular season. Lee Lowenfish, Marty Adler, Dick Updegraff, Bob Edwards, Robert Creamer, and numerous others helped me to track down authors and/or their family members. My agent, Peter Ginsberg, moved extraordinarily quickly to actuate this idea. Tsuyako Uehara at Dutton Signet answered permission inquiries. My editor, Deb Brody, offered enthusiastic encouragement throughout. My wife, Luise Custer, offered her unquestioning love and support, to which, as always, I reply in kind.

# INTRODUCTION

Extraordinary lives often reveal ordinary truths. Jackie Robinson was born in 1919 and died in 1972. He crammed into these brief 53 years a legacy of accomplishment, acclaim, controversy, and influence matched by few Americans. He was, even before his historic baseball breakthrough, an athlete of legendary proportions. He won fame and adulation as the first African-American to play in the major leagues in the twentieth century, launching an athletic revolution that transformed American sports. He garnered baseball's highest honors: Rookie of the Year, Most Valuable Player, and first-ballot election to the Hall of Fame. More significantly, Robinson became a symbol of racial integration and a prominent leader in the civil rights struggle of the 1950s and 1960s. Yet Jackie Robinson's half century among us illuminates not just the contours of an exceptional life, but much about the broader African-American experience of those years.

Jackie Robinson was born in Georgia in the heart of the segregated South, the grandson of a slave and the son of sharecrop farmers. While Jackie was still an infant, his father, Jerry Robinson, abandoned the family. His mother, Mallie, seeking a better life for Jackie and his four older siblings, joined the post–World War "great migration" of African-Americans out of the South. Most blacks traveled to the eastern metropolises: New York, Philadelphia, Washington, or to Midwestern manufacturing centers like Chicago and Detroit. Mallie Robinson, on the advice of a brother, headed west to California.

African-Americans were relatively rare in California in the 1920s. Although Mexican-born blacks had figured prominently in the early settlement of the region, by the early twentieth century blacks accounted for only one percent of the state's population. Those who lived there confronted a pattern of discrimination common to the American West. Although few laws addressed the issue of black-white relations, widely established and accepted practices defined the limits of tolerance. Few hotels, restaurants, or recreational facilities accepted African-Americans. Restrictive covenants and other less formal practices barred blacks from living in most neighborhoods. Job discrimination impeded economic advancement. African-Americans met hostility at almost every turn from strangers, neighbors, and police.

Thus Jackie Robinson grew up in an environment quite similar to that of other children of the great migration. Raised in a family without a father and sustained by their mother's income from domestic work—the most commonly available job for an African-American woman—the Robinsons lived in poverty, held together by their mother's indomitable spirit and strong sense of Methodist moralism. As a teenager in Pasadena, Robinson ran with local street gangs and experienced inevitable confrontations with the easily provoked local police, resulting in at least one arrest.

However, if southern California offered a harsh existence, it also proffered opportunities unavailable in most other locales. The absence of tenements and the predominance of single-family houses allowed Mallie Robinson to buy a home for her family. The lack of restrictions on black athletic participation opened an avenue of success to her sons. First, Jackie's older brother Mack, who starred at the University of Oregon and at the 1936 Olympic Games, and then Jackie, who won renown in four sports at Pasadena City College and UCLA, took advantage of this option.

Robinson's years at UCLA introduced him to high-level interracial competition. Unlike his later career, Robinson was not "the first" African-American athlete at UCLA. All-American Kenny Washington, like Robinson an extraordinary all-around athlete, who starred in football, baseball, and basketball, and future movie actor Woody Strode both preceded Robinson at UCLA. Robinson's childhood friend, Ray Bartlett, was the fourth black starter on the 1939 football team. While most black athletes of the era played for Negro colleges or in Negro Leagues and on clown teams like the Harlem Globetrotters, Robinson achieved his initial stardom on integrated playing fields.

Even more significantly, in his senior year at UCLA, Robinson met his future wife, Rachel Isum. Rachel, a freshman, was five years younger than Jackie, and came from a more secure black middle-class background. She was a third-generation Californian, a rare status among African-Americans, had earned an academic scholarship to UCLA, and maintained a straight *A* average. Rachel's calm, warm, thoughtful manner complemented Jackie's fiery impetuousness. They formed an enduring bond of mutual love and support that would gird them through the challenging years ahead.

Like others of their generation, Jackie and Rachel found their courtship interrupted by World War II. Robinson's army career typified the African-American military experience. Drafted in April 1942 and assigned to Fort Riley, Kansas, Robinson ran an endless gauntlet of racial discrimination. He was barred from Officers' Candidate School, blocked from playing on the camp baseball team, and restricted to segregated facilities. Robinson, however, applied both his aggressiveness and celebrity to demand better treatment. He rose to the rank of lieutenant and waged a campaign to improve conditions for black soldiers at Fort Riley. After his transfer to Fort Hood in Texas, Robinson refused to move to the back of a military bus and defied the officers who attempted to discipline him, resulting in a court-martial that might have led to dishonorable discharge. A military tribunal acquitted Robinson of all charges, but the episode nonetheless left its mark and intensified Robinson's commitment to racial justice.

Upon his release from the army, Robinson faced a familiar dilemma for African-Americans. Although at the peak of his athletic talents and good enough to star in any of the major American team sports, Robinson, like his brother Mack and Kenny Washington before him, had few professional options. Neither organized baseball, the National Football League, nor most major basketball teams accepted black players. Robinson's best alternative was to cast his lot with baseball's Negro Leagues, and in the spring of 1945 he signed with the Kansas City Monarchs.

There can be little doubt that, at their best, the Negro Leagues played a high level of baseball, featuring some of the game's greatest stars. Robinson's own 1945 Monarch team included standout pitchers Satchel Paige and Hilton Smith. Opposing players included future Baseball Hall of Famers Buck Leonard, Josh Gibson, Roy Campanella, and Martin Dihigo. For Robinson, however, the Negro Leagues proved a distasteful experience. Accustomed to the highly structured training and scheduling of major college sports and hostile to all forms of segregation, Robinson considered the Negro Leagues a step down rather than a leg up. The long, hot bus rides through the South, the degrading treatment at gas stations and other white-owned facilities, and the players' own informal approach to most non-league contests frustrated Robinson. An intensely private individual who neither smoked, drank, nor enjoyed what Paige called the "social ramble," Robinson never really fit in among the Monarchs. Although Robinson performed well with Kansas City, batting .387 and starting as shortstop in the East-West All-Star Game, and despite the fact that he gained invaluable training and exposure to top-flight baseball competition, Robinson, unlike most of his teammates and rivals, always disparaged his brief stint in the Negro Leagues.

Unbeknownst to Robinson, his performances with the Monarchs attracted intense scrutiny. Brooklyn Dodger president Branch Rickey had secretly decided to bring blacks into the major leagues and, under the guise of forming a new Brown Dodger squad, assigned his top scouts to evaluate Negro League talent. From the start, Robinson was high on Rickey's list of prospects. In April *Pittsburgh Courier* sportswriter Wendell Smith arranged a tryout with the Boston Red Sox for Robinson and two other Negro League stars. The Red Sox, who agreed to the audition in the face of local political pressure, never considered signing Robinson. Shortly thereafter, Rickey met with Smith and quizzed him about potential players for the Brown Dodgers. Smith, who might have suspected Rickey's true intentions, recommended Robinson.

Branch Rickey often offered conflicting reasons for his historic decision to desegregate baseball. At times he spoke of the need to eradicate the memory of a black college player whom he had coached in 1904 who had wept when barred from staying with his teammates at a Midwestern hotel. At others he expressed moral and religious concerns. Almost as frequently, he denied any noble intentions, and invoked his desire to field the best possible team. "The Negroes will make us winners for years to come," he accurately predicted. In addition, he surely recognized that in attracting fans from New York City's growing African-American population and by fielding winning teams, he would boost Dodger attendance. A combination of these factors, and a desire to make a mark in history beyond the boundaries of baseball, motivated Rickey.

What is often forgotten in light of the unequivocal success of the Rickey–Robinson alliance are the extraordinary risks that Rickey assumed in signing Robinson. Although Rickey correctly perceived that integration would bring profits, most major league magnates believed that luring more blacks to the ball park would, in the words of New York Yankee owner Larry Mac-Phail, "result in lessening the value of several major league franchises." While Rickey felt that fears of player opposition and fan violence were exaggerated, he could exert minimal control over these possibilities.

Furthermore, in selecting Jackie Robinson, Rickey took a great gamble. Although a seasoned athlete, Robinson had minimal baseball experience. Other than his five months with the Monarchs, Robinson had not played serious competitive baseball since leaving U.C.L.A. five years earlier. Few considered him the best player in the Negro Leagues. More ominously, Rickey—who had traveled to California and done extensive research on Robinson's background—was well aware of the athlete's tempestuous nature and capacity for controversy. "Jackie had a genius for getting into extracurricular scrapes," wrote one Los Angeles sportswriter. His problems in the army, also known to Rickey, reinforced this image. Rickey discounted many of these reports, noting that most of Robinson's difficulties stemmed from asserting his rights or in response to discrimination. If Robinson were white, Rickey reasoned, his aggressiveness, both on and off the field, would have been "praised to the skies." This behavior by an African-American, however, was "offensive to some white people." Rickey believed that rather than offend whites, Robinson's racial pride and combativeness, if consciously curbed, would rally them to his cause.

Other elements of Robinson's history and personality appealed to Rickey. Robinson boasted a college education and had been an army officer. He was intelligent, articulate, and comfortable in the limelight. He had, unlike most Negro League players, extensive experience in high-level interracial competition. In addition, Robinson had the type of athletic skills that Rickey always admired in a ballplayer: speed (the only crucial skill that Rickey believed could not be taught), daring, and a fierce competitive drive.

Before signing Robinson, however, Rickey elicited a promise from the young African-American. Regardless of the vile insults he might face from opposing players, fans, or off the field during his early years in baseball, Robinson would not respond. He would curb his naturally combative instincts and "turn the other cheek." Robinson, who fully understood and welcomed the magnitude of the challenge confronting him, readily agreed.

In February 1946 Jackie Robinson married Rachel Isum in a church wedding in Los Angeles. Shortly thereafter, they departed for spring training in Florida to launch "baseball's great experiment." The South that Jackie Robinson entered in 1946 was a land of rigid segregation, lynchings, and racial oppression, the dismantling of Jim Crow a seemingly distant dream. Two years later, President Harry S Truman would order the desegregation of the armed forces. Eight years would pass before the U.S. Supreme Court would issue its landmark *Brown* v. *Board of Education* decision. Seventeen-year-old Martin Luther King, Jr., was attending classes at Morehouse College. Robinson thus became what one writer has called, "a one man civil rights movement."

From the moment of their arrival in Florida, the Robinsons encountered the specter of Jim Crow. In Pensacola, airline officials removed them from their scheduled flight. At Sanford, threats of violence forced Jackie and Rachel out of town. In Jacksonville and Deland, public officials refused to allow him to play. On one occasion a local sheriff paraded onto the field and demanded Robinson's ouster in mid-game. Yet Robinson, assigned to the Montreal Royals of the International League, the Dodgers' top farm club, participated freely in games at the Dodger home base in Daytona Beach and fans, both black and white, greeted his appearances enthusiastically. Local business leaders in many Florida communities, cognizant of the profits and publicity generated by baseball training camps, courted the integrated Dodgers for future seasons. While Rickey would shy away from bringing Robinson and the Dodgers back to Florida in 1947, Robinson had established an important precedent. Within just three years, cities throughout Florida and the rest of the South would clamor to host the Jackie Robinson Dodgers.

Throughout the ensuing 1946 season, Robinson, in the words of *New York Amsterdam News* columnist Joe Bostic, "ascended the heights of excellence to prove the rightness of the experiment. And prove it in the only correct crucible for such an experiment—the crucible of white hot competition." In the Royals' opening game at Jersey City, Robinson unveiled his charismatic ability to convert challenges into transcendent moments. The Montreal second baseman garnered four hits, including a three-run home run, scored four times, stole two bases, and twice scored from third by inducing the opposing pitcher to balk.

This extraordinary debut proved a prologue for an equally remarkable season. Despite a rash of brushback pitches, spiking attempts, threats of race riots in Baltimore (the league's southern-most city), and vile harassment by opposing players, Robinson led the International League in batting average (.349) and in runs scored (113). He finished second in stolen bases and registered the highest fielding percentage of any second baseman. Behind Robinson's inspirational play, Montreal won the league pennant by nineteen and a half games, returning to the South to meet, and ultimately defeat, the Louisville Colonels in the Little World Series for the championship of the minor leagues.

Robinson's spectacular season at Montreal dispelled most doubts about his right to play in the major leagues. Branch Rickey, however, kept Robinson on the Royals roster throughout spring training in 1947. Rickey had embarked on several strategems that he hoped would ease Robinson's way onto the

Dodgers. He avoided the pitfalls of Florida segregation by dispatching the Dodgers and Royals to Cuba and Panama. He transformed Robinson into a first baseman, the Brooklyn club's greatest need. Rickey believed that a demonstration of Robinson's undeniable skills would generate a groundswell of support for his promotion among the Dodger players.

Robinson responded with a .429 spring batting tear, but rather than demand his ascension, several Dodgers, led by Southerners Dixie Walker, Kirby Higbe, and Bobby Bragan circulated a petition to keep him off the team. Several key players, however, most notably Kentucky-born shortstop Pee Wee Reese, refused to sign the protest and Rickey and manager Leo Durocher quickly quelled the rebellion. On April 10, five days before the start of the season, with no groundswell yet in sight, Rickey simply elevated Robinson to the parent club as the Dodger first baseman.

Around the National League, Robinson's arrival prompted undercurrents of dismay. The Philadelphia Phillies, under the leadership of manager Ben Chapman, subjected Robinson to an unconscionable stream of racial abuse. Rumors circulated that the St. Louis Cardinals and Chicago Cubs would strike rather than compete against a black player. Opposing pitchers targeted Robinson regularly with brushback and beanball pitches, hitting him a league-leading seven times in the first half of the season. Hotels in Philadelphia and St. Louis barred Robinson; in Cincinnati the hotel compelled him to take his meals in his room for fear his presence might offend other guests.

Amidst this backdrop of pressure and challenge, Robinson carved out not just an extraordinary rookie season, but a monument to courage and equal opportunity. After an early slump, Robinson relentlessly removed any remaining justifications for the exclusion of blacks in baseball. Robinson batted over .300 for most of the season. He led the league in stolen bases and trailed just one other player in runs scored. He paced the Dodgers in home runs and led them to the pennant. The *Sporting News*, which had consistently opposed the inclusion of blacks in organized baseball, awarded him its Rookie of the Year Award.

Yet Robinson's statistics and honors, impressive as they were, failed to capture his achievement. By injecting the more aggressive and flamboyant baserunning and batting styles of the Negro Leagues, Robinson transformed major league baseball. In the process, Robinson transformed the nation's consciousness as well.

Robinson had begun the 1947 season as a curiosity; he emerged as a national phenomenon. Wherever the Dodgers played, fans turned out in record numbers to witness the integration spectacle. Robinson doubtless benefited from the liberalized racial attitudes that had emerged during the Great Depression and World War II, but he simultaneously helped to forge a new consciousness that would accelerate the civil rights movement of the 1950s. African-Americans saw Robinson as their standard-bearer leading the onslaught against segregation. Whites confronted in Robinson an individual who not only won their admiration as an athlete, but as a man, compelling them to reassess their views of both African-Americans and American race relations.

Although few people realized it at the time, Robinson had also launched a revolution in American athletics. Only two other major league teams signed African-American players in 1947 and the pace of integration, in retrospect, seems agonizingly slow. Yet within a decade, blacks from the United States and Caribbean countries appeared on all but one team and had emerged as the dominant stars of the game. This pattern proved even more pronounced in other team sports. By the late 1960s, African-Americans predominated in the National Football League and National Basketball Association. The black influx in college football and basketball forced Southern universities to first abandon policies barring competition against integrated squads and ultimately to recruit African-Americans themselves. Sports became the primary symbol of social mobility in the black community, prompting concern about an overemphasis on athletics among African-American youth.

In the wake of his triumphant rookie season, Robinson transcended baseball and sports to become an American icon. Both on and off the field Robinson symbolized the promise of integration and equal opportunity. Numerous articles profiled not just Robinson the ballplayer, but the Robinson family, with Jackie and Rachel living in integrated neighborhoods, their children attending predominantly white schools, vanguards of the new racial enlightenment. As the nation's foremost representative of impending interracial improvement, Robinson found himself embroiled in 1949 in a cold war confrontation with singer-actor Paul Robeson, whose more pessimistic assessment of American race relations led him to an ill-fated flirtation with Soviet communism.

Robinson's dynamic play for the Dodgers reinforced his charismatic appeal. In 1949 Robinson led the National League in hitting, winning the Most Valuable Player Award, and began a string of six consecutive All-Star Game appearances. With the addition of catcher Roy Campanella, pitcher Don Newcombe, and other former Negro League stars, the Dodgers continued to showcase the benefits of integration. Equally important was the fact that Robinson, the proud, fierce African-American firebrand, was clearly the leader and dominant personality on the National League's most accomplished and celebrated squad.

Yet amidst these growing achievements, Robinson's "genius for getting into extracurricular scrapes" reasserted itself. Upon signing with the Dodgers in 1945, Robinson had guaranteed Branch Rickey that he would ignore insults and assaults during the experimental phase of his career. By 1949 both Rickey and Robinson agreed that this chapter had ended. Robinson no longer needed to unnaturally restrain his responses to opposing players or anyone else.

The "new" Robinson seemed forever surrounded by a swirl of controversy. He complained that some umpires had it in for him. He warred with Giants manager Leo Durocher. He objected to the failure of the Yankees to sign black players, protested the continuing discrimination faced by black athletes in spring training, and demanded that blacks be considered as managers. His unrepentant outspokenness and civil rights militancy alternately attracted criticism and acclaim both inside and outside of baseball.

In January 1957, after ten tempestuous seasons, Jackie Robinson retired as a player. It is fitting testimony to his baseball prowess that his career record alone, without any consideration of his pioneering social role, merited his first-ballot election to the Hall of Fame five years later. His lifetime batting average was .311. His .410 on-base percentage ranks among the top twenty-five players of all time. The Dodgers won pennants in six of Robinson's ten years with the club and finished second three times. In addition, the color line had likely robbed Robinson, already twenty-eight years old when he joined the Dodgers, of at least five years of prime productivity.

Unlike most athletes, Robinson never retreated from the public eye after his retirement. He accepted a job as vice-president of Chock Full O' Nuts, a chain of New York City fast-food restaurants that employed many African-Americans. He chaired the NAACP Freedom Fund Drive and became one of that organization's primary spokespersons and fundraisers. He immersed himself in the civil rights movement as an ardent supporter of the Reverend Martin Luther King, Jr., raised funds for the Student Non-Violent Coordinating Committee (SNCC), and marched in many of the signpost demonstrations of the 1960s.

Yet Robinson also became engulfed in the turbulently shifting racial and generational tides of that decade. Always defiantly independent in thought and action, Robinson forged his own distinctive and controversial path in politics and protest. In 1960 he endorsed Richard Nixon for president over John F. Kennedy, the favorite of most civil rights activists. Although the vast majority of African-Americans supported the Democrats, Robinson allied with New York Governor Nelson Rockefeller and became the nation's most prominent black Republican. As white and black radicals increasingly attacked the American economic and political system, Robinson reaffirmed his faith in "black capitalism" as the vehicle for African-American progress, establishing the Freedom National Bank and other black-owned enterprises.

In 1960 young SNCC activists successfully approached Robinson for assistance, seeing him as a kindred spirit. By the late 1960s, however, Robinson had publicly feuded with Malcolm X and subsequent black power advocates and split with Martin Luther King, Jr., over King's opposition to the Vietnam War. Indeed, Robinson came to be regarded by many militants as a pillar of the mainstream establishment; in some quarters as an Uncle Tom. Ironically, these attacks coincided with Robinson's resignation from the NAACP as a result of its domination by a "clique of the Old Guard" and failure to incorporate "younger, more progressive voices."

Accustomed to contention, Robinson could confidently navigate these controversies. Personal tragedy, however, took a far deeper toll. On March 6, 1968, police arrested twenty-one-year-old Jackie, Jr., recently returned from Vietnam where he had been wounded in action, for possession of drugs and a firearm. Where Jackie Sr. had been a herald of the "New Negro" of the civil rights movement, his son became a harbinger of the devastation that would decimate African-American males in the 1980s and 1990s. Addicted to heroin in Vietnam, the younger Robinson had turned to a life of crime. Jackie Jr. entered Daytop Village, a Staten Island drug rehabilitation center. He emerged cured of his addiction and devoted to helping others afflicted by drugs. Fate would allow him little time to savor his triumph. In the early morning hours of June 17, 1971, the sports car he was driving veered out of control and crashed on the Merritt Parkway near the Robinson home in Connecticut, killing twenty-four-year-old Jackie Robinson, Jr.

His son's ordeal and death transformed the elder Robinson. The tragedy had been played out, as had most of his adult life, in public view. "I guess I had more of an effect on other people's kids than I had on my own," rued Robinson after Jackie Jr.'s arrest, as unsparing in his self-criticism as in his attacks on others. Robinson's physical condition declined precipitously. Plagued for a decade with diabetes, Robinson found his eyesight failing. He suffered a heart attack, and poor blood circulation made it difficult for him to walk. The amputation of his left leg grew imminent. In addition, coming closely on the heels of the 1968 King assassination and election of Richard Nixon, with whom Robinson had long since parted company, the trials of Jackie Jr. led Robinson, like many other African-Americans, to reevaluate his faith in America's ability to overcome its history of racism and discrimination.

This reassessment culminated in the 1972 publication of Robinson's remarkable final testament, his bluntly titled autobiography *I Never Had It Made*. Robinson remained characteristically frank and outspoken. He expressed pride in his accomplishments, but nonetheless acknowledged where he had erred—in his castigation of Robeson, his endorsement of Nixon, his split with King over Vietnam, and other episodes. He wrote honestly and movingly about Jackie, Jr. Most tellingly, Robinson, who for a quarter of a century had symbolized the possibility of integration in America, now sounded a profoundly pessimistic note. "There was a time I believed deeply in America. I have become bitterly disillusioned," he wrote. Although he acknowledged that "Personally, I have been very fortunate. . . . I cannot say I have it made while our country . . . speeds along a course toward more and more racism."

Yet the image of Robinson in his final years as broken and dispirited belies the reality of his indomitable personality. The publication of Roger Kahn's *The Boys of Summer* in 1971 reawakened a new generation to the power and the glory of the Robinson saga. Those who saw and spoke to Robinson in 1972 describe him as ever ebullient and optimistic, despite his personal grief and physical difficulties. Kahn, in a final telephone conversation, found Robinson "as enthusiastic as a twenty-year-old" in discussing his latest business venture. When major league baseball, at the 1972 World Series, chose to honor the twenty-fifth anniversary of Robinson's debut, he joked with his former teammates about his impending amputation, needling Pee Wee Reese that he would return to best him on the golf course. Then before a national television audience Robinson offered America one final enduring memory. After accepting the accolades of the dignitaries, he challenged organized baseball to fulfill his legacy by hiring black managers.

Nine days later, on October 24, 1972, Robinson died of a heart attack. He was only fifty-three years old. For the eulogy Rachel Robinson, who had shared Jackie's triumphs and heartbreaks, chose not someone from Robinson's baseball past, nor one of his long-standing allies from earlier civil rights struggles, but thirty-one-year-old Reverend Jesse Jackson, an African-American leader who embodied the hopes of the future rather than the disappointments of the past.

Jesse Jackson, like Rachel Robinson, understood Robinson's

true final testament. Robinson, preached Jackson, had "created ripples of possibility," "turned stumbling block into stepping stone," and bequeathed the "gift of new expectations." In his autobiography Robinson had vented his disappointment with the state of race relations in the 1970s, but he also reaffirmed the message that has made him such an enduring figure: That individuals of courage and commitment can confront bigotry and create change. In *I Never Had It Made*, Robinson had tempered his disillusionment with a far more uplifting epitaph: "A life is not important except in the impact it has on other lives." By that measure, one quarter century after his death and one half century after his historic feat, the import of Jackie Robinson's life continues to resound.

# Pepper Street, Pasadena

## MAURY ALLEN

*A*lthough born in Georgia, Jackie Robinson grew up in
southern California during the 1920s and 1930s. Carey
McWilliams, writing in 1946, claimed that "Negro
migrants have made perhaps a better adjustment in Los
Angeles than in any other American city." But the experiences of
the Robinson family, living in nearby Pasadena, amply demonstrate the limits of toleration in California. Jackie, his mother
Mallie, his three brothers, and his sister shared a life of poverty,
hard work, and recurrent discrimination. In 1986 veteran sportswriter Maury Allen spoke to Robinson's surviving siblings, Willa
Mae and Mack, about Jackie's formative years in the California
crucible that shaped his character and described their responses
in Jackie Robinson: An American Life.

● ● ● ● ● ● ●

The late afternoon sun glistened above the hills of Mount
Wilson in the bucolic quiet of Pasadena, California. It was a soft
summer day in 1986, and as Willa Mae Robinson Walker, Jackie

Robinson's only sister, crossed the street from Jackie Robinson Park to the Jackie Robinson Community Center at 1020 North Fair Oaks, she smiled gently and remembered a time some sixty years ago.

"This very street, North Fair Oaks, that was the dividing line between blacks and whites. We lived over there on the black side in that big house at 121 Pepper Street, and we couldn't even cross to this side, the white side," she said.

Pasadena is some fifteen miles north and east of downtown Los Angeles, a bedroom community for Hollywood stars in the old days, a setting for many movies, an area of fine stores, expensive homes, and much movie history. Its most famous buildings are probably the Pasadena Playhouse and the Rose Bowl. Jackie Robinson starred in the Rose Bowl. He was not allowed to enter the Playhouse.

Jackie Robinson was born in the early evening of January 31, 1919, in a small sharecropper's farmhouse outside Cairo, Georgia. He was the fifth child of Jerry and Mallie Robinson. The other children were Edgar, Frank, Mack, and Willa Mae, three years older than Jackie, the baby of the Robinson clan.

"Jack was a mama's boy," says Willa Mae. "Always was. When he finished Pasadena Junior College, he had scholarship offers from dozens of schools. He chose to stay home and go to UCLA. Why? Because he didn't want to leave his mama."

Jack Roosevelt Robinson. Why Roosevelt?

"I don't really know about that," says Willa Mae. "I didn't even know about that Roosevelt part until years later. One day when Jack was seventeen, eighteen years old, he got in trouble with the cops over some traffic speeding problem. They made him go to court, and he sat there all day. They never called his name. He was really angry at that and finally went up and asked when they were going to call him.

" 'What's your name?' the court officer asked.

" 'Jack Robinson,' he said.

" 'We don't have a Jack Robinson. We have a Roosevelt Robinson.'

" 'I guess that's me,' Jack said."

In the spring of 1919, Jerry Robinson announced that he was

through being a farmer. He wanted to move into town and get a job there. Mallie was concerned that her brood would grow hungry without being able to grow their own turnips, raise their own chickens, and eat their own eggs. They argued. Mallie also heard rumors around that Jerry Robinson was eyeing another man's wife and planned to take up with her. Tensions increased in the small farmhouse. Mallie, a deeply religious woman, prayed for guidance. When Jerry announced that he was taking off to look for a job, maybe as far away as Texas, Mallie did not plead for him to stay. He ran away to Florida, rumor had it, with the other woman.

"We never saw him again," says Willa Mae, "but after Jack became famous he did show up one time. Jack didn't have anything to do with him and that was it."

Mallie Robinson had a brother Frank who had served in the Army in World War I and was stationed in California. He returned late in 1919 for a visit, extolled the conditions in California, and told his sister she would do better there with her family than she ever could in Georgia.

Promised housing by the brother, Mallie Robinson collected her family in the spring of 1920, scraped together the necessary fare by selling some of her furniture and clothes to neighbors, and boarded a train headed west to California.

"I was six or seven when we got there," says Mack Robinson, a silver medalist at the 1936 Berlin Olympics and a second-place finisher to Jesse Owens in the 200 meters. Mack Robinson, retired now, worked as a construction laborer a good part of his adult life.

"What my mother didn't know when she brought us here, what none of us knew, was that Pasadena was as prejudiced as any town in the South. They let us in all right, but they wouldn't let us live. It isn't much better today.

"When we first came here we lived at 45 Glorietta Street. It wasn't much of a place and we were all squeezed in there, but we managed."

Mallie worked as a domestic, and as the children grew up they contributed financially to the family. The Robinson family was on and off welfare several times but finally saved enough money to purchase the house on Pepper Street. It had been owned by a black who had a niece who looked white. The niece had made the original purchase. There would eventually be three Robinson-family houses on the Pepper Street site as the children grew and married, sort of a Pasadena version of the Kennedy compound at Hyannis.

"It was an all white neighborhood, and this lady across the street, this Mrs. Carey, was actually afraid of black people," says Willa Mae. "She complained to police and would slam her door when one of us appeared on the street to play. My mother got us to walking in the other direction when we needed to go to a store to avoid trouble."

There were also, as there almost always are, decent people willing to help the Robinsons.

"There was a bakery down the block, and at the end of the day one of us would be sent there to collect the old bread for free. They used to say 'Leave it for the Robinson Crusoe family.' Then there was the milkman who would stop by at the end of his day's route and drop off a few containers of milk without charge. People did help."

While many of the neighbors, including the Careys, gave the Robinsons a hard time, Mack Robinson explains why peace finally settled on the area.

"We just kicked some white ass," Mack says. "Kids aren't so tough when you can knock them down with a punch."

Mack is angered that Pasadena has never seen fit to properly honor Jackie or himself for their athletic deeds. The only official city money spent on a Jackie Robinson memorial is the plaque on the ground in front of where the Pepper Street house once stood. The house was torn down years ago as part of a redevelopment. The sign reads: "JACKIE ROBINSON resided on this Site with his Family from 1922 to 1946."

"I went to a fiftieth reunion in Columbus, Ohio, of the 1936 Olympic team," Mack says. "It was quite an event. In Pasadena it meant nothing."

Mallie soon had regular jobs as a domestic, and the children worked after school. The biggest problem in the early years was baby Jackie, too small to leave at home alone and too young for school.

"My mother figured I could take him to school with me and he would play in the sandbox all day. There was a little fuss about that, but after a while they let us do it and it worked out fine," Willa Mae says.

Finally young Jack was old enough to enter Grover Cleveland School. He was well behaved in school and did his work but was not an exceptional student.

"In those days he would come home from school, gulp down a glass of milk, put his books on that old dresser, and be out the door playing ball with the kids. How that boy loved playing ball," Willa Mae says.

With three older brothers, Jack often played in street games and in the neighborhood lots as the youngest player on the teams. His brother thinks it helped his professional career.

"When he was playing with older boys, he had to learn how to make up for his lack of size and strength," says Mack. "I have to think the quickness did it."

All of the Robinson kids, including Willa Mae, were terrific athletes. "I used to pitch in the baseball games and played soccer and field hockey and ran track. I really enjoyed sports," she says.

Bill Brown, a retired cement mason, remembers something else the boys did but the girls were not allowed to participate in.

"We used to play cards in the alleyways behind the houses," says Brown. "Jack was a little young for it, but he wanted to play so I taught him cards. We played all kinds of card games for a penny out there. I also taught him how to play bridge when he was about ten or twelve. He got real good at it."

Following in the footsteps of his brothers, young Jack soon became a recognized athlete around Pepper Street and at the Grover Cleveland School, the George Washington Junior High, and Muir High School. Jack got his first taste of professional sports at the age of seven or eight when kids in school bribed the talented Robinson to play on their teams by offering him part of their lunches or even a dollar. He would rush home from school with that dollar and quickly offer it to Mallie for the family funding.

"There were a lot of days we were hungry," says Mack. "We all worked after school to make a few dollars, cutting lawns, shining shoes, delivering groceries, running errands."

"I guess that you would call Jack hyper," says Willa Mae. "I could never remember him walking when he could run. He just seemed on the go all the time."

With Mallie working as a cleaning woman for neighborhood women, with all of the children pitching in financially as best they could, with an occasional gift from the neighborhood bakery or milk wagon, and with a rare gift from the welfare department, Mallie kept the family together.

"I think it was her religion that did it," says Willa Mae. "Not a day passed that Mama didn't pray to God for help."

In some few years Pepper Street began changing in ethnic makeup. Several more black families moved into the area. Mexicans moved in, Orientals moved in, poor whites moved in. All of these groups were bound together—by their poverty rather than by their race.

"They called it the Pepper Street gang," says Willa Mae, "but it isn't what they call a gang today. They weren't out to do trouble or rob anybody. They just were a bunch of kids who enjoyed being together and mostly playing ball games."

"I think it was 1933 when he was in junior high school that we began to notice what an athlete Jack was," says Mack. "He was uncanny. He just took up a sport and he was the best in the neighborhood before anybody knew it. I think the first time he played Ping-Pong he won the city championship. I think that was the first time he got his name in the papers."

Mack Robinson is a handsome man with a brush mustache and white hair. He is a broad-shouldered, husky gentleman who has a little trouble moving around these days because of a recent knee operation, the result of years of running track and working on his feet. He lives with his second wife, Del, in a small house on McDonald Street in Pasadena, a few blocks away from the original house on Pepper Street. Del is busy in the backyard feeding the chickens and rabbits. There are photographs everywhere of the children, ten in all, and the dozen grandchildren, many of whom live nearby and march through the house to attack the cookie jar. He orders a few of the smaller ones to deliver a hug and a kiss before they can get that cookie and props his leg up on a recliner and talks of a time half a century ago. There is, leaning against a side wall, a huge blowup of a 1936 photograph of Mack as an Olympian teammate of Jesse Owens and another photograph of brother Jackie in his rookie season in Brooklyn. . . .

MACK ROBINSON: "What hasn't changed is the prejudice in the world. That's still the same. The white man doesn't recognize what he is doing to the world. If he doesn't recognize it soon there might not be any world. I'm not a politician but I know enough to see what's going on. Blacks are better off in some ways today than they were when we were kids, but in a lot of ways we aren't. There's no adequate housing, there are no good jobs, there is still prejudice in a lot of ways. When I was a kid they wouldn't let us in the swimming pool but one day a week. Now, at least, we have our own swimming pools.

"I went to Pasadena Junior College and then I went to the Olympics in 1936. I finished second to Jesse and when I got back I could only get a job as a street sweeper. I lost that when they had a fuss over the pools. Then I got into construction labor. I worked on building the Rose Bowl. Jack played there later, and I always took pride in that.

"My life always seemed to be one step ahead or one step behind the times. I never was able to make full use of my athletic skills. We didn't think of making money in sports then. We just thought of enjoying ourselves and competing for the fun of it. I think we were better people for it. . . .

"The reason Jackie made it was the strength he got from our mother. She instilled that pride in him. She wouldn't take anything from anybody. She was a real strong woman. It took a lot of guts to come out to California with five small kids. Her grandfather had been a slave and now she was setting out on her own to build a new life. Jackie inherited a lot from her; we all did. . . .

"Jack was the baby of the family and things got better when he was growing up. We even had a car by the middle 1930s, and he used to borrow my car to take out his girlfriends. We had this 1936 Ford and that's the car we still had in 1947 when Jack played for Brooklyn and five of us drove cross-country to see him play.

"People asked me through the years why he made it with the Dodgers. Was he better than anybody else? I can't say that. Maybe he was just the right man at the right time. Sometimes that is more important than who is best." . . .

A few blocks away, in a small house on Worcester Street, Willa Mae Robinson Walker lives with her daughter and grandson. She is a widow. Her husband, James, a school custodian, died several years ago of a heart attack. She is a thin woman with gray hair. She has a warm smile and an outgoing personality. She welcomes a visitor warmly and is proud to talk about her baby brother.

WILLA MAE: "I moved out of the Pepper Street house in the early 1940s into this house. Jack had his bachelor party right here the night before he married Rachel in 1946. He had all his old friends from the Pepper Street gang and they had a great time. Jack didn't drink or smoke, but he didn't stop other people from doing it and they drank a lot that night.

"When we first moved to Pepper Street we had a bad time. Nobody wanted us out there since the neighborhood was all white. [It is now a neighborhood of mixed heritage, blacks, poor whites, Latins, Asians—all living peacefully in these small, neat houses.] They did everything they could to get us out of there. One night we even had a cross-burning. We didn't know who did it, but there was one family, the Careys, we always suspected. They were just mean. They used to call the cops all the time on us for the silliest things, mostly for being out on the street. Jack was the one who was out the most. He just didn't enjoy playing indoors. He wanted to be outside.

"He would come out, bounce a ball on the street, and they would yell, 'Get off the street, nigger.' He would yell back at them, 'Shut up, cracker.' That kept up for a long while but finally they saw that we wouldn't move, we wouldn't give in and they would have to live with us or move themselves. They decided to live with us. I can't say we became friends, but they stopped bothering us. That was all we ever wanted.

"A neighbor woman, Mrs. Eva Armstrong, would come in once in a while to help us out while my mother was at work cleaning houses, but most of the time I was in charge of the house. I did the cooking and the cleaning, looked after Jackie, ran the errands for shopping, and kept us all clean and neat.

"Jack was only interested in sports. He wasn't a great student, but that was only because somewhere along the line he decided sports would be his life. He always talked of coaching teams in football and baseball, and I think that's what he would have done if he hadn't become a baseball player.

"People used to ask me how Jack got so good throwing a baseball and a football, and I said it was from throwing rocks at the other kids who threw rocks at him. That was something we all did. It was more of a game than anything else. I don't think anybody was trying to hurt anybody else. We went through plenty with our neighbors after we moved to the house on Pepper Street, but it ended after a few years for two reasons. We all got older, and they all got tired of it.

"A lot of that changed, of course, after Mack became a famous athlete around here, and then Jack. Then they all started bragging how they knew the famous player from Pasadena Junior College, Jackie Robinson, and you would think they were great buddies. That's how people are, I guess.

"Jack played at Pasadena and then went to UCLA because he didn't want to be away from his mama. After that, he played some professional football in Hawaii, came back to get a coaching job, and went in the Army. When he came back from the Army, I acted as his secretary and he wrote letters to a lot of colleges looking for jobs. He was hired by three or four until they found out he was a Negro. Some never had asked on the application. Then he did get a coaching job. He also had sent a letter to the Kansas City Monarchs about playing for them, and one day a letter arrived while he was out. I opened it and it offered a job, and I talked to Mack and he called Jack and Jack asked what we thought. 'Take it,' Mack said, and he wrote them back he would take the job if they offered more money.

"Jack went to Brooklyn, and I used to go there every year for a visit. I went to every World Series he was in except the

1955 World Series, and that's the one they finally won. In those early days in Brooklyn I don't think we ever stopped worrying about him. He got so much hate mail and so many threats on his life and he talked about quitting, and we worried all the time about him. We used to read some things in the paper about the hate mail and the people trying to get him out of baseball, and the phone would ring and we would be afraid to pick it up. We used to think it would be a call from somebody saying Jackie was dead. Jackie's mama was scared all the time, but she wouldn't really ever let on. She just prayed he would be all right and she trusted in God. One time in spring training he had to be snuck out of the ballpark with two Negro sportswriters, and when he called later he told us if they didn't get him out of there in time a gang was coming after him. 'I might have been lynched,' he said, and we just sat down and cried. Was it worth it? There were lots of times we just thought he should come home and coach at a black school and be done with it. But that wasn't Jack. He was determined to do it so he did it.

"We always worried about him because he was so quick to anger if somebody said something that was insulting. I don't think Jack ever looked for a fight, but I don't think he ever walked away from one, neither."

# THE GOAL DUST GANG

## WOODY STRODE AND SAM YOUNG

*H*ad Jackie Robinson never played major league baseball, he would still be remembered as perhaps the
greatest all-around athlete this nation has ever produced. Los Angeles sportswriter Vincent X. Flaherty
called him "the Jim Thorpe of his race," but Robinson was
arguably a better athlete than the fabled Native-American
Olympian. During his collegiate career, first at Pasadena City
College and later at UCLA, Robinson reigned as a record-setting
broad jumper, an all-American football player, and two-time
conference leading scorer in basketball. Ironically, baseball was
Robinson's weakest sport at UCLA.

In 1939, Robinson joined two other great African-American
athletes, Kenny Washington and Woody Strode, on the UCLA
football squad. The color barrier blocked Washington and Strode
from entering the professional ranks, but in 1946, after Robinson
had signed with the Montreal Royals, they reintegrated the
National Football League (which had allowed blacks prior to
1933) as teammates on the Los Angeles Rams. Strode later
went on to a successful acting career in Hollywood, appearing in

*many films including* The Man Who Shot Liberty Valance *and* The Professionals.

*The following excerpt, drawn from Strode's autobiography,* Goal Dust, *describes the athlete's life at UCLA, Jackie Robinson on and off the field, and the climactic 1939 gridiron showdown between UCLA and USC.*

● ● ● ● ● ● ●

Bill Ackerman was the graduate manager at that time and his goal was making UCLA a national name. . . . As far as Bill was concerned we were all Christian, all went to church on Sundays, and took our baths on Saturday.

In 1940 he was manager of the track team that went back to the Midwest for the NCAA's. Jackie Robinson was a member of that track team. He was the best all-around athlete UCLA ever had. The people back there wanted Jackie to sleep somewhere else. Bill said, "No soap, you treat him just like the white boys or I'll take the team home. You won't have a track meet." They weren't too happy about it, but they finally agreed to let Jackie sleep in their hotel.

Bill Ackerman was the Godfather; he helped integrate us into society. He provided us with a cultural education, so that if we were to go to the White House, we'd know how to dress and how to act. When we got to places like Oregon or Washington we never had any problems staying with the team because Bill had made all the arrangements. And there was no discrimination at UCLA; the students would bend over backwards to have it equal for everybody. . . .

UCLA ended up taking care of me and my whole family while I was in school. They gave me one hundred dollars a month and an eleven-dollar meal ticket. Every week they gave me twenty bucks under the table so I could pay the bills at home. They gave Kenny Washington and me a car, all my books free from Campbell's book store and all my clothes free from Desmond's. They gave us tickets to the home games which I would sell. I was always after Bill Ackerman to give me more tickets, but he always said no. And Bill had my daddy do some brick work out at his house; he was always looking out for us. Well, you can imagine what a candy store that was for me. . . .

But UCLA was tough; you had to have the units to get in. There was no bullshit from upstairs; we had to work to get our grades before we could play football. . . .

All the years I was at UCLA I had to earn my scholarship. All the guys who were on scholarship did some kind of maintenance work for the school. A lot of the great athletes were janitors; they scrubbed toilets. Kenny and I had good jobs; we used to walk around campus with a stick picking up papers, and we did a little gardening, too. That's how I earned my hundred bucks a month. . . .

When Kenny and I got back to school that fall there were a lot of changes on the Bruins' football team. Except for Kenny, we had a whole new backfield. Ned Matthews became our first-string quarterback. Izzy Cantor's little brother, Leo, took over the fullback job. And the school recruited Jackie Robinson to replace Hal Hirshon at right halfback. We had the best backfield talent on the coast and it was up to our new coach, Babe Horrell, to figure out how to make us winners. . . .

Babe Horrell was high class, cultured and civilized. He always dressed right; he always talked right. . . . Babe was a nice guy, and he was more like a friend than our coach.

When Babe took over after the 1938 season, his first goal was recruiting Jackie Robinson out of Pasadena Junior College. Jackie was probably the most sought-after athlete on the West Coast. I hadn't met Jackie at that point; I had only read about him. Of course in those days Jackie was famous as a football player.

Jackie Robinson was the first of the Gayle Sayers/O. J. Simpson/Eric Dickerson-type running backs. He had incredible breakaway speed coupled with an elusiveness you had to see to believe. He could change direction quicker than any back I had ever seen. Stop on a dime: boom; full speed in the other direction. They didn't have to do a lot of blocking for him because he was so instinctive. He was shifty and quick and would just outmaneuver everybody.

Pasadena Junior College used to play in the Rose Bowl and

Jackie would draw crowds of 20–30,000 people to watch him play. I remember the game Jackie played against Compton Junior College in 1938; that was one of his greatest football games.

He ran back a kick 85 yards for a touchdown. He scored two more touchdowns on runs of 50 and 60 yards and threw for another. The way Jackie ran the sidelines you'd have thought he was playing on a fifty-acre field. Bill Ackerman and Babe Horrell had gone to that game to see if Jackie was good enough to attend U CLA. They took one look at this kid and said, "Yeah, he's good enough," just like their reaction to Kenny Washington. And Jackie Robinson was very pigeontoed, so when he ran alongside Kenny, with his knock-knees, they made quite a pair.

Pasadena Junior College won all eleven of their games in 1938 and the Junior College Championship. Jackie was the unanimous choice as most valuable player. He scored 131 points and gained over 1,000 yards. He and Ray Bartlett, who played end and was Jackie's best friend growing up, were both named to the All-Southern California Eleven. That was pretty unusual: the two guys who got all the honors were black.

Pasadena Junior College had a pretty unusual team. There were five blacks and six Southerners on the team. Their coach was Tom Mallory from Oklahoma, and he brought the six Southerners with him. At first the Southerners tried to sock hard and hurt and all that stuff, but Jackie and Ray had the same attitude as Kenny and me; if you hit me hard, I'm going to hit you just as hard or harder next time. They had to learn how to respect each other. Then again it helps to have an outstanding team, and the kid that made them great was Jackie Robinson. . . .

At that time, Jackie's brother Mack was the really famous athlete in the family. He was a hell of a track-and-field man. At Pasadena Junior College he set the junior college long-jump record at 25 feet. Then he moved up to the University of Oregon and set a world record in the 220-yard dash. That record stood until Jesse Owens broke it at the 1936 Olympics. Of course, Mack finished second to Jesse Owens in Berlin. . . .

Growing up, Jackie idolized Mack. One of Jackie's first athletic goals was to break Mack's long-jump record at the junior college, which he did. That story became part of the legend of

Jackie Robinson, because the National Junior College Track Championships and the Southern California Junior College Baseball Championships were being held on the same day. The track meet was in Pomona, the baseball game was in Glendale, and it took a couple of hours to get from one place to the other. They gave Jackie permission to arrive at the track meet and jump an hour early. On his third jump, Jackie went 25 feet 6 1/2 inches, breaking Mack's record.

They had a car waiting, and as soon as he broke the record, they rushed him out to Glendale. He got there in the middle of the third inning, and his team was down by a few runs. Well, he got a couple of key hits, stole a couple of bases, and basically won the game by himself. He finished the season batting .417, stole twenty-five bases in twenty-four games, and was voted the most valuable player in Southern California junior college baseball.

Jackie also lettered in basketball in Pasadena. In 1938 they won the championship and Jackie led the Western Division in scoring. Altogether he lettered in four varsity sports. When it came to athletics, Jackie Robinson could do anything he wanted.

That's why UCLA wanted him. And Oregon wanted him pretty bad, too. They figured they owned Jackie because Mack had gone to school there. Some friends of the school came down and threw the keys to a brand-new Dodge on his porch. And there was an alumnus from Stanford who offered to pay Jackie's way to any school back East just so he wouldn't stay on the West Coast and possibly beat Stanford playing for another school.

Lucky for us we had Babe Horrell, because Babe had considerable prestige, influence, and reputation in Pasadena. He used it all in persuading Jackie to come to UCLA, and Babe made him give the car back. But Jackie wanted to stay close to home anyway. When he announced his decision, he said, "I choose UCLA because I plan to get a job in Los Angeles after I finish school, and I figure I'll have a better chance if I attend a local university."

Jackie came out to UCLA in the summer of 1939. They put him in the extension school so he could make up some units and become eligible to play football in the fall. We also recruited his friend Ray Bartlett, and they became the fourth and fifth black players on our team. The black community liked to point to us as a symbol of achievement.

I never knew Jackie that well. . . . We were only together that one year. But Jackie was a very intelligent and good-looking young man. He had a very dark complexion with thin, straight features. He had a perfect white smile and steely hard eyes that could flash angry in a heartbeat. To be honest, Jackie Robinson was not well-liked when he was at UCLA. He would never believe there'd be a statue of him sitting out there right now, at the baseball stadium UCLA named after him.

Jackie was not friendly. He had been in a few scuffles in Pasadena with the law, minor trouble. When he came to UCLA he was very withdrawn. Even on the football field he would stand off by himself.

People used to ask me, "Why is Jackie so sullen and always by himself?"

Well, for one thing, Jackie's brother Frank was killed in a motorcycle accident just before Jackie got to UCLA. People hardly ever mention that. But Jackie and Frank were very close. . . . Frank encouraged and advised Jackie. I remember Jackie said, "I wanted to win, not only for myself but also because I didn't want to see Frank disappointed." . . .

To someone like Kenny or me, Pasadena seemed like a million miles away based on the crude transportation of that time. It was like Paris, France, as far as I was concerned. Pasadena was where all the rich white people lived. Orange Grove Avenue was millionaires' row. Those people controlled the community, and Pasadena was a segregated and prejudiced town. So it was much harder for someone like Jackie Robinson growing up than it was for someone like Kenny Washington, who grew up with nothing but poor Italians.

See, Jackie Robinson knew where he was from. That's the other reason Jackie had an angry personality. . . .

Right before Jackie arrived at UCLA, a little story hit the papers that created some tension. Jackie and Ray Bartlett used to play on a softball team sponsored by Pepsi-Cola. They were in what was known as an Owl League, playing overhand softball down at Brookside Playground. They were going home after a game, heading up Mountain Avenue. Jackie had borrowed an old Plymouth from somewhere, and he was giving his teammates a lift home. Ray Bartlett was riding on the running board. When they got to Fair Oaks and Mountain they passed a white guy who started shouting insults at them, called them a bunch of niggers. Eventually they got to a traffic signal and both cars stopped. Ray, without saying anything, reached out and slapped the guy across the face with his baseball glove. The white guy realized the mistake he had made when he saw how many angry kids there were in Jackie's car. When the light changed, he hightailed it.

Well, Jackie was hotheaded, and he wasn't going to leave it alone. He chased the guy and forced him off the road. You can imagine how scared that man was. Ray tried to cool Jackie off, but Jackie wouldn't back down. He was in a rage and ready to kick this guy's ass, but right then the police showed up. Jackie started to defy them, and they ran him in.

Ray, being Jackie's best friend, went down to the police station to see what they were going to do with him. Jackie was yelling, "Ray, get my mother!"

So Ray went and told Mallie what happened. She called Babe Horrell, who, like I said, had considerable influence in Pasadena. Babe got hold of the judge assigned to the case, and I don't know exactly what happened in court, but Jackie was released. They probably put him on some kind of probation. That story followed Jackie out to UCLA and hurt his reputation.

When I went to talk to Bill Ackerman the other day, he told me, "Jackie always seemed to have a chip on his shoulder. I wasn't close to Jackie like I was to you guys. Maybe he was rather ahead of his time in his thinking with regard to the blacks' situation. I think it hurt him emotionally to see how some of his friends were treated. The result was he kept pretty much within himself; to a certain extent he was a loner.

"Of course, all you kids used to fight for your rights. Ray Bartlett used to be a good fighter for that. I called him Red, you know, because he had that head full of red hair. But Kenny wasn't as vocal as Jackie. Jackie was a nine, and Kenny was a three.

"But Jackie was the best all-around athlete UCLA has ever

had, and that includes everybody, even the people playing there now. He was well-coordinated, he had great speed, a lot of strength, and he was very quick."

Jackie became the only man in UCLA history to letter in four varsity sports: track, baseball, basketball, and football. He was the national long-jump champion in 1940, and he was the basketball team's highest scorer the two years he played. Baseball was his weakest game, but in football he excelled. In 1939 he led the nation in average yards per carry, a little over 12 yards per run from the line of scrimmage.

With Jackie Robinson on the right side and Kenny Washington on the left, we had the two greatest halfbacks the West Coast had ever seen. . . .

We were a tough group of dead-end kids, and we came together that year to form UCLA's first great football team. And, to the best of my knowledge, UCLA was the first major university to have four black kids playing key roles. Kenny and Jackie were the first one-two black backfield men, I started every game, and Ray Bartlett saw considerable playing time as a reserve. We were unique in America.

Our success started when we faced Texas Christian University in the first game of the season. TCU was a football powerhouse which hadn't been defeated in their last fourteen games. They finished the 1938 season ranked no worse than third in the nation and a lot of people thought they were the number-one team. Going into our game the bookies had them favored by nine points. We looked at the game as a test to see what our potential really was.

### NEGRO STARS LEAD ATTACK
#### By Bob Hunter (*Examiner*)

Kenny Washington and Jackie Robinson—UCLA's dynamic Goal Dust Twins—went wild in the third quarter last night to spark a inspired Bruin team to a thrilling 6-2 triumph over mighty Texas Christian!

Outside of a decisive 71-yard drive, staged almost single handedly by Washington and Robinson, the Horned Frogs held the upper hand.

We didn't lose a game for the rest of the season. Going into our last game with USC, we were undefeated and so were they. If we could beat them, we'd win the conference championship and go to the Rose Bowl for the first time ever. The showdown was December 9, 1939, and it was the biggest, the most colossal, the greatest game ever seen in these parts. Three dollars-thirty cents for reserved, two-twenty for general admission, and a dollar sixty-five at the Peristyle end. . . .

The week before the big game we practiced in secret. Both schools had spies, and we caught two of theirs with binoculars and notebooks. We had guards patrolling the perimeter of the field, and they caught these guys hiding in the bushes. They tied them up and took them out to fraternity row. The kids out there shaved UCLA in their hair, painted them blue and gold, and sent 'em home. That's how the war escalated.

There was always a pre-game rally that was held around a huge bonfire, which, if you look it up, means fire of bones. We didn't burn any bodies; we built a structure out of telephone poles set about thirty feet apart. The week prior to the game, all the kids would search the city of Los Angeles looking for wood to fill this structure. They'd steal all the wooden crates from the markets, they'd go up into the hills and collect brush and deadfall. And one year, the USC kids stole all the outhouses from all the construction sites.

The night before the game, they would set off this fire and the flames would shoot hundreds of feet into the sky, thick black smoke would pour out, and sparks would fly at random like fireworks. It may sound dangerous, but we had a lot of vacant lots and land, and it wasn't hard finding a big open area for one of these fires. The kids would stand around and dance while the yell leaders stood on a platform and said whatever they could think of to get the crowd worked up. It was like an Indian war dance, but it was clean fun. There were no drugs; maybe some of the kids drank, but it wasn't a problem.

That year, we sabotaged USC's rally before the big game. A couple of our kids snuck over there early. They soaked the tips of towels in gasoline and lit them. As they ran past USC's woodpile, they flicked the flaming gas off their towels and started their bonfire early. Later I found out from our spies the USC kids had burned Kenny, Jackie, and me in effigy.

"Hey, they burnt you guys up last night, Woody!"

"That's because we're going to kick their asses tomorrow!"

They made figures out of straw, hung us, and burned us. That wasn't racial, that was fear. . . .

To this day, it was the biggest crowd in the history of the Coliseum. When I ran out of the tunnel onto the field the sight nearly took my breath away; I nearly hyperventilated. There were 103,500 paid admissions and there must have been another 5,000 when you counted all the press people, the vendors, the officials, and the gate crashers. It was a splashy, colorful ocean of people.

There were thirty American flags flying around the top of the bowl; how many places had room for that? The student sections faced each other across the field and they competed to see who could do the best yells or the best stunts with the color cards. The USC band was on the field, and they were pretty slick. They dressed up like soldiers from Troy with crimson skirts and capes with gold piping. And they had shiny gold helmets with side flaps and red mohawks on the top.

All the Hollywood royalty showed up. Douglas Fairbanks and Joe E. Brown. Jane Wyman . . . But nobody paid them any attention. This was a big game; everybody was a fan. And the noise was deafening, like the static from a blank TV station times a hundred thousand. Russell Newland of the *San Francisco Chronicle* wrote:

> The fans made more noise per 100 pounds than any we've heard this season. Even the "hot dogs" were half again as thick as the one-handed "bow-wow" lunches Northern Californians bit into submission.

Our heads were so full of thoughts that nobody spoke before the game. We were like soldiers on their way to the front. By the time we finished all our warm-ups and drills, I was 100 percent concentration towards the job at hand. This time we were ready, and we were in great shape because nobody got to fall off the log. We were ready to go the whole sixty minutes.

We won the coin toss, and Kenny took the opening kickoff on the 10-yard line and ran it out to the 30. On fourth down we punted. USC took over the ball and tried to ram it down our throats. Granny Lansdell and Harry Smith put on a show, with Harry providing the best blocking I ever saw.

He cut Kenny Washington down cold, in the open, twice. The first time, Kenny was on defense, and Harry just laid him out as Granny went on by. That was the first time Kenny had been knocked off his feet by one man all year.

The second time, Kenny was running with the ball and Harry was maneuvering into position to make the tackle. Kenny must have said to himself, "Screw it, let's see how strong this guy really is." Kenny put his head down and drove at Harry as hard as he could. When they hit, all three of them, Kenny, Harry and the ball, hung there, like they were suspended in time. Then Kenny went over backwards, and Harry recovered the ball. I think that's when we realized we were up against the best.

Right after that fumble, USC almost scored. They got the ball down to our 11-yard line. . . .

They snapped the ball to Lansdell and he cut back over center. He was past our secondary before we knew what happened. Then suddenly Jackie Robinson came flying out of the corner. He put 180 pounds of wiry body behind his helmet and planted it right on the ball. This is what Dick Hyland wrote for the *Times*:

> The ball shot off the Trojan's chest like it had been blown from a gun barrel. No man's arm could have withstood that blow from Robinson's body, no bag of wind incased in leather could have done anything but react violently when compressed as that football was between Robinson and Lansdell. There was no individual fault in that play. Concerned, instead, were laws of physics pertaining to reactions.

It seemed like the ball laid there in the end zone for hours. Finally, I got down and scooped it up. Once I had it in my hands, I woke up quick like I had stuck my finger in a socket. I saw a picture of myself in the papers; my eyes looked like a frightened deer's, and I was striding the goddamnedest stride.

Two guys hit me right off. I got to the goal line and somebody else hit me; I kept on going. Suddenly I was in the clear and charging. I was thinking six points when Bob Hoffman brought me down on the 13. To this day, I don't know where he came from, but he saved a sure touchdown.

The first half ended scoreless. USC outplayed us, and we were lucky to still be in the game. . . .

In the second half [Kenny] came out throwing. He just missed on two touchdown passes to Jackie, and he threw a 44-yard pass the referee ruled I caught out-of-bounds. We started to click and gain momentum.

There were about five minutes left in the game when we took over on our own 20-yard line. Kenny went to the pass. He threw an 18-yarder to me. Then he hit Jackie Robinson for another first down on the USC 26. He threw another to me for a first down on the 15 and a fourth to Ned Mathews for 5 yards. Then Leo and Kenny, like a couple of bulldozers, picked up our last first down on the USC 3-yard line. . . .

It was first and goal on the USC 3-yard line. The whole series depended on Ned Mathews, just twenty years old, to call the right plays. On first down he called on number thirteen, and Kenny tried to crash through the left side of the Trojan line. That was Harry Smith's territory, and he stopped Kenny for no gain.

Ned decided to try the right side. We opened a hole four feet wide, and Leo Cantor was halfway through it when Bob Hoffman hit him and stood him straight up. After a second, Leo just plopped right where he was.

We called time-out to let Leo recover his senses. We got into our huddle, and Ned decided we'd try to surprise USC and call the same play. That was a mistake, because Leo was still woozy, and he lost 2 yards. It was fourth down on the 4-yard line. The ball was directly in front of the goal post. A little over thirty seconds were left in the game. [According] to Davis J. Walsh:

It wasn't just one of those things that cry aloud. Crying aloud, as a matter of fact, would have been

empty, footless, vapid in the midst of all the bluster and
uproar that went on yesterday. The situation didn't
even brusquely demand a field goal try. It fairly
shrieked for it, bellowed, trumpeted, clamored,
screamed and bleated almost obscenely in a shrill,
insensate falsetto.

We didn't kick it. Babe Horrell could have called time-out
and told us to kick, but he figured Ned had gotten us that far, he
might as well take us the rest of the way. In the huddle we took a
vote, should we go for six points or three?

Five of us voted touchdown, five of us voted field goal. It
was up to Ned to cast the deciding vote. He voted touchdown. All
his life Ned wanted to be part of the Thundering Herd; now he
had a chance to beat them. He wanted to do it right. He wanted
the touchdown.

Ned called a play designed to trick them. Kenny got the ball
and faked a run to the left. Jackie, Leo, and I all decoyed to draw
the defense away. While Kenny was moving left, he threw the
ball back across the field to Don McPherson, who was standing
all alone in the end zone. He had his fingertips on the ball when
Bob Hoffman stepped in front and knocked the ball to the ground.
The game ended scoreless.

# THE COURT-MARTIAL
# OF JACKIE ROBINSON

## JULES TYGIEL

*J*ackie Robinson dropped out of UCLA in the spring of
1941, just four months shy of graduation, to take a job
with the National Youth Administration. During the next
year he appeared in the college All-Star football game in
Chicago and played on semi-professional football teams in Los
Angeles and Hawaii. Following the outbreak of World War II, he
was drafted into the army.

Like many of his fellow African-American soldiers, Robinson fought his worst battles not in Europe or Asia, but on the
home front; his antagonist not Hitler nor Tojo, but Jim Crow.
From his early efforts to enter Officers' Candidate School to the
refusal to accept segregated seating on a military bus that led to
his court-martial, Robinson enlisted as a combatant in what the
Pittsburgh Courier called the "Double-V" campaign: victory at
home, as well as abroad, in the battle against racism. If, as most
historians argue, World War II was a crucial turning point for
the civil rights movement, it was due in no small part to the
courageous protests of Robinson and many other African-American

*military personnel who bravely challenged the racial status quo
amidst the cauldron of war.*

● ● ● ● ● ● ●

On July 6, 1944, Jackie Robinson, a twenty-five-year-old
lieutenant, boarded an Army bus at Fort Hood, Texas. Sixteen
months later he would be tapped as the man to break baseball's
color barrier, but in 1944 he was one of thousands of blacks thrust
into the Jim Crow South during World War II. He was with the
light-skinned wife of a fellow black officer, and the two walked
half the length of the bus, then sat down, talking amiably. The
driver, gazing into his rear-view mirror, saw a black officer seated
in the middle of the bus next to a woman who appeared to be
white. "Hey, you, sittin' beside that woman," he yelled. "Get to
the back of the bus."

Lieutenant Robinson ignored the order. The driver stopped
the bus, marched back to where the two passengers were sitting,
and demanded that the lieutenant "get to the back of the bus
where the colored people belong." Robinson refused, and so
began a series of events that led to his arrest and court-martial
and, finally, threatened his entire career.

Jackie Robinson was already a national celebrity in 1944.
During a spectacular athletic career at the University of California at Los Angeles, he had starred in basketball, football,
track, and baseball. He was drafted in April 1942, and during the
following year a study of blacks in the Army singled him out.
"Social intercourse between the races has been discouraged," it
was reported in *Jim Crow Joins Up*, "yet Negro athletes such as
Joe Louis, the prizefighter, and Jack Robinson, the All-American
football star . . . are today greatly admired in the army."

Initially, Robinson had been assigned to a cavalry unit at
Fort Riley, Kansas, where he applied for Officers' Candidate
School. Official Army policy provided for the training of black
officers in integrated facilities; in reality, however, few blacks
had yet gained access to OCS. At Fort Riley, Robinson was
rejected and told, off the record, that blacks were excluded from
OCS because they lacked leadership ability.

Robinson took his plight not to Army officials but to an even more commanding figure—Joe Louis, the heavyweight boxing champion of the world. Louis was also stationed at Fort Riley, and although he was not a commissioned officer, his status was somewhat higher than that of a raw recruit. Louis investigated the situation and arranged a meeting for black soldiers to voice their grievances in the presence of a representative of the secretary of war. Within a few days of this session, several blacks, including Robinson, were enrolled in OCS.

Robinson's Army career, however, continued to be stormy, and a good part of the tempest revolved around sports. Athletics were an important part of military life; teams from different Army forts competed against one another and against college teams. Professional and college athletes, once drafted, often found themselves spending the war on the baseball diamond or the gridiron. The coaches of Fort Riley's highly competitive football team tried to persuade Robinson—at the time more renowned for his football prowess than for his baseball skills—to join the squad.

Robinson had other ideas. Earlier in his Army career he had wanted to try out for the camp baseball team. Pete Reiser, who was to be Robinson's teammate on the Dodgers and who played on the Fort Riley squad, later recalled Robinson's humiliating rejection: "One day a Negro lieutenant came out for the ball team. An officer told him he couldn't play. 'You have to play for the colored team,' the officer said. That was a joke. There was no colored team. The lieutenant stood there for a while watching us work out. Then he turned and walked away. I didn't know who he was then, but that was the first time I saw Jackie Robinson. I can still remember him walking away by himself."

Refused the baseball field, Robinson balked at representing Fort Riley as a running back. A colonel threatened to order him to participate, but Robinson remained adamant. To the dismay of the Fort Riley football fans, the best running back in camp refused to suit up.

In January 1943 Robinson was commissioned a second lieutenant and appointed acting morale officer for a black company at Fort Riley. As might be expected, the principal obstacles to high morale were the Jim Crow regulations governing the camp. Particularly upsetting were conditions at the post exchange, where only a few seats had been set aside for black soldiers. Robinson telephoned the base provost marshal, Major Hafner, to protest this situation; the major said that taking seats away from the white soldiers and giving them to black would cause a problem among the white troops. Furthermore, he could not believe that the lieutenant actually wanted the races seated together.

"Let me put it this way," Robinson remembered the officer as saying: "How would you like to have your wife sitting next to a nigger?"

Robinson exploded. "Major, I happen to be a Negro," he shouted, "and I don't know that to have anyone's wife sitting next to a Negro is any worse than to have her sitting next to some of these white soldiers I see around here."

"I just want you to know," said Hafner, "that I don't want my wife sitting close to any colored guy."

"How the hell do you know that your wife hasn't already been close to one?" asked Robinson as he launched into a tirade against the major.

The provost marshal hung up on him, but Robinson's protest was not fruitless: although separate areas in the post exchange remained the rule, blacks were allotted additional seats.

Robinson was never punished or disciplined for being insolent to his superior officer, but he was soon transferred to the 761st Tank Battalion at Fort Hood, Texas. It was not an improvement. "The prejudice and discrimination at Camp Hood made [other bases] seem ultraliberal in [their] attitude," recalled Harry Duplessis, one of Robinson's fellow black officers. "Camp Hood was frightening. . . . Segregation there was so complete that I even saw outhouses marked White, Colored, and Mexican."

Nevertheless, Robinson's performance was so outstanding that even though he was on "limited service" because of an old ankle injury, his commanding officer requested that he go overseas with the battalion. In order to do so, Robinson was required to sign a waiver relieving the Army of all responsibility in the event of injury. Robinson agreed, but Army medical authorities insisted the ankle be examined before giving their approval.

The medical examination took place at a hospital thirty miles from Fort Hood. While waiting for the results, Robinson got a pass to visit with his company. He arrived at the base to find the battalion off on maneuvers, so he stopped at the officers' club, where he met Mrs. Gordon H. Jones, the wife of another black lieutenant. Since she lived on the way to the hospital, they boarded the bus together.

For black soldiers in the South, the shortest bus trip could be a humiliating and even dangerous experience. According to the *Pittsburgh Courier*, which cited a "mountain of complaints from Negro soldiers," "frustrations on buses in the South was one of the most fruitful sources of trouble for Negro soldiers." In Durham, North Carolina, only weeks before, an altercation had ended with the driver shooting and killing a black soldier who had refused to move to the back of a bus. The driver was tried and found not guilty by a civilian jury. Unable to change the rules on civilian bus lines, the Army began to provide its own, nonsegregated buses on Southern bases. The action was given no publicity at first and was ignored at many bases. In June 1944, however, the story had been made public, and the resulting furor had brought the Army policy to the attention of many black soldiers.

When Robinson boarded the bus with Mrs. Jones on July 6, he was aware that military buses had been ordered desegregated. As he wrote to the National Association for the Advancement of Colored People two weeks later, "I refused to move because I recalled a letter from Washington which states that there is to be no segregation on army posts." In his autobiography Robinson stated that the boxers Joe Louis and Ray Robinson had also influenced his actions by their recent refusals to obey Jim Crow regulations at a bus depot in Alabama. In any event, Lieutenant Robinson told the driver: "The Army recently issued orders that there is to be no more racial segregation on any Army post. This is an Army bus operating on an Army post."

The man backed down, but at the end of the line, as Robinson and Mrs. Jones waited for a second bus, he returned with his dispatcher and two other drivers. The dispatcher turned to the driver and asked, "Is this the nigger that's been causing you trouble?" Leaving Mrs. Jones, Robinson shook a finger in the driver's face and told him to "quit f——— with me." As Robinson started walking away, two military policemen arrived on the scene and suggested that he explain the situation to the provost marshal.

Lieutenant Robinson was driven to military police head-quarters by two MP's. They were met there by Pvt. Ben W. Mucklerath, who asked Cpl. George A. Elwood, one of ten MP's, if he had a "nigger lieutenant" in the car. Robinson told the enlisted man that "if he ever called me nigger again I would break him in two." The first officer on the scene was Capt. Peelor Wig-ginton, the officer of the day. When Wigginton began to take Mucklerath's story, Robinson interrupted. He was ordered out of the room until the assistant provost marshal, Capt. Gerald M. Bear, came to take over the investigation.

When the Southern-born Captain Bear arrived, Robinson started to follow him into the guard room, only to be told, "Nobody comes into the room until I tell him." Why then, asked Robinson, was Private Mucklerath already in the room? When Captain Wigginton began briefing Captain Bear on Mucklerath's testimony, Robinson, standing by the door, complained that the account was inaccurate.

The hostility grew with the arrival of a civilian woman named Wilson who was to record Robinson's statement. Robinson later recalled that the stenographer continually inter-rupted his statement with her own questions and comments, such as, "Don't you know you have no right sitting up there in the white part of the bus." Robinson challenged the right of a Texas civilian to interrogate him and finally snapped at her to stop inter-rupting. Captain Bear growled something about his being "uppity," and when Robinson insisted on making corrections in the written statement before signing it, the civilian stenographer jumped up and said, "I don't have to take that sassy kind of talk from you."

As a result of the evening's events, camp officials were determined to court-martial Robinson. When his commanding officer, Col. R. L. Bates, refused to endorse the court-martial orders, the authorities transferred Robinson to the 758th Tank Battalion, whose commander promptly signed. Robinson was charged with insubordination, disturbing the peace, drunkenness, conduct unbecoming an officer, insulting a civilian woman, and refusing to obey the lawful orders of a superior officer.

Faced with so many counts, Robinson feared that there was a conspiracy against him at Fort Hood and that he would be dishonorably discharged. He wrote to the NAACP for "advice or help on the matter.

"The people have a pretty good bunch of lies," he reported. "When I read some of the statements of the witnesses I was certain that these people had got together and was going to frame me." While admitting that he had cursed after the bus dispatcher had called him a "nigger," he denied "calling the people around all sorts of names." "If I didn't respect them," he protested, "I certainly would have Mrs. Jones."

Robinson was particularly upset because officials had not even asked Mrs. Jones to give a statement. He felt that he was "being unfairly punished because I wouldn't be pushed around by the driver of the bus," and was "looking for a civilian lawyer to handle my case because I know he will be able to free the truth with a little technique."

His fear of a conspiracy was not groundless. During World War II, according to the historian Jack D. Foner, "many black soldiers were unjustly convicted by courts-martial, either because their officers assumed their guilt regardless of the evidence or because they wanted to 'set an example' for other black soldiers." The demand on the NAACP for assistance for black soldiers was so great that they had to turn down most requests unless the case was deemed to be "of national importance to the Negro race." In a letter actually dated one day after the trial, the NAACP informed Robinson that "we will be unable to furnish you with an attorney in the event that you are court-martialled."

Meanwhile, among black soldiers in the Southwest, "Jackie Robinson's encounter with a cracker bus driver" had become, according to Lieutenant Duplessis, the "racial cause célèbre." Robinson's hasty transfer from the 761st Tank Battalion to the

758th led many black officers to believe that the Army was attempting to try him in secrecy. A group of them wrote letters to the NAACP and to two of the more influential black newspapers, the *Pittsburgh Courier* and the *Chicago Defender*. Lt. Ivan Harrison recalls the campaign as follows: "The NAACP, his fraternity, and the Negro press soon learned about Jackie and the messages began to pour in demanding to know what happened. They moved Jackie to another camp, then answered he was no longer a member of the 761st. Of course, the black underground soon notified them where he could be found. . . . It was beginning to be such a hot potato that they held what I am sure was the shortest court-martial in the history of the armed services."

Harrison was wrong about that; the court-martial proceedings lasted more than four hours. And although the black press made scant mention of the Robinson case, the officers' campaign did have some notable success. All charges stemming from the actual incident on the bus and Robinson's argument with the civilian secretary were dropped. He had still to face a court-martial, but on the two lesser charges of insubordination arising from his confrontation in the guardhouse.

Although the dismissal of the more serious charges was to Robinson's advantage, it also made his defense more difficult. He was being tried for insubordination, but no mention of the event which caused this rebellious behavior—the encounter on the bus—was to be allowed. Nor were the actions of the stenographer to be considered. Robinson was no longer on trial for refusing to move to the back of a bus, which was within his rights, or for responding to the racial slurs of a civilian, but for acting with "disrespect" toward Captain Bear and disobeying a lawful command given by that officer.

In the meantime, a problem had arisen regarding Robinson's defense. Unable to get help from the NAACP, he had been assigned a young Southern lawyer to act as his counsel. Before Robinson could even protest, the lawyer withdrew from the case: having been raised in the South, he said, he had not "developed arguments against segregation" that were necessary to defend Robinson adequately. He did, however, arrange for Robinson to engage Lt. William Cline, a lawyer from the Midwest who was eager to handle the case.

The court-martial of 2d Lt. Jackie Robinson took place on August 2, 1944. The heart of the prosecution's case was presented by Captains Bear and Wigginton, who told essentially the same story. As they had attempted to ascertain the facts of the events of July 6, Robinson continually interrupted them and acted disrespectfully. When ordered from the room, according to Bear, Robinson continued to stand by the half-gate door, "leaning on the half gate down in a slouching position with his elbows resting on the gate, and he kept interrupting." Several times, said Bear, he told the black lieutenant to get away from the door, and in response, Robinson bowed and said, "O.K., sir. O.K., sir. O.K., sir." Bear demonstrated the way in which Robinson bowed as he "kind of smirked or grimaced his face."

Captain Bear testified that he gave Robinson a direct order to remain seated until called upon. Instead the lieutenant went outside and was "pitching rocks" and talking to the driver of a jeep. When ordered back inside, said Bear, Robinson complied "reluctantly . . . with his hands in his pockets, swaying, shifting his weight form one foot to the other."

When Robinson was brought into the orderly room to make his statement, said Bear, "everything he said seemed facetious to him, and he seemed to be trying to make fun of it . . . he would raise and lower his words, and he would say, 'Oh, yeah' when I would ask him a question, and several times I asked him not to go so fast and to tone his language down." He seemed "argumentative" and asked questions such as, "Well, do I have to answer that?" When asked to speak more slowly, according to Bear, Robinson began to "baby talk," exaggerating the pause between each word.

Once Robinson's statement had been taken, Bear arranged transportation for him back to the hospital, but the lieutenant stated that he did not want to go back, since he had a pass until eight in the morning. In Captain Wigginton's opinion, Robinson was "very disrespectful," which led the officer of the day to threaten to arrest him for insubordination.

In his own testimony Robinson countered most of the accusations against him. He admitted breaking in on the conversation between Captain Wigginton and Private Mucklerath, but "to my mind I was not interrupting at all; Pvt. Mucklerath stated something that I did not think was quite right and I interrupted him to see if I could . . . get him to correct his statement." After complaining that Mucklerath had called him a "nigger lieutenant," he was asked if he knew what a nigger was. "I looked it up once," said Robinson, "but my grandmother gave me a good definition, she was a slave, and she said the definition of the word was a low, uncouth person, and pertains to no one in particular; but I don't consider that I am low and uncouth. . . . When I made this statement I did not like to be called nigger, I told the Captain, I said, 'If you call me a nigger, I might have said the same thing to you. . . .' I do not consider myself a nigger at all. I am a Negro, but not a nigger."

Robinson denied most of the specific accusations made against him and stated that Bear had been "not polite at all" from the moment he arrived, and "very uncivil toward me" when taking the statement. "He did not seem to recognize me as an officer at all. But I did consider myself an officer and felt that I should be addressed as one." And, he added bitterly, "they asked that private to sit down."

Robinson's testimony held up better under cross-examination than did Bear's or Wigginton's. There were several flaws and omissions in the accounts of the two captains. Referring to the "argumentative" questions Robinson had raised in giving his statement, Cline asked Bear if it was "improper for an accused to make such inquiry as that." When prodded, Bear stated that it was not. Had not Bear ordered Robinson to "be at ease," asked one of the judges presiding. If so, he continued, "I do not see the manner in which he leaned on the gate had anything to do with you."

The questions of whether Robinson had been placed under arrest on July 6 and whether he had refused to accept the transportation that Bear had ordered for his return to the hospital were also targets of the cross-examination. Defense questioning revealed that the vehicle provided was, in reality, a military police pickup truck. Yet Bear had testified that he had informed

Robinson that he was being placed under arrest in quarters, in which case, no bodily restrictions were allowed. Robinson was within his rights to protest.

Lieutenant Cline was not totally successful in discrediting the witnesses for the prosecution. Efforts to relate Robinson's behavior to the incident on the bus were disallowed. Both Bear and Wigginton denied that there had been any unusual exchange between Robinson and the stenographer, preventing the defense from exploring this aspect of the case. Nonetheless, by the time the two men left the witness stand, key segments of their testimony had been either repudiated or placed in doubt.

The prosecution's cross-examination of Lieutenant Robinson was far less effective. Robinson denied having had any drinks that evening, though "evidently they thought I had." He also stated that he had not willfully disobeyed a direct order. The only reason that he had argued with Bear, he explained, was that he had asked the captain half a dozen times whether he was under arrest—and if he was not, Robinson wanted to know why he was being escorted back to the hospital under guard. By his own admission, Bear had given Robinson ambiguous answers. Unlike Bear and Wigginton, Robinson was subjected to virtually no examination by the court-martial board.

The defense also presented several character witnesses from Robinson's battalion. The most significant testimony came from Colonel Bates. Bates stated that Robinson was an officer he would like to have under his command in combat, and several times the prosecution and the court itself reprimanded the colonel for volunteering unsolicited praise of Robinson.

When the defense had rested, the prosecution called a few additional witnesses. All supported the story told by Captains Bear and Wigginton but none proved to be particularly effective. Private Mucklerath was notably lacking in credibility. While he recalled Robinson's vow that if the private ever "called him a nigger he would break [me] in two," he denied having used that term and could not explain why the black lieutenant had said this. He was followed to the stand, however, by Corporal Elwood, who, while generally supporting the testimony of the other whites, admitted that Mucklerath had indeed asked him if he had a "nigger lieutenant" in the car.

Elwood was the last witness to be heard. The attorneys then made their closing arguments, and Robinson later recalled: "My lawyer summed up the case beautifully by telling the board that this was not a case involving any violation of the Articles of War, or even of military tradition, but simply a situation in which a few individuals sought to vent their bigotry on a Negro they considered 'uppity' because he had the audacity to exercise rights that belonged to him as an American and a soldier."

Robinson and his lawyer then settled down to await the verdict. They did not have long to wait. Voting by secret written ballot, the nine judges found Robinson "not guilty of all specifications and charges."

The ordeal that had begun almost a month earlier on a military bus was finally over. To some extent the acquittal was due to the fact that Robinson was a renowned figure—his conviction might have proven an embarrassment for the Army. For most other black soldiers, however, neither military nor Southern justice was likely to have produced such a conclusion.

Robinson was now free to resume his service career, but his Army experiences had taken their toll on his patriotic fervor. A month earlier he had been willing to waive his rights to compensation for injury and go overseas, but now his main desire was to leave the service altogether. With Colonel Bates and his tank battalion already on the way to Europe, Robinson did not wish to join another unit. He asked to be released from the Army. He was quickly transferred to Camp Breckinridge, Kentucky, where he coached black athletic teams until he was honorably discharged in November 1944.

Had the court-martial of Jackie Robinson been an isolated incident, it would be little more than a curious episode in the life of a great athlete. His humiliating confrontations with discrimination, however, were typical of the experience of the black soldier; and his rebellion against Jim Crow attitudes was just one of the many instances in which blacks, recruited to fight a war against racism in Europe, began to resist the dictates of segregation in

America. As Robinson later wrote of his acquittal at Fort Hood, "It was a small victory, for I had learned that I was in two wars, one against the foreign enemy, the other against prejudice at home."

Even Robinson could not have realized how high the personal stakes were when he refused to move to the back of the bus in 1944. Had he been convicted of the more serious charges and, as he feared, dishonorably discharged, it is doubtful that Branch Rickey, general manager of the Brooklyn National League Club, would have chosen him to integrate organized baseball in 1946. In the climate of postwar America, a black man banished from the Army could have found little popular support. It is not unreasonable to suppose that Robinson, who was already twenty-eight years old when he joined the Brooklyn Dodgers, might never have made it to the major leagues had he been forced to wait for another man to act as trailblazer. Fortunately, his defiance had precisely the opposite effect. His Army experiences, which graphically illustrated the black man's lot in America, also demonstrated Jackie Robinson's courage and pride. These were the very qualities that would prove essential in making the assault on baseball's color line.

# "He Did Far More for Me . . ."

## RED BARBER WITH ROBERT CREAMER

*I*n early 1945, as World War II drew to a close, Brooklyn Dodgers president Branch Rickey had determined to break baseball's longstanding color barrier. No one outside of Rickey's immediate family and (contrary to the following recollections) the Dodgers board of directors knew of these plans. Significantly, the first Dodger employee that Rickey took into his confidence was not manager Leo Durocher, nor the front-office personnel, but radio announcer Red Barber.

Red Barber, first with the Cincinnati Reds and after 1937 with the Brooklyn Dodgers, had pioneered the craft of baseball broadcasting. His popularity with the Brooklyn fans rivalled that of the players. But Barber had been born and raised in the South and had never questioned the racial assumptions of his upbringing. Rickey's revelation that a black player would soon be joining the Dodgers precipitated a crisis of conscience, causing Barber to reassess not only his beliefs on race, but the meaning of Christianity.

In the following passage, from his book Rhubarb in the Cat-bird Seat, Barber recounts his shocking conversation with Rickey *and movingly re-creates how his tortured decision to "broadcast the ball" taught him about love and tolerance. Barber's reaction also reinforced Rickey's conviction that individuals, even those raised in the South, would be able to overcome long-held prejudices in a quest for the common good.*

● ● ● ● ● ● ●

Mr. Rickey and I left Cashmore's office in Borough Hall and walked around to Joe's Restaurant, which was an old landmark in Brooklyn. It was just around the corner from the Dodger offices at 215 Montague Street. When we went in the place, it was practically empty because it was well past the luncheon period. Mr. Rickey walked to a table way in the back of the restaurant, and I followed. We sat down and gave our order, and the waiter left. We were completely alone.

I recall very distinctly that he picked up a hard roll and broke it into pieces, and that he kept jabbing his knife into the butter and dabbing the butter onto the pieces of roll and then eating them.

He said, "I'm going to tell you something. I'm going to tell you something that even my board of directors doesn't know. No one knows outside of the family."

He chewed another piece of roll and then he said, "When I was baseball coach at the University of Michigan—I coached baseball there while I was getting my law degree—the best player I had one year was a catcher. He was a splendid young man. He was a Negro from Upper Michigan and his family was the only Negro family in that area. When he came to Ann Arbor he was by and large unaware that he was a Negro in a white world. He had had no unpleasant experiences.

"Early in the season we went down to South Bend, Indiana, to play Notre Dame. We were staying at the Oliver Hotel. I stood at the desk registering my players, saying this is so-and-so, and this is so-and-so, and getting their room keys for them and sending them off to their rooms. When the catcher came up the room clerk pulled back the register and he said, 'We do not take Negroes here.'

"I was stunned, and the boy didn't know what hit him. I explained to the room clerk that this was the catcher for the University of Michigan team, and that the University of Michigan team had complete reservations. We were guests of the University of Notre Dame.

"The room clerk was blunt and rude and vocally firm. He said they did not register Negroes, and that they were not going to register this one, and he didn't care if it was the University of Michigan baseball team or football team or what. Quite a crowd had gathered around by now, listening and watching. I said to the room clerk, 'Well, now. We have to have some way out of this. He has to have a place to sleep. Would you object if he slept in the extra bed in my room, as long as you don't have to register him?' And the clerk said, 'All right. You can do that.'

"He turned and got the key and handed it to me, and I gave it to my catcher. I said, 'Now you go up to the room, and you stay there until I come up. I'll be up just as soon as I can finish registering the rest of the team. It won't be but a couple of minutes. You go ahead.'

"When I finished registering the rest of the team, I went up to the room, pushed open the door, and went inside. And there was this fine young man, sitting on the edge of a chair, crying. He was crying as though his heart would break. His whole body was racked with sobs. He was pulling frantically at his hands, pulling at his hands, pulling at his hands. He looked at me and he said, 'It's my skin. If I could just tear it off, I'd be like everybody else. It's my skin. It's my skin, Mr. Rickey.' "

There in Joe's Restaurant in Brooklyn, this bear-shaped man with the dark, bushy eyebrows broke another hard roll, spilled crumbs all over the place, jabbed at the butter. He was angry all over again. He was back in the Oliver Hotel in South Bend.

Then he leaned forward across the table and said, "You know, I have formed a Negro baseball team called the Brooklyn Brown Dodgers."

I said, "Is that the team that's going to go into the Negro League?"

He said, "Yes. I have all my Dodger scouts out looking for Negro players. They're scouting them all over the Caribbean.

They're scouting them all over the United States. I've got Sukey [he meant Clyde Sukeforth, who was his best scout] and all the others out working on this. They are scouting Negro players only."

He chewed on a piece of roll. "They think they're scouting them for the Brown Dodgers."

I didn't react at all. I really didn't understand what he was talking about.

Abruptly, he said, "I have never been able to shake the picture of that fine young man tearing at his hands, and telling me that it was his skin, and that if he could just tear it off he would be like everybody else. As the years have come and gone, this has hurt me inside. And I have made up my mind that before I pass on I am going to do something about it."

He looked at me. "What I am telling you is this: there is a Negro ballplayer coming to the *Dodgers*, not the Brown Dodgers. I don't know who he is, and I don't know where he is, and I don't know when he's coming. But he is *coming*. And he is coming soon, just as soon as we can find him."

Again, I didn't say a word. I couldn't.

"Needless to say," he went on, "I have taken you into my confidence in telling you this. I have talked about it only with my family. Jane is utterly opposed to my doing it. The family is dead set against it. But I have got to do it. I must do it. I will do it. I *am* doing it. And now you know it."

This was a year before I heard the name Robinson. It was a full year later—Rickey never talked to me about it again—that I picked up the paper and saw that Jackie Robinson had been signed and was going to play that season with Montreal, Brooklyn's number one farm team. I said to myself, "Well, he said he was going to do it."

I have often wondered why this man told *me* about his earth-shaking project that afternoon in Joe's Restaurant. You could argue that the thing had become so much a part of him, and the opposition of his family was so complete and he was carrying all of this inside himself, that he had to have some human being to speak out loud to, that he had to have some other human being hear him say what was inside him. You could say he paid me a

high compliment in choosing me as the human being that he
would trust to listen to him and respect his confidence.

But Rickey's strength was such that he could walk his way
alone. I don't think he needed me as his confessor. And, certainly, when he spoke to me about it, I gave him back no support.
I gave him back 100 percent silence, because he had shaken me.
He had shaken me to my heels.

And I think *that* is why he told me, because he knew it would
shake me. He always told me that I was the most valuable person
in Brooklyn to him and the ball club. He never let me forget that
I had a great public relations worth to him and the Dodgers,
and that I was doing valuable work. He saw to it that I was left
alone, that I was free to do my job the way I wanted to do it. I
don't believe anyone was able to go to Rickey and say something
critical of my broadcasting. He stopped them. He wouldn't listen
to them. He would say, "You don't know his job and his problems. He does. He handles things in his own way. You leave him
alone."

Rickey saw to it, in other words, that I had sole occupancy
of the catbird seat, but he shook me that afternoon in Joe's
Restaurant. He needed me in Brooklyn, or he *wanted* me in
Brooklyn, which is more accurate. But he knew that the coming
of a Negro ballplayer could disturb me, could upset me. I believe
he told me about it so far in advance so that I could have time to
wrestle with the problem, live with it, solve it. I was born in Mississippi. I grew up in Florida. My father was from North Carolina. My mother's people were long-time Mississippians. My
entire heredity and environment was of the Deep South. Florida is
not Deep South in the sense that Mississippi, Alabama, Georgia
and South Carolina would be considered Deep South—Florida
has always been a more cosmopolitan state—but make no mistake about it, it is still a southern state. So I was raised southern. I
was raised by wonderful, tolerant people who taught me never to
speak unkindly to anyone or to take advantage of anyone. The
Negroes who came and went through our lives were always
treated with the utmost respect and a great deal of warmth and a
great deal of affection. But there was a line drawn, and that line
was always there.

I know that it gave me great pause when I first went to Cincinnati, the first time I went north to live. I wondered how I could get along in a northern city. Well, I got along all right, because I tended strictly to my own business. But what Mr. Rickey told me in Joe's Restaurant meant that this was now part of my business. I would still be broadcasting baseball, with all its closeness and intimate friendships and back-and-forth and give-and-take, but now a Negro player would be part of all that. And if he meant one Negro player, he meant more than one. He meant that the complexion (and this is no play on words) in the dugout and the clubhouse was going to be drastically and permanently changed.

I went home that night to Scarsdale and as soon as I got in the house I told my wife what Mr. Rickey had said. (That was in no sense a violation of confidence: Rickey believed in wives and husbands sharing each other's lives.) I told her about it, and I said to her, "I'm going to quit. I don't think I want—I don't know whether I can—I'm going to quit."

She said, "Well, it's your job and you're the one who's going to have to make the decision. But it's not immediate. You don't have to do anything about it right now. Why don't we have a martini? And then let's have dinner."

So time went by and, as I said, Mr. Rickey never referred to it again. But the thing was gnawing on me. It tortured me. I finally found myself doing something I had never really done before. I set out to do a deep self-examination. I attempted to find out who I was. This did not come easily, and it was not done lightly.

I had to face the economic side of things. That was a great job in Brooklyn and, other things being equal, I did not want to leave it. I was very happy in my work, very happy at Brooklyn. (That's why I left in 1953, when I found I could not be happy broadcasting in Brooklyn under Walter O'Malley—the happiness that I had in Ebbets Field was too precious to me to dilute and vitiate, so I left.) Even so, when I was thinking about the impending arrival of the man who turned out to be Jackie Robinson and saying to myself, "Don't be in such a hurry to walk away from a great job," I wasn't afraid of leaving. I was only thirty-seven years old. I still had the confidence of youth. I have always felt that I could make a living. My father used to tell me, "Son, don't let anybody ever tell you that the job you have is the *only* job you can have. And don't ever let a man make you afraid of your job." My father told me that when I was a boy, and he repeated it during my adolescence, and whenever anybody has threatened me, his words come back and I react rather strongly. So it wasn't so much the loss of the job itself. It was leaving something I loved.

But then I had to ask myself, what is it that is so upsetting about the prospect of working with a Negro ballplayer? Or broadcasting the play of a Negro ballplayer? Or traveling with a Negro ballplayer? What is it that has me so stirred up? Why did I react the way I did when Rickey told me he was bringing in a Negro player? Why did I go straight home and tell my wife I was going to quit?

Well, I said, I'm southern. I'm trained. Of course, that answer came to me more clearly some years later when I saw *South Pacific*; I didn't know it at the time I was struggling to find the answer. In that great show there was a song, "You've Got To Be Carefully Taught." That was my problem. I had been carefully taught, and not just by my parents. I had been taught by everybody I had been around. I had been carefully taught by Negroes and whites alike. I was a product of a civilization: that line that was always there was indelible. All right, I said, I'm southern.

And then—I don't know why the thought came to my mind—I asked myself the basic question that a human being, if he is fair, ought to ask. How much control did I have over the parents I was born to? The answer was immediate: I didn't have any. By an accident of birth I was born to Selena and William Barber, white, Protestant, in Columbus, Mississippi, February 17, 1908. And due to circumstances over which I had no control, I stayed in Columbus, Mississippi, until I was ten and then I stayed in Florida until I was a grown man. The first time I had something to do with what I was doing was when I left Sanford and went up to work my way through the University of Florida. For the rest of it, I had some vote in the matter.

Then, of course, I worked out that but for an accident of

birth I could have been born to black parents. I could have been born to any parents. Then I figured out that I didn't have anything to be so proud of after all, this accident of the color of my skin.

Just about that time, the rector of the church of St. James the Less in Scarsdale asked me to do a radio talk for him out in Westchester County. You look back and you say to yourself, how marvelous it is the way things synchronize in your life, how they fit and mesh together, the timing. I had been brought up in a family that believed in religion. I had gone to Sunday School as a regular thing, and later, as a young man, I taught Sunday School briefly myself. But I lost the habit of going to church after I got involved in broadcasting, and it wasn't until after the birth of our daughter Sarah that I became interested again. My father was a Baptist and my mother was a Presbyterian, but I married an Episcopalian and when I went back to church I went back as an Episcopalian. And so, while I was trying to work out this thing of who I am, and this accident of birth, and losing a lot of false pride, the Reverend Harry Price, an Episcopal clergyman I had gotten to know, asked me to do this radio talk. The talk, built on a sentence from St. Paul, was to be called "Men and Brothers." And what the rector wanted me to talk about was a problem that was coming to a head then. It was just about the time that it was beginning to get attention, and later it got to be quite serious and it hasn't diminished. It was the problem of the relationship between the Jews and the non-Jews in the wealthy community of Scarsdale, New York. It was going pretty good—and it still is. A lot of people forgot that Jesus was a Jew. Some embarrassingly sickening things were beginning to happen. Sad things were being said. Things were being done to children. And so the rector asked me to talk about men and brothers, with the idea being that whether you were a Jew or a Christian, you were brothers. You were men, and you were men and brothers together, and you should get along together.

Well, when I worked out that talk I suddenly found that I wasn't nearly so interested in the relationship between Christians and Jews, Jews and Christians, as I was about the relationship between one white southern broadcaster and one unknown Negro ballplayer, who was coming. That talk—working it out, preparing it, giving it—I don't know how much help it gave to anyone who was listening, but it helped me a great deal. What was my job? What was my function? What was I supposed to do as I broadcast baseball games? As I worked along on that line, I remembered something about Bill Klem, the great umpire. Klem always said, "All there is to umpiring is umpiring the ball." When you think about it, that is the one thing you must tell a fellow who wants to umpire. Just umpire the ball. There are a couple of other technicalities that you have to know, of course, but the ball is the basic thing. Is the ball foul or fair? Is the ball a good pitch or a bad pitch? Did the ball get to the base before the runner did, or did it not? Did the ball stick in the fielder's glove, or did it bounce out? An umpire doesn't care anything about how big the crowd is or which team is ahead or who the runner is on third or whether this is the winning run that is approaching the plate. All he does is umpire the ball. It doesn't matter whether the man at bat is a great star or a brand-new rookie. It doesn't even matter what color he is.

I took that and worked over it a little bit, and I said, "Well, isn't that what I'm supposed to do? Just broadcast the ball? Certainly, a broadcaster is concerned with who is at the plate— you're deeply concerned. You're concerned about the score, and the excitement of the crowd, and the drama of the moment. You do care if this is the winning run approaching the plate. But still, basically, primarily, beyond everything else, you broadcast the ball—*what* is happening to it. All you have to do is tell the people what is going on."

I got something else in my head then. I understood that I was not a sociologist, that I was not Mr. Rickey, that I was not building the ball club, that I was not putting players on the field, that I was not involved in a racial experiment, that I did not care what anybody else said, thought, or did about this Negro player who was coming and who's name I still did not know. All I had to do when he came—and I didn't say *if* he came, because after Rickey talked to me I *knew* he was coming—all I had to do when he came was treat him as a man, a fellow man, treat him as a ballplayer, broadcast the ball.

I had this all worked out before I ever read that Jackie

Robinson was signed and going to Montreal. And when he did come, I didn't broadcast Jackie Robinson, I broadcast what Jackie Robinson did. Sometimes it was quite interesting. But it was what *he* did that made it interesting. All I did was broadcast it, which was my job. . . .

If I did do anything constructive in the Robinson situation, it was simply in accepting him the way I did—as a man, as a ballplayer. I didn't resent him, and I didn't crusade for him. I broadcast the ball.

It was a sensitive, even delicate, situation. After all, I had the microphone, and I had the southern accent, and I had millions of people listening to every word I said. And this thing was not something that you were suddenly confronted with one day, and then didn't have to worry about anymore. It had to be handled inning by inning, game by game, month by month. It was there all the time because when Robinson came, he came to stay.

I think I did it the right way. I know that Jack told me he appreciated what I did, and Mr. Rickey said he thoroughly approved. Other people were kind in their comments, too. It's been written about in newspapers and magazines and in a couple of books. I never had any backlash from my listeners, to use a word that has come into popular use but which no one ever thought of using in that context then. To my knowledge, the Brooklyn broadcasters never had any backlash, either white or black, in the slightest degree. I know I never heard of any.

And so I am proud—in that meaning of self-respect—of this. But I would like to say something else. While I deeply appreciate it when Jack Robinson thanks me, I know that if I have achieved any understanding or tolerance in my life, if I have been able to implement in any way St. Paul's dictum of men and brothers, if I have been able to follow a little better the second great commandment, which is to love thy neighbor, it all stems from this. That word "love," in the Biblical sense, comes from the Greek word, *agape*. In Greek, the language that the New Testament was written in, the word *agape* means "to have concern for." That is the sense in which Christ used it when he said the second great commandment was like the first—the first was to love God, and the second was to love your fellow man. It means

that far from "loving" him, you can hate his guts, but if he's hurting, you're to help him. If he falls, you pick him up. If he's
hungry, you feed him. You don't have to like him. It has nothing
to do with love in the romantic, physical sense. Jesus dramatized
this in his story about the Good Samaritan. A man was jumped
on and beaten and robbed by thugs and left lying in a road. A
rich man, of the same racial strain, came along and saw the
wounded man and ignored him, left him lying there. A priest, a
priest of the man's own religion, passed him by. But a fellow
who was foreign and of a different religion and of a different
color skin—there was fear and bitter hatred between the different
peoples there in the Holy Land, and it continues to this day—
when this fellow saw the man lying there he turned back from
where he was going, helped the man to an inn, and had him bandaged and fed and put to bed. He told the innkeeper to take care
of him and whatever the bill was, he would pay it. That is concern, that is love. It is a great thing to have.

So, if I have been able to implement to any degree the
second great commandment, to have concern. . . . Well, what I
am trying to say is, if there is any thanks involved, any appreciation, I thank Jackie Robinson. He did far more for me than I did
for him.

# "Oh, They Were a Pair"

## Clyde Sukeforth as Told to Donald Honig

C lyde Sukeforth spent parts of ten seasons as a light-hitting reserve catcher in the major leagues. During those years he hit only two home runs and drove in a total of ninety-six runs. Sukeforth's near-legendary reputation, however, evolves not from his playing days, but from his acumen as a scout during a career that spanned a half-century after his catching days had ended.

In 1945 Branch Rickey instructed Sukeforth and other major Dodgers scouts to assess Negro League players as part of an alleged plan to create an all-black club called the Brooklyn Brown Bombers. That August Rickey dispatched Sukeforth to check out the shortstop for the Kansas City Monarchs. If Sukeforth liked the way the shortstop threw, Rickey instructed him, he was to bring the player back to Brooklyn to meet with Rickey. Sukeforth's subsequent scouting trip and the resulting summit at the Dodgers offices on Montague Street have become a part of American sports forklore.

In an interview with oral historian Donald Honig in Baseball: When the Grass Was Real, Sukeforth described these fateful *events, and, with the fine eye that made him such an effective scout, also captured life in the Negro Leagues, American racial mores, and the dynamic personalities of Rickey and Robinson.*

● ● ● ● ● ● ●

Well, I've been in baseball for about fifty years now, and it's never been dull. Disappointing sometimes, yes; frustrating sometimes, certainly; and sometimes it's been downright infuriating. But never dull. I've been a player, coach, manager, scout. So I've seen the game from every possible angle.

I stayed with the Brooklyn organization after my playing days were over. I did some scouting, minor-league managing, coaching, even managed the Dodgers for a couple of games at the beginning of the 1947 season, after Durocher was suspended and before Burt Shotton came in. That was a job I was glad to get *out* of. That wasn't for me. You've got to have the right temperament to manage a big league ball club.

Branch Rickey took over as general manger during the war, and we got along fine. . . .

Mr. Rickey sent me out on an assignment which I guess you might describe as memorable. This was in August, 1945. We were still with Brooklyn. He called me into his office one day and told me to have a seat.

"The Kansas City Monarchs are playing the Lincoln Giants in Chicago on Friday night," he said. "I want you to see that game. I want you to see that fellow Robinson on Kansas City. Talk to him before the game. Tell him who sent you. Tell him I want to know if he's got a shortstop's arm, if he can throw from the hole. Ask Robinson to have his coach hit him some balls in the hole."

Mr. Rickey had been talking about establishing a Negro club in New York called the Brooklyn Brown Bombers, and we had been scouting the Negro Leagues for more than a year. But you know, there was always something strange about it. He told us he didn't want this idea of his getting around, that nobody was supposed to know what we were doing. So instead of showing our credentials and walking into a ball park, as we normally would have done, we always bought a ticket and made ourselves as inconspicuous as possible.

"Now, Clyde," the old man went on, "if you like this fellow's arm, bring him in. And if his schedule won't permit it, if he can't come in, then make an appointment for me and I'll go out there."

Mr. Rickey go out there? To see if some guy named Robinson was good enough to play shortstop for the Brooklyn Brown Bombers? Well, I'm not the smartest guy in the world, but I said to myself, *This could be the real thing.*

So I went to Chicago and started calling every hotel I thought a Negro club might be staying at. But I couldn't contact him. Later I found out why—they'd come in from somewhere out in Iowa the night before by bus, saving themselves a hotel bill.

I went out to Comiskey Park the next day and bought myself a ticket. I sat down front and began studying my scorecard. This was in August, and those scorecards are so often inaccurate that late in the year; but I seemed to remember that this fellow Robinson's number was eight. A few fellows came out, and one of them had number eight on him. I stood up and said, "Hey, Robinson." He walked over. I introduced myself and told him just what I was supposed to tell him.

He listened carefully and when I was through, he spoke right up—Jackie was never shy, you know.

"Why is Mr. Rickey interested in my arm?" he asked. "Why is he interested in me?"

And I said, "That is a good question. And I wish I had the answer for you. But I don't have it."

"Well," he said, "I'd be happy to show you what arm I have, but I'm not playing. I've got a bad shoulder, and I can't throw the ball across the infield."

I talked to the guy for a while, and I thought to myself: Mr. Rickey has had this fellow scouted. The only thing he's concerned about is his arm. Is it a shortstop's arm? Well, I had heard reports that he was outstanding in every way. A great athlete. So I thought: Supposing he doesn't have a shortstop's arm? There's always second base, third base, outfield. I liked this fellow.

"Look," I said, "you're not in the lineup. If you could get away for two or three days, it won't arouse anybody's suspicions. Tell your manager that you'll be back in a few days. We'll go into New York; I think the old man would like to talk to you."

Now this is Friday night, and Sunday I have to see a second baseman in Toledo. So I asked Robinson to meet me down at the Stevens Hotel after the game, and we would talk some more. He said all right.

Later it occurred to me that they might not let him in. This was 1945, remember. So when I got to the hotel, I saw the bellman out front, and I gave him a couple of bucks and said, "There's going to be a colored fellow coming along here, and I want you to show him to the elevator." He said he would do that.

Evidently Jackie had no trouble getting in, because he came up to the room later on. And he starts right off.

"Why is Mr. Rickey interested in my arm? Why does he want to see me?"

"Jack," I said, "I can't answer that. I don't know."

"You can't blame me for being curious, can you?"

"I can't blame you," I said, "because I'm just as curious as you are."

You could feel it boiling inside of him: *Why is Mr. Rickey interested in my arm?*

"Look, Jack," I said, "you know that the old man has originated a lot of things, he's revolutionized a lot of things, and I'm hopeful it's something along those lines . . . but I just don't know."

But he wouldn't let up. He kept pressing me.

"Tell me what he said."

"I told you," I said.

"Tell me again."

"He told me to come out and see if you've got a shortstop's arm. He *also* said that if you couldn't come to Brooklyn to see him, he would come to see you."

The significance of that last part wasn't lost on him. I could see that. He was no fool, this fellow. Don't ever sell Robinson cheap. No, sir!

The more we talked, the better I liked him. There was something about that man that just gripped you. He was tough, he was intelligent, and he was *proud*.

"Mr. Sukeforth," he said, "what do *you* think?"

I was honest. I'd learned in a short time that that was the way you had to deal with Robinson.

"Jack," I said, "this could be the real thing."

It evidently sat well with him. It pleased him. Was he afraid of the idea? He was never afraid of anything, that fellow.

Then I told him I had to be in Toledo on Sunday. I asked him if he would meet me in the Toledo ball park, and in the meantime I would make transportation arrangements to New York.

"I'll meet you in Toledo," he said.

"You got money?" I asked.

"I've got money," he said.

So I'm in Toledo on Sunday. I look up between games of the doubleheader, and there's Robinson, sitting back up in the stands, watching me. I don't know how long he'd been sitting there, his eyes on me. I waved to him to come down and join me.

"I'm glad you made it," I said when he sat down.

He didn't say much; he was pretty quiet. Evidently this thing had been going around in his mind.

We boarded the sleeper for New York that night. I got up the next morning, somewhere in New York State, and he's already up.

"Jack," I said, "let's go get some breakfast."

"No," he said, "I'll eat with the boys." He meant the porters.

I didn't make an issue of it. I went and got breakfast and came back, and we sat and talked on the way in. When we got to New York, I took him straight out to the Brooklyn Dodgers' office, at 215 Montague Street.

I brought him into Mr. Rickey's office and made the introductions. Then I said, "Mr. Rickey, I haven't seen this fellow's arm. I just brought him in for you to interview."

But the old man was so engrossed in Robinson by that time he didn't hear a damn word I said. When he met somebody he was interested in, he studied them in the most profound way. He just stared and stared. And that's what he did with Robinson—stared at him as if he were trying to get inside the man. And Jack stared right back at him. Oh, they were a pair, those two! I tell you, the air in that office was electric.

Listen, Mr. Rickey was under a lot of pressure too for signing Robinson. He was criticized by a lot of people, including some of the big wheels in the Brooklyn organization. They thought it was a bad move. But he was always that much ahead of everybody else. He knew this thing was coming. He knew that with the war over, things were going to change, that they were going to *have* to change. When you look back on it, it's almost unbelievable, isn't it? I mean, here you've had fellows going overseas to fight for their country, putting their lives on the line, and when they come back home again, there are places they're not allowed to go, things they're not allowed to do. It was going to change all right, but not by itself, not by itself. Somewhere along the line you needed a coming together.

Do you know for how long the idea was in Mr. Rickey's head? More than forty years. For more than forty years he was waiting for the right moment, the right man. And that's what he told Robinson.

"For a great many years," he said, "I have been looking for a great colored ballplayer. I have reason to believe that you're that man. But what I'm looking for is *more* than a great player. I'm looking for a man that will take insults, take abuse—and have the guts *not to fight back!* If some guy slides into second base and calls you a black son of a bitch, you're coming up swinging. And I wouldn't blame you. You're justified. But," Mr. Rickey said, "that would set the cause back twenty years."

He went on along those lines, talking about turning the other cheek and things like that. He told Jack that he wanted to sign him for the Brooklyn organization, to play at Montreal. He described some of the things Robinson would have to face—the abuse, the insults, from fans, newspapermen, from other players, including some of his own teammates.

When the old man was through, Robinson just sat there, pondering it, thinking about it. I'd say he sat there for the better part of five minutes. He didn't give a quick answer. This impressed Mr. Rickey.

Finally Jackie said, "Mr. Rickey, I think I can play ball in Montreal, I think I can play ball in Brooklyn. But you're a better judge of that than I am. If you want to take this gamble, I will promise you there will be no incident."

Well, I thought the old man was going to kiss him.

Yes, that's about thirty years ago now, since those two came together. I guess you could say that history was made that day.

What was I doing while it was going on? Listen, I was pretty uneasy—remember, I hadn't seen the guy's arm!

# THE NEGRO AND BASEBALL: THE NATIONAL GAME FACES A RACIAL CHALLENGE LONG IGNORED

## ARTHUR MANN

*T*he following article, the manuscript of which was discovered in the Arthur Mann Papers at the Library of
Congress, has never previously been published. Mann
was a New York sportswriter, renowned among his
fellow baseball scribes for his uncanny impersonations of Branch
Rickey at the annual baseball writers' show. He would later work
for Rickey as the Dodgers press secretary and author fine biogra-
phies of both Rickey and Robinson.

In September 1945, Rickey gave Mann an exclusive scoop
on the Robinson story. The article was clearly written with
Rickey's close cooperation. (His handwritten comments and corrections appeared in the margins of the manuscript.) It thus provides the first authorized account of Rickey's rationale for
signing African-Americans, his critique of the Negro Leagues,
the talent search that led to Robinson, their first meeting, and
other surprising revelations about the integration saga. It is also
full of errors (Robinson becomes a naval officer!) and exaggera-
tions with which Rickey sought to embellish the story. (Compare,

*for example, this version of Sukeforth's role to Sukeforth's own in
the preceding selection.)*

    *Originally intended to be published in* Look *magazine,
simultaneously with the Dodgers' announcement of the Robinson
signing, Mann's piece was cancelled when political pressures in
New York City forced Rickey to reveal his bold experiment earlier
than he wished. For the story of these pressures, Rickey's marginal comments, and a critical analysis of Mann's article, see the
next selection, "Jackie Robinson's Signing: The Untold Story."*

● ● ● ● ● ● ●

    For the second time in a quarter-century, Branch Rickey has
revolutionized organized baseball. Back in 1920 it was the chain-
store system of player-development. Today he has taken an even
more daring pioneer step by bringing the Negro into the ranks
of a sport governed by two Commissioners who were born in
Kentucky, a state that has never ratified the 13th, 14th or 15th
amendments.

    Even the most progressive in organized baseball have long
ignored the growing shadow of Negro playing ability. When an
outright charge of racial prejudice loomed, and when states and
Congress considered anti-discrimination laws, the big leagues
directed Rickey and Larry MacPhail, president of the New York
Yankees, to form a committee of four whites and four blacks to
"study" the question. When half-formed, that body was super-
seded at the suggestion of New York's Mayor LaGuardia by a
ten-man group containing only two Negroes. Before the new
committee had met, MacPhail issued an unofficial masterpiece
of ambiguity, interpreting the Negroe's relation to the pure-
white playing fields of the game. MacPhail prophesied vague and
eventual consideration of Negro playing talent on the basis of
population ratio, national, of course.

    During all this, Brooklyn scouts were completing a three-
year search, ostensibly in behalf of Rickey's dormant Brown
Dodgers. They had combed the Caribbean area, Panama, Mexico
and the entire United States, evaluating thousands of black
players. On August 29 last, the fruit of the costly search appeared

at the Brooklyn Dodger offices to become the first Negro chattel in the history of the so-called national pastime. He was track and football star, Jackie Robinson, graduate of the University of California in Los Angeles and, until his recent discharge, a lieutenant in the United States Navy.

Determined not to be charged with merely nibbling at the problem, Rickey went all out and brought in two more Negro players, Donald Newcombe, of Newark, a pitcher; and Sam Jethro, of Cleveland, an outfielder. He consigned them, with Robinson, to the Dodgers' top farm club, the Montreal Royals, current International League champions, and back door to Ebbets Field. While they may not make the big-league grade in 1946 or even at all, they will have every chance to do so, and Rickey has high hopes of seeing one or all three in a Dodger uniform next Summer.

Just what organized baseball and the rest of the country would say or do about the matter has concerned Rickey far less than how the signing of the game's first colored players would affect the general interests of the Negro race. During a speech at a Rotary Club luncheon in Brooklyn last April, he said:

"Most vital in considering the Negro and organized baseball is the question of immaturity. Admitting that racial equality in the sport must be an eventual fact, is this the right time to proclaim it in baseball? Is it too soon? Would the Negro cause—and he has a cause—be thrown for a loss, as the cause of temperance was thrown back at least fifty years by the premature acceptance of national prohibition?"

Rickey's surprising decision, which has caught everybody else in baseball on the other side of the fence or straddling it uncomfortably, throws an atomic bombshell into a situation which baseball itself has made untenable. The game has traded on the term "national pastime" while failing to accept Negro players even in the smallest of leagues. Steadfastly maintaining that they "simply aren't good enough," all club owners now face Rickey's challenge, along with the Jim Crow grandstands in all the ball parks of the South.

While the announcement was necessarily guarded and sudden, Rickey has long been troubled by the fact that money from the Negro has been acceptable at the box office, while his playing ability has been ignored on the field. He first came to grips with the problem about forty years ago as football coach of his alma mater, Ohio Wesleyan. He was shocked when West Virginia University refused to play with his backfield star, Charlie Thomas, in the lineup. "Tommy's" crime against collegiate society consisted of having a six-foot-three, 200-pound body covered with black skin.

But a bigger jolt came at South Bend, where Rickey took his team to play Notre Dame. The hotel manager refused a room for Tommy, and did so with embarrassing emphasis. Rickey argued that Ohio Wesleyan honestly believed the Negro a creature made in God's image, with blood, brains and feelings like white mortals, but the manager refused. He finally consented with great reluctance to put a cot in the coach's room. . . .

"Whatever mark that incident left on the blackboy, it was no more indelible than the impression made on me. Tommy is now a successful dentist in Albuquerque, New Mexico, but for forty years I've had recurrent visions of him 'wiping off his skin,' " [recalls Rickey].

Until last Spring when some under-average and over-age Negro players appeared to demand tryouts at big-league training camps, they had never been aggressively anxious to play white baseball. There was never a moment to "invade." However, Negroes wanted to play baseball and did. Their activity and following is such that upwards of a half-million dollars pour annually into the coffers of big-league ball parks as rent for the Negro's so-called league contests and the many lucrative exhibition games for which the Negro American and National Leagues are a somewhat brazen front. Larry MacPhail admitted recently that the New York Yankees realized $100,000 a year from this type of Negro baseball.

Rickey's interest in the Negro player lay dormant until he took over the Dodgers in late 1942. Without warning or apparent reason, he was besieged with telephone calls, telegrams and letters of petition in behalf of black ball players. They were from Negro clubs, churches, the Clergy and recognizable communist groups. The staggering pile of missives were so inspired as to convince him that he and the Dodgers had been selected as a kind of guinea pig. Curious, he looked into the Negro baseball situation, first with an inspection of the two so-called National and American Leagues.

"They are the poorest excuse for the word league," Rickey announced in a press release, "and by comparison with organized baseball, which they understandably try to copy, they are not leagues at all. I failed to find a constitution or a set of bylaws. I failed to find a single player under contract, and learned that players of all teams became free agents at the end of each season."

Records of the past season confirmed Rickey's belief, for the two leagues, National for East and American for the West, served as little more than an excuse for booking the twelve teams as attractions. And they have attracted as many as 50,000 to a single game. The better teams play from 30 to 40% more league games than the poorer teams. For instance, this year the Homestead Grays, of Pittsburgh, National League Champions, played 45 league contests. The next three teams played 42, 39 and 40, respectively, but the two trailers, New York Cubans and New York Black Yankees, played only 27 and 33 games respectively. The Grays then met and lost to the Cleveland Buckeyes in the "black world series."

These league meetings were sandwiched in among countless exhibition games, mostly spontaneous. Teams were booked whenever idle, and anywhere. It is nothing for a good black team to be booked for nine exhibition games in a week, with the public seldom knowing whether the games are official or otherwise. The exhibition games will number five or six for every league contest during a playing period that begins in April and continues through October—some 200-odd days.

The subterfuge of this traffic would be less odious, were it not poured through three privileged bottlenecks known as bookers. William Leuschner controls metropolitan New York dates. Edward Gottlieb holds exclusive rights to Philadelphia and environs. You must see Abraham Saperstein of Chicago, for the western clubs.

Organized baseball rents its parks for Negro league games at the Yankee Stadium and Polo Grounds in New York, Comiskey

Park and Wrigley Field in Chicago, in Cincinnati, Washington, Cleveland, Birmingham, Kansas City, Pittsburgh, Philadelphia, Memphis and Newark. Only three Negro clubs, Memphis, Philadelphia and Baltimore, have their own parks, while the first two also use organized baseball grounds for big games.

Most big-league parks exact a guarantee of $1000 against a percentage of the gross that is usually 25% though occasionally 20%. This is in addition to expense of the operating staff at the parks, which, in most cases, must be paid by the renter. The three booking agents exact 15% for their work. Players are supposedly paid from $300 to $900 a month, but Rickey's three-year search for a player-contract was in vain.

As president of the Brooklyn Dodgers in 1943, it was Rickey's duty to operate at a profit, if possible, and one channel of revenue lay in filling Ebbets Field with attractions on those days or nights when the Dodgers were away from home. His efforts to rent the field to the New York booking agent, Leuschner, for Negro games, night or day, failed. He demanded the same guarantee exacted by the two other New York clubs and it was considered outrageous.

Feeling the chill of a freeze-out, Rickey embarked on the task of combing the Western hemisphere for Negro players with the idea of putting a team in Ebbets Field and calling it the Brooklyn Brown Dodgers. He dispatched a man to Mexico and Cuba incognito, where $5000 was spent obtaining exhaustive reports, especially of the large number of Negro teams in Mexico.

Coincident with this, he was approached by one José Sada, athletic director of a Puerto Rican school, who was completing work for his masters degree at New York University. He needed funds. Dodger money saw him through, and in return he scouted Puerto Rico baseball thoroughly and turned in a report on every player of even fair ability on the island.

A year later José Sada accompanied one of the regular Dodger scouts into Mexico for a second survey of the growing number of Negro teams there. The two were instructed to size up recruits for the Brooklyn Brown Dodgers. The total spent for this purpose in 1944 was $6000.

Last Spring the two Negro players, both well over 30, who

demanded and received a tryout at the Dodgers' Bear Mountain training camp set the stage for an effective smoke screen of Rickey's activities. The aspirants weren't signed, but the mere fact that they had broken the ice of organized baseball with a tryout attracted attention. Rickey then set out to help form not only a baseball team, but a new Negro circuit, called the United States League. He met with eight colored men and seven whites at the Hotel Theresa in Harlem and listened to their plans. Brooklyn provided a substantial sum of money to start. He rented Ebbets Field to a promoter. The Brooklyn Brown Dodgers became a fact, and had a modest schedule. It cost $5000 more.

But it was then possible for Rickey to send his regular scouts out to find the best Negro players in the land "for the Brown Dodgers." George Sisler and Tom Greenway took separate routes. The job was not an easy one, because considerable skill and cunning are required to catch up with teams of the two Negro leagues. You cannot find their schedules, which wouldn't be much good anyway, because, taking pot luck at big league parks, they suffer unexpected cancellations when big-league teams adjust their own schedules. And the exhibition games are booked without warning or consistency, making them fly-by-night and -day as well.

But Sisler and Greenway stuck to their task and managed to see all of the teams more than once. Neither scout, by the way, knew what the other was doing, and Rickey kept them apart. Yet, both turned in an enthusiastic report on the same player, the shortstop of the Kansas City Monarchs.

Rickey called in another scout, Clyde Sukeforth, and sent him to Chicago to cover the Negro games, again for the purpose of getting the best player for the Brown Dodgers. Sukeforth knew nothing of what Sisler and Greenway had done. After a week in Chicago, he telephoned that he really had something: the shortstop of the Kansas City Monarchs!

"How does he play *off* the field?" Rickey asked.

"Didn't scout him that way," Sukeforth replied. "Do you want to know?"

Rickey demanded every possible fact about the boy—his speech, habits, conduct, thoughts and ambitions. It required a week of hard work, but Sukeforth called back with news. The boy stood up.

"If you want to see him, you can," the scout announced. "He hurt his finger, and he'll be out of action several days."

"Bring him in!" Rickey said.

Jackie Robinson, 24 years old, six feet tall, 190 pounds, lean and wide-shouldered, represented an expenditure of $25,000. Facing Rickey, he was soft-spoken and just a bit self-conscious. . . .

For two hours Rickey talked, studied and listened. He wasn't sure of what he was listening for; perhaps something to change his mind. What right, he asked himself, had he to subject this boy to the ordeal that necessarily follows the violation of a caste system, be it oriental or democratic? Robinson talked of his future, of the Navy, his education, his dreams, mother and girl friend. Rickey ordered him to pace the floor, and studied his build, carriage and movements. Finally he said:

"Do you know why you're here?"

Robinson nodded and replied, "To play for the Brown Dodgers."

"I've brought you here," Rickey said, "to play *white* base-ball . . . if you will."

The boy's chin sagged momentarily. He blinked in under-standable amazement. Rickey talked fast.

"This is not a hasty decision," he said. "It's not being done for mere money. I'm doing it because I can't help it; because I can't face my God much longer knowing that His black creatures are held separate and distinct from His white creatures in a game that has given me all that I can call my own. I'll be excoriated, ridiculed, torn apart in the press, hated by many of my friends. I'll be accused of race-baiting in order to swell my ball club's trea-sury. I'm not a young man, and the strain of the coming months may affect my health, my meagre wealth and what I've worked for. But all that is nothing to what confronts you, Jack Robinson. Will you do it? *Can* you do it?"

The player nodded and whispered. "I can do it, Mr. Rickey."

"Why?" Rickey thundered. "Why will you do it? Why are you willing to subject yourself to ridicule, insult, perhaps injury and all the indignities that men are capable of? Why? Do you want to be white?"

"No, sir," Robinson said, "but doing this will help my people. It'll encourage colored boys who haven't had my chances. They'll work harder, Mr. Rickey . . . and better. They don't need much more incentive!"

Rickey felt the boy's sincerity, and knew that the words came from deep in his soul. He watched the hands, the bandaged finger, and his thoughts returned again to the South Bend Hotel . . . to Charlie Thomas trying to rub off his black skin. Rickey warned Robinson further of what might happen on ball fields, in club houses, at the hands and tongue of those who refuse to believe that racial equality can be created by legislation.

Then, in his swivel chair, Rickey posed as a hotel manager and simulated the treatement that had ben meted out to Charlie Thomas. He portrayed an outraged headwaiter and heaped derision upon Robinson. He became a ball player from the South, a southern sports writer in training camp, assuming the Dodgers would be permitted to train in the South.

In all instances Robinson's reactions and replies were those of unmistakable understanding, tolerance and fortitude that only a strong young man could have. Rickey warned him that the cross of the black race was on his broad shoulders, that they must be brothers together in this crusade, that neither could have secrets from the other, and that Robinson had to be both a Job and a Christ in this memorable start.

"You may start with me, Mr. Rickey," he said grimly, picking up a pen, "but you won't finish with me."

Robinson signed an agreement to accept the terms, then specified, of a uniform player-contract to be proffered on or before November 1, 1945. The signed agreement contained a statement that Robinson was *not* under contract to any team or individual, which substantiated Rickey's criticism of Negro baseball affairs. An outstanding player of the race, according to unanimous opinion of Brooklyn scouts, wasn't considered good enough for a contract from a Negro team or league.

As Rickey recruited additional players from the unsigned ranks, Negro teams began offering contracts in anticipation of a

later big-league raid. Whether or not any desirable Negro talent
will be unsigned when or if other big league clubs lower the bars,
Branch Rickey doesn't know. Having three of the best, he doesn't
even care.

# Jackie Robinson's Signing: The Untold Story

## John Thorn and Jules Tygiel

*I*n the process of historical research, unexpected discoveries
can provide enlightenment into even the most familiar of
stories. While rummaging through some previously
unopened boxes at the Baseball Hall of Fame in 1987, forty
years after Robinson's Dodgers debut, John Thorn found a set of
photographs that led to new insights into the signing of Jackie
Robinson. The resulting article elaborates on Arthur Mann's
"The Negro and Baseball" and sheds additional light on
Rickey's 1945 strategies.

It also demonstrates how historians often act as detectives.
At the time of its initial publication in Sport magazine, many of
the conclusions about the "secret" photo session described were
based on informed guesses. The authors were thus gratified when
photographer Maurice Terrell—whom they had been unable to
locate—wrote and confirmed their account. "I knew that Branch
Rickey intended to sign Jackie Robinson as the first black,"
explained Terrell, "but I was told that not even Jackie knew this
and I was sworn to secrecy."

● ● ● ● ● ● ●

It was the first week of October, 1945. In the Midwest the Detroit Tigers and Chicago Cubs faced off in the final World Series of the World War II era. Two thousand miles away photographer Maurice Terrell arrived at an almost deserted Lane Field, the home of the minor league San Diego Padres. Terrell's assignment was as secretive as some wartime operations: to surreptitiously photograph three black baseball players wearing the uniforms of the Kansas City Royals, a Negro League all-star team. Within three weeks one of these players would rank among the most celebrated and intriguing figures in the nation. But in early October 1945, as he worked out with his teammates in the empty stadium, Jackie Robinson represented the best-kept secret in sports history.

Terrell shot hundreds of motion-picture frames of Robinson and his cohorts. A few appeared in print but the existence of the additional images remained unknown for four decades, until unearthed in 1987 at the Baseball Hall of Fame by John Thorn. This discovery triggered an investigation which has led to startling revelations regarding Brooklyn Dodger President Branch Rickey's original plan to shatter baseball's longstanding color line; the relationship between these two historic figures; and the still controversial issue of black managers in baseball.

The popularly held "frontier" image of Jackie Robinson as a lone gunman facing down a hostile mob has always dominated the integration saga. But new information related to the Terrell photos reveals that while Robinson was the linchpin to Branch Rickey's strategy, *in October 1945 Rickey intended to announce the signing of not just Jackie Robinson, but several stars from the Negro Leagues at once.* Political pressures, however, forced Rickey's hand, thrusting Robinson alone into a spotlight which he never relinquished.

The path to these revelations began with Thorn's discovery of the Terrell photographs in a collection donated to the Hall of Fame by *Look* magazine in 1954. The images depict a youthful, muscular Robinson in a battered hat and baggy uniform fielding from his position at shortstop, batting with a black catcher crouched behind him, trapping a third black player in a rundown between third and home, and sprinting along the basepaths more like a former track star than a baseball player. A woman with her back to the action is the only figure visible in the vacant stands. The contact sheets bore the imprinted date October 7, 1945.

The images perplexed Thorn. He knew that the momentous announcement of Jackie Robinson's signing with the Montreal Royals had not occurred until October 23, 1945. Before that date his recruitment by Brooklyn Dodger President Branch Rickey had been a tightly guarded secret. Why, then, had a *Look* photographer taken such an interest in Robinson two weeks earlier? Where had the pictures been taken? And why was Robinson already wearing a Royals uniform?

Thorn called Jules Tygiel, the author of *Baseball's Great Experiment: Jackie Robinson and His Legacy*, to see if he could shed some light on the photos. Tygiel had no knowledge of them, but he did have in his files a 1945 manuscript by newsman Arthur Mann, who frequently wrote for *Look*. The article, drafted with Rickey's cooperation, had been intended to announce the Robinson signing but had never been published. The pictures, they concluded, had doubtless been shot to accompany Mann's article, and they decided to find out the story behind the photo session. Tygiel set out to trace Robinson's activities in early October 1945. Thorn headed for the Library of Congress to examine the Branch Rickey papers, which had been unavailable at the time Tygiel wrote his book.

The clandestine nature of the photo session did not surprise the researchers. From the moment he had arrived in Brooklyn in 1942, determined to end baseball's Jim Crow traditions, Rickey had feared that premature disclosure of his intentions might doom his bold design. Since the 1890s, baseball executives, led by Commissioner Kenesaw Mountain Landis, had strictly policed the color line, barring blacks from both major and minor leagues. In 1943, when young Bill Veeck attempted to buy the Philadelphia Phillies and stock the team with Negro League stars, Landis had quietly but decisively blocked the move. Rickey therefore moved slowly and deliberately during his first three years in Brooklyn. He informed the Dodger owners of his plans but took few others into his confidence. He began to explore the issue and devised elaborate strategies to cover up his attempts to scout black players.

In the spring of 1945, as Rickey prepared to accelerate his scouting efforts, integration advocates, emboldened by the impending end of World War II and the recent death of Commissioner Landis, escalated their campaign to desegregate baseball. On April 6, 1945, black sportswriter Joe Bostic appeared at the Dodgers' Bear Mountain training camp with Negro League stars Terris McDuffie and Dave "Showboat" Thomas and forced Rickey to hold tryouts for the two players. Ten days later black journalist Wendell Smith, white sportswriter Dave Egan, and Boston city councilman Isadore Muchnick engineered an unsuccessful audition with the Red Sox for Robinson and two other black athletes. In response to these events the major leagues announced the formation of a Committee on Baseball Integration. (Reflecting Organized Baseball's true intentions on the matter, the group never met.)

Amidst this heated atmosphere Rickey created an elaborate smokescreen to obscure his scouting of black players. In May 1945 he announced the formation of a new franchise, the Brooklyn Brown Dodgers, and a new Negro League, the United States League. Rickey then dispatched his best talent hunters to observe black ballplayers, ostensibly for the Brown Dodgers, but in reality for the Brooklyn National League club.

A handwritten memorandum in the Rickey Papers offers a rare glimpse at Rickey's emphasis on secrecy in his instructions to Dodger scouts. The document, signed by Charles D. Clark and accompanied by a Negro National League schedule for April–May 1945, is headlined "Job Analysis," and defines the following "Duties: under supervision of management of club:

1. To establish contact (silent) with all clubs (local or general).
2. To gain knowledge and abilities of all players.
3. To report all possible material (players).
4. Prepare weekly reports of activities.
5. Keep composite report of outstanding players. . . . To travel and cover player whenever management so desire."

Clark's "Approch" [sic] was to "Visit game and loose [sic] self in stands; Keep statistical report (speed, power, agility, ability, fielding, batting, etc.) by score card"; and "Leave immediately after game."

Curiously, Clark listed his first "Objective" as being "to cover Negro teams for possible major league talent." Yet according to his later accounts, Rickey had told most Dodger scouts that they were evaluating talent for a new "Brown Dodger" franchise. Had Rickey confided in Clark, a figure so obscure as to escape prior mention in the voluminous Robinson literature? Dodger superscout and Rickey confidante Clyde Sukeforth has no recollection of Clark, raising the possibility that Clark was not part of the Dodger family, but perhaps someone connected with black baseball. Had Clark himself interpreted his instructions in this manner?

Whatever the answer, Rickey successfully diverted attention from his true motives. Nonetheless, mounting interest in the integration issue threatened Rickey's careful planning. In the summer of 1945 Rickey constructed yet another facade. The Dodger President took Dan Dodson, a New York University sociologist who chaired Mayor Fiorello LaGuardia's Committee on Unity, into his confidence and requested that Dodson form a Committee on Baseball ostensibly to study the possibility of integration. In reality, the committee would provide the illusion of action while Rickey quietly completed his own preparations to sign several black players at once. . . .

Thus by late August, even as Rickey's extensive scouting reports had led him to focus in on Jackie Robinson as his standard bearer, few people in or out of the Dodger organization suspected that a breakthrough was imminent. On August 28 Rickey and Robinson held their historic meeting at the Dodgers' Montague Street offices in downtown Brooklyn. Robinson signed an agreement to accept a contract with the Montreal Royals, the top Dodger affiliate, by November 1. Rickey, still concerned with secrecy, impressed upon Robinson the need to maintain silence until further preparations had been made. Robinson could tell the momentous news to his family and fianceé, but no one else.

For the conspiratorial Rickey, further subterfuge was

necessary to keep the news sheltered while continuing the arrangements. Rumors about Robinson's visit had already spread through the world of black baseball. To stifle speculation Rickey "leaked" an adulterated version of the incident to black sportswriter Wendell Smith. Smith, who had recommended Robinson to Rickey and advised Rickey on the integration project, doubtless knew the true story behind the meeting. On September 8, however, he reported in the Pittsburgh *Courier* that the "sensational shortstop" and "colorful major league dynamo" had met behind "closed doors."

"The nature of the conferences has not been revealed," wrote Smith. "It seems to be shrouded in mystery and Robinson has not made a statement since he left Brooklyn." Rickey claimed that he and Robinson had assessed "the organization of Negro baseball," but did not discuss "the possibility of Robinson becoming a member of the Brooklyn Dodgers organization."

Smith hinted broadly of future developments, noting that "It does not seem logical [Rickey] should call in a rookie player to discuss the future organization of Negro baseball." He closed with the tantalizing thought that "it appears that the Brooklyn boss has a plan on his mind that extends further than just the future of Negro baseball as an organization." But the subterfuge succeeded. Neither black nor white reporters pursued the issue further.

Rickey, always sensitive to criticism by New York sports reporters and understanding the historic significance of his actions, wanted to be sure that his version of the integration breakthrough and his role in it be accurately portrayed. To guarantee this he expanded his circle of conspirators to include free-lance writer Arthur Mann. In the weeks following the Robinson meeting, Mann, Rickey's close friend and later a Dodger employee, authored at the Mahatma's behest a 3000-word manuscript to be published simultaneously with the announcement of the signing.

Although it is impossible to confirm this, it seems highly likely that Maurice Terrell's photos, commissioned by *Look*, were destined to accompany Mann's article. Clearer prints of the negatives revealed to Thorn and Tygiel that Terrell had taken the

pictures in San Diego's Lane Stadium. This fits in with
Robinson's fall itinerary. In the aftermath of his meeting with
Rickey, Robinson had returned briefly to the Kansas City Monarchs. With the Dodger offer securing his future and the relentless
bus trips of the Negro League schedule wearing him down, he
had left the Monarchs before season's end and returned home to
Pasadena, California. In late September he hooked up with Chet
Brewer's Kansas City Royals, a postseason barnstorming team
which toured the Pacific Coast, competing against other Negro
League teams and major and minor league all-star squads. Thus
the word "Royals" on Robinson's uniform, which had so piqued
the interest of Thorn and Tygiel, ironically turned out not to relate
to Robinson's future team in Montreal, but rather to his interim
employment in California.

For further information Tygiel contacted Chet Brewer, who
at age eighty still lived in Los Angeles. Brewer, one of the great
pitchers of the Jim Crow era, had known Robinson well. He had
followed Robinson's spectacular athletic career at UCLA and in
1945 they became teammates on the Monarchs. "Jackie was
major league all the way," recalls Brewer. "He had the fastest
reflexes I ever saw in a player." With Brewer's Royals, Robinson
was always the first in the clubhouse and the first one on the field.
"Satchel Paige was just the opposite," laughs Brewer. "He would
get there just as the game was about to start and come running on
the field still tying his shoe."

Robinson particularly relished facing major league all-star
squads. Against Bob Feller, Robinson slashed two doubles. "Jack
was running crazy on the bases," a Royal teammate remembers.
In one game he upended shortstop Gerry Priddy of the Washington Senators. Priddy angrily complained about the hard slide
in an exhibition game. "Any time I put on a uniform," retorted
Robinson, "I play to win." The fire in his playing notwithstanding, Robinson maintained his pledge to Rickey. Neither
Brewer nor any of his teammates suspected the secret that
Robinson faithfully kept inside him.

Brewer recalls that Robinson and two other Royals journeyed from Los Angeles to San Diego on a day when the team
was not scheduled to play. He identified the catcher in the photos

as Buster Haywood and the other player as Royals third baseman Herb Souell. Souell is no longer living, but Haywood, who, like Brewer resides in Los Angeles, has vague recollections of the event, which he incorrectly remembers as occurring in Pasadena. Robinson had befriended Haywood the preceding year while coaching basketball in Texas. He recruited the catcher and Souell, his former Monarch teammate, to "work out" with him. All three wore their Royal uniforms. Haywood found neither Robinson's request nor the circumstances unusual. Although he was unaware that they were being photographed, Haywood still can describe the session accurately. "We didn't know what was going on," he states. "We'd hit and throw and run from third base to home plate."

The San Diego pictures provide a rare glimpse of the pre-Montreal Robinson. The article which they were to accompany and related correspondence in the Library of Congress offers even rarer insights into Rickey's thinking. The unpublished Mann manuscript was entitled "The Negro and Baseball: The National Game Faces a Racial Challenge Long Ignored." As Mann doubtless based his account on conversations with Rickey and since Rickey's handwritten comments appear in the margin, it stands as the earliest "official" account of the Rickey-Robinson story and reveals many of the concerns confronting Rickey in September 1945.

One of the most striking features of the article is the language used to refer to Robinson. Mann, reflecting the blind racism typical of postwar America, insensitively portrays Robinson as the "first Negro chattel in the so-called national pastime." At another point he writes, "Rickey felt the boy's sincerity," appropriate language perhaps for an eighteen-year-old prospect, but not for a twenty-six-year-old former army officer.

"The Negro and Baseball" consists largely of the now familiar Rickey–Robinson story. Mann re-created Rickey's haunting 1904 experience as collegiate coach of black baseball player Charlie Thomas, who, when denied access to a hotel, cried and rubbed his hands, chanting, "Black skin! Black skin! If I could only make 'em white." Mann described the search for the "right" man, the formation of the United States League as a cover for scouting operations, the reasons for selecting Robinson, and the fateful drama of the initial Rickey-Robinson confrontation.

Other sections, however, graphically illustrate which issues Rickey deemed significant. Mann repeatedly cites the financial costs incurred by the Dodgers: $5,000 to scout Cuba, $6,000 to scout Mexico, $5,000 to establish the "Brooklyn Brown Dodgers." The final total reaches $25,000, a modest sum considering the ultimate returns, but one which Rickey felt would counter his skinflint image.

Rickey's desire to dispel the notion that political pressures had motivated his actions also emerges clearly. Mann had suggested that upon arriving in Brooklyn in 1942, Rickey "was besieged by telephone calls, telegrams, and letters of petition in behalf of black ball players," and that this "staggering pile of missives were so inspired to convince him that he and the Dodgers had been selected as a kind of guinea pig." In his marginal comments, Rickey vehemently objected to this notion. "No!" he wrote in a strong dark script. "I began all this as soon as I went to Brooklyn." Explaining why he had never attacked the subject during his two decades as general manager of the St. Louis Cardinals, Rickey referred to the segregated conditions in that city. "St. Louis never permitted Negro patrons in the grandstand," he wrote, describing a policy he had apparently felt powerless to change.

Mann also devoted two of his twelve pages to a spirited attack on the Negro Leagues. He repeated Rickey's charges that "They are the poorest excuse for the word league" and documented the prevalence of barnstorming, the uneven scheduling, absence of contracts, and dominance of booking agents. Mann revealingly traces Rickey's distaste for the Negro Leagues to the "outrageous" guarantees demanded by New York booking agent William Leuschner to place black teams in Ebbets Field while the Dodgers were on the road.

Rickey's misplaced obsession with the internal disorganization of the Negro Leagues had substantial factual basis. But in transforming the black circuits into major villains of Jim Crow baseball, Rickey had an ulterior motive. In his September 8 article, Wendell Smith addressed the issue of "player tampering," asking, "Would [Rickey] not first approach the owner of these Negro teams who have these stars under contract?" Rickey, argued Smith in what might have been an unsuccessful preemptive strike, "is obligated to do so and his record as a businessman indicated that he would." As Smith may have known, Rickey maintained that Negro League players did not sign valid contracts and became free agents at the end of each season. The Mahatma thus had no intention of compensating Negro League teams for the players he signed. His repeated attacks on black baseball, including the Mann article, served to justify this questionable practice.

The one respect in which "The Negro and Baseball" departs radically from common perceptions of the Robinson legend is in its depiction of Robinson as one of a group of blacks about to be signed by the Dodgers. Mann's manuscript reveals that Rickey did not intend for Robinson, usually viewed as a solitary standard bearer, to withstand the pressures alone. "Determined not to be charged with merely nibbling at the problem," wrote Mann, "Rickey went all out and brought in two more Negro players," and "consigned them, with Robinson, to the Dodgers' top farm club, the Montreal Royals." Mann named pitcher Don Newcombe and, surprisingly, outfielder Sam Jethroe as Robinson's future teammates.

As Mann's report indicates, and subsequent correspondence from Rickey confirms, *Rickey did not plan to announce the signing of just one black player*. Whether the recruitment of additional blacks had always been his intention or whether he had reached his decision after meeting with Robinson in August is unclear. But by late September, when he provided information to Mann for his article, Rickey had clearly decided to bring in other Negro League stars.

During the first weekend in October Dodger Coach Chuck Dressen fielded a major league all-star team in a series of exhibition games against Negro League standouts at Ebbets Field. Rickey took the opportunity to interview at least three black pitching prospects, Newcombe, Roy Partlow, and John Wright. The following week he met with catcher Roy Campanella. Campanella and Newcombe, at least, believed they had been approached to play for the "Brown Dodgers."

At the same time Rickey decided to postpone publication of Mann's manuscript. In a remarkable letter sent from the World Series in Chicago on October 7, Rickey informed Mann:

> We just can't go now with the article. The thing isn't dead,—not at all. It is more alive than ever and that is the reason we can't go with any publicity at this time. There is more involved in the situation than I had contemplated. Other players are in it and it may be that I can't clear these players until after the December meetings, possibly not until after the first of the year. You must simply sit in the boat. . . . There is a November 1 deadline on Robinson,—you know that. I am undertaking to extend that date until January 1st so as to give me time to sign plenty of players and make one break on the complete story. Also, quite obviously it might not be good to sign Robinson with other and possibly better players unsigned.

The revelations and tone of this letter surprise Robinson's widow, Rachel, forty years after the event. Rickey "was such a deliberate man," she recalls, "and this letter is so urgent. He must have been very nervous as he neared his goal. Maybe he was nervous that the owners would turn him down and having five people at the door instead of just one would have been more powerful."

Events in the weeks after October 7 justified Rickey's nervousness and forced him to deviate from the course stated in the Mann letter. Candidates in New York City's upcoming November elections, most notably black Communist City Councilman Ben Davis, made baseball integration a major plank in the campaign.

Mayor LaGuardia's liberal supporters also sought to exploit the issue. Professor Dodson's Committee on Baseball had prepared a report outlining a modest, long-range strategy for bringing blacks into the game and describing the New York teams, because of the favorable political and racial climate in the city, as in a "choice position to undertake this pattern of integration." LaGuardia wanted Rickey's permission to make a pre-election announcement that "baseball would shortly begin signing Negro players," as a result of the committee's work.

Rickey, a committee member, had long ago subverted the panel to his own purposes. By mid-October, however, the committee had become "an election football." Again unwilling to risk the appearance of succumbing to political pressure and thereby surrendering what he viewed as his rightful role in history, Rickey asked LaGuardia to delay his comments. Rickey hurriedly contacted Robinson, who had joined a barnstorming team in New York en route to play winter ball in Venezuela, and dispatched him to Montreal. On October 23, 1945, with Rickey's carefully laid plans scuttled, the Montreal Royals announced the signing of Robinson, and Robinson alone.

The premature revelation of Rickey's racial breakthrough had important ramifications for the progress of baseball's "great experiment." Mann's article never appeared. *Look*, having lost its exclusive, published two strips of the Terrell pictures in its November 27, 1945 issue accompanying a brief summary of the Robinson story. The unprocessed film negatives and contact sheets were loaded into a box and nine years later shipped to the National Baseball Hall of Fame, where they remained, along with a picture of Jethroe, unpacked until April 1987.

Newcombe, Campanella, Wright, and Partlow all joined the Dodger organization the following spring. Jethroe became a victim of the "deliberate speed" of baseball integration. Rickey did not interview Jethroe in 1945. Since few teams followed the Dodger lead, the fleet, powerful outfielder remained in the Negro Leagues until 1948, when Rickey finally bought his contract from the Cleveland Buckeyes for $5,000. Jethroe had two spectacular seasons at Montreal before Rickey, fearing a "surfeit of colored boys on the Brooklyn club," profitably sold him to the Boston Braves for $100,000. Jethroe won the Rookie of the Year Award in 1950, but his delayed entry into Organized Baseball foreshortened what should have been a stellar career. To this day, Jethroe remains unaware of how close he came to joining

Robinson, Newcombe, and Campanella in the pantheon of integration pioneers.

Beyond these revelations about the Robinson signing, the Library of Congress documents add surprisingly little to the familiar contours of the integration saga. There is one letter of interest from Rickey to Robinson, dated December 31, 1950, in which the old man offers some encouragement to Jackie's budding managerial ambitions. But by the time he retired in 1956, Robinson's personal ambition to manage had faded, though he never flagged in his determination to see a black manager in the majors. The Rickey Papers copiously detail his post-Dodger career as general manager of the Pittsburgh Pirates, but are strangely silent about the critical 1944–48 period. Records for these years probably remained with the Dodger organization, which claims to have no knowledge of their whereabouts. National League documents for these years remain closed to the public.

In any case, Robinson's greatest pioneering work came as a player. Though Rickey apparently intended that Jackie be just one of a number of black players signed at one time, the scuttling of those plans laid the success or failure of the assault on Jim Crow disproportionately on the capable shoulders of Jackie Robinson, who had always occupied center stage in Rickey's thinking. While this greatly intensified the pressures on the man, it also enhanced his legend immensely. Firmly fixed in the public mind as the sole pathfinder, rather than group leader, he became the lightning rod for supporter and opponent alike, attracting the responsibility, the opprobrium, and ultimately the acclaim for his historic achievement.

# IT WAS A GREAT DAY IN JERSEY

## WENDELL SMITH

*O*n April 18, 1946, all eyes were on Roosevelt Stadium *in Jersey City, where Jackie Robinson, playing for the Montreal Royals, a Dodger farm team, would make his debut in organized baseball. Many commentators expressed grave doubts as to Robinson's chances of success. The hostile reception that he and black teammate John Wright had received during spring training in Florida (see "Il a gagné ses épaulets"), had further dampened their optimism.*

*Among those watching most closely was African-American sportswriter nonpareil Wendell Smith. Athletes were not the sole victims of baseball segregation. Black newsmen also found themselves relegated to the lower-paying, less prestigious realm of Jim Crow, their chances for advancement blocked, their audiences limited in size. Wendell Smith, sports columnist for the* Pittsburgh Courier, *was one of the finest journalists of his generation. Along with fellow African-American sportswriters Sam Lacy, Joe Bostic, Fay Young, and others, he reported on black athletes while waging a tireless campaign for sports integration. Yet their work reached few white Americans.*

*Smith's role in the Robinson saga went beyond journalistic advocacy. In April 1945 he arranged for a tryout for Jackie Robinson and two other Negro League stars with the Boston Red Sox. When that mock trial produced no results, he recommended Robinson to Branch Rickey. Smith was a close advisor to both Rickey and Robinson during the early years of integration, giving Rickey tips on Negro League players and traveling with Robinson and living as his roommate on Royal and Dodger road trips. In 1948 he co-authored* Jackie Robinson: My Own Story, *the first of three autobiographical accounts of Robinson's life.*

*In the early 1950s, Smith became a pioneer in his own right, joining the* Chicago American, *the first black sportswriter for a major urban daily newspaper. After 1963 he worked as a television broadcaster in Chicago until he died at age fifty-eight in November 1972, just one month after the passing of Jackie Robinson. His extraordinary skills won belated recognition in 1993 when he was named to the writers' wing of the Baseball Hall of Fame.*

*The following selection, an impassioned description of Jackie Robinson's triumphant 1946 debut with the Montreal Royals, showcases Smith's talent and captures one of the greatest moments in sport history. It originally appeared in the* Pittsburgh Courier.

● ● ● ● ● ● ●

JERSEY CITY, N.J.—The sun smiled down brilliantly in picturesque Roosevelt Stadium here Thursday afternoon and an air of excitement prevailed throughout the spacious park, which was jammed to capacity with 25,000 jabbering, chattering opening day fans. . . . A seething mass of humanity, representing all segments of the crazy-quilt we call America, poured into the magnificent ball park they named after a man from Hyde Park—Franklin D. Roosevelt—to see Montreal play Jersey City and the first two Negroes in modern baseball history perform, Jackie Robinson and Johnny Wright. . . . There was the usual fanfare and color, with Mayor Frank Hague chucking out the first ball, the band music, kids from Jersey City schools putting on an exhibition of running, jumping and acrobatics. . . . There was also the hot dogs, peanuts and soda pop. . . . And some guys in the distant bleachers whistled merrily: "Take Me Out to the Ball Game". . . . Wendell Willkie's "One World" was right here on the banks of the Passaic River.

The outfield was dressed in a gaudy green, and the infield was as smooth and clean as a new-born babe. . . . And everyone sensed the significance of the occasion as Robinson and Wright marched with the Montreal team to deep centerfield for the raising of the Stars and Stripes and the "Star-Spangled Banner". . . . Mayor Hague strutted proudly with the henchmen flanking him on the right and left. . . . While the two teams, spread across the field, marched side by side with military precision and the band played on. . . . We all stood up—25,000 of us—when the band struck up the National Anthem. . . . And we sang lustily and freely, for this was a great day. . . . Robinson and Wright stood out there with the rest of the players and dignitaries, clutching their blue-crowned baseball caps, standing erect and as still as West Point cadets on dress parade.

## What Were They Thinking About?

No one will ever know what they were thinking right then, but I have traveled more than 2,000 miles with their courageous pioneers during the past nine weeks—from Sanford, Fla., to Daytona Beach to Jersey City—and I feel that I know them probably better than any newspaperman in the business. . . . I know that their hearts throbbed heavily and thumped a steady tempo with the big drum that was pounding out the rhythm as the flag slowly crawled up the centerfield mast.

And then there was a tremendous roar as the flag reached its crest and unfurled gloriously in the brilliant April sunlight. . . . The 25,000 fans settled back in their seats, ready for the ball game as the Jersey City Giants jogged out to their positions. . . . Robinson was the second batter. As he strolled to the plate the crowd gave him an enthusiastic reception. . . . They were for him. . . . They all knew how he had overcome many obstacles in the deep South, how he had been barred from playing in Sanford,

Fla., Jacksonville, Savannah and Richmond. . . . And yet, through it all, he was standing at the plate as the second baseman of the Montreal team. . . . The applause they gave so willingly was a salute of appreciation and admiration. . . . Robinson then socked a sizzler to the shortstop and was thrown out by an eyelash at first base.

The second time he appeared at the plate marked the beginning of what can develop into a great career. He got his first hit as a member of the Montreal Royals. . . . It was a mighty home run over the left field fence. . . . With two mates on the base paths, he walloped the first pitch that came his way and there was an explosive "crack" as bat and ball met. . . . The ball glistened brilliantly in the afternoon sun as it went hurtling high and far over the left-field fence. . . . And, the white flag on the foul-line pole in left fluttered lazily as the ball whistled by.

## He Got a Great Ovation From Team, Fans

Robinson jogged around the bases—his heart singing, a broad smile on his beaming bronze face as his two teammates trotted homeward ahead of him. . . . When he rounded third, Manager Clay Hopper, who was coaching there, gave him a heavy pat on the back and shouted: "That's the way to hit that ball!". . . . Between third and home-plate he received another ovation from the stands, and then the entire Montreal team stood up and welcomed him to the bench. . . . White hands slapping him on his broad back. . . . Deep Southern voices from the bench shouted "Yo sho' hit 'at one, Robbie, nice goin', kid!". . . . Another said: "Them folks 'at wouldn't let you down in Jacksonville should be hee'ah now. Whoopee!". . . . And still another: "They cain't stop ya now, Jackie, you're really goin' places, and we're going to be right there with ya!". . . . Jackie Robinson laughed softly and smiled. . . . Johnny Wright wearing a big, blue pitcher's jacket, laughed and smiled. . . . And, high up in the press box, Joe Bostic of the *Amsterdam News* and I looked at each other knowingly, and we, too, laughed and smiled. . . . Our hearts beat just a bit faster, and the thrill ran through us like champagne bubbles. . . . It was a great day in Jersey. . . . It was a great day in baseball!

But he didn't stop there, this whirlwind from California's gold coast. . . . He ran the bases like a wild colt from the Western plains. He laid down two perfect bunts and slashed a hit into rightfield. . . . He befuddled the pitchers, made them balk when he was roaring up and down the base paths, and demoralized the entire Jersey City team. . . . He was a hitting demon and a base-running maniac. . . . The crowd gasped in amazement. . . . The opposing pitchers shook their heads in helpless agony. . . . His understanding teammates cheered him on with unrivaled enthusiasm. . . . And Branch Rickey, the man who had the fortitude and courage to sign him, heard the phenomenal news via telephone in the offices of the Brooklyn Dodgers at Ebbetts Field and said admiringly—"He's a wonderful boy, that Jackie Robinson—a wonderful boy!"

## They Mobbed Him After the Game

When the game ended and Montreal had chalked up a 14 to 1 triumph, Robinson dashed for the club house and the showers. . . . But before he could get there he was surrounded by a howling mob of kids, who came streaming out of the bleachers and stands. . . . They swept down upon him like a great ocean wave and he was downed in a sea of adolescent enthusiasm. . . . There he was—this Pied Piper of the diamond—perspiration rolling off his bronze brow, idolizing kids swirling all around him, autograph hounds tugging at him. . . . And big cops riding prancing steeds trying unsuccessfully to disperse the mob that had cornered the hero of the day. . . . One of his own teammates fought his way through the howling mob and finally "saved" Robinson. . . . It was Red Durrett, who was a hero in his own right because he had pounded out two prodigious home runs himself, who came to the "rescue." He grabbed Robinson by the arm and pulled him through the crowd. "Come on," Durrett demanded, "you'll be here all night if you don't fight them off. They'll mob you. You can't possibly sign autographs for all those kids."

So, Jackie Robinson, escorted by the red-head outfielder, finally made his way to the dressing room. Bedlam broke loose in there, too.... Photographers, reporters, kibitzers and hangers-on fenced him in.... It was a virtual madhouse.... His teammates, George Shuba, Stan Breard, Herman Franks, Tom Tatum, Marvin Rackley and all the others, were showering congratulations on him.... They followed him into the showers, back to his locker and all over the dressing room.... Flash bulbs flashed and reporters fired questions with machine-gun like rapidity.... And Jackie Robinson smiled through it all.

As he left the park and walked out onto the street, the once-brilliant sun was fading slowly in the distant western skies.... His petite and dainty little wife greeted him warmly and kindly. "You've had quite a day, little man," she said sweetly.

"Yes," he said softly and pleasantly, "God has been good to us today!"

# Il a gagné ses épaulets

## JULES TYGIEL

**B**efore Jackie Robinson could join the Brooklyn Dodgers, he had to prove himself in the minor leagues. For the 1946 season, Branch Rickey assigned Robinson and former Negro League pitcher John Wright to the Montreal Royals, the top Dodger farm team, where he hoped the African-American players would be somewhat sheltered from the racism that prevailed in the United States. Ironically, however, Robinson both began and ended his trial season in the segregated South—first at spring training in Florida and later at the Little World Series in Kentucky. Throughout the intervening months, beanball-throwing pitchers, hostile base runners, and taunting fans and opponents tested his determination. Robinson responded in heroic fashion, rising to the challenge with a performance, which, given the pressures and circumstances, has few equals in the annals of sport. This article is excerpted from Baseball's Great Experiment: Jackie Robinson and His Legacy.

● ● ● ● ● ● ●

In the waning days of February 1946, Jackie and Rachel Robinson boarded an American Airlines plane in Los Angeles; their destination, the Brooklyn Dodger training camp at Daytona Beach, Florida. Eight years would pass before the Supreme Court's school desegregation decision would begin to unravel the threads of racial discrimination, nineteen before Congress would pass a comprehensive Civil Rights Act. For Rachel, married but a few weeks and raised in California, it would be her first exposure to southern society and she approached the journey with trepidation. "I had heard so many stories about the treatment of Negroes in the Deep South that I was bewildered," she later recalled. Rachel also knew of "how quickly Jack's temper could flare up in the face of a racial insult. . . . I could not be sure but what some incident might occur in which we would both be harmed or killed."

In the unsettled environment of the postwar South, Rachel's fears of physical harm were well founded. Although southerners did not repeat the orgy of violence that had left scores of blacks murdered after World War I, reports of atrocities still emanated from the region. At least thirty lynching attempts occurred in 1946. As if to reinforce the Robinsons' apprehensions, one of the worst outbreaks of anti-black rioting had erupted in Columbia, Tennessee, that week. Before it ended, one hundred blacks would be summarily arrested and two killed "while trying to escape."

To reach Daytona Beach, the Robinsons took an all-night flight to New Orleans where they were to change planes. In New Orleans, however, they encountered a seemingly innocuous obstacle. Bumped off their connecting flight, they had to wait for another plane. Stranded at the airport, Jackie and Rachel made the acquaintance of Jim Crow. They discovered that none of the restaurants would serve blacks unless they took their food elsewhere to eat. The Robinsons, related Jackie, "decided to skip food until we reached a place where we could be treated like human beings." Since the airport provided no places for blacks to rest, they went to a nearby hotel. "We entered this place," Rachel vividly remembered, "and I was almost nauseated. It was a dirty, dreadful place and they had plastic mattress covers. Lying on the bed was like trying to sleep on newspapers." Twelve hours passed before they resumed their journey.

The Robinsons' ordeal had just begun. At Pensacola airline officials instructed them to deplane "so more fuel could be added on." Two white passengers replaced them. Despite Jackie's vociferous protestations, the Robinsons were helpless. Needing a place to stay overnight, the Robinsons sought to rent a room in a home recommended by a cab driver. When they arrived they found the house "overrun with children." Rather than impose upon the occupants and anxious about their already delayed arrival at the training camp, the couple decided to ride a bus to Jacksonville, where they could make connections to Daytona Beach.

On the bus Jackie and Rachel sat down in reclining seats and tried to sleep. Within a few miles the driver stopped the bus and motioned them to the rear. "The seats at the back," wrote Robinson many years later, "were reserved seats—reserved for Negroes—and they were straight backed. No little buttons to push. No reclining seats." For Rachel, on her first visit to the South, the trip seemed a nightmare. "For sixteen hours we bounced and jogged at the back of the bus and often I was almost nauseated by the engine fumes that wafted in through the open window. . . . The Jim Crow section got so jammed that we took turns standing and sitting, although there were several empty seats in the white section."

At Jacksonville they waited in a bus station that Rachel described as a "wretched hell hole," crowded into a black waiting room with few seats and numerous flies. Unwilling to ask for food at the back doors and windows of restaurants, the Robinsons went hungry throughout the long ordeal. Finally, Wendell Smith and Pittsburgh *Courier* photographer Billy Rowe drove from Daytona Beach to pick them up and deliver them to the Dodger camp. As they arrived three days late, Robinson exclaimed, "Well I finally made it, but I never want another trip like this one."

Four months had elapsed since the Brooklyn Dodgers had shocked the nation with the announcement of Robinson's signing. Team President Branch Rickey, the architect of the integration strategy, had carefully planned each aspect of the historic break-through, seeking to minimize wherever possible the difficulties that Robinson would face. He assigned Robinson to the Montreal Royals, a team which ventured no farther south than Baltimore during the regular season. But Robinson's baptism under fire would nonetheless take place not in the friendly environment of Canada or the northern United States, but in Florida, where the white baseball leagues held their annual preseason training. . . .

Rickey also had to select a manager for the Montreal Royals. His choice surprised the baseball world. In December 1945, he announced that Clay Hopper, a forty-four-year-old cotton broker from Greenwood, Mississippi, would manage the Royals. "Hopper is a gent with a drawl from the deep South and he is going to have to handle Jackie Robinson," noted Canadian sportswriter Baz O'Meara. "Oh! Oh!" commented the Baltimore *Afro-American*.

Two frequently cited quotations illustrate Hopper's alleged distaste for his new assignment. The Mississippian, it is said, pleaded with Rickey to send Robinson elsewhere. "Please don't do this to me," he reputedly told Rickey. "I'm white and I've lived in Mississippi all my life. If you're going to do this, you're going to force me to move my family and home out of Missis-sippi." On a later occasion, when Rickey described a Robinson catch as a "superhuman play," Hopper reportedly responded, "Mr. Rickey, do you really think a nigger's a human being?"

These stories may be true, but Rickey, who had so carefully orchestrated the integration scenario, had not rashly cast Hopper in this critical role. The new Royal manager epitomized the career baseball man. Since graduating from Mississippi A. & M. he had played for or piloted nineteen different teams before coming to Montreal. Although a spectacular slugger, an almost total inadequacy in the field had short-circuited Hopper's playing career. Rickey, while still directing the St. Louis Cardinal organi-zation, had spotted young Hopper's leadership qualities. He handed the Mississippian the reigns of his first minor league club in 1929, when Hopper was only twenty-seven years old. For the next seventeen years Hopper could be found at the helm of a Rickey farm club. In 1942 when Rickey moved to Brooklyn,

Hopper followed him into the Dodger organization. Soft-spoken with a good sense of humor, Hopper earned a reputation for handling and developing young players. Eight times he rewarded Rickey with championship teams.

Rickey knew Hopper well and trusted the integrity of his longtime confederate. He also hoped that Hopper's Mississippi origins might mute dissension and serve as an example of a white southerner willing to accept blacks on his team. Nor does it appear that Rickey forced the role of civil rights pioneer on Hopper. Hopper earned a substantial income from his cotton enterprises and did not depend upon baseball for his livelihood. The timing of his appointment is equally significant. He agreed to manage the Royals after the Dodgers had publicized their integration venture. "We signed Robinson before we signed Hopper," said Rickey, Jr., "so he must have been forewarned." . . .

On March 4 Robinson and Wright made their long-awaited spring training debut. The Dodgers had directed preparations for their stay in Florida primarily at Daytona Beach, where most workouts would take place. But their initial brush with southern hospitality occurred at the Dodger pre-training camp at Sanford, a small celery-growing town, twenty miles from the central Brooklyn outpost.

Barred from the Mayfair hotel where other Dodger hopefuls boarded, Robinson and Wright donned their Montreal uniforms at the home of David Brock, a local black doctor, before proceeding to the Sanford training grounds. "I didn't need an introduction when [Robinson] came through the door," Hopper later told Red Barber. "I said to myself, 'Well, when Mr. Rickey picked one he sure picked a black one.' " The Mississippian shook Robinson's hand and greeted him pleasantly. "I was relieved to see him stick out his hand," recalled Robinson, "for even in those days a great number of southerners would under no circumstances shake hands with a Negro."

On his first day Robinson's rendezvous was neither with destiny nor baseball players, but with the media. Newsmen surrounded Robinson and fired a myriad of questions, while photographers demanded dozens of poses. . . .

The following day included fewer questions and more

baseball as events seemed to be progressing smoothly. But at the Brock home, Robinson and Wright found black newspapermen Smith and Rowe anxiously awaiting their return. Several times Smith made phone calls to Rickey. Suddenly he turned to the Robinsons and Wright and told them, "Pack your bags, we're going to Daytona Beach." Robinson feared that Rickey had decided to end the experiment and inwardly fumed as he gathered his belongings. As the carload of blacks left Sanford, Smith explained the reason for the hurried flight. A delegation from the town had told Rickey that they would not allow blacks and whites on the same field. They demanded that the Robinsons and Wright, as well as Smith and Rowe, leave Sanford. . . .

These early difficulties failed to discourage the Robinsons. "What it did for us," recalls Rachel, "was not only enlighten us and open our eyes to what things were going to be like, but it also mobilized a lot of fight in us. We were not willing to think about going back. It gave us the kind of anger and rage to move ahead with real determination." In addition the experiences strengthened their relationship. "Because we were a newly married couple," she relates, "I think it had a lot to do with quickly solidifying our marriage."

Following the hurried departure from Sanford the Robinsons and Wright settled into Daytona Beach. The Dodgers had divided their training base in the resort community into two camps. Ironically, the parent club worked out on the white side of town, while the Royals practiced in the black district. Local officials raised no objections to Robinson and Wright training in Daytona Beach, but widespread speculation persisted that they would be barred from actual competition. The test occurred on March 17 when the Royals and Dodgers met in an exhibition clash.

"Southern tradition and precedent will go by the boards," reported the *New York Times* that morning. But rumors flew that the game would be cancelled. Robinson himself doubted that city officials would allow him to perform. New York sportswriter Bill Corum, a part-time Daytona Beach resident who had encouraged Rickey to encamp in the city, also "began to worry . . . that some untoward incident" might occur. Four thousand fans, including an overflow crowd in the section reserved for blacks, poured into the ball park to witness events.

Robinson took the field "thinking so many other things, I didn't know what I was doing." When he strode to the plate in the second inning, he expected to be jeered. Corum, fearing the same thing, had recruited a contingent of friends "to cheer him no matter what." Corum's precautions proved unnecessary. Widespread applause drowned out scattered boos leaving Robinson "with a warm glow of hope and confidence." He played five relatively uneventful innings. "Aside from the fact that one man on the ballfield had a complexion shades darker than every other player present," commented Buster Miller in the New York *Age*, "there was absolutely nothing to remind the observer that 'something different' was occurring."

"Something different," however, happened in Jacksonville, where the Royals were scheduled to play against the Jersey City Giants on March 23. The *Florida Times-Union*, the local newspaper, noted the probability that Robinson would be in the lineup, marking "the first time a member of his race had played with white ball players at the Jacksonville park." In a city in which blacks constituted almost half the population and substantial numbers of blacks attended baseball games, the *Times-Union* predicted "one of the largest crowds ever to see an exhibition game will turn out . . ." and that the "colored stands" would probably prove inadequate to handle the local black fans.

The problem of seating Jacksonville's black spectators never had to be faced, as another Robinson entered the picture. Two days before the scheduled game, George C. Robinson, the executive secretary of the Jacksonville Playground and Recreation Commission, announced that Robinson and Wright would not be permitted to play. "It is part of the rules and regulations of the Recreational Department that Negroes and whites cannot compete against each other on a city-owned playground," he told the *Times*.

Initially the Dodgers offered a conciliatory response. Rickey announced that the Dodgers "have no intention of attempting to go counter to any government's laws and regulations. If we are notified that Robinson cannot play at Jacksonville, of course he cannot play." The Giants requested that the Royals leave Robinson and Wright at Daytona Beach. Rickey countered with a demand that he be notified of the ruling on the "official stationery of the city of Jacksonville" so that "neither the Montreal club nor the Brooklyn club would bear the onus." Instead, the Jacksonville Parks Commission voted unanimously to cancel the game.

The barring of Robinson and Wright drew widespread criticism throughout the North. "Jacksonville got more bad press banning [them] than any city in Florida has experienced since the Jesse Payne lynching at Madison, Florida, last October," wrote Wendell Smith. New York and Boston writers were described as "quite upset," while the Brooklyn *Eagle* decried the act as "deplorable." Baz O'Meara of the Montreal *Daily Star* called it a "terrible thing" but noted that Canadians "can hardly appraise these things from an American standpoint." Fifty-eight members of a northern Presbyterian church wrote a letter protesting the Jacksonville decision as a "great injury to democracy and brotherhood" in violation of the "Gospel of Jesus Christ." Robinson commented philosophically, "Well, I think all of us will sleep just as well tonight, eat just as well tomorrow and feel just as good the next day. I think the world will keep moving in the same general direction—forward."

Two days later, however, on March 25 the Royals arrived at Deland, Florida, to find the game cancelled due to a malfunction in the lighting system; the game had been scheduled for the afternoon. The *Eagle* reported that "Officials of Southern cities are uniting today in a lockout campaign against the Montreal Royals." Red Smith recalls that before a scheduled Dodger-Athletics contest at West Palm Beach, a sportswriter asked Connie Mack, "Suppose they bring Jackie Robinson along?" Mack angrily flared, "I wouldn't play him. I used to have respect for Rickey. I don't anymore." Another reporter convinced Mack to take these comments "off the record" and the outburst received no publicity.

Later that week Hopper and his team journeyed to Jacksonville hoping to play their scheduled game despite the earlier cancellation. Outside the stadium they found a large crowd awaiting them, but the park itself, wrote Wendell Smith, "was as closed and quiet as a funeral parlor at three o'clock in the morning." City officials had padlocked the gate and a contingent of city police barred further entry. When Montreal General Manager Mel Jones telephoned for an explanation, the receiver went dead. The Royals reluctantly retreated to Daytona Beach.

Undeterred, the Montreal club again tried to play outside of Daytona Beach. On April 7 the Royals were scheduled to play the St. Paul Saints at Sanford, where townspeople had expelled Robinson and Wright earlier. City officials asked Rickey to leave the black second baseman at the Dodger camp. Rickey ignored the request and the Royals again boarded their little-used bus for the twenty-mile ride to Sanford. Robinson nervously took batting practice and, to everyone's surprise, appeared in the starting lineup. As the second batter in the first inning Robinson beat out an infield single. He proceeded to dance off first base to the chagrin of the distracted pitcher. As the hurler threw to the plate, Robinson broke for second, stealing the base easily. When the next batter singled, the former track star flashed around third base and headed for a close play at the plate. With the crowd roaring, Robinson slid safely under the tag with the first run of the game.

Basking in the moment and the cheers of the Florida fans, Robinson fielded his position in both of the first two innings. As he returned to the dugout at the end of the second frame, his reverie came to an abrupt end. "Vicious old man Jim Crow stepped right on the baseball diamond," wrote Wendell Smith. The chief of police walked on to the field and informed Manager Hopper that Robinson and Wright had to be removed from the ball park. Caught in the middle of a game, Hopper saw little point in resistance and the two blacks withdrew from the dugout.

Robinson's appearance at Sanford and the Royals' abortive trek to Deland and Jacksonville marked a distinct shift in Rickey's strategy. Initially, he had pledged not to take the black athletes where they were unwanted. After the first Jacksonville ban, however, Dodger spokesmen became more strident and militant. "We don't care if we fail to play another single exhibition game," declared Mel Jones. "If they don't want to play us with our full team, they can pull out of the games." Club President Hector Racine proclaimed, "It will be all or nothing with the

Montreal club. Jackie Robinson and John Wright go with the team, or there's no game." In assessing his position, Rickey had undoubtedly realized that he held a strong hand. With national public opinion on his side, he could force the issue and shift responsibility for any incidents to Florida city officials. Nor did the Montreal club suffer. The Royals simply transferred their road games to Daytona Beach and missed few training contests. . . .

Dodger strategists had feared fan reaction in Florida, but they also worried about the response of white athletes. Under the best of circumstances, spring training represents a difficult period for baseball players. For all but a handful of established major leaguers, the Florida camps are pressure-filled testing grounds in which career hopes may be realized or dashed. The crowded postwar Dodger camp intensified competition and the presence of Robinson and Wright added disruptive elements. Yet little outward evidence of resentment surfaced among white players. . . .

Several players went out of their way to assist the two blacks. "Everyone has been helpful," said Robinson. "I've been told how to play different hitters and John here picked up a lot of pointers on pitching." Lacy cited the example of one unnamed player who initially refused to have his picture taken with the blacks but later could be seen passing along helpful hints. Robinson seemed to be most readily accepted by those with whom he directly competed. Signed as a shortstop, Jackie was quickly introduced to Stan Breard, the popular French-Canadian who had starred at that position for the Royals in 1945. Robinson posed for pictures with Breard and his wife. Later, when a ground ball took a bad hop and slammed Robinson in the face, Breard ran over to make sure his rival was uninjured, offering words of reassurance. After the Royals switched Robinson to second base, Lou Rochelli, a returning war veteran and one of the top candidates at that position, instructed Robinson in his new assignment. . . .

The case of Clay Hopper, whom Rickey hired as Montreal manager despite his southern background, typified the response of baseball people. Whatever Hopper's personal feelings, he did not display them. He treated both Robinson and Wright fairly. He never spoke out publicly against the experiment and when called upon to take his integrated squad to various Florida cities, he did not balk. By the time the Royals arrived in Montreal, Hopper spoke glowingly of Robinson, calling the black second baseman a "regular fella and a regular member of my baseball club." While skeptical about Robinson's hitting abilities, Hopper regaled Montreal reporters with stories of Robinson's fielding and base running prowess. When the Montreal *Daily Star* ran an opening day layout picturing Abraham Lincoln surrounded by Rickey, Racine, Robinson, and Hopper, the southerner asked for the original for his home in Mississippi.

The ultimate measure of the spring efforts, however, lay not with the manager, nor the white players, nor the fans, but in the performances of the two black athletes. "Mr. Rickey never over-assured us," says Rachel Robinson. "He never said, 'Look, I'll fix it.' He implied quite the contrary. Jackie would have to make a place for himself on the team." In his desire to impress, Robinson quickly developed a sore arm that plagued him through much of spring training. Unable to make the long throw required of a shortstop, Robinson shifted to second base, a move that Rickey had planned all along. But, with his arm "throbbing like a sore thumb," he proved equally ineffective at that position. It appeared that the injury might curtail Robinson's career.

But Rickey would not allow a minor ailment to undermine his efforts. He handed Robinson a first baseman's mitt and ordered Hopper to play him at that position where he would not have to throw. As a result, Robinson made his Florida debut at first base. the position, ironically, at which he would begin his major league career a year later. A full week passed before Robinson could return to second base.

As Robinson's arm healed, his poor hitting posed a more serious problem. Robinson failed to bat safely in his first seven times up in intrasquad games and also went hitless in another four-game stretch. His early performances seemed to confirm the standing opinion that Robinson was a "sunbeam afield, but not too husky a hitter." A Montreal writer reported that Jackie "chases the curve à la Jim Thorpe," the great Indian athlete who had failed to achieve stardom in baseball. After viewing Robinson's early efforts, a sportswriter wrote, "It is do-gooders like Rickey that hurt the Negro because they force inferior Negroes on whites and everybody loses. Take this guy Robinson. If he was white they'd have booted him out of camp a long time ago."

"Jackie couldn't perform well that spring," recalled Rachel, "because the pressure was unbearable. . . . He was trying too hard; he was overswinging; he couldn't sleep at night; he had great difficulty concentrating." But Robinson resourcefully compensated for his slump. In his first game against the Dodgers he reached base on a fielder's choice, stole second, and scored a run. A similar sequence occurred in his aborted Sanford appearance. The black speedster fattened his average with bunt singles and infield hits, always an important facet of the Robinson diet, and treated Florida observers to a preview of the baserunning excitement that would characterize his career. In one game opponents caught Robinson between first and second and according to Hopper, "The whole ball club . . . tried to run him down. . . . None of us was surprised when he reached second base safely; we'd have been surprised if they'd got him out."

By the beginning of April, Robinson had "shed his early spring nervousness" and showed daily improvement. In the Royals last game against the parent Dodger club, Robinson slashed two singles against major league pitchers and threw "like a man with a brand new arm." Facing the Jersey City Giants, he tripled and scored. In another contest he stroked two hits against St. Paul. While his performance had not erased all doubts about his hitting ability, when the Royals headed north, Robinson had clearly earned a slot in the starting lineup. . . .

Before the teams broke camp, Branch Rickey assessed Robinson's first spring training. "I'm not discouraged," said Rickey. "I was told that Robinson and Wright would be reviled and shunned by other ball players. They haven't been. I was told that they would be thrown at and spiked. That hasn't happened. I was told that they couldn't live down here . . . that I couldn't get transportation for them in the South . . . that fans would boo them off the field, but the crowds treated them with no discourtesy." Rickey's actions, however, speak louder than his optimistic words. He cancelled plans to bring Don Newcombe and Roy Campanella to spring training. Fearing further incidents, the Royals called off scheduled exhibition games in Georgia and

Virginia. The following year when Rickey prepared to promote Robinson to the Dodgers, he set up training camp in Havana, Cuba, rather than in Florida. . . .

Beyond the human drama of the Robinsons and John Wright, what stands out in retrospect is the extent to which baseball's first integrated spring training unveiled a strategy for later civil rights advocates. Aided and abetted by sympathetic whites, a handful of individual blacks shouldered the physical risks inherent in a policy of direct confrontation with the institutions of Jim Crow. In the face of opposition from local public officials, baseball's integration coalition refused to retreat.

JIM CROW DIES AT SECOND hailed a newspaper headline in the aftermath of Jackie Robinson's heroic 1946 opening day performance. Yet Robinson's dramatic debut resolved neither the issue of blacks in baseball nor his future with the Montreal Royals. In athletics one day's triumph may be washed away in the daily flood of competition that follows. . . . Robinson's inaugural achievement notwithstanding, the recurrent pressures of the lengthy International League campaign confronted him with an ongoing test of his abilities, stamina, and perseverance.

League schedulers had stiffened Robinson's task by placing the Royals on the road for the first two weeks of the season. After a pair of games at Jersey City, the Royals would travel to Newark, Syracuse, and Baltimore, the league's southernmost locale, before arriving in Montreal.

Robinson faced his first crisis in Newark, the second stop on the Royals itinerary. Following a Sunday doubleheader against Montreal, Newark Bears outfielder Leon Treadway jumped the club. Many assumed that Treadway, a North Carolinian who had spent the preceding two seasons with the Yankees, refused to play against Robinson. . . . The furor that inevitably followed Robinson notwithstanding, he continued to perform well. In five games against the two New Jersey teams he batted .417, scoring ten runs and driving in five.

The Royals migrated northward to Syracuse where cold weather and an even chillier reception for Robinson and Wright greeted them. With the exception of Baltimore, Syracuse proved the most inhospitable of cities. Fans booed Robinson when he appeared at the plate and the Chiefs players jeered him mercilessly from the dugout. As Robinson knelt in the batter's circle waiting to hit, a Syracuse player pushed a black cat in his direction, shouting, "Hey Jackie, there's your cousin clowning on the field." The umpire stopped the game and ordered the Syracuse manager to silence Robinson's tormentors. The first contest against the Chiefs marked the first game in which Robinson failed to hit safely; the second night he rebounded with two hits in five at-bats. . . .

Wright and Robinson had one further port of call before finding safe harbor in Montreal. Their opening odyssey concluded in Baltimore. Even before the season had begun, International League President Frank Shaughnessy had telephoned Rickey and begged him not to bring the black players to the southern city. Predicting "rioting and bloodshed" that would "wreck organized baseball in that city," Shaughnessy beseeched Rickey, "For God's sake, Branch, don't let that colored boy go to Baltimore. There's a lot of trouble brewing down there." The two baseball officials met on opening day at Jersey City and Shaughnessy reiterated his plea. When the Mahatma dismissed his fears with one of his customary sermons, Shaughnessy exploded, warning the Dodger executive that "this is not the time for philosophical mouthings and silly platitudes. The people are up in arms in Baltimore."

Rickey later admitted that had he believed that a serious possibility of violence and bloodshed existed he doubtless would have retreated. He felt, however, that Shaughnessy had greatly exaggerated the dangers. "We solve nothing by backing away," he told the league president. "In fact, we'll encourage every agitator in Maryland if we show fear." In Baltimore, Oriole officials seemed more concerned with the financial consequences of Robinson's presence than with the prospect of violence. Rumors abounded in the city of a threatened fan boycott.

On a frigid April Saturday night Robinson debuted in Baltimore. "You know they told me this was the Southernmost city in the league," he remarked, "but last night I thought I was playing in Alaska." Only 3,415 "frozen fans" attended the game, reinforcing reports of a boycott. Those who appeared made their presence known. For Rachel Robinson, sitting behind the Royal dugout, this experience seemed worse than the humiliating journey to Florida. When Jackie appeared on the field, the man sitting behind her shouted, "Here comes that nigger son of a bitch. Let's give it to him now." The Baltimore fans unleashed an unending torrent of abuse. All around her people engaged "in the worst kind of name-calling and attacks on Jackie that I had to sit through." For one of the few times Rachel feared for Jackie's physical safety. That night as she cried in their hotel room, Rachel thought that perhaps Jackie should withdraw from the integration venture. . . .

The following day, with warmer weather and a Sunday doubleheader in the offing, Baltimore fans dispelled all fears of a boycott. Over 25,000 people filled the stadium, including an estimated 10,000 blacks. The volume of insults increased as white fans roundly booed Robinson. Unlike opening day, Robinson did not respond to the Baltimore challenge with his best performance. During the first three games of the series he registered only two hits in ten at-bats and committed two errors. The Royals lost the second game of the Sunday doubleheader due to Robinson's poor fielding.

The following night, in the series finale, Robinson atoned for his earlier showing. He had three hits in three official times at bat, scoring four runs to pace the Royals to a 10–0 victory. He also received his unofficial baptism into organized baseball when a fastball by pitcher Paul Calvert smashed him on the wrist. Whether negative feelings or simply Robinson's effectiveness at the plate motivated Calvert (ironically a Montreal native) is impossible to determine.

The Monday night triumph over Baltimore concluded the grueling two-week road trip. For the beleaguered Robinson the tour represented a spectacular success. Despite the pressure of the Jersey City opener, the Treadway desertion in Newark, and the hostility of fans and players in Baltimore and Syracuse, he performed remarkably well. While the Royal team compiled only a 6–6 record, Robinson had hit safely in ten of the twelve contests and boasted a .372 batting average. He had scored seventeen runs and stolen eight bases. As April drew to a close, and with spring training and the initial road trip behind him, Jackie Robinson finally arrived in Montreal.

Robinson's presence in Canada posed an unmistakable irony: the integration of baseball, the national pastime of the United States, would be enacted largely outside that country's borders. Canadians, observes historian Robin Winks, "[tend] to view their neighbors in the midst of their racial dilemma with a certain air of moral superiority." They therefore reacted with a mixture of puzzlement and pride. "Local sports fans didn't seem to appreciate how monumental and revolutionary a move the Brooklyn and Montreal clubs had made," reported Montreal sportswriter Dink Carroll, adding, "The absence here of an anti-Negro sentiment among sports fans . . . was what Mr. Rickey doubtless had in mind when he chose Montreal as the locale of his history-making experiment." . . .

French Canadians predominated in Montreal, accounting for 75 percent of the population, and their influence permeated the city. In Delormier Downs, the ball park where the Montreal populace lavished fanatic affection on the hometown Royals, the public address announcer spoke both French and English and signs were translated into both languages. . . .

The hospitality that the Robinsons received in their neighborhood was, in part, an extension of the adulation at Delormier Downs. From the first, the French-Canadian fans had taken to Robinson. Despite his impressive play on the first road trip, many in Montreal still questioned his abilities and staying power when the Royals arrived in Canada. Local sportswriters doubted that Robinson would hit well enough to maintain a position with the International League club. Lloyd McGowan wrote that Robinson had been "fattening up" on left-handed pitching and predicted that his average would drop when he faced righties. As late as May 16 Baz O'Meara of the *Star* wrote, "There's a widespread belief that in a month or so, Jackie will not be hitting with any degree of consistency."

Throughout the month of May, Robinson silenced his detractors. "The critics have cowered, scampered for cover," wrote McGowan on May 28. "Robinson has proved that there is nothing he can't do on the diamond with a fair amount of éclat, not to mention elan." The "dark destroyer" continued to hit at an impressive pace, his average consistently above the .340 mark. He impressed observers even more with his baserunning and fielding skills. Robinson ranked second in the league in stolen bases and, after committing seven errors in the first three weeks of the season, he began a string of seventy-nine errorless games. Robinson's growing skill as a pivot man on double plays also evoked praise. Before joining the Royals, Robinson had always played shortstop. Yet once he adjusted to fielding at second base, few matched him at turning the double play. In the team's twenty home games during May, Robinson, working with two different shortstops, engineered thirty-two double plays prompting McGowan to boast, "Nobody can chase Robbie off his keystone job—nobody you've seen playing baseball lately." . . .

Supplementing their winning ways with an exciting style (within one two-day period, for example, four different players, including Robinson, stole home safely), the Royals attracted Montreal fans in record numbers. Robinson provided the primary lure. "The Canadian people loved him," remembers shortstop Al Campanis. "He would prepare a show for them. He'd be on first base and he'd hear the chant '*Allez!* Steal that base.'" Commenting on the fanaticism surrounding Robinson, a visiting sportswriter remarked, "Montreal fans are as fair and generous as any I've ever seen, but they don't seem to be helping Robinson by making that furor over him every time he comes to bat."

His admirers followed the easily recognizable Robinson wherever he went. Pittsburgh *Courier* correspondent Sam Maltin reported, "On the streetcar, on the way home from the stadium, Jackie is surrounded by admirers. . . . In restaurants, Jackie's food gets cold. He's too busy signing autographs, never refusing requests for his signature. He's in great demand as a speaker at youth gatherings." In mid-June he joined a contingent of the Montreal Canadiens, the reigning world hockey champions, in a visit to ailing servicemen. Even among the heroes of Canada's own national pastime, Robinson remained the prime attraction.

*   *   *

As long as Jackie Robinson remained anchored at Montreal, the travails of racial pioneering seemed less ominous. For both him and Rachel the interludes in Canada provided a necessary, if limited, respite from the seasonal tempests. In other cities, however, Robinson's reception remained unpredictable and threatening.

Buffalo ranked perhaps as the most hospitable of other International League cities. On Jackie's initial appearance, according to a Buffalo sportswriter, "He received an ovation he can never forget." Between games of a June doubleheader, the president of the Buffalo City Council hosted a ceremony honoring Robinson. . . . The two men received gifts including cash, wallets, wrist watches, and traveling bags. Throughout the season Robinson could depend upon a warm reception in Buffalo.

On the other hand, Syracuse, the league's other New York city, persisted as one of Robinson's worst stops. The problem arose not from the fans, but from the opposing athletes. Bench jockeying was common practice in baseball, but directed at Robinson, its ugly racial overtones exceeded the accepted bounds of propriety. At the season's end Montreal General Manager Jones berated his Syracuse counterpart for the Chiefs' treatment of Robinson. "You've got the worst bunch of jockeys in the league from your club," fumed Jones. "He had to take a worse ride from your club than any other."

The taunts of the Syracuse players paled beside the threats of violence that always accompanied a trip to Baltimore. "There was a lot of tension there," recalls teammate Johnny "Spider" Jorgenson. "People no doubt liked to see him play, but there was still that tension there that anything could happen." The ominous crowd reaction that had so terrified Rachel Robinson during the first series in Baltimore resumed in each of the Royals subsequent appearances. On the second journey to the southern city, Robinson, injured earlier, appeared in only one game. On the final play of that contest a brawl erupted at home plate and fans came pouring out of the stands in support of the hometown Orioles. Robinson had already reached the clubhouse when the melee began, but fans surrounded the dressing room. "Those fans were there, I would say, until one o'clock in the morning," remembers Jorgenson, "and they'd say 'Come out here Robinson, you son of a bitch. We know you're up there. We're gonna get you.' " Jorgenson and two other players, southerners Tatum and Rackley, remained with Robinson until the crowd had dispersed and then, unable to get a cab, they escorted Robinson to his hotel on a city bus. . . .

The games at Baltimore displayed the terrors of baseball integration; they also demonstrated the undeniable economic benefits. "Although many of them came for the sole purpose of booing him," wrote Lacy, "it remains a matter of record that Jackie Robinson was the outstanding factor which drew more than 67,000 fans to the city stadium last week." Long before the final series at Baltimore, Robinson had become the leading drawing card in minor league baseball. "Not since Dizzy Dean has Rickey had a man in the fold with as much crowd appeal," reported J. Taylor Spink in the *Sporting News*. The Royals shattered International League attendance records in the wake of Robinson's march through the circuit. Montreal established a new standard for home attendance, but on the road Robinson had an even more dramatic impact. Almost three times as many fans in other cities saw Montreal play in 1946 as had appeared the preceding year. Baltimore, largely on the strength of its contests with Montreal, attracted more fans than any club in International League history. Counting the regular schedule and post-season play-offs, over a million people saw the Royals perform in 1946, a remarkable figure in a minor league in which most arenas seated between ten and twenty thousand spectators. . . .

People in the International League ball parks, both black and white, came to see Jackie Robinson. Dink Carroll, commenting on the record attendance pace established by Baltimore pointed out, "The Orioles are not the attraction away from home that the Royals are—nor is any other club in the league. There are a couple of reasons for this—first, the Royals are the league leaders . . . and second, they have Jackie Robinson. . . . Everyone wants to see him after reading so much about him."

No one wanted to see Robinson more than his fellow black Americans. Large numbers of blacks flooded International League ball parks wherever Robinson appeared. On his first road trip thousands of blacks descended upon tiny Ruppert Stadium in Newark for the initial contest between the Royals and the Bears. In Buffalo and Baltimore blacks consistently accounted for between 40 and 50 percent of the throngs who massed at the playing fields. . . .

In the eyes of black America, Robinson became a larger-than-life figure. On May 18 Sam Lacy described his hopes for his son's future. "I'd want him to combine the wisdom of Joe Louis with the courage of Jackie Robinson," eulogized Lacy. "I'd hope for him to have Jackie's ability to hold his head high in adversity, the willingness to withstand the butts and digs and meanness of those who envy him." A prominent society of blacks selected Robinson as one of the ten great Negroes of his era. Rachel Robinson was also elevated to the pinnacle of black worship. An article by Lula Jones Garrett about the wife of the pioneer athlete concluded, "The only person I know who can equal her is that first citizen of the world, Mrs. Eleanor Roosevelt."

In International League grandstands, Robinson could rely on his black supporters to partially offset white hostility; on the playing field, he stood alone. When confronted by opposing players who objected to his presence, Robinson relied on his own skills and self-control to withstand their onslaughts. Verbal taunts and bench jockeying could be ignored or silently absorbed. But the physical weapons in a ballplayer's arsenal could be less readily dismissed.

The brushback pitch, a fastball thrown right at the batter at speeds approaching or exceeding 90 miles an hour, represents baseball's ultimate intimidator. The inability to recover from the fear implanted by the brushback has ruined many promising careers. Pitchers commonly test young players by throwing at their heads, but in Robinson's case, the consequences of this test were magnified. In the eyes of many, not only was Robinson's personal courage in question, but that of all ballplayers of his race.

"He's been thrown at more than any batter in the league," said teammate Curt Davis, a veteran of thirteen years in the majors. "If he hasn't been then there are a flock of pitchers in this league who have inexplicable lapses in control." Larry MacPhail later admitted to Wendell Smith that he ordered pitchers on the

On October 5, 1945, three weeks before the Montreal Royals announced the signing of Jackie Robinson, *Look* photographer Maurice Terrell staged a secret photo session with Robinson. Robinson, ironically, was wearing the uniform of the Kansas City Royals, an African-American barnstorming team.
(BASEBALL HALL OF FAME LIBRARY)

This triptych offers a reminder that Jackie Robinson was not just a great baseball player but perhaps the most outstanding all-around athlete in the nation's history. At UCLA, he excelled in basketball, football, and track as well as in baseball.
(BASEBALL HALL OF FAME LIBRARY/ROCHESTER TIMES UNION)

Jackie Robinson and pitcher John Wright, the first blacks to play in organized baseball since the 1890s, arrive for spring training with the Montreal Royals in February 1946.
(BASEBALL HALL OF FAME LIBRARY)

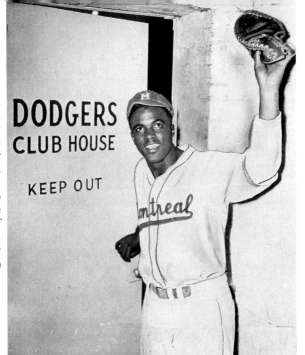

On April 9, 1947, the Brooklyn Dodgers officially called up Jackie Robinson from their Montreal farm team to the parent club. This posed photo captured both the irony and triumph of this historic event. (BASEBALL HALL OF FAME LIBRARY)

Jackie Robinson, still wearing the Montreal Royals uniform, signs autographs at Ebbetts Field on the day before he is called up to the Brooklyn Dodgers for the 1947 season. (UPI/BETTMAN)

In 1948, the Dodgers shifted Robinson to second base, where he played for most of his career. (BASEBALL HALL OF FAME LIBRARY)

Jackie and Rachel Robinson in Washington, D.C., after Jackie's controversial appearance before the House UnAmerican Activities Committee on July 18, 1949. (UPI/BETTMAN)

Jackie and Rachel Robinson celebrate Jackie Jr.'s third birthday on November 18, 1949. (BROOKLYN PUBLIC LIBRARY, BROOKLYN COLLECTION)

Jackie always sought to be a model for American youth. Here he poses with a young boy in a Dodger uniform. (BASEBALL HALL OF FAME LIBRARY)

Brooklyn manager Chuck Dressen shows his elation after Robinson's fourteenth-inning game-winning home run on the final day of the regulation 1951 season. Robinson still looks stunned in the aftermath of his heroic performance.
(BROOKLYN PUBLIC LIBRARY, BROOKLYN COLLECTION)

Jackie at the plate with characteristic intensity. (BASEBALL HALL OF FAME)

Robinson reaches out to teammate Jim Gilliam during a game against the New York Giants in the heat of the pennant race in 1956, Robinson's final year in the major leagues. (GEORGE SILK/LIFE MAGAZINE © TIME INC.)

After his retirement from baseball in 1957, Robinson became a vice-president with the Chock Full o' Nuts restaurant chain. Here he sits at his desk, the epitome of the business executive. (BASEBALL HALL OF FAME LIBRARY)

At Jackie Robinson's induction into the Baseball Hall of Fame in 1962, he is flanked by his former boss, Branch Rickey, wife Rachel, and his mother, Mallie Robinson. (BASEBALL HALL OF FAME LIBRARY)

Jackie Robinson's funeral in 1972. Rachel Robinson joins hands with their son, David, and Reverend Jesse Jackson, who delivered the eulogy. (UPI/BETTMAN)

Yankees' Newark farm team to throw at Robinson. One anony-
mous manager stated, "I offered to buy a suit of clothes for any
pitcher on our club who knocks him down."

Statistics do not entirely bear out these reports. Pitchers hit
Robinson only six times during the season, with hurlers on Baltimore and MacPhail's Newark franchise striking him three times
each. Statistics, however, can be misleading. One cannot determine how often Robinson relied on his agile reflexes to duck out
of the way of the oncoming pitch. "I've seen him dusted off at
least 30 times," reported Joe Page, a veteran Royal rooter who
attended most of their home games. His experiences in one late
season game illustrate the point. In a game at Montreal, Oriole
pitcher Stan West, who had hit Robinson once earlier in the
season, forced Robinson to fall to the dirt in his first at bat and hit
him on the wrist in his second time up. On his next appearance at
the plate, West threw two more fastballs aimed at Robinson,
drawing the vocal wrath of the Montreal fans.

The brushback pitch is intended to intimidate the batter and
make him less effective at the plate. With Robinson it usually
achieved the opposite effect. "Jackie can take it," related teammate Davis. "He brushes himself off and comes back as if
nothing happened." "He always picked himself up smiling," said
Page. The manager who offered a suit of clothes for knocking
down Robinson found no takers. "We had a tough enough time
with the colored boy to get him without wasting pitches," complained one hurler. Robinson explained his counter strategy as
follows: "After you have ducked away from a close one, you can
expect a curve ball. Nine out of ten pitchers come back to the
plate after they drive you away from the plate." . . .

"They might have throwed at him a little more," concedes
Tom Tatum, "but they took potshots more at second base." A
second baseman is in a highly vulnerable position. In making the
pivot on the double play, he generally has his back to the runner,
who attempts to prevent the fielder from completing the throw to
first base. In this situation baserunners unleashed their aggres-
sions against Robinson. "I've seen the time when if it'd been me,
well, the fight would've started," recalls Tatum. Robinson, however, usually went out of his way to stress that the rough-and-

tumble play at second base was a part of the game. After one incident in which Robinson had to be helped from the field, he defended the baserunner. "He didn't rough me up," said Robinson, "he only came in hard and fast. That's the way to play baseball."

But several times plays around second base sorely tested Robinson's self-discipline and promise to Branch Rickey. "You could see sometimes that he'd like to, oh boy . . . ," muses Tatum. Al Campanis recalls one instance in which an opposing player "really wanted to get him at second base, but [Robinson] was too quick." Robinson grew furious and Campanis quickly intervened. "I threw my glove down," relates the current vice-president of the Los Angeles Dodgers. "I said, 'You want to challenge somebody?' " The baserunner backed off. "I think that time [Robinson] might have wanted to beat the hell out of him," says Campanis, "but he just walked around in front of him and got about five yards away and got a grip on himself and backed off." On another occasion, Jackie exchanged words with Baltimore first baseman Eddie Robinson, whom he accused of kicking him in the back on a double play. The Oriole Robinson claimed that the blow had been accidental and the incident passed without further conflict. . . .

By June, Robinson had won most of his teammates over with his quiet courage and determined play. Tom Tatum admitted that at the start of the season many of the players were concerned about having a black man on the team. "There's some of the boys that were uptight maybe a little because they were from the South." Robinson felt that the Southerners "didn't know how to take me at first." Those who objected, however, kept their misgivings private. "If they don't like the notion of his being on the club," wrote Dink Carroll, "they are hiding their true feelings successfully."

Robinson always exercised diplomacy in discussing his teammates with the press. After the opening game he credited their support for his outstanding performance. Later in the season, he told J. Taylor Spink, "It wasn't a question of the players getting along with me. I was on the spot to see if I could get along with them." Speaking of the southern players, he added, "It wasn't my privilege to make friends with them at first."

Robinson never forced himself on his teammates. "He was very quiet, never said much," recalls Spider Jorgenson. Campanis remembers the team stopping for a meal at a cafeteria in Buffalo during the early part of the season. After Robinson came through the food line, he hesitated before choosing a table until Campanis invited Jackie to join him. As shortstop and second baseman, the two men talked frequently on the field. "But he still had that respect that maybe this guy doesn't want to eat with me," says Campanis. "I think he wanted to be asked rather than come right over. . . . He didn't want to sit there unless somebody wanted him there." As the season progressed, the Royals accepted Robinson more readily. "As soon as he won his first ballgame for us, they started pulling for him," says Tatum, "especially when he'd get knocked down at second base or thrown out at the plate."

One Jackie Robinson was not enough for Jersey City manager Bruno Betzel. "I'd like to have nine Robinsons," Betzel told J. Taylor Spink. "If I had one Jackie, I'd room with him myself and put him to bed nights to make sure nothing happened to him." Betzel's enthusiastic appraisal echoed the sentiments of most observers who had watched Jackie slash his way through the International League. "The greatest performance being put on anywhere in sports," wrote newsman Ted Reeves, "is being supplied by colored boy Jackie Robinson of Montreal." "Robinson has been the 'fair haired' lad of the league champions," Sam Lacy wrote, tongue lodged comfortably in cheek.

Robinson's statistics at Montreal still speak eloquently of his triumphant season. He led the league in hitting with a .349 average and in runs scored with 113. He finished second in stolen bases and drove in sixty-six runs, a remarkable figure for a player batting second in the lineup. He also recorded the highest fielding percentage of any International League second baseman. Yet these statistics fail to provide an adequate measure of Robinson's performance. Robinson missed almost thirty games due to injury and played many others in less than complete health. As late as mid-August he was batting in the .370s before a late slump dropped his average. "There doesn't seem to be anything he can't do," marvelled Dink Carroll.

In all departments, Robinson drew accolades. "His most obvious stock in trade is his noodle," lauded Joe Page. "I don't think there is a smarter player in the International League." "Much of his popularity is due to the fact that Robbie is always coming up with something new," wrote Lacy after Robinson evaded a rundown play by confounding Jersey City third baseman Bobby Thomson with a "football roll" that sent Thomson hurtling over him without making the tag. Robinson's running skills awed his admirers. "The real trouble starts when he gets on base," said Page. "Then the boys start throwing the ball around trying to get him. He seems to have the knack of sensing what the pitcher is going to do, like Cobb used to."

Robinson reminded many observers of Ty Cobb, the Georgia-born baseball great who had had little use for blacks. The analogy seemed particularly appropriate with regard to Robinson's bunting abilities. Betzel called him a better bunter than the legendary "Georgia Peach." Hopper described him as a "real artist" in his ability to lay the ball down. By one account, bunts accounted for almost 20 percent of Robinson's hits. While some saw this as a sign of weakness at the plate, most dismissed this criticism. "He can hit the curve and while a natural right-handed pull-hitter, he can power the ball to all fields and has proved he can hit behind the runner," wrote McGowan. . . .

Outwardly, Robinson had borne his ordeal with "effortless dignity," as Jimmy Cannon remarked. Robinson's composure, however, masked the tremendous strain that he had endured. "All season I have been under terrific pressure," he admitted in October. "It required all my stamina and determination to justify the faith Mr. Rickey and others had in my ability. I knew that every move was being watched and everything I did required deepest concentration." Rachel Robinson recalls that although she and Jackie faced minimal frustrations after spring training, "There were the stresses of just knowing that you were pulling a big weight of a whole lot of people on your back. . . . I think Jackie really felt, and I agreed, that there would be serious conse-quences if he didn't succeed and that one of them would be that nobody would try again for a long time." Jones also knew of the pressures affecting Robinson. "He came into my office more than once," said the Montreal general manager, "and he'd say, 'Nobody knows what I'm going through.' But he never mentioned quitting."

At home, Rachel knew that her husband was not well. Unable to eat or sleep, Jackie often felt nauseated. In late August both she and Hopper urged the second baseman to see a doctor. The physician concluded that Jackie verged on a nervous breakdown. Since the club had already clinched the pennant, the doctor ordered Robinson to remain home for ten days. Two playing days after his rest period began, however, Robinson returned to action. Two factors motivated his hasty return. As the league's leading hitter, he feared speculation that he was protecting his average in order to win the batting title. More importantly, the doctor's diagnosis had provided its own relief. "As soon as the doctor told me that I wasn't dying of anything horrible, like cancer, that it was just my nerves," Robinson told Hopper, "I was all right. I wasn't nervous anymore."

The Montreal Royals won the International League pennant by nineteen and one-half games. In the play-offs they experienced no difficulty defeating the Newark Bears and Syracuse Chiefs to emerge as league champions. The Little World Series, which pitted the victors in the International League against the American Association for the championship of the minors, remained their only test. In 1946 the Louisville Colonels won the American Association title. Jackie Robinson headed South once again. . . .

As the likelihood of a Louisville-Montreal series grew apparent, many expressed concern that Robinson might be barred from playing in the southern city. Bruce Dudley, the president of the Colonels, had opposed the Robinson signing the previous year. Nonetheless, he quickly squelched rumors that the black second baseman would not be allowed to participate. As long as organized baseball accepted Robinson, reasoned Dudley, he could appear in the Louisville Stadium.

Local officials could not as easily resolve the problem of

handling the massive demand for play-off tickets among the black community. The Jim Crow section of Parkway Field held only 466 people and the Colonels' management, citing fears of racial violence, refused to make accommodations for those who wished to see Robinson. "I saw thousands turned away," protested a letter writer in the Louisville *Courier-Journal*, "yet there were plenty of seats in the bleachers. But they were held for white patrons." Even the black press faced similar difficulties. Sam Lacy had telephoned ahead several days earlier for a press reservation. At the ball park, however, he found that a " 'press' ticket entitles you to a spot, smack dab against the rightfield wall . . . located at the extreme end of the covered stands . . . which are 'reserved for colored.' "

Louisville blacks resourcefully overcame these obstacles. Some paid high prices to whites for their tickets. Others sought vantage points outside the ball park. One person climbed a tele-phone pole beyond the center-field fence. About 300 others were "clinging precariously to the sloping roof of a dilapidated shack in view of the rightfield wall." A similar number stood atop a tool house of the L & N Railroad, while another group climbed some freight cars on a siding behind them.

Lacy, sitting in his "spot" in the right-field stands, knew precisely when Robinson entered the playing area from the "crescendo of boos emanating from the huge amphitheater," which struck him "with the force and positive meaning of a punch in the nose." The black sportswriter likened the southern response to a baby forced to take cod-liver oil or a drinker faced with an inferior brew. "It amuses you to see them turn up their noses and move to push the stuff away when they're forced to try a blend after so many years of having it 100 proof," he jibed.

"They called him everything under the sun," recalls John Welaj, who played for the Colonels. "They probably called him watermelon eater, chicken thief, crap shooter, nigger, every-thing." . . .

Each time Robinson came to the plate during the three games at Louisville a chorus of boos rained down on him from the almost all-white stands. "He took it most gracefully and con-ducted himself in his every move as a gentleman," said Tommy

Fitzgerald, a sympathetic Louisville sportswriter. The tension of the series, however, affected Robinson's play. In three games he stroked only one hit, though he did turn in several stunning fielding plays. Deprived of Robinson's demoralizing speed on the bases, the Royals lost two of the three contests played in the southern city. . . .

"Robinson hasn't played too well down here," Al Campanis warned the Colonels as the teams departed Louisville. "Wait until you see him in Montreal where the fans are his friends." In Montreal a seven-inch blanket of snow awaited the teams. Delormier Downs, appropriately laid out for the football season, had snow piled along the foul lines. Despite the cold weather, a large crowd appeared to wreak vengeance on Louisville players for Robinson's treatment in Kentucky. As each Colonel approached the plate, they roundly jeered him.

Nonetheless, it appeared that the Colonels would easily register their third victory of the series. At the end of four and one-half innings they led 4-0 and going into the bottom of the ninth, they still held a 5-3 lead. A streak of wildness by Louisville pitchers, however, allowed Montreal to even the score, with Robinson scoring the tying run. In the bottom of the tenth inning, an error, fielder's choice and a sacrifice, placed Royal runners on second and third. The Colonels elected to walk Marv Rackley intentionally to load the bases and pitch to Robinson. Then, as Tommy Fitzgerald described it, "On this frigid, football striped baseball diamond tonight, Jackie Robinson, former All-American halfback at Southern California [*sic*] intercepted one of Mel Deutsch's pitches from the 15-yard line to give Montreal a 6-5 victory over Louisville."

The Montreal *Gazette* called Robinson's game winning single "revenge," but his retribution had just begun. The next night the "dark destroyer" slashed a double in the first inning and scored the first Royal run. With the score tied 3-3 in the seventh, he led off the inning with a booming triple and then scored on a double by Lew Riggs. In the eighth inning, with the bases loaded and two out, Robinson surprised everyone with a squeeze bunt, which scored Campanis from third with the final run in the Royals 5-3 victory. "Quicker than you can say Jack Robinson, the

Colonels have changed from favorites to underdogs in the Little World Series," lamented Fitzgerald.

For the sixth game, over 19,000 people jammed Delormier Downs in the hopes that the Royals would bring the momentous season to a close. Forty-two-year-old pitcher Curt Davis obliged with a 2-0 shutout. Robinson collected two of Montreal's six hits and started two rally-ending double plays, including one in the ninth with two runners on base. The Royals reigned as Little World Series Champions.

As the spectators poured onto the field Robinson fought his way to the clubhouse to join the Royal celebration. The French-Canadian fans refused to leave, chanting for Robinson to rejoin them and singing *"Il a gagné ses épaulettes."* When he appeared in his street clothes they gathered around him, kissing and hugging him, and tearing at his street clothes. As they lifted Robinson to their shoulders, tears appeared in his eyes. The crowd remained after he retrieved his belongings from the locker room and they chased him deliriously for three blocks as he attempted to leave. A passing motorist finally rescued Robinson and spirited him home. To Sam Maltin, who had shared so much of the magical season with Jackie and Rachel, it provided a fitting climax. "It was probably the only day in history," he wrote, "that a black man ran from a white mob with love, instead of lynching on its mind."

# The Race Question

## The Major League Steering Committee
## (August 27, 1946)

*W*hile Jackie Robinson conquered and captivated the International League, major league owners, still reluctant to accept black players, attempted to address how to handle the "race question." At their meeting on August 27, 1946, a steering committee consisting of the two league presidents and two owners from each league submitted a report, most likely written by New York Yankees owner Larry MacPhail, on issues confronting major league baseball in the post–World War II era. The bulk of the report dealt with labor relations, but Section E addressed what MacPhail defined as "Methods to protect baseball from charges that it is fostering unfair discrimination against the Negro for reasons of his race and color."

In this never-before published document, MacPhail, exercising perilous logic, sought to defend the absence of blacks from the major leagues, fixing blame not on the baseball establishment, but on ignorant protesters, inadequate black athletes, and selfish Negro League owners. Although written as Robinson was making integration a reality, the report suggests no strategy and indicates no desire to further the process of integration. Although

*MacPhail never addresses Branch Rickey or the Dodgers by
name, his indirect criticism of "the individual action of any one
club" barely conceals MacPhail's contempt for Rickey's actions.*

*Eighteen months later, in February 1948 Rickey charged
that his fellow owners had unanimously approved a secret 1946
report condemning his efforts to integrate the game. His fellow
owners denied Rickey's allegations. Whether or not a vote was
actually taken and if so, whether the section on the "race question" was approved either separately or as part of the larger
report is impossible to determine. Yet it remains a damning document demonstrating the segregationist attitudes held by many
major league owners. As late as 1953 most of the owners present
at that meeting had yet to add African-Americans to their major
league squads.*

● ● ● ● ● ● ●

The appeal of Baseball is not limited to any racial group.
The Negro takes great interest in baseball and is, and always has
been, among the most loyal supporters of Professional Baseball.

The American people are primarily concerned with the excellence of performance in sport rather than the color, race or creed
of the performer. The history of American sport has been enriched
by the performance of great Negro athletes who have attained the
mythical All-American team in football; who have won world
championships in boxing; and who have helped carry America to
track-and-field victory in the Olympic games. Fifty-four professional Negro baseball players served with the Armed Forces in
this war—one player was killed and several wounded in combat.

Baseball will jeopardize its leadership in professional sport
if it fails to give full appreciation to the fact that the Negro fan
and the Negro player are part and parcel of the game. Certain
groups in this country including political and social-minded
drum-beaters, are conducting pressure campaigns in an attempt to
force major league clubs to sign Negro players. Members of these
groups are not primarily interested in Professional Baseball. They
are not campaigning to provide a better opportunity for thousands
of Negro boys who want to play baseball. They are not even

particularly interested in improving the lot of Negro players who are already employed. They know little about baseball—and nothing about the business end of its operation. They single out Professional Baseball for attack because it offers a good publicity medium.

These people who charge that baseball is flying a Jim Crow flag at its masthead—or that racial discrimination is the basic reason for failure of the major leagues to give employment to Negroes—are simply talking through their individual or collective hats. Professional baseball is a private business enterprise. It has to depend on profits for its existence, just like any other business. It is a business in which Negroes, as well as Whites, have substantial investments in parks, franchises, and players contracts. Professional baseball, both Negro and White, has grown and prospered over a period of many years on the basis of separate leagues. The employment of a Negro on one AAA League Club in 1946 resulted in a tremendous increase in Negro attendance at all games in which the player appeared. The percentage of Negro attendance at some games at Newark and Baltimore was in excess of 50%. A situation might be presented, if Negroes participate in major league games, in which the preponderance of Negro attendance in parks such as the Yankee Stadium, the Polo Grounds and Comiskey Park could conceivably threaten the value of the Major League franchises owned by these Clubs.

The thousands of Negro boys of ability who aspire to careers in professional baseball should have a better opportunity. Every American boy, without regard to his race or his color or his creed, should have a fair chance in baseball. Jobs for half a dozen good Negro players now employed in the Negro leagues is relatively unimportant. Signing a few Negro players for the major leagues would be a gesture—but it would contribute little or nothing towards a solution of the real problem. Let's look at the facts:

(1) A major league baseball player must have something besides great natural ability. He must possess the technique, the co-ordination, the competitive aptitude, and the discipline, which is usually acquired only after years of training in the minor leagues. The minor league experience of

players on the major league rosters, for instance, averages 7 years. The young Negro player never has had a good chance in baseball. Comparatively few good young Negro players are being developed. This is the reason there are not more players who meet major league standards in the big Negro leagues. Sam Lacy, Sports Editor of the Afro-American newspapers, says, "I am reluctant to say that we haven't a single man in the ranks of colored baseball who could step into the major league uniform and disport himself after the fashion of a big leaguer. . . . There are those among our league players who might possibly excel in the matter of hitting or fielding or base-running. But for the most part, the fellows who could hold their own in more than one of these phases of the game, are few and far between—perhaps nil." Mr. Lacy's opinions are shared by almost everyone, Negro or White, competent to appraise the qualifications of Negro players.

(2) About 400 Negro professionals are under contract to the 24 clubs in 4 Negro leagues. The Negro leagues have made substantial progress in recent years. Negro baseball is now a $2,000,000 business. One club, the Kansas City Monarchs, drew over 300,000 people to its home and road games in 1944 and 1945. Over 50,000 people paid $72,000 to witness the East-West game at the White Sox Stadium in Chicago. A Negro league game established the all-time attendance record at Griffith Stadium in Washington. The average attendance at Negro games in the Yankee Stadium is over 10,000 per game.

These Negro leagues cannot exist without good players. If they cannot field good teams, they will not continue to attract the fans who click the turnstiles. Continued prosperity depends upon improving standards of play. If the major leagues and big minors of Professional Baseball raid these leagues and take their best players—the Negro leagues will eventually fold up—the investments of their club owners will be wiped out—and a lot of professional Negro players will lose their jobs. The Negroes who own and operate these clubs do not want to part with their outstanding players—no one accuses them of racial discrimination.

(3) The Negro leagues rent their parks in many cities from clubs in Organized Baseball. Many major and minor league clubs derive substantial revenue from these rentals. (The Yankee Organization, for instance, nets nearly $100,000 a year from rentals and concessions in connection with Negro league games at the Yankee Stadium in New York—and in Newark, Kansas City and Norfolk). Club owners in the major leagues are reluctant to give up revenues amounting to hundreds of thousands of dollars every year. They naturally want the Negro leagues to continue. They do not sign, and cannot properly sign, players under contract to Negro clubs. This is not racial discrimination. It's simply respecting the contractual relationship between the Negro leagues and their players.

## Summary:

Your Committee believes that the relationship of the Negro player, and/or the existing Negro Leagues to professional baseball is a real problem—one that affects all Baseball—and one that should have serious consideration by an Executive Council.

There are many factors in this problem and many difficulties which will have to be solved before any generally satisfactory solution can be worked out. The individual action of any one Club may exert tremendous pressures upon the whole structure of professional baseball, and could conceivably result in lessening the value of several Major League franchises.

Your Committee does not desire to question the motives of any organization or individual who is sincerely opposed to segregation or who believes that such a policy is detrimental in the best interest of professional baseball.

Your Committee wishes to go on record as feeling that this is an overall problem which vitally affects each and everyone of us—and that effort should be made to arrive at a fair and just solution—compatible with good business judgment and the principles of good sportsmanship.

# The Betrayal of Robinson

## Harold Parrott

*A*s the traveling secretary of the Brooklyn Dodgers in
1947, Harold Parrott was both eyewitness and partici-
pant to Jackie Robinson's tempestuous rookie season. In
April and May Robinson faced a petition drive among his
teammates to keep him off the team, a reported strike by the St.
Louis Cardinals, verbal abuse from Ben Chapman's Phillies, and
at least one death threat. Parrott's accuracy with regard to
chronology, conversations, and even some facts is somewhat sus-
pect, but this feisty excerpt from his acerbic exposé, The Lords of
Baseball, captures the heated intensity of Robinson's first months
in the major leagues.

● ● ● ● ● ● ●

Right from the very first time he saw this black man run wild
on the bases and get up to rip the ball after they knocked him down
with a duster, [Dodger manager] Leo [Durocher] had Jackie Robinson tabbed as a winner. The Lip figured Jackie could put them all in

the World Series, the big dough, the endorsements and commercials, and all that went with winning.

I had heard him bark this at his unhappy Dodger players in a bizarre midnight meeting in an Army barracks in Panama, where we had gone to play exhibition games against Robinson and the rest of the Montreal squad in the spring of 1947. We were there because we daren't bring this black-and-white show into any of the Southern states.

By now it was a cinch that the Negro was too good to be kept off the Dodgers. When would he be brought up? That was the question.

Bobby Bragan and Dixie Walker and a few more of the hominy-grits boys decided to beat Rickey to the punch. They made up a petition saying they would not play on the same team with a Negro, and they were trying to get a few patsies like Carl Furillo to take it around and get others to sign it. The only south in Furillo's background was southern Italy; he wouldn't have known Mason and Dixon from the Smith Brothers.

Kirby Higbe, a strongarm pitcher, didn't like the aroma of the whole thing, even though he was from South Carolina. He tipped me off over a few beers in a Panama bar one night.

I phoned Rickey in Brooklyn, and the Old Man jumped into a plane within the hour, heading to Panama to quell the rebellion.

Rickey wasn't needed this time. Durocher handled the whole thing.

When I told Leo about the plot, he had exploded. He called the midnight meeting in the barracks, and I can still hear him as he challenged the mutineers. He was wrapped in a yellow bathrobe, and he looked like a fighter about to enter the ring. He stared down Walker and Bragan and started punching out the words.

"I don't care if the guy is yellow or black, or if he has stripes like a fuckin' zebra," Durocher rasped, glaring around the room. "I'm the manager of this team, and I say he plays. What's more, I say he can make us all rich." After a pause, the Lip added, "An' if any of you can't use the money, I'll see that you're traded!" . . .

There had been dollar signs dancing in Durocher's eyes from the very first day he saw Robinson. Leo wanted the black man right then. He thought Jack could ring the cash register for us all. . . .

I remember the Old Man telling me to pick up an extension telephone in his Brooklyn Dodger office less than a week before we—Robinson and the other players to whom I acted as confessor, valet, and nursemaid as the team's traveling secretary—were to make our first road trip of 1947.

We'd been looking forward to sleepy Philadelphia as a relief from the big-city pressure cooker that New York became when Robinson broke the color line.

After all, this *was* the City of Brotherly Love, wasn't it?

Nothing ever seemed to happen in Philadelphia, good *or* bad. The Futile Phillies, as the writers liked to call them in the quaint sports-page jargon of the day, had been the caboose of the National League for years—undistinguished and unnoticed, but quite necessary to fill out the eight-team league.

Robinson had never had any trouble when he played there before thousands of Negroes as the shortstop of the Kansas City Monarchs.

Even the Benjamin Franklin Hotel, the second-rate house the Dodgers had used for years, didn't figure to be a problem. They'd had my rooming list, with the black man's name on it, for almost a month, and they hadn't called me to complain. It all seemed to add up to a pleasant visit.

All these things were running through my mind as Rickey was motioning for me to pick up the extension phone. "Herb Pennock is calling from Philadelphia," he whispered, holding a hand over his own mouthpiece. "I want you to hear this . . ."

Pennock, known as the Squire of Kennett Square during his Yankee days as a southpaw pitching great, was now the suave, silver-thatched general manager of the Phillies, who were being revived by Bob Carpenter and the DuPont millions.

". . . just can't bring the Nigger here with the rest of your team, Branch," I heard Pennock saying. "We're just not ready for that sort of thing yet. We won't be able to take the field against your Brooklyn team if that boy Robinson is in uniform."

"Very well, Herbert," replied the always-precise Rickey. "And if we must claim the game nine to nothing, we will do just that, I assure you."

That was the official score of a forfeited game: 9 to 0.

When we arrived in Philadelphia and took cabs to the Franklin, I was bluntly told that there were no rooms for us. "And don't bring your team back here," the manager snapped, "while you have any Nigras with you!"

While the bellboys stacked our luggage on the sidewalk, I tried to call Carpenter and Pennock to see if they had any pull at the other hotels in town. No answer on either line, the Phillies' switchboard said. No, sorry, they couldn't be found anywhere.

I hired a truck to load the bags, got cabs to take the players and the newspapermen to the ballpark where they could twiddle their thumbs for a few hours, and prepared to search for a hotel that would take in my homeless band. The thought crossed my mind that we might have to take the train back to New York after that night's game and become commuters for the rest of the series.

Higbe, the carefree Carolinian, didn't make matters easier when he asked Robinson in a loud voice if there weren't some of Jack's friends in town who'd take us in as boarders. Robbie managed a weak smile, but it was obvious he was smarting inside, knowing we were pariahs because of him. Worse yet, the other players knew the reason, and he knew they knew.

I very nearly didn't try the second hotel my cabbie took me to, because the fashionable Warwick looked too plush; but I brazened it out and asked anyway, mentioning our black problem boy. Delighted to have us, the manager told me. Of course the rates were almost twice those at the crummy Franklin, but any port in a storm, no matter how expensive. We stayed at the Warwick for many seasons after that one. The food was great, by a master chef named George Lamaze.

That night Pennock had the nerve to ask me if I'd found a hotel. I didn't tell him of our good fortune, just to see if he'd come up with any helpful suggestions, but he remained silent. All the talking for the Phillies was done a few hours later by their Southern-born and -bred manager, Ben Chapman, and at no time in my life have I ever heard racial venom and dugout filth to match the abuse that Ben sprayed on Robinson that night.

Chapman mentioned everything from thick lips to the supposedly extra-thick Negro skull, which he said restricted brain growth to almost animal level compared to white folk. He listed the repulsive sores and diseases he said Robbie's teammates would become infected with if they touched the towels or the combs he used. He charged Jackie outright with breaking up his own Brooklyn team. The Dodger players had told him privately, he said, that they wished the black man would go back into the South where he belonged, picking cotton, swabbing out latrines, or worse.

Chapman sang this hate song almost alone at first, but soon he picked up an infantile chorus behind him on the bench. These were guys who had acquired some bravery after listening to their fearless leader clobber the defenseless black, and who now hoped to make a hit with the boss man by parroting his lines.

Suddenly it dawned on me how many people whom I had previously regarded as normal and rational weren't about to give an even break to a black boy who wanted only to be a part of this thing all we "sportsmen" had always called the "Great American Pastime."

Meanwhile, there wasn't a peep out of Robinson. Everybody knew he had been muzzled by Rickey. The whole thing was as one-sided as a mugging.

I noted where Carpenter and Pennock sat, and I was sure they could hear just about everything that came out of their team's dugout. Certainly the fans in the stands nearby were in on this verbal lynching.

I felt sure that Chapman would tone down his attacks the second night, perhaps after some discreet hints from his embarrassed superiors. But no, Ben raved on without a letup. At this point Eddie Stanky, a gutsy little Dodger infielder who was out of Mobile, Alabama, himself, could take it no more. "Why don't you guys go to work on somebody who can fight back?" he barked. "There isn't one of you has the guts of a louse!"

But the jibes went on, even more vicious than before, if possible.

Years later, after I had written some of the details of this "riding" in the *Sporting News*, the paper sent a reporter to Chapman's home to check up on the story. They couldn't believe it, I guess.

Ben denied nothing. Rather lamely, he pointed out that Robinson had been a rookie when they worked him over. "We always gave rookies a baptism like that first time around the league, to see how they could take it. You wouldn't have wanted us to treat Robinson any different from the white boys, would you?"

On top of everything else, Robinson wasn't doing much on the field. He was pressing, trying too hard, and he had a sore throwing arm. It wasn't as bad as the spring before, when he had pulled a ligament trying to make a throw across his body from behind second base too early in training. Now he was playing first, and he could cover up the arm, because not many hard throws are called for there.

At the plate, he was popping everything straight up in the air.

"It's a home run!" screeched one of the Phillies derisively when Robbie popped up right in front of the plate with two men on. "Yeah," cracked Puddinhead Jones as the ball dropped into catcher Andy Seminick's big mitt, "if you're playing in an elevator shaft!"

"You can't play ball up here, you black bum," came out of the Phils' dugout. "You're only up here to draw those Nigger bucks at the gate for Rickey—"

Chapman's tagline hurt worst of all: "If you were a white boy, you'd have been shipped down to Newport News long ago!"

After that first series in Philadelphia was over, we took the train back to New York, and I raced to Rickey's home in Forest Hills. I burst in on the Old Man and blurted out all that had happened in the City of Brotherly Love.

"Nobody can take vile stuff like this for very long," I said. "We'll have a nervous breakdown on our hands—"

"Ho, ho, ho," was Rickey's only reply. It wasn't just a chuckle, but a belly laugh; he doubled up as I poured out the shabby details.

I was hurt, and Rickey saw it. I guess I bit my lip and got red in the face.

"Don't you see what's happening, son?" he said, getting up out of his chair and putting a kindly arm around my shoulder.

Of course I saw. More than he did, I thought bitterly. I couldn't make out why Rickey was acting this way. What did he think I was, an imbecile?

"You and mother"—he meant Mrs. Rickey—"weren't very

strong for this Robinson thing at the start," he began. "Now all of a sudden you're both fans of Jackie, and you're actually worrying about him. What do you suppose has happened?"

I thought it best to keep my mouth shut if I wanted to hang onto my job. I was seething inside.

"On this team, on any team," B.R. went on, "there are some fair-minded men of quality who will rebel against the treatment Robinson is getting, and they'll do something about it. There will be an incident, perhaps a small one, perhaps something big. But they'll be drawn closer to him and become a protective cordon around him. You'll see. . . ."

It occurred to me right then that I hadn't even told him about Stanky taking Robinson's side against the Phillies. I had wanted to make the situation sound as bleak as possible, I guess. . . .

At St. Louis, we ran into a threatened strike by Cardinal players who said they wouldn't go on the same field with the "Nigra." We were running into this same white bigot fence everywhere. Sam Breadon, the Cardinal owner, didn't raise a finger to squelch the revolt, but Ford Frick, the league president, had to. All eyes were on him, and he threatened to slap a long suspension and big fine on any Cardinal player who went on strike.

Not all the Cardinals went along with Enos Slaughter and the other red-hots from the sowbelly and sorghum belt. Stan Musial gave Robbie some kind words of encouragement and even some tips about shifting his feet to take throws around first base. Musial's folks had been poor as church mice in the mine country around Donora, Pennsylvania, and the Polish boy remembered very well the putdowns he had received before he made it big.

By this time Robbie had started to knock the hell out of the ball. And even when he wasn't hitting, he had proved he could run; he had stolen the third game in that Philadelphia series from Chapman just as cleanly as a pickpocket lifting a farmer boy's wallet at the county fair. But now he had started spraying base hits to all fields, and they were shots that the players called blue darts or frozen ropes. Jack held both arms extended as far from his powerful body as possible, gripping at eye level the handle of a bat he carried high, almost proudly, and very still, above the level of his head. He looked almost like a big black bird about to take off, with those arms held that way. Every time I see Joe Morgan of today's Reds flap that rear arm of his while waiting to attack a pitch, I think of Jack.

They tried knocking him down, but the dusters only made him a tougher hitter, and the word on that soon got around. When he got up out of the dirt after a knockdown and rearranged himself with his eyes flashing, "ferocious" is the only word you could use to describe him as a hitter.

The news that Robinson was "making it" spread fast, and the little ballpark in Cincinnati, Crosley Field, which then had less than thirty thousand seats, was jammed with whites who had come to see if this Nigra could really do it, as well as blacks there to cheer their new trailblazer on.

There had been a sack of mail for Robinson at our hotel, and I went through it the morning we hit town. Three of the letters contained threats that Jack would be shot in his tracks if he dared to take the field. I handed these over to the FBI, which got pretty excited about it and searched every building that overlooked the ballpark and would afford a sniper a shot at Number 42.

Usually I didn't show Robbie the hate mail, most of which was scrawled and scribbled like the smut you see on toilet walls. But this time I had to warn him, and I could see he was frightened. . . .

Mind you, all this really happened, not in the Dark Ages nor the black days of the Spanish Inquisition or Atilla the Hun; nor was it some history-book tale of the Nubian slaves who were chained to their oars in the galleys of Egyptian princes. This was the year 1947 in supposedly civilized Philadelphia and St. Louis and Cincinnati and New York. By all means let us not forget New York.

The Polo Grounds was in the middle of Harlem, and even Frick wanted to back off when it came time for Robinson to appear there against the New York Giants. He suggested to Rickey that it might be unwise to press "too hard" by putting the black man in the very first series up there in such a highly inflammable black environment. How about leaving him at home in Brooklyn for a few days with a "sprained ankle"?

Rickey wouldn't hear of it. This was no time to pussyfoot,

he said. He pushed boldly ahead with his Black Experiment and backed Robinson in every way he could. . . .

In Philadelphia, Ben Chapman, the manager, cornered me under the stands for a heart-to-heart talk.

I knew him well, for he had pitched for our team in a fruitless and embarrassing comeback attempt after all those years of glory in the Yankee outfield. Ben was a charming man, intelligent, often witty. We had played a lot of bridge on the long Dodger road trips, and he had far-out bidding ideas, which he called the "Winslow System." I always called him Winslow after that.

"Poor Parrott," he said with mock concern as we stood there under the stands. "Know how you're going to end up?" We were alone as we chatted, for it was early. But Robinson had already stolen one game of the series with his daring running, and the ballpark would be jammed in a few hours to see if the black Ty Cobb was for real.

I begged my old friend to read my future for me: What did Ben use, a Ouija board or tea leaves?

He severely ignored my joke. "You'll be the nursemaid to a team of twenty-four niggers," Ben rasped, "and one dago." He didn't like Furillo, either.

Now it was my turn.

"If I was short a hotel room, and had the choice of bunking with you or with Number 42 [that was Robinson], know what I'd do?"

Chapman played straight man, just as I had, and waited for my answer.

"I'd room with Robinson, Winslow."

For a moment, I thought Ol' Ben was going to pop me, but he didn't. . . .

To those who still bad-mouth the black man, I would say he was nicer to Ben Chapman than I could have been, after all the unspeakable abuse Ben had spouted his way. When Chapman was in a jam, Robinson even tried to save his job for him, and I am sure Ben would admit that today.

This all came up because Broadway columnist Walter Winchell . . . had suddenly found out that Ben Chapman, from Alabama, suh, did not like black people, and particularly black ballplayers. The powerful peeping-tom columnist got a big anti-Chapman crusade going, and hardly a day passed when the Phillies' manager didn't get a jab as a racist in Winchell's syndicated column, which was big in Philly, with its large black population. . . . It got so hot for Chapman in Philadelphia that he was about to lose his job.

On [a] visit to Philly in 1947, Winslow sidled up to me and, with a sickly smile, got out something that was obviously very hard for him to say: "For old times' sake, will you do me a big favor? Ask Robinson if he'll agree to have a picture taken shaking hands with me?"

It was hard, but I resisted the urge to tell Ben that was the first time I'd ever heard him call Jack by a decent name. Usually, it had been something unprintable. I must have looked stunned, though, for Chapman added, as a humbling afterthought: "A picture like this in the newspapers may save my job. I'll come over to your dugout this evening to have it taken, if he'll agree."

Robinson smiled wanly when I told him of Chapman's request and—to my surprise—quickly agreed.

"Tell Ben he doesn't have to come over to our dugout, either; I'll meet him halfway, behind the plate during batting practice."

"I'll go with you," I said, thinking to make the chore easier. I had often been Jack's ice-breaker.

"No," said Robinson. "This is something I should do alone, not as if I'm being urged."

Dixie Walker, Chapman's pal from Alabama, and a fine man through and through, had listened to this whole conversation, from the moment I relayed the strange request to Robbie. Dixie watched wide-eyed—we both did, in fact—as Robinson and Chapman, each marching from his own dugout, met on the neutral ground behind home plate. Ben extended a hand, smiling broadly as if they had been buddy-buddy for a lifetime. Robinson reached out and grasped it. The flicker of a smile crept across his face as the photographer snapped away, getting several shots.

Beside me Walker gasped, groping for words.

"I swear," he said softly, "I never thought I'd see Ol' Ben eat shit like that!"

# ROOKIE OF THE YEAR

## *Time* magazine
### (September 22, 1947)

*B*y the end of his rookie year, which had begun so ominously, Jackie Robinson had become a national phenomenon. Fans, both black and white, overflowed stadiums to see him play. A postseason poll would name him the second most popular man in America. Only crooner Bing Crosby had received more votes. On September 22, as the season drew to a close, with the Dodgers in first place and Robinson having just won baseball's first Rookie of the Year Award, Time magazine recognized Robinson's celebrity with a cover story. The cover art featured Robinson's handsome dark face amidst a sea of white baseballs. The article inside traced not only "the sociological experiment that Robinson represented," but gives a vivid portrait of Robinson's baseball skills and his emergence as the most exciting baseball player of the era. Forty years later, the annual prize for the best first-year player was renamed the Jackie Robinson Rookie of the Year Award in his honor.

●　●　●　●　●　●　●

It was only a month since Speedster Enos Slaughter of the St. Louis Cardinals, galloping into first base, had spiked First Baseman Jackie Robinson. Jackie, the first avowed Negro in the history of big-league baseball, looked at his ripped stocking and bleeding leg. It might have been an accident, but Jackie didn't think so. Neither did a lot of others who saw the play. Jackie set his teeth, and said nothing. He didn't dare to.

Last week the Brooklyn Dodgers faced the Cards again, and this time the pennant—and the Dodgers' none-too-healthy $4\frac{1}{2}$-game lead—was at stake. The Cards, somewhat housebroken descendants of the rough-&-tumble Gashouse Gang, were fighting back, late and hard. In the second inning, Jackie Robinson was spiked again—this time by trigger-tempered Catcher Joe Garagiola.

Next inning, at the plate, there was a face-to-face exchange of hot words between Robinson and Garagiola—the kind of rough passage that fans appreciatively call a "rhubarb." Umpire "Beans" Reardon hastily stepped between the two and broke it up. That was the end of it: no fisticuffs on the field, no rioting in the stands. But it was a sign, and an important one, that Jackie had established himself as a big leaguer. He had earned what comes free to every other player: the right to squawk.

That change of attitude showed, as nothing else could, the progress of Jackie Roosevelt Robinson in the toughest first season any ballplayer has ever faced. He had made good as a major leaguer, and proved himself as a man. Last week *The Sporting News*, baseball's trade paper, crowned him the rookie of the year. *The Sporting News* explained, carefully and a little grandiloquently, that it had made the choice solely on the basis of "stark baseball values." Wrote Editor J. G. Taylor Spink:

"Robinson was rated and examined solely as a freshman player in the big leagues—on the basis of his hitting, his running, his defensive play, his team value. The sociological experiment that Robinson represented, the trail-blazing he did, the barriers he broke down did not enter into the decision."

The "sociological experiment" may not have been foremost in Taylor Spink's mind, but it was never out of Jackie's. He, his team-mates and the National League had broken baseball's 60-year color line. Only two years had passed since Rogers Hornsby declared, and baseball know-it-alls everywhere had nodded in assent: "Ballplayers on the road live close together . . . it won't work."

## Wobbling Rabbit

The man who had made it work is a well-muscled, pigeon-toed, 28-year-old rookie from Pasadena, Calif., who, along with Glenn Davis and Babe Didrikson Zaharias, is one of the great all-round athletes of his day.

He looks awkward, but isn't. He stops and starts as though turned off & on with a toggle switch. He seems to hit a baseball on the dead run. Once in motion, he wobbles along, elbows flying, hips swaying, shoulders rocking—creating the illusion that he will fly to pieces with every stride. But once he gains momentum, his shoulders come to order and his feet skim along like flying fish. He is not only jack-rabbit fast, but about one thought and two steps ahead of every base-runner in the business. He beats out bunts, stretches singles into doubles. Once Jackie made second on a base-on-balls; he saw that the catcher had lost the ball, so he just kept on going.

He has stolen 26 bases this season, more than any other National Leaguer. He dances and prances off base, keeping the enemy's infield upset and off balance, and worrying the pitcher. The boys call it "showboat baseball." He is not, in his first year, the greatest baserunner since Ty Cobb, but he is mighty good. Cobb made a practice of coming in with spikes aimed at anyone brave enough to get in his way. It wouldn't have been politic for Jackie to do it that way very often. Robinson's base running, which resembles more the trickiness of "Pepper" Martin, is a combination of surprise, timing and speed. Says Jackie: "Daring . . . that's half my game."

## Turnstile Sociology

Jackie's daring on the baselines has been matched by shrewd Branch Rickey's daring on the color line. Rickey gave Robinson his chance. As boss of the Brooklyn Dodgers, Rickey is a mixture of Phineas T. Barnum and Billy Sunday, who is prone to talk piously of the larger and higher implications of what he is doing.

There were large implications, of course, in signing Jackie Robinson, but the influence on the box office was a lot easier to figure. Jackie Robinson has pulled about $150,000 in extra admissions this season.

Where the Dodgers have played, Negroes have turned out in force to see their hero. In Chicago, where Negro fans sported Jackie Robinson buttons, Jackie's fans came early and brought their lunch. In Jim Crowish St. Louis, where Negroes must sit in the right-field pavilion, the Robinson rooting section was more noticeable. Their adulation embarrassed Robbie: it made it harder for him to act like just another ballplayer. Rickey had promised to treat Jackie "just like any other rookie," and he certainly did on the payroll. Though he may have to pay Jackie more next season, so far Rickey has paid the crowd-pulling rookie-of-the-year only $5,000. Under league rules that is the least that the poorest rookie can be paid.

This week, as the Dodgers raced toward the finish seven games ahead, it was at least arguable that Jackie Robinson had furnished the margin of victory. The Dodgers are certainly not a one-man ball club. They have a bull-necked powerhouse of a catcher named Bruce Edwards, 24, whose special talents are steadiness and hustle. In Pee Wee Reese and Eddie Stanky, both short of height but long on skill, they have the best keystone combination in the league. The Dodgers also have a special affection for 34-year-old relief pitcher Hugh Casey, who has come onto the hill to save game after game, and is held in higher esteem by his team mates than strong-arm Ralph Branca, the Dodgers' only 20-game winner. And of course there is Dixie Walker, the "Pee-pul's Cherce," who at 36 still hits when it will do the most good—with men on base. In a locker-room gab-fest a few weeks ago, the Dodgers agreed among themselves that Jackie Robinson was the team's third most valuable player—behind Edwards and Reese.

## No Drink, No Smoke

Branch Rickey, the smartest man in baseball, had looked hard and waited long to find a Negro who would be his race's best foot forward, as well as a stout prop for a winning ball team.

Rickey and his men scouted Robinson until they knew everything about him but what he dreamed at night. Jackie scored well on all counts. He did not smoke (his mother had asthma and cigaret fumes bothered her); he drank a quart of milk a day and didn't touch liquor; he rarely swore; he had a service record (as Army lieutenant in the 27th Cavalry) and two years of college (at U.C.L.A.). He had intelligence, patience and willingness. He was aware of the handicaps his race encounters, but he showed it not by truculence or bitterness, and not by servility, but by a reserve that no white man really ever penetrated. Most important of all Robinson's qualifications, he was a natural athlete. Says Rickey: "That's what I was betting on." . . .

## Do's & Don'ts

Montreal had been won over, but that cut no ice in Flatbush. Branch Rickey, who knows his fellow citizens, set out to soften them up. He organized a group of Brooklyn's leading Negro citizens, including one judge, into a formal "how-to-handle-Robinson committee." In every other city in the National League, Rickey set up similar committees. The Brooklyn committee drew up a list of do's and don'ts a yard long; Jackie's deportment in public & private was to be supervised as thoroughly as Princess Elizabeth's.

He could not, like other ballplayers, endorse breakfast foods (or any other product, for that matter) at the usual $1,000 per endorsement. He could sign his name to no magazine or newspaper articles. When he got what he considered a bad decision from the umpire, he was not to object. When another player insulted him, he was to grin and bear it. He had to leave the ballpark after games by a secret exit. It was as important to avoid adulation as it was to avoid brickbats; there were to be no Jackie Robinson Days at Ebbets Field. He was not to accept any social invitations, from whites or blacks, and he was to stay away from night spots.

Jackie Robinson had already learned, by a lifetime's practice, the lesson another Robinson—soft-shoe dancing Bojangles—once laid down while acting as the unofficial Mayor of Harlem.

Bojangles' formula: "Do the best you can with what you've got . . . and get along with the white folks." Jackie had no desire to be a martyr for his race; he was just a young fellow anxious to make a living as a ballplayer. Though he barely knew Joe Louis, he sought him out for advice. He got an earful which boiled down to three words: "Don't get cocky."

Jackie lives a long way from Harlem's high life, in a five-room, second-floor flat on Brooklyn's McDonough Street, in a Negro neighborhood. His name is not on the door, and he knows few of his neighbors. How he feels about them shows through the guarded brevity of his speech, which sometimes carries a suggestion of dryness. Says he: "I don't want to bother with too many people who want to be my relatives."

Jackie's idea of a fine way to spend a night off is to go to bed early. He averages ten hours' sleep. He likes neither music nor dancing. "You know," he says, "colored people do not like music and dancing any better than white people . . . the white people just think they do." At home, he carefully takes his vitamin pills, spends a lot of time baby-sitting with his nine-month-old son, and according to his wife (whom he met at U.C.L.A.), always has his face buried in a paper. Like most ballplayers, he soaks up every word in every newspaper in town that concerns him and his team. His reader reaction: "Some reporters write nice things about me and mean them, and others write nice things and don't mean them. I can always tell."

So that Jackie would have company when the Dodgers were on the road, Rickey persuaded a Negro newsman, Wendell Smith, to travel with the club. In two cities, Jackie said, he had hotel trouble; he was not welcome at the Chase, where the Brooklyn club stays in St. Louis, or at Philadelphia's Benjamin Franklin. ("They fooled me," said Jackie. "I thought it would be St. Louis and Cincinnati.")

## No Help at First

Branch Rickey's do's & don'ts, strangely enough, did not include any instructions on how to play baseball. Although Jackie had played second base or shortstop all his life, he was handed a

first-baseman's mitt and sent out to sink or swim at a new position—first base. Being right-handed was no help: first base is a
left-hander's position. It is easier for a left-hander to throw from
first to any other base, and easier to pick a man off the bag. Only
a few great first basemen (among them the Cubs' Frank Chance
and the Giant's George Kelly) were right-handed. But Robinson,
with a tricky "scissors" pivot, manages to get rid of the ball as
quickly as any southpaw first baseman in the league.

His biggest difficulty is trying to forget that he is a shortstop.
Fielding ground balls, he scoops them up as if he had a quick
throw to make. And because he does not crouch down to block
the ball, a lot of grounders dribble between his legs. He also can't
seem to break his habit of catching put-out throws two-handed.
The Cardinals' Stan Musial, for example, gets a far longer reach
by taking throws single-handed.

A right-handed hitter, Jackie has a habit of swinging too
soon and his motion is half chop, half lunge. As a result, he fouls
off a lot of balls to the left. But his batting average at week's end
was a solid .301. The wise boys who judge a hitter by his Runs
Batted In totals are apt to take too fast a look at Jackie's R.B.I.
and grumble that Jackie can't hit in a tight spot. But as the club's
No. 2 hitter in the line-up, Jackie's job is either to push along the
lead-off man by a sacrifice, or to get on base himself. Jackie's
R.B.I. total (44) is higher than most No. 2 hitters'—including
Philadelphia's Harry Walker, who is baseball's current batting
king with an average of .362.

Actually, Jackie at bat is most dangerous when the odds are
against him. When the count gets to two strikes, as he explains
it: "Then I begin to crowd the plate a little." Says Branch
Rickey: "He is the best batter in the game with two strikes on
him." Pitchers capitalize on his hasty swing by feeding him slow
stuff. "I just can't hit those nuthin' pitches," Jackie complains.
Because he is the best bunter in the game, the Dodgers "cut him
loose" at the plate (i.e., let him decide for himself whether to
take, hit or bunt). He and Pete Reiser are also the only Dodgers
good enough to be "cut loose" on the bases, allowed to steal
without waiting for a signal.

## Timing & Tricks

By now, Robbie has carefully catalogued pitchers' weaknesses. He has, for example, discovered that when Boston's Si Johnson crooks his neck in a certain way, Si has stopped worrying about the base-runner and is about to pitch. This discovery gives Jackie a split-second head start on his way to second.

A similar mixture of timing and careful study enabled him to steal home last month against the New York Giants. (It was the second time this year he had pulled off the most spectacular base-running trick of them all.) Standing on third, Jackie carefully watched Pitcher Joe Begg's windup. Robinson ran in with the pitch as far as he dared, then slammed on the brakes and began to count: "One-two-three-four. . . ." He ticked off how long it took Beggs to get the ball across the plate. Satisfied that he could have made it in that time, Jackie scurried back to third base and took a deep breath. Next pitch, as Beggs involved himself in another slow-motion windup, Robinson was off like an express, rushing for the plate. The pitcher froze like a man with a high-voltage electric wire in his hand. Jackie went home standing up.

Who taught him to do things like that? Says Branch Rickey: "Primarily God."

## The Other Cheek

It is impossible to measure how much better, or how much worse, Jackie's first season might have been had his handicaps been fewer. It was not just that he was playing an unfamiliar position, or that at 28 he was pretty old for a rookie. He also had to turn the other cheek to abuses and insults. First he had to overcome the attitude of his fellow Dodgers, which ranged from mere wait-&-see stand-offishness to Southern-bred hostility.

And the rough stuff from rival teams began early and has never stopped. The first time the Dodgers played St. Louis, the Cards grumbled about playing on the same field with a Negro. They changed their minds—under pressure. Philadelphia was worse, because there the opposition had the open support of Phillies Manager Ben Chapman. He bawled insults at Robinson from the dugout. Chapman's second-division Phillies, notoriously the cruelest bench-jockeys in baseball, chimed in. Says Rookie Robbie: "I'd get mad. But I'd never let them know it." The Phillies management finally called down Chapman. He had his picture taken with Robinson to prove to everyone that the ugly reports weren't true.

It was Robinson's own Dodger mates who first came round. One or two of his fellow Dodgers began to say "Hello" to him in the locker room. Jackie wrote to his high-school baseball coach: "It isn't too tough on me. I have played with white boys all my life. But they hadn't played with a Negro before, and it sure was rough on some of them." Soon he was invited to play cards on trips, but though he didn't like the deuces-wild type of poker the boys played, he joined in a few games of hearts.

As Branch Rickey had foreseen, if Jackie played good baseball, the rest took care of itself. Some of the southerners on the squad shared the attitude of an Atlanta newsman who, when asked what he thought of Jackie Robinson, replied "He's good, damn him." But they were ready to back any player, black or white, who might help bring them the bonus (about $6,000 for winners, $4,000 for losers) that each gets for playing in a World Series.

After Slaughter did his spiking job a month ago, a group of Brooklyn players came to Jackie and said: "If they give you the works, give it back to them—and the team will be behind you 100%." That was the day Jack Roosevelt Robinson won his long, patient battle.

# THE INTEGRATION OF
# NEGROES IN BASEBALL

## DAN W. DODSON

*N*ew York University sociology professor Dan W. Dodson
was the tall, rangy son of white Texas sharecroppers.
He spoke with a deep Southern accent, but the message
his voice carried from the 1930s on was one of tolerance and integration. Dodson's writings, reported the New York
Times *in his 1995 obituary, provided "the underpinnings for the
movement to achieve racial and ethnic harmony." He also played
an active role in a variety of integration struggles.*

*In 1944 New York City Mayor Fiorello LaGuardia named
Dodson the executive director of the Mayor's Committee on
Unity. Shortly thereafter Dodson became a behind-the-scenes
advisor to Rickey's efforts to integrate the national pastime. In
the following article, which appeared in the* Journal of Educational Sociology *in 1954, shortly after the Supreme Court's
Brown v.* Board of Education *decision that declared segregated
schools unconstitutional, Dodson describes the role he played
and the risks he took. More significantly he assesses the strategies employed by Rickey and their relevance to the impending
struggle in the broader society. Dodson's analysis captures the*

*optimism that the Robinson experience engendered among integration advocates.*

● ● ● ● ● ● ●

At the present time there are 22 Negroes playing on Major League Baseball teams, and some seventy or eighty in the totality of organized baseball. Thus in eight years America's most prominent national sport has moved from a tradition of seventy years discrimination to almost complete integration. Only six clubs have no persons of the Negro race. (They are the New York Yankees, Baltimore Orioles, Washington Senators, Boston Red Sox and Detroit Tigers of the American League and the Philadelphia club of the National League).

The beginning of this undertaking, which started with the Brooklyn Dodgers in 1945 is of considerable significance to educators and community workers who are to assume the leadership in integrating school systems and other agencies as a result of the desegregation decision of the United States Supreme Court. It is proposed in this account to relate some of the steps involved in the crash of the color line with the employment of Jackie Robinson in October 1945, by the Brooklyn Club, and follow it through the three years that this author had a relationship to it. The analysis will be as it was seen from the vantage point of the Executive Director of the Mayor's Committee on Unity of New York City—the administrator of a program designed to improve relations between the racial and religious in that community— while he served as advisor to Branch Rickey, the President of the baseball club.

## Background Climate

America was at war, presumably to defeat racism. Riots had occurred in New York City, Detroit, and Beaumont, Texas, in the summer of 1943. The President of the United States had issued the 8802 order creating the Fair Employment Practices Committee. Negro baseball clubs had developed with considerable investment and equity in the perpetuation of the segregated pattern. In fact, they had asked for a committee from organized baseball to work with them toward better scheduling and perhaps eventual recognition of them as a part of the organized baseball structure, and Rickey of the Dodgers and MacPhail of the Yankees had been appointed by their respective leagues to represent organized baseball in negotiating with them.

In spring training in several instances, during the previous seasons try-outs had been asked for by Negro players, but nothing had ever come of it. The Negro press was complaining bitterly that there was discrimination against Negro players, for their own segregated clubs were beginning to demonstrate that they had baseball talent. In addition, many of the Negro players had played with or against "barnstorming" groups of white players in off season games and some, particularly Satchel Paige, had shown up to a good advantage.

In the spring of 1945 a new pressure group was formed in New York City called the "End Jim Crow In Baseball Committee." They were holding street meetings and receiving considerable publicity. Abroad, America's treatment of Negroes was becoming increasingly embarrassing as she tried to square domestic practice with war aims. Thus there was set a situation pregnant with possibilities for social change.

## The Role of Personality

It would be hard to assess the forces that went into the success of this venture, without reckoning with the personality of Branch Rickey. He is often called "The Deacon." He is of Methodist persuasion, and very active in his church's affairs. He had never seen his teams play on Sunday at the time I worked with him.

My impression was that he was intensely interested in youth and wanted to help them get their chance. He seemed to have little interest in men who had made the grade. He was always selling men when they became famous stars, but he had built in St. Louis, and was to repeat in Brooklyn, one of the strongest baseball organizations in the business. This interest in youth was contagious among those with whom he worked. Rickey had a great sense of concern about the discrimination against Negroes in baseball. . . .

In contrast to this response was that of MacPhail of the Yankees. When I called on him, in his inimitable way he said:

"You d—d professional doogooders know nothing about baseball. It is a business. Our organization rented our parks to the Negro Leagues last year for about $100,000. That is about the return we made on our investment. The investment of the Negro Clubs is also legitimate. I will not jeopardize my income nor their investment until some way can be worked out whereby it will not hurt the Negro Leagues for the major leagues to take an occasional player of theirs." He had no suggestion, however, as to how this could be done. It was clear he was thinking of maintaining segregation in the minor leagues and expecting the Negroes to get the training that would fit them for participation in the "big show" of the majors.

I am convinced that without the intelligence, personality, and dedication of a Rickey, it would have been very hard, indeed, to have successfully crashed the color line in baseball.

## Assessing Opposition

In the first interview with Rickey, he indicated what he thought would be the major sources of opposition. They were as follows:

1) The players. He thought of the three major obstacles this would be the least, provided he could find a good enough player that they would be convinced would help them win a pennant. He thought they would resent a player hired simply because he was a Negro.
2) The other owners. He said they could never attack him openly, but in a thousand ways from scheduling to policy formation—they would give him trouble.
3) The thing he feared most was the venom of some of the sports writers. He said many of them were from the South. They were always ready to criticize breaks with tradition. They, too, could never attack him openly, but obliquely they

would make it as hard for him as possible. Since success of baseball as an amusement depends upon good public relations, this would be most hazardous of all.

That these three assessments were about right, time substantiated. Only one player asked to be traded. He later asked for the letter of request to be returned to him.

The other clubs sent their scouts through the South and told young players they would have to play with Negroes if they signed with the Dodgers. In the first year, while Robinson was attracting 300,000 extra to the gate, Rickey estimated that he lost $500,000 in player production because of this advantage over his scouts. One of them left the organization the next year, because of the handicap under which he labored.

The second season after the signing of Robinson (Robinson's first in the majors) Happy Chandler, the Baseball Commissioner, banished the Dodger manager, Leo Durocher, for one year, on charges made by MacPhail, but which MacPhail said later were much less severe than the penalties given. It was in this year that Rickey brought Shotten in as manager and won the pennant. In loyalty to Durocher, however, he brought his banished manager back the next year in face of heavy criticism. Many of us will always believe that it was Chandler's way of getting at Rickey, whom he could not touch personally, but whose manager was vulnerable.

At a meeting of the owners in the winter of 1945 one is alleged to have made an impassioned speech to the effect that Rickey had ruined baseball by what he had done. I asked Mr. Rickey what he did. He said, "I started at first to answer. Then I said to myself, 'It's water over the dam and they can't pour it back.' " This capacity to see things in perspective is characteristic of the man.

The first barrage of the newspaper men was to the effect that he had robbed the Negro League. Robinson swore he was not under contract, but this seemed to make no difference. A large section of the sports press was favorable to the action. Many were not convinced, however, that Rickey meant business. Others took up the chant that he was merely exploiting the Negroes for publicity, and had no intention of carrying through.

After this first barrage, the opposition of the fourth estate attacked him for his miserliness. Powers, of the *Daily News* rarely referred to Rickey for over a year except in terms such as "El Cheapo." He wrote a scurrilous article from Florida in spring training season of 1946 raising the fears and doubts about what would happen if integration were attempted. The Chairman of the Mayor's Committee on Baseball and I, as its secretary, released a statement challenging his position. It is interesting to note with regard to the charge of miserliness, that the players on the club made Rickey a gift of a boat in a public ceremony in the park in the fall of 1946. At least his players, I am sure, never thought of him as a "penny pincher."

## Planning Strategy

The remainder of the summer from July 1945 to October's end was a time of strategy planning. The whole climate of community had to be changed. The job could not be done in a climate of controversy and acrimony. Mr. Rickey believed the End Jim Crow In Baseball Committee to be Communist inspired. He had no confidence in them. He had investigated me before he ever acknowledged my letter which asked for an appointment to discuss this problem with him. Apparently, after he had spent thirty minutes quizzing me, he decided he could trust me.

He needed help. Could we get this Committee out of the way until he had a chance to do something? Could I help him get together the material on Negroes in other sports? What about the new Law against Discrimination? To whom could he turn for guidance in the larger community? In the Negro Community? When should the signing of a contract be announced? What did we know about how integration is accomplished? What experience was there?

## Changing Community Climate

The first problem was obviously that of community climate. As Executive Director of the Mayor's Committee on Unity I suggested that we seek the aid of the newly formed State Commission Against Discrimination In Employment. With this Mr. Rickey agreed. They declined the invitation to work on the problem, saying they were an official body and there might be a formal complaint against the baseball clubs, and if they were working with them and then had to sit as judges over them they would be embarrassed.

I then went to the chairman of our committee, Mr. Charles Evans Hughes, Jr. and asked if we could not persuade Mayor LaGuardia to appoint such a committee. LaGuardia agreed. In addition to the citizens of the community, Mr. Rickey and Mr. MacPhail were also asked to join the committee as representatives of the two leagues. The appointment of the committee gave Rickey access to a few men whom he could consult—notably Dr. John H. Johnson of St. Martin's Episcopal Church of Harlem, Judge Edward S. Lazansky, and such help as I and my staff could give.

In addition, the appointment of the committee made it possible for me to go to the End Jim Crow group and ask that they call off their operations—especially a demonstration they had planned both at Ebbetts Field and the Polo Grounds. Further it assuaged feelings in the community that "nothing was being done."*

This symbolic action—the appointment of a committee—is a standard technique for delaying action. Someone should develop criteria for determining conditions under which such action is a justifiable risk as against a deliberate stall of social action.

It would have been disastrous to the outcome of the enterprise—in my judgment—had the appearance been given that a Negro was employed in Organized Baseball either because of the new law or because of a pressure group program. Undoubtedly, however, both contributed to the initiation of the venture, and the venture was less difficult, no doubt, because both were realities.

---

* Parenthetically, this was one of the toughest decisions I ever had to make while in office. The major purpose I could see for the committee was that it was a stall for time. You could not tell its members this. Yet had Mr. Rickey not delivered—had he been bluffing, as so many contended—I would have been totally discredited and the Mayor's Committee on Unity would have been impaired immeasurably through the loss of public confidence.

# The Integration Process

How [to] proceed with process?

Mr. Rickey had already spent about $5,000.00 scouting the Negro players. He thought he had found the man he wanted to start with, Jackie Robinson. He didn't think he was the best player. (He probably changed his mind later), but he was the best for the integration experiment. He was a college man—culturally the peer of any man on his team. He had played with and against whites. (This was of great significance later. His organization thought two subsequent players did not "make the grade" because they were Southern Negroes who tended to "freeze" when the whites started insulting them. Robinson, on the other hand, tended to be his best when he was under such pressure. He was what they called a "money player.")

The story of Rickey's sessions with Robinson have been widely publicized. He used what came to be called "role playing" situations with him to test his reactions to some social situations. He was anxious that Robinson cooperate in being a ball player and not try to be a social reformer. He tried to impress on him that his greatest reform service would be to perform so well and control himself so completely that he and those of his race to follow would be accepted. This pattern was followed religiously for the first year and one-half.

The next integration problems were:

1) What should be the timing of the announcement? I urged that it be after the 1945 season, but before contract signing time, in order that every player, when he returned to negotiate his contract, would understand that he might play with a Negro. If it were announced after contracts were signed they might feel they had been taken advantage of.

2) Where should he be assigned? Rickey felt he would assign a white man under comparable circumstances to a farm club. He so assigned Robinson. Montreal was ideal. It was a community in the North, a large French-Canadian population without so much prejudice, etc.

3) How to deal with the players? All the information we

possessed said, "You don't ask the players if they *want* to play with Negroes." You assume you have the right to employ qualified people. Obviously to have hired a Negro simply because he was a Negro, and put a "bush leaguer" on the field and have him "slaughtered" (figuratively) would have set race relations back and discredited the entire undertaking. "Firmness of policy" was also urged on Mr. Rickey. This he followed, but with intelligence. With his persuasiveness, he overcame many doubting Thomases.

4) Rickey didn't ask players to accept a minority player. Instead, he tried to create climate conducive to his acceptance. A few illustrations will suffice. In the year in Montreal, Robinson made a good record. At one stage he was benched with a "Charley Horse." The team was behind in the game. Mr. Rickey had ordered that he be rested. When he picked up the morning paper he noted that he had been sent in the game at a late stage, and had been instrumental in the win. He called the manager to find out why. The manager apologized but said, "The players asked for him, because he could help them pull the game out." Robinson thereupon volunteered to go into the game. The acceptance because of team need did not occur by happenstance.

A second illustration. After the year in Montreal, now bring him into the Majors? The strategy was carefully planned. The Dodgers were sent in spring training to the Caribbean. There they played against local teams with many Negro and dark Spanish members. The Montreal Club with Robinson was left in Florida.

Then the Dodgers were brought to Florida and played exhibition games with the Montreal Club in Florida and later at Ebbetts Field. Then Robinson's contract was sold to Brooklyn on the eve of three exhibition games with the Yankees—the last games preceding the opening of the season. Thus the team had been conditioned to playing against Negroes, then introduced to Robinson—then he was given a chance to play as a Dodger three games before the season started. In this strategy (all planned before spring training), it was hoped the team would be led by successive stages to want Robinson as a man who could help win a pennant.

A third illustration. At first Robinson had to take all the abuse the opposing team heaped on him. However, the time came about mid-season when some of the players told him to take no more; they would back him up.

Thus I believe there is illustrated a vital point—You don't worry about prejudices people possess too much. You create situations which bring them together for common purposes and allow them to work out their relations to each other in the best climate you can create.

5) In this climate problem it is important to keep in mind competitive relationships. I was concerned because Robinson was a second baseman. The Dodgers already had about the best second baseman in the League in Eddie Stanky. I was afraid that if the press carried a continuous chatter about whether Robinson could take Stanky's job away from him that morale would suffer. I suggested that he should not be put in a competitive role, and raised this problem. Mr. Rickey winked and said, "I have first base open. I think he can play that." Later when Stanky was sold, Robinson was moved to second base. Thus there was averted one of the oldest fears, namely, "The Negro is going to take the white man's job and vice versa."

## Meeting New Sets of Changed Relationships

Once this process was started whole sets of changed relationships emerged. I shall mention these and comment on them briefly.

1) Response of the Negro community. As could be expected, the Negro community received the movement with great enthusiasm. Special trains ran from Chicago and Detroit to see Robinson play in Buffalo. Mr. Rickey feared that over-enthusiasm might hurt the cause. Hence a meeting was held with Negro community leadership at which only four of us who were white were present. Here he laid his fears before

them. As a result, cards were printed and widely distributed saying, "Don't spoil Jackie's chance." Ministers cautioned from their pulpits. Negro newspaper sport columns carried good articles interpreting the importance of Negroes behaving responsibly at games. Herbert Miller was enlisted to go to other National League towns to do a comparable job.

2) The problem of hotel accommodations and eating facilities on trips. The position was taken that the Brooklyn Club could not assume that responsibility for discrimination in these places. However, as time went on these places of accommodation were held up to ridicule by the press. Most communities now (Baltimore is still an exception) accept baseball teams as teams.

3) Local communities were faced with new examination of local policies. In spring training the first year, the Dodgers were scheduled to play another club in a Florida town. The opposing club called up to say there was a law in that town to the effect that racially mixed groups could not play together in the city limits. Hence, Rickey would have to cancel the game. He replied, "I will not cancel the game. I will not leave my Negro players behind. We will be there at 2:00 p.m. as scheduled. Whoever cancels the game will take the responsibility for it. I won't make their moral compromise for them."

Significantly, two years later when spring training schedules were being arranged one of the large Georgia towns wanted the Dodgers to play their local club. To this Rickey responded, "If I can bring my whole team." "What do you mean by that?" they asked. "My Negro players," said Rickey. "Hell, that's who we want to see play," they responded.

4) Organized Baseball had to readjust. The best illustration relates to an exceptionally fine person—Ford Frick, then President of the National League, now Commissioner of Organized Baseball. My notes say that when I interviewed him in July of 1945 he showed interest, but was dubious of the wisdom of immediate integration. "Baseball is highly competitive. Many players are from the South. (My research reveals 35% were from 13 southern states.) A Negro player

sliding into a white man at second base might start a fight—
this might produce a riot. We should begin way down in the
Minor leagues and get them accustomed to playing together
before they reach the Majors." Almost two years to a day the
St. Louis Cardinals came to Ebbetts Field and threatened to
revolt rather than play against Robinson. Whereupon Frick
is reported to have said: "This is the United States of
America. If it wrecks the National League for five years, the
man is going to have his chance." Needless to say there was
no revolt. The growth of the persons in power positions is a
significant dimension of this case study.

## Principles of Integration

Since space does not permit further description of this action
the following tentative principles are listed as possible conclusions:

1) Don't ask people if they would like to change. Undoubtedly
   the great majority of people in baseball would have said
   "No" had they been polled.

2) Begin with a firm statement of policy and don't equivocate.
   Once opposition thinks you will listen, you are headed for
   trouble.

3) Don't worry about attitudes of people who are asked to
   accept new members. Set new relationships on basis of factors other than those in which prejudice is involved, e.g.
   winning the pennant was a issue, not integrating baseball.

4) Don't make moral compromises for those whose responsibility is that of decision making. The refusal to shield the
   policy makers in Florida hastened their own moral growth as
   they wrestled with the issues in which they had to accept
   moral responsibilities attendant on their choices.

5) Don't accept defensive role for your behavior. A student of
   mine asked Mr. Rickey why he had hired Robinson. He
   replied, "I don't have to answer that question. You have to
   answer instead, 'Why shouldn't I?' He was good enough to
   wear Uncle Sam's uniform. He is a qualified ball player.

Why shouldn't I?" This type of approach can't be answered and cannot be challenged publicly.

6) Use community resources. Rickey used Mayor's Committee on Unity, Y.M.C.A., the churches, the Negro press, etc.

7) Be sensitive to timing. Integration could not have happened ten years earlier, perhaps.

8) Produce best climate possible in which people relate to each other. The position played, spring training strategy, work on neutralizing End Jim Crow Committee in Baseball, etc. All were involved in this aspect of the program.

9) Bring representatives together as peers. Some thought Negroes should be pitchers only because they would not be associating with whites in the same way as they would as regular players. This would have been almost a Jim Crow position and probably would have been disastrous.

10) Don't meddle with relationships between members, once integration starts. Let members work out their own relationships. Forcing relationships makes for trouble.

11) Assess opposition and try to meet it positively.

12) Be prepared for oblique attacks. Opposition can rarely attack frontally and openly. It is at other points that they seek to undermine your leadership.

# THE PAUL ROBESON–JACKIE ROBINSON SAGA AND A POLITICAL COLLISION

## RONALD A. SMITH

*P*erhaps no episode in Jackie Robinson's life has provoked more criticism than his 1949 testimony before the
House Un-American Activities Committee (HUAC) condemning singer-actor Paul Robeson. The confrontation
occurred during Robinson's third and finest season in the major
leagues. Established as the Dodger second baseman and team
leader, Robinson paced the National League in batting with a
.342 average, scored 122 runs and drove in 124 runs, en route to
winning the Most Valuable Player Award. Along with fellow
Negro League veterans Roy Campanella and Don Newcombe,
Robinson spearheaded the Dodgers to another pennant. He had
become, along with world heavyweight boxing champion Joe
Louis, the most renowned African-American in the nation and a
symbol of optimism on race relations.

Paul Robeson, on the other hand, had grown disenchanted
with the prospects for equality in the United States. The spectacu-
larly multitalented Robeson—a former all-American football
player, lawyer, singer, and actor—had long been at the forefront
of the battle for integration, but during the post–World War II

*years he increasingly came to see communism as a panacea for
the nation's ills and the Soviet Union as a beacon of tolerance.
Amidst the heated anti-communist passions of the cold war,
Robeson increasingly became a pariah, barred—often violently—
from performing and hounded by protests wherever he appeared.*

*On April 20, 1949, Robeson told a Paris audience that "It is
unthinkable that American Negroes would go to war on behalf of
those who have oppressed us for generations against the Soviet
Union ..." Both at the time, and in retrospect, the statement
seemed a foolish rhetorical sally. Nonetheless, Robeson's comments ignited a firestorm. Many of the nation's foremost African-
American leaders, including Walter White, president of the
National Association for the Advancement of Colored People;
Mary McLeod Bethune, who had led President Franklin D. Roosevelt's "Black Cabinet"; and Lester Granger, the head of the
National Urban League, rose to criticize Robeson's comments.
But Robinson's testimony before HUAC remains the most cele-
brated—and subsequently castigated—of the attacks.*

*In this article Pennsylvania State University Professor
Ronald A. Smith examines the Robeson–Robinson collision
within the historical context of the postwar era. Smith, like most
who have commented on these events, sees Robeson as the more
sympathetic figure. As Smith notes even Robinson himself, in his
1972 autobiography, reconsidered the wisdom of his participation in the Robeson–HUAC affair. What is often lost, however, is
both the inherent naivete of Robeson's flirtation with the Soviet
Union and the powerful condemnation of segregation delivered
by Robinson before his HUAC inquisitors. "The fact that . . . it is
a Communist who denounces injustice in the courts, police brutality and lynching when it happens, doesn't change the truth of
his charges," asserted Robinson. ". . . white people must realize
that the more a Negro hates communism because it opposes
democracy, the more he is going to hate any other influence that
kills off democracy in this country—and that goes for racial discrimination in the Army, and segregation on trains and buses,
and job discrimination because of religious beliefs or color or
place of birth."*

● ● ● ● ● ● ●

Two Afro-American performing heroes, Paul Robeson and Jackie Robinson, collided politically during the turbulent anti-communist days of the early Cold War era. The House Un-American Activities Committee erected a stage for star athletic performer Jackie Robinson, the twentieth-century desegregator of professional baseball. At the same time it attempted to construct the political gallows for ex-athletic great and premier singer and actor, Paul Robeson, who was praising the Soviet Union's race relations as he fought for the rights of blacks in America. The political collision of two black heroes tells us much about the nature of American society and of the place of sport and the performing arts during the precipitous years of the communist-hunting post–World War II era. For symbolic reasons, Jackie Robinson was asked by government officials to help obliterate Paul Robeson's leadership role among Americans. So successful were Robinson and others that for a generation Paul Robeson remained for most Americans a non-person.

It is ironic that Paul Robeson (1898–1976), who had been involved himself in the desegregation of professional baseball, should have the desegregator, Jackie Robinson (1919–1972), play an important role in Robeson's departure from the public forum. Robeson, who was over fifty years old when the confrontation occurred, was a product of the latter nineteenth and early twentieth centuries. The fact that Robeson's early life and career took place in the depths of Jim Crowism in America may help explain why he developed certain racial and political positions perceived as radical and became a target for Robinson and others in the desegregation movement of the Cold War Years.

Paul Robeson was born the same decade that baseball, then the unquestioned national pastime, rid itself of all blacks playing the professional game. At about the same time, the League of American Wheelmen, a key amateur bicycle association, inserted a whites-only clause in its constitution; John L. Sullivan, the first great American boxing champion, refused to fight blacks; and the newly formed Jockey Club of New York began to restrict the

licensing of black jockeys. Two years before the birth of
Robeson, the historic 1896 Supreme Court *Plessy* v. *Ferguson*
"separate but equal" decision judicially sanctioned the segregation of blacks from whites. This was followed during Robeson's
first year by Supreme Court decisions to uphold literacy tests and
poll-tax qualifications for voting; policies devised to keep the
Negro out of politics. Justice Henry Brown rationalized these
decisions when he wrote in the *Plessy* decision: "If one race be
inferior to the other socially, the Constitution of the United States
cannot put them on the same plane. . . ." It would have been
natural for blacks born at the time to be socialized in believing
that they were inferior. Even the evolutionary theory of natural
selection, struggle for existence, and survival of the fittest indicated to many Americans that blacks were placed low on the evolutionary ladder.

The belief in the racial inferiority of blacks at the time of
Robeson's birth influenced the racial question in at least two
important ways. First, Jim Crow laws multiplied greatly so that in
the leisure domain, recreational facilities such as swimming
pools, playgrounds, and public parks were segregated, though
almost never equally. Especially in the South, laws mandated
separate entrances, ticket windows, and seating arrangements and
created such curiosities as an Oklahoma ban on blacks and whites
fishing together in the same boat and a Birmingham, Alabama,
ordinance prohibiting racially mixed play at dominoes or
checkers. Second, the hue and cry of voices proclaiming racial
superiority of whites affected the way blacks thought of themselves. Increasingly, Negro leaders and masses turned toward an
accommodation with the Jim Crow system rather than protest
against it. The dominant Negro leader of the turn-of-the-century
America, Booker T. Washington, led the way toward accommodation with the whites. In his famous Atlanta Compromise speech
in 1895, Washington held up his hands, fingers outstretched, to a
mixed crowd of blacks and whites, and proclaimed that "in all
things that are purely social we can be as separate as the fingers. . . ." Washington believed that it was more valuable for
blacks to prove their worth by their own productivity than to
demand either political or social rights.

If most blacks became accommodated to the unjust system, some, such as W. E. B. Du Bois, the historian and social critic, attacked racial prejudice where they found it. Du Bois criticized Booker T. Washington's views arguing that they represented "in Negro thought the old attitude of adjustment and submission . . . [which] practically accepts the alleged inferiority of the Negro races." Du Bois called for "work, culture, liberty,—all these we need, not singly but together, not successively but together, each growing and aiding each, and all striving toward that vaster ideal that swims before the Negro people, the ideal of human brother-hood, gained through the unifying ideal of Race. . . ." Said Du Bois: "All that makes life worth living—Liberty, Justice, and Right, [should not be] marked 'For White People Only.' "

Paul Robeson was raised with beliefs more in sympathy with Du Bois than with Washington. From an early time, his preacher-father, a former runaway slave, ingrained in the boy a sense of pride and worth as a black man. He soon found that in mental and physical qualities he was superior to most whites. As one of only three blacks graduating from his high school in Somerville, New Jersey, Robeson scholastically headed his class of 250 students. He was a skilled debator in his high school, was a soloist of the glee club, acted in the drama club, and excelled in several sports. During his senior year he achieved the highest score on a statewide examination for a scholarship to attend Rut-gers College. From that day on, he later recalled, "Equality might be denied but I *knew* I was not inferior."

Indeed, Robeson was not inferior physically or mentally, and he showed remarkable abilities during his college years and after. He was an all-American football player at Rutgers in 1917 and 1918, and was called the greatest defensive end of all time by Walter Camp, the so-called father of American football. Robeson won twelve varsity letters in football, basketball, baseball, and track-and-field. He led his class academically and was elected to Phi Beta Kappa in his junior year. After college, he played pro-fessional football on the first championship team of what today is the National Football League. He took a law degree at Columbia University, before becoming a Shakespearean actor and a world renowned singer. Yet, by the 1960s and 1970s, he had become for most, a forgotten man. While Jackie Robinson was generally recognized for desegregating professional baseball, Robeson was not widely remembered even among blacks.

Jackie Robinson was born on a share-cropper farm in Cairo, Georgia, in 1919, the year Babe Ruth was sold to the New York Yankees and the Black Sox scandal took place. The same year saw Jack Dempsey winning the heavyweight boxing championship and immediately announcing that he would pay "no attention to Negro challengers." Both Robeson and Robinson grew up in a Jim Crow society in which social and legal separation was readily apparent.

While Jackie Robinson moved to southern California with his mother and older brothers and sisters in 1920, Paul Robeson attended Columbia Law School. On weekends, he traveled to Ohio and played football with another black, Fritz Pollard, on the championship Akron Pros. Later, as he was completing his law degree, he competed for the Milwaukee Badgers in the fledgling National Football League. Upon graduation from Columbia, the American Bar Association denied him membership, and he suffered other severe limitations on his chosen profession. He soon withdrew from law practice and launched an acting and singing career. The summer before his last term at Columbia Law School, he had toured Great Britain singing and acting in a play titled *Voodoo*. By the mid-1920s, Robeson starred in Eugene O'Neill's plays, *The Emperor Jones* and *All God's Chillun Got Wings*. Robeson portrayed a black man who married a white woman in *All God's Chillun*. Reaction to his involvement in a racially mixed drama in Jim Crow America included hate mail and threats to both Robeson and playwright O'Neill from the Ku Klux Klan and individuals with equally harsh racist feelings. Favorable audience reaction and reviews, however, brought Robeson recognition among both whites and blacks. He gained further public recognition from musical concerts featuring his rich voice singing Negro spirituals.

Robeson spent increasing periods of time in Europe and England in the 1920s and 1930s. Especially in London he found less racial hatred and greater personal freedom than in America. Becoming more politically aware as areas of the world moved toward fascism during the 1930s, Robeson began to question the imperialistic policies of European nations and America toward colonial Africa, of fascist Italy toward Ethiopia, and of Nazi Germany toward the Spanish Civil War. By the mid-to-late 1930s, Robeson took the side of those who favored freedom for blacks in Africa. He campaigned for the Republican cause against totalitarian Franco in Spain, and deeply opposed fascism in Italy and especially in Germany. In Nazi Germany in 1934, on his way to Russia to confer with a film director, Robeson was threatened and racially abused by German storm troopers near Berlin.

In Moscow, Robeson was greatly impressed with the Russian people and what he considered their lack of racial prejudice. He wrote: "I, the son of a slave, walk this earth in complete dignity." From that point on, Robeson continued his praise of the Soviet Union while speaking out against fascist thought wherever he found it. He found much to criticize in America. Two decades later he would testify before the House of Representatives Committee on Un-American Activities, stating:

> I would say in Russia I felt for the first time a full human being, and no colored prejudice like in Mississippi and no colored prejudice like in Washington and it was the first time I felt like a human being, where I did not feel the pressure of color as I feel in this committee today.

In September 1939, Paul Robeson returned to live in the United States after spending most of the previous twelve years abroad. This was the same month that Jackie Robinson began attending college at UCLA. . . .

During the time Robinson starred in athletics at UCLA, Robeson was attaining new heights of popularity as a singer and actor. When the United States entered World War II as an ally of the Soviet Union, little was said about Robeson's praise of life in the Soviet Union—most saw him as a strong opponent of fascism. He helped conduct war bond drives as he continued to sing Russian folk songs and speak out for black rights everywhere. Like a number of civil rights leaders, he saw World War II as having a positive effect in breaking down Jim Crow laws and customs. Robeson even had a part in the attempt to desegregate professional baseball in the midst of the war.

Segregation existed in professional baseball during World War II as it had for more than a half-century when it had first drawn the color line. It seemed hypocritical to Robeson and others that America would fight to end the myth of Aryan supremacy in Germany while the nation preserved its own myth of racial supremacy at home. A movement to end baseball segregation began soon after Pearl Harbor. It is not surprising that the American Communist Party took a lead in the agitation for integrating baseball and in accepting any role Paul Robeson would play in it.

The American Communist Party organ, the *Daily Worker*, had called for breaking the color line in the 1930s, but in early 1942 its sports editor, Lester Rodney, began attacking the Commissioner of Baseball, Kenesaw Mountain Landis, for not eliminating Jim Crowism in America's most visible sport. After the great black pitcher Satchel Paige and his Kansas City Monarchs defeated a group of Major Leaguers, who were in military service and headed by pitcher Dizzy Dean, Rodney wrote contemptuously:

> Can you read, Judge Landis? . . . The Stars could get only two hits off Satchel Paige in seven innings of trying. Why does your silence keep him and other Negro stars from taking their rightful place in our national pastime at a time when we are at war and Negro and white are fighting and dying together to end Hitlerism?

The *Daily Worker* quoted Jimmy Dykes, manager of the Chicago White Sox, as saying to Jackie Robinson, the young Negro shortstop: "I'd love to have you on my team and so would all the other big league managers. But it's not up to us. Get after Landis." To a similar statement, Commissioner Landis replied that if any managers "want to sign one, or 25 Negro players, it is all right with me. That is the business of the managers and the club owners." . . .

Pressure to change baseball's six decades of segregation continued to be exerted during the first summer of America's entry into World War II. There was one report of a heated discussion of club owners over blacks in baseball at the time of the Major League All-Star game and of the meeting transcripts being ordered destroyed. That same summer the president of the Pittsburgh Pirates announced that blacks would be given tryouts for his team. There is, however, no evidence that blacks of the stature of Josh Gibson, a catcher, or Sammy Bankhead . . . of the nearby Homestead Grays Negro team—or any other—were given the opportunity. Thirty-five-year-old Satchel Paige, the best known and highest paid black player of the times, indicated that he would only come into white baseball if it were on a team of all blacks because the racial tension in both the South and the North would be too high if a white team were desegregated. A writer from Los Angeles mocked the scene: "Let the Negro have his name in the casualty lists of Pearl Harbor or Bataan or Midway. But, for heavensakes, let's keep his name out of the boxscores." Indeed, the old argument of possible race riots, as had occurred after the Jack Johnson-Jim Jeffries Great White Hope fight of 1910, was still brought up in discussions of desegregation in American sport.

Agitation continued into 1943, eventually involving Paul Robeson. A resolution was introduced in the New York State legislature protesting the unwritten ban against blacks in baseball, and Brooklyn's communist councilman, Peter V. Cocchione, introduced a resolution calling for desegregation of baseball. The Negro Publishers Association became involved and requested Commissioner Landis to discuss the question of blacks in organized baseball at the annual meeting of Major League teams. The Commissioner agreed, and for the first time in its history professional baseball officially examined the desegregation issue in its December meeting. Eight black newspapermen and Paul Robeson attended the meeting. Robeson's presence dominated the session.

Robeson was one of three blacks to address the club owners. He was introduced by Landis who said that he had brought Robeson to the meeting "because you all know him. You all know that he is a great man in public life, a great American." Robeson told the owners: "I come here as an American and former athlete. I come because I feel this problem deeply." He expressed his belief that the time had come for baseball to change its attitude toward the Negro and told them he had become the first black actor to play in Shakespeare's *Othello* on Broadway less than two months before. He declared that if he could be a black in an otherwise all-white play, then a Negro in a white cast should no longer be incredible to baseball owners. Robeson said that though he understood the owner's fears of racial disturbance if baseball were desegregated, "my football experience showed me such fears are groundless." When he finished, the owners gave him what a black writer called a "rousing ovation," but the owners neither questioned Robeson nor the other two speakers. Landis did reiterate a previous statement that "each club is entirely free to employ Negro players to any extent it pleases and the matter is solely for each club's decision without any restrictions whatsoever."

While Jackie Robinson endured the torture of desegregating organized baseball, Paul Robeson entered the post–World War II era criticizing American racial policies and praising those of the socialistic Soviet Union. Robeson had noted during the war the influence that he believed would be brought on the United States' racial policies from abroad. "We in America," Robeson said, "criticize many nations. We know that international conscience has great influence in spite of wars. One important part of the solution of the Negro problem here will be the pressure of other countries on America from the outside." These were prophetic remarks in light of the effect of the Cold War politics on breaking down America's Jim Crow policies in the 1950s and 1960s. After World War II, Robeson was much involved in that external influence, probably giving it more visible support than any other black American. His outspoken stance for black rights and his procommunist ideology created a furor wherever he went as America turned to a hate-Russia campaign in the post-war era.

As Jackie Robinson attempted to make his impact in baseball with his base hits and effective fielding, Paul Robeson plowed forth on his own crusade. The day after Robinson made his first Major League base hit, Robeson's scheduled concert appearance in Peoria, Illinois, was unanimously banned by the city council. Not long after that incident, the Albany, New York, Board of Education withdrew permission previously granted to Robeson for a concert in its school auditorium. Said a board member: "The color of Paul Robeson's skin has nothing to do with this case, but the color of his ideologies has." Retorted Robeson: "Whether I am a communist or a communist sympathizer is irrelevant. The question is whether American citizens, regardless of their political beliefs or sympathies, may enjoy their constitutional rights." The Albany case was eventually taken to the New York Supreme Court, which granted Robeson the right to sing in the Albany school. Robeson gave his concert, and that same day Jackie Robinson revealed hate letters written to him threatening his life if he did not quit baseball.

It was in context of Robinson's desegregation of baseball under white terms and Robeson's stand for human rights under free political terms that a collision arose between Robinson and Robeson. The catalyst was the House Un-American Activities Committee (HUAC) of the United States Congress. In the late 1930s, HUAC had been established principally to investigate fascist and communist activities. It became an inquisitorial committee which ferreted out political deviants for public exposure and ridicule. Organizations and individuals which HUAC considered heretical were singled out to be destroyed or at least immobilized. Extended hearings were conducted in which accused and accusers were questioned at length. One historian has written that the accused would leave HUAC hearings "with a mark of Cain," while the accuser would depart "the tribunal with a halo of potential market value." Another has concluded that HUAC's "endless harassment of individuals for disagreeable opinions and actions has created anxiety, revulsion, indignation, [and] outrage. . . ."

Paul Robeson was one of HUAC's targets. He had been chastised previously by HUAC, but in 1949 the Committee, representing American fear of and hysteria over the Cold War political left, attacked Robeson violently. This vendetta came as a result of a comment made by Robeson at the World Congress of

Partisans held in Paris, France, on April 20, 1949. Robeson, along with W. E. B. Du Bois, directed the American delegation to the communist-led meeting. Both men spoke to the 1800 delegates from about sixty nations, and both condemned America's international actions. It was Robeson, however, whose rhetoric drew the attention of the American press and the ire of governmental officials. One of Robeson's unwritten statements caught the ear of the press:

> It is unthinkable that American Negroes would go to war on behalf of those who have oppressed us for generations against the Soviet Union which in one generation has raised our people to full human dignity.

The next day the nation's newspapers reported Robeson's remarks indicating that blacks would never fight against the Soviet Union. As one Negro leader, Lester B. Granger, commented: "A nation-wide 9-day sensation was manufactured." Most black leaders were quick to castigate Robeson for his Paris speech. "We American Negroes," declared Max Yergan, a black who had once led the Council of African Affairs with Robeson, "can be deeply grateful Mr. Paul Robeson did not speak for us in Paris a few days ago." Exclaimed Walter White, head of the National Association for the Advancement of Colored People: "We will not shirk equal responsibilities. . . . We will meet the responsibilities imposed upon all America." Robeson is "an ingrate" chided Dr. Channing Tobias, a member of the NAACP board of directors. Wrote Mary McLeod Bethune, President of the National Council of Negro Women: "I am chagrined at his presumption. . . . I think he has missed his cue and has entered the stage during the wrong scene." Edgar G. Brown, Director of the National Negro Council, went further by calling Robeson's speech communist propaganda while quoting Stephen Decatur's "In peace and war—my country, right or wrong." To all of this a black columnist stated that "we all know that our professional leaders had to say officially that Paul does not speak for Negroes as a group." He then criticized others for joining the bandwagon which he believed was essentially saying, "Deed, Boss, that bad old Paul ain't speaking for me and you know I'll fight for democracy, if I ain't been lynched first."

Newspapers intended for a Negro audience were almost as unequivocal in their stands against Robeson as were white newspapers and black leaders, and their immediate reaction to Robeson's Paris statement clearly showed that Robeson did not speak for all American blacks, probably not even most blacks. The *Pittsburgh Courier* editorialized that Robeson's declaration that blacks would never fight the Soviets was a "pathetic statement." The *Chicago Defender* snapped "Nuts to Mr. Robeson," and the less hostile *Philadelphia Afro-American* stressed that "Robeson does not speak for us and millions of other colored people." Some black columnists, though, sided with Robeson. This was only natural, for at the time Robeson spoke in Paris, lynchings were still prevalent in the South while anti-lynching bills before Congress died; Jim Crow conditions existed in the nation's capital; segregation continued in the military; and the Ku Klux Klan persisted in America. One writer, while condemning Robeson's "fat-headed" statement about fighting the Soviets, nevertheless commented that the "racial consciousness of Americans sorely needs to be stirred up." Another believed that the "fear of Russia and of communism, as well as outside criticism of the United States, have been the Negro's greatest benefactor in recent years." Few took the stance of Robeson's friend, W. E. B. Du Bois, who praised Robeson and condemned the "sheep-like disposition, inevitably born of slavery" which Negroes showed in following white leadership.

Most reaction by both blacks and whites was hostile to Robeson, but there was an uneasy feeling exposed in the American press that there was some truth to what Robeson was saying. Would blacks fight for America in a war against the Soviet Union? In a sample of whites in several Northern cities, over 50 percent questioned Negro's loyalty to America. Members of HUAC, who had used Robeson previously as a favorite target, believed that they could attack the problem positively and leftist Paul Robeson negatively at the same time. They would conduct a hearing on the communist infiltration of minority groups and invite prominent blacks to testify about Negro loyalty and

Robeson's disloyalty. Invited to testify before HUAC, among others, were Lester Granger, National Urban League head; Dr. Charles S. Johnson, President of Fisk College; Thomas W. Young, Negro publisher; and Clarence Clark, a disabled Negro veteran of World War II. Of greatest importance because of his popular stature as desegregator of America's "National Pastime," was the invitation sent to Jackie Robinson. Chairman of HUAC, John S. Wood of Georgia, telegrammed Robinson asking him to testify before his Committee "to give the lie" to statements by Paul Robeson.

By 1949, Jackie Robinson was probably the best known black in America with the possible exception of Joe Louis and Paul Robeson. At the time of the HUAC hearings on communist infiltration of minority groups, Robinson was leading the National League in batting with a .360 average and was also the top vote getter in the annual all-star balloting in his league. It was not unexpected that HUAC would ask a black of Robinson's public exposure to testify against another prominent black. According to Alvin Stokes, a black investigator for HUAC, the Committee felt it was necessary to get someone of the popular stature of Robinson to discredit Robeson.

The decision to speak out against Robeson was not an easy one for Robinson. He recounted his dilemma. If he testified he might merely be the black pawn in a white man's game which pitted one black against another, and he might be considered a "traitor" to his own people. If he did not testify he feared that Robeson's statement might discredit all blacks in the eyes of whites. At that time, Robinson had faith that whites would ultimately render justice to blacks. He chose to testify before HUAC. With advice from Branch Rickey and Lester Granger, Robinson prepared a statement which he delivered before HUAC on July 18, 1949.

Seated before the Committee, Robinson testified, rather naively but with good effect, that baseball was "as far removed from politics as anybody can possibly imagine." Referring to Robeson's statement which he had been called upon the HUAC "to combat," Robinson said:

I can't speak for any 15,000,000 people any more than any other one person can, but I know that I've got too much invested for my wife and child and myself in the future of this country, and I and other Americans of many races and faiths have too much invested in our country's welfare, for any of us to throw it away because of a siren song sung in bass.

Robinson continued:

But that doesn't mean that we're going to stop fighting race discrimination in this country until we've got it licked. It means that we're going to fight it all the harder because our stake in the future is so big. We can win our fight without the Communists and we don't want their help.

With those strong words he closed his testimony. Earlier in his statements he had qualified his harsh remarks by stating that Robeson should have a "right to his personal views, and if he wants to sound silly when he expresses them in public, that is his business and not mine." Acknowledging that Robeson was "still a famous ex-athlete and a great singer and actor," Robinson said that "Negroes were stirred up long before there was a Communist party and they'll stay stirred up long after the party has disappeared—unless Jim Crow has disappeared by then as well." Robinson saw progress, though slow, in black rights, pointing out that there were only seven blacks out of 400 Major League players and that only three of the sixteen Major League teams were desegregated. "We're going to keep on making progress," Robinson told the probers, "until we go the rest of the way in wiping Jim Crow out of American sports."

Robinson's testimony against Robeson was predictably praised by HUAC, which for the first time that year allowed motion and still photographers free access in the room during Robinson's testimony. The Committee obviously knew the publicity value of a sports performer well-known to Americans. Major newspapers emphasized the anti-Robeson comments of

Robinson while giving little space to the pro-civil rights state-
ments of the all-star second baseman. Newspaper accounts
accomplished HUAC's objective of discrediting Robeson's Paris
statement. Headlines of "ROBESON SILLY, JACKIE ROBIN-
SON TELLS RED QUIZ" and "DODGER STAR RAPS
ROBESON 'SIREN SONG' " appeared in leading Chicago and
Philadelphia newspapers. The *New York Times* editorialized:
"Jackie Robinson scored four hits and no errors" testifying before
HUAC, while the *Washington Post* editor praised Robinson and
denigrated Robeson for his "insulting libels."

Opinions expressed by blacks were not as consistent. First,
some blacks were suspicious of HUAC, questioning why it had
never thoroughly investigated the Ku Klux Klan or any other
American fascist group. They also distrusted HUAC because its
committee chair had been held by Southern racists of the likes of
Martin Dies (Texas) and John Rankin (Mississippi). Commented
one black writer: "How come your committee can investigate
everything from Reds to second basemen, and can't investigate
the Ku Klux Klan?" Second, one of their own black heroes Paul
Robeson, even though tainted, was being attacked by the white
establishment. However questionable were some of Robeson's
beliefs, he was one of their own. While major white newspapers
were cheering Robinson for castigating Robeson, black papers
were generally cheering Robinson for advocating black civil
rights and criticizing HUAC's investigation for dividing blacks
against each other. "LYNCHERS OUR CHIEF ENEMY
JACKIE TELLS 'RED' PROBERS" headlined the *Philadelphia
Afro-American*. One of its writers claimed that the hearings were
a "witchhunt." Meanwhile a Pittsburgh writer asserted that
Robinson had been a "stooge" for HUAC and had put Negroes on
the defensive, hamstringing the civil rights movements. Others,
too, criticized Robinson. A woman from the west coast chided
Robinson claiming that "the habit of 'bad mouthing' is a slavery
trait and should have been outgrown ere this time." An angry
individual from Boston wrote that "Paul Robeson was fighting
for his people's rights when Jackie Robinson was in knee pants."
If HUAC had been successful in creating a negative climate

around Robeson's name, it had also created division among blacks over two of their heroes.

The Robeson–Robinson confrontation added to the mounting pressure in America to cleanse itself of any sympathy for the Soviet Union. Robeson soon began his rapid decline to near oblivion. A Robeson concert in Peekskill, New York, later in the summer of 1949, brought about a united effort by several military veterans groups to stop it. Concert-goers were prevented from attending the first concert attempt, and after it was given a week later, a riot resulted with hundreds injured, numerous autos and buses wrecked, and crosses burned as if it were a Ku Klux Klan rally. Concert managers soon refused to book him, and his recordings were often taken out of record shops. There was even a move by Rutgers University alumni to remove his name from the college rolls. The *American Sports Annual* deleted Robeson's name from its list of football all-American selections for the years 1917 and 1918. The Federal Bureau of Investigation continually harassed Robeson, and the Secretary of State, John Foster Dulles, had his passport cancelled—two methods used by the federal government to deny Robeson personal freedom and economic independence. The vicious attacks upon Robeson were part of the hysteria created out of the Cold War ideology of the post–World War II era. It was the same hysteria which gave rise to the demogogic character of Joseph McCarthy, who as Senator used character assassination involving the issue of communism in his rise to prominence around 1950.

By the mid-1950s, the anti-communist excesses diminished considerably. Though HUAC was still active, the Senate's censuring of McCarthy helped to control the most outrageous charges of communism in America. Robeson was still effectively blacklisted in America, however, and the denial of a passport for almost a decade placed him in a difficult economic position. He, like the Communist Party which had been legislated out of existence, was successfully silenced. But the question of equal political and social rights for blacks, for which Robeson had been active for a generation, was beginning to come to a head. The landmark Supreme Court decision of 1954, *Brown* v. *Board of Education*, overturned the earlier "separate but equal" decision.

Other court actions and federal legislation soon brought resistance and physical confrontation as America faced the proposition of equal rights for all its citizens regardless of race.

Jackie Robinson increasingly spoke out for black rights and, like Robeson before him, was classified by some as an "uppity nigger." Unlike Robeson, Robinson kept his remarks within a more conservative framework. When Robinson announced publicly after the 1956 baseball season that he was retiring from baseball, he wrote:

> I don't regret any part of these last 10 years. There's no reason why I should. Because of baseball I met a man like Branch Rickey and was given the opportunity to break the major-league color line. Because of baseball, I was able to speak on behalf of Negro Americans before the House Un-American Activities Committee and rebuke Paul Robeson for saying most of us Negroes would not fight for our country in a war against Russia.

Although Jackie Robinson never became reconciled to the beliefs of Paul Robeson, he saw something more positive in Robeson shortly before his own death. Writing in his autobiography published in 1972, titled *I Never Had It Made*, Robinson stated that he never regretted his statements about Robeson made two decades before. "But," Robinson wrote:

> I have grown wiser and closer to painful truths about America's destructiveness. And I do have increased respect for Paul Robeson who, over a span of that twenty years, sacrificed himself, his career, and the wealth and comfort he once enjoyed because, I believe, he was sincerely trying to help his people.

When Jackie Robinson died on October 24, 1972, his place in history was almost assured. Paul Robeson died on January 23, 1976. Because he had tied the black rights movement in America to what he considered was a positive Soviet racial policy, he had become a political leper and was in almost total eclipse in the 1950s and 1960s. There was, indeed, a curtain of silence surrounding him. By the 1970s, and especially after his death, a growing number of individuals began to see greatness in Robeson. Even politicians, who often fear to speak out on controversial individuals and issues, began to speak of Robeson's historic concern for humanity. One of the outspoken was Congressman Andrew Young, a black who later became Ambassador to the United Nations under President Jimmy Carter. He wrote:

> Paul Robeson was the hero of my youth. . . . I can never forget the strength of conviction that helped strengthen our backs and set our feet in the path of self-liberation as a people. Paul loved people of all colors and of many nations. He loved justice, freedom, and compassion. He had no tolerance for injustice, oppression, or tyranny. Few men in their lifetime bequeath a legacy to the living.

If both Paul Robeson and Jackie Robinson, as performers, were on the cutting edge of racial reform in America, it appears that they were approaching change from different directions. Robeson wanted reform on his own terms, not necessarily those of white society. Robinson was more willing to compromise with white society for a time to accomplish positive racial goals and his own advancement. Robeson was more idealistic and unyielding, and because of it he was politically, economically, and socially alienated from the greater American society. Robinson was more realistic and pragmatic, and he fared far better socially and financially than did Robeson. What was common to both Robeson and Robinson was that they were both black performers, one an ex-athlete and an actor and singer and the other solely an athlete, who in their own ways fought for equal rights for blacks. Robinson's position as desegregator of professional baseball seems assured. Robeson's status as a crusader for black rights everywhere seems likely to rise with time. If "men will judge men by their souls and not by their skins," as W. E. B. Du Bois advocated in the early twentieth century, it appears that both Paul Robeson and Jackie Robinson, despite their acknowledged differences, will be judged not only as athletic and performing champions but as leaders in race relations as well.

# September 30, 1951

## MILTON GROSS

*B*obby Thomson's three-run home run on October 3, 1951, that catapulted the New York Giants over the Brooklyn Dodgers in their pennant playoff series is arguably the most famous single moment in baseball history. This epic (or, for Dodger fans, tragic) clout would not have come to pass, however, if not for the spectacular play of Jackie Robinson three days earlier in the regular season finale in Philadelphia. The Dodgers, who had compiled a twelve-and-a-half game lead on August 12, had watched the Giants, managed by Robinson's arch-rival, Leo Durocher, win sixteen straight games after that date, and then inexorably close the remaining gap in September.

On Sunday, September 30—the final day of the season—the two clubs were tied for first place. The Giants defeated the Boston Braves, 3–2, necessitating a Dodger win over the Phillies to force a playoff. The Dodgers fell behind 6–1 after three innings. Going into the eighth inning, the Phillies still led, 8–6, but a pinch hit two-run double by Rube Walker tied the game and forced it into extra innings. The score remained tied into the twelfth. Then

*Jackie Robinson, in a sequence that more than any other demon-
strated his competitive greatness, took control of the contest.*

*New York Post sportswriter Milton Gross captured the ten-
sion of the game and Robinson's heroics in his column the next
day. Journalist Arch Murray dubbed Robinson's game-winning
blow the "shot that would be heard around the baseball world."
Ironically, this sobriquet would become more familiarly attached
to Thomson's home run three days later.*

● ● ● ● ● ● ●

Now as you look back at it, it seems it had to be this way.
Hollywood could have taken a hand and written a bit, but destiny did it better because it's come down not to baseball alone, a
playoff for the pennant race pairing the Dodgers and Giants, but
Jackie vs. Leo. The enmity that exists between them would
make any part of the world go round, let alone Brooklyn and
New York.

It is a real and bitter thing, this feeling between Robinson
and Durocher, and what it presages is something for the future,
because Jackie and Leo are as unpredictable as the National
League season has been.

Here, perhaps, are the two best competitors baseball has
known. Leo, making up in determination, callousness to taunts,
ridicule and defamation what he lacks in ability. Jackie, doing
what no other man in the history of the game had done before,
doing it, despite, or maybe because of, the color of his skin; but
coming up to this day the foremost competitive spirit these eyes
have ever seen.

Maybe this is why Leo hates him so. Because he fears him.
Because Leo has never been able to guide his feeling about this
one man into sensible channels he has tried to challenge
Robinson, goading him into unbelievable heights of performance
that Jackie, left alone, might never have achieved.

This is just baseball. It is a game at which even children
can play, but to Durocher this is a way of life and to Jackie it is a
crusade.

\* \* \*

I watched Robinson perform in Philadelphia yesterday in the most exciting game of baseball I have ever seen, and I came away from it with a lump in my throat. Sentimentally I was for the Giants because of the fantastically successful run they have made for the flag, when all gave up on them but themselves. But emotionally I had to be for the Dodgers because of what Jackie had done.

When it was over I rode back to New York with Jackie and his lovely wife, Rachel. The game was done and they could kid each other, but their voices still shook and Jackie said there was something that felt like a brick in his solar plexus.

Rachel reached into her pocketbook and extracted a scorecard.

"Here it is," she said to her husband. "I kept score for the full 14 innings. For the first time I followed a full game. I'm framing this, Jack, and I'm putting it in your den."

Robby looked at her and smiled. "You couldn't have watched it the whole way," he said. "I looked over at you several times and you didn't see anything. I thought you were crying."

There were real tears in Rachel Robinson's eyes when she said, "Maybe I was. You would be crying, too, if you looked out there at your man and he looked as though he were lying there dead."

Jackie wasn't dead, but the Dodgers would have been if he hadn't thrown himself at Eddie Waitkus' line drive just a few steps to the right of second base and speared the shot. The bases were filled with two out in the 12th, and all the runners were moving. But Jackie got his hands on the ball and as he did he jammed his own elbows into his stomach and fell to the ground. The wind was knocked from his body, but Robby instinctively got rid of the ball in a shovel pass to Pee Wee Reese as he fell, not knowing how umpire Lon Warneke would call it.

The homer he was to hit two innings later provided the Dodgers' margin of victory and the stepping stone into the playoff against the Giants; but to me this fielding gem, the unthinking reaction to get rid of the ball despite the pain within him, typified Jackie.

Robby plays baseball with his whole being. He flubbed a ground ball by Richie Ashburn in the second and gave the Phils two runs. He tripled to drive one in in the fifth, but in the seventh and 11th there were runners in scoring position and Jackie left them there. Another man, dog tired and in pain going into the 14th when the tide appeared to be turning irrevocably against the Dodgers with Robin Roberts pitching brilliantly, would have let down. This is not an ordinary man, however. This is one man who must forever remain unique in the sports and social history of our land. This is one who did what no other had ever done before. This is Robinson.

He was slumped in the Dodger dugout, and the others were looking at him, wondering whether or not he could go on after knocking himself out on that superlative play in the 12th inning. Doc Wendler, the Dodger trainer, had a piece of cotton soaked in ammonia under Jack's nose. The horrible, penetrating smell of the medication brought Jackie around.

"Let's go," Pee Wee Reese shouted to the Dodgers. They all ran from the dugout to their positions in the field except Reese and Robinson. Pee Wee paused at the top of the dugout steps and said, "Push him out here, Doc. He'll be all right once he gets on the field."

Doc looked questioningly at Jackie and heaved him to his feet. And Jackie went out on the field in uncertain steps.

Reese knew Robinson. He knew what this game meant to Jackie—if for no other reason than that Leo Durocher's Giants would get the chance at the Yankees if the Dodgers failed. Then Jackie did it.

On the train coming back Robinson said, "It's more than a baseball game to me. It's something personal."

No more had to be said. I had heard Jackie and I had heard Leo. I knew this was meant to be. Destiny had a hand in this vendetta, and it must be contested to an end—hand to hand, if need be.

# NOW I KNOW
# WHY THEY BOO ME!

## JACKIE ROBINSON

*B*y 1955 Jackie Robinson had spent eight years in the
major leagues. He had become, along with Stan
Musial, the dominant player in the National League,
leading the Dodgers to four pennants and three second-
place finishes. But during these years Robinson appeared in the
headlines as much for controversies, both on and off the field, as
for his stellar performances. Often these episodes resulted from
Robinson's intense competitive fires, but many revolved around
issues of racial adjustment in the newly integrated game and
Robinson's outspoken advocacy of civil rights issues.

In a series of three revealing articles that appeared in Look
magazine in January and February 1955, Robinson assessed his
career and explained why, unlike other players who could navigate the game unscathed by conflict, he remained a lightning rod,
attracting bolts of attention wherever he turned.

● ● ● ● ● ● ●

From the Dodger bench at Wrigley Field, I watched the ball Duke Snider had slammed into left field. I saw it clear the wall. Then it struck a spectator and dropped onto the playing field. This was a home run. There couldn't be any doubt about it—we saw the spectator double up, clutching at his stomach in pained surprise.

But when the ball bounced back, I knew what would happen. Sure enough, when umpire Bill Stewart saw Ralph Kiner, the Cubs' left fielder, picking up the ball, the umpire, apparently thinking it had hit the wall and not cleared it, called Snider's hit a ground-rule double.

I leaped out of the dugout. The Dodger bench jumped up too, and I thought they were with me. Then I ran out on the field to argue. We needed the game and were trailing by three runs. After a minute of argument, I saw I was alone. No one had followed me out to protest. And the boos had begun. (Newspaper photographs later showed the spectator being hit by Snider's "double.")

Our manager, Walt Alston, stood silently on the third-base coaching line. Walt is a calm man. Apparently, he also thought Stewart's call was right.

Out there alone, with the fans riding me more every second, I felt foolish. I wanted to find a hole and crawl into it. The Chicago players in the dugout were enjoying my predicament. One held up his hands to show that the ball had cleared the wall by two feet. If the umpires saw the signal, they gave no sign. I was ignored, and they waved the game on.

I had to walk back across the infield, with the boos ringing in my ears. Jackie had done it again. I knew I had no right to be out there arguing about a play in which I hadn't figured at all. But my team had. It kills me to lose, and when I ran out to question Stewart's decision, I never took a second to think. That's the way I am about winning. I can't stand to watch a baseball game unless I'm playing.

Last season, in a year when every game counted, I lost my head more than I ever had in my eight years as a major-leaguer. Fans—and some sportswriters—began calling me a "sorehead" and a "loudmouth" who wanted every break to go my way. I have puzzled for a long time now, and maybe I've got it figured out. If I'm a troublemaker—and I don't think that my temper makes me one—then it's only because I can't stand losing. Some baseball players have an easy disposition, no matter which way the score goes. But not me. Even as a boy, and later as a football player at U.C.L.A., all I ever wanted to do was to finish first.

I admit that I challenge umpires and tell off opposing players. But I'm no more aggressive in this respect than Ty Cobb or John McGraw or Frankie Frisch. Leo Durocher and Eddie Stanky kick up fusses all the time. But if I do it, I'm stepping out of line. Many people think that a Negro, because he is a Negro, must always be humble—even in the heat of sports competition. But, in my case, maybe it goes deeper than that.

They have resented me especially ever since I came up to the Dodgers, not just because I am a Negro but because I was *the* Negro who broke the color line in baseball. It's a theory that is not entirely mine too. Tom Meany once wrote: "When he protests a decision, it becomes an issue. When Roy Campanella, Larry Doby or Monte Irvin protest, not too much is made of it. Robinson is simply paying the price which always accompanies a trail blazer."

If I've been resented since the beginning in 1947, why did the fans get on me more than usual last year? Well, during the last season, when it appeared that I was slipping, the people who didn't boo when I was on top felt free to let go, and did.

The worst booings I got in the National League last season were in Milwaukee. My unpopularity can be traced to two incidents that happened there. One time, I was involved in a hot exchange with a few Braves after Joe Adcock was hit by a pitched ball. While describing the scene to the radio audience, Earl Gillespie, the Milwaukee broadcaster, denounced me as an "agitator." Afterwards, Gillespie—and I quote him directly—told me that he was "emotionally upset" and "didn't know" what he had been talking about. But I think his remarks did turn many Milwaukee fans against me.

Another time in Milwaukee, the Braves' Johnny Logan was batting with a 2-and-2 count on him. He fouled the next pitch, but the scoreboard gave him a ball: on the next pitch, he got a base on balls. The next time I came to bat, I asked umpire Lee Ballanfant: "Can I get a walk on three balls the way Logan did?"

"Get in there and hit or get out of the game," Ballanfant said.

I told him it might be of little use because his decision had already cost the Dodgers the game. He threw me out. Walking away from the plate, I flipped the bat toward the dugout. It was a wet night, and the bat slipped. It landed on the roof of the dugout, bounced into the stands and hit three spectators. So my reputation as a sorehead and a poor sport was clinched in Milwaukee, where the fans are the noisiest.

Everybody close to the scene knew it was an accident. Ballanfant reported to National League president Warren Giles that I wasn't angry, that I didn't throw the bat wildly on purpose. The usher who was hit said that the bat struck him so lightly that he thought it was a spectator tapping him on the side of the head because he was blocking the view. The next time I came to Milwaukee, I apologized to him and the other people who were hit. No one sued me, though at first it was threatened. But the incident has made enemies for me.

I was on the spot when Branch Rickey signed me, the first Negro to get a chance in organized baseball. He told me that one wrong move on my part would not only finish the chance for all Negroes in baseball, but it would set the cause of the Negro in America back 20 years. So, in my first year in organized baseball with Montreal, the Brooklyn farm team, I had to hold my temper. . . .

Throughout these two seasons, I had to keep my mouth shut and take it. I couldn't protest to an umpire and I couldn't get back at players who taunted and insulted me with racial remarks. Keeping myself in hand while I was playing ball was tough enough, but I also had to be extra careful about my life outside of the ball park. While traveling with the club, I was afraid to accept invitations to parties in strange towns or even to eat in a restaurant where I wasn't known. I worried about getting into a situation that would result in bad publicity. I was on guard night and day. . . .

There was a noticeable chill in the air when I first joined the Dodgers. Even though certain fellows like Pee Wee Reese did their best to make me feel at home, I kept my distance. I didn't mix. (By nature, I'm not gregarious, and I do not drink or smoke.) At Ebbets Field, I dressed quickly after each game and left the clubhouse as soon as I could. On the road, I stayed away from the card games. I didn't want to rush things. I figured that the others were having a harder time getting used to me than I was adjusting myself to them. At U.C.L.A., I had been on teams with white boys, but no Dodger had ever shared a locker room with a Negro. It was an uneasy, touch-and-go situation.

Pee Wee is a Southerner, born in Ekron, Ky., and he took a lot of abuse because of his consideration for me. He was great to me in 1948 when Eddie Stanky went to the Braves and I moved to second base. Because he was a Kentuckian, the bench jockeys all over the circuit rode him, a great shortstop, asking him how it felt playing next to a Negro. In our first game at Boston, the Braves tried to give us a real bad time. But Pee Wee shut them up. He walked over to me, put his arm around me and talked to me in a warm and friendly way, smiling and laughing. His sincerity startled the Braves, and there was no more trouble after that from them. Later, he did the same for me in other ball parks. . . .

. . . . Until last year, the Negroes on the club were separated from the white players when we stayed in St. Louis. They were put up at the Chase and we were quartered at the Adams, a Negro hotel that wasn't air-conditioned. When you are trying to sleep in St. Louis in July and August, air conditioning becomes an important item.

Partly because of the air conditioning and partly because of the principle of the thing, I took up the Chase matter with Walter O'Malley, president of the Dodgers, last winter when I was signing my contract. He straightened it out, and the doors were opened to the Negro players in the spring. At first I was the only one who went there. The other Negroes took a defensive attitude. If they weren't good enough for the Chase for the past six years, they didn't want to go there now. The way I look at it, if a hotel takes a ban off Negroes, the Negroes should go there for the sake of the progress that's being made in racial relationships. Later in the season, the other Negro players with the Brooklyn club changed their minds and moved to the Chase too.

During the first three years I traveled with the Dodgers, I was told that our hotel in Cincinnati, the Netherland Plaza, did not serve Negroes in its dining room. So I always had my meals brought to my room. Then one time when Rachel was traveling with me, there was a fire in the room-service kitchen at the Netherland Plaza and room service was discontinued. At dinnertime, Rachel and I went downstairs. In the lobby, we met a club official of the Dodgers and he asked us where we were planning to eat.

"We'll just have to eat in the dining room," I said.

"I don't think you should do that," he said. "Go across the street and down two blocks to the left. There's a cafeteria there where you'll be served."

Rachel looked at me and asked me what I thought we should do about it. I was annoyed.

"We'll go to the dining room," I said.

Rachel felt uneasy about it and so did I. We walked toward the door of the dining room. The headwaiter saw us coming and walked toward us with a big smile.

"Mr. Robinson," he said to me, "where have you been? You've been staying in this hotel for years, and we've been wondering why you've never eaten in our dining room. I'm glad you finally decided to come here. . . ."

Today, I can't help thinking how much these things have changed in the past eight years. When I came to the Dodgers, I didn't see how I would be able to last for the first season. Because I was the only Negro in the League, I felt as lonely and as out of place as I had felt the previous year at Montreal, where I had almost suffered a nervous breakdown in August.

Early last season, on a day when Don Newcombe was warming up to pitch for the Dodgers, manager Walter Alston made a change in the Brooklyn line-up that started an exchange of comment between a couple of newspapermen.

I was moved from my regular position at third base to left field, usually covered by Sandy Amoros, the Negro rookie, and Amoros was put on the bench for the day. Dick Young, who always has both eyes open for a good story, spoke to me about the coincidence of the benching of Amoros while Newcombe was pitching.

Dick went on to remark that if Amoros remained in the line-up with Junior Gilliam and Roy Campanella and me while Newcombe was pitching, the Negroes in the Dodger line-up would have outnumbered the whites, five to four. It would have been a situation unprecedented in the history of major-league baseball. Ten years ago, I never expected this would happen.

None of us really believed, however, that Sandy was taken out of that game because of his color, but I wasn't certain. Sure enough, later in the season, Alston used all of Brooklyn's five Negro players as a unit on several occasions. That was enough to convince me that the Brooklyn management wanted to win ball games—period.

At the beginning of the year, when Newcombe returned from the Army and Amoros came up from the International League, I wondered how the Dodgers' front office felt about having so many Negroes on its roster. Within baseball, there had been talk about it. I had heard that one National League manager, trying to make a player deal, had said to the officials of a Southern minor-league club, "You don't want to do business with those Negro-loving Dodgers, do you?" The same argument had been used by scouts from other major league organizations while talking business with the parents of teenage white Southern base-ball prospects.

I never hesitate to speak up about anything that's on my mind. So I asked Dodger president O'Malley if he would ever set a limit on the number of his Negro players. Mr. O'Malley told me that the club wouldn't hesitate to put nine Negroes on the field if they were the nine best available players.

But it is a fact that the increase in the number of Negroes among the first-string players in Brooklyn caused an outbreak of open resentment in the club only two years ago. That was the first time I had seen a display of racial feeling among the Dodgers since 1947, when a group of players signed a petition of protest against Branch Rickey's proposal to bring me up to Brooklyn from the farm club at Montreal.

The trouble in 1953 arose when Junior Gilliam took over my

position at second base during spring training. Charlie Dressen, who was then the Brooklyn manager, moved me over to third base to make room for Gilliam. Some of the white players felt it was unfair to oust Billy Cox from third base in order to bring another Negro into the infield. They complained about it to Roger Kahn, who was covering the Dodgers at the time for the New York *Herald-Tribune*. When Roger wrote the story for his paper, they never denied it.

Roger came to me and asked me how I felt about it. I told him that if the players supporting Cox's candidacy for the third-base job were doing it because they felt he was the best third baseman on the club, I was all for them. But, I then added, if they were backing Cox only because they didn't want another Negro in the infield, I had no sympathy for them.

A few of the highly respected older players, whose opinions carry weight in the clubhouse, took the same stand on the matter. Thanks to them, the unpleasantness gradually died out. (Billy was traded to the Orioles last December. Paul Richards is getting one of the game's great infielders, and I'm sure the color situation had nothing to do with Billy's being traded.)

On those days last summer when five Negroes appeared in the Brooklyn lineup, the one thing about it that impressed me most was the lack of comment. Here was a major-league club which had created a national uproar only eight years ago by signing one Negro. Now, its Negroes in some games outnumbered its white players, and nobody in the ball park seemed to be giving it a second thought. I couldn't help thinking that maybe democracy in the U.S.A. is doing better right now than many people are willing to believe.

Most people probably don't realize how much racial prejudice has been broken down by Mr. Rickey's determination to put Negroes into major-league baseball. The game of baseball has always been loved and respected in this country. During the last eight years, when Negroes became identified with baseball, a lot of other Americans began to look upon them in a new light. . . .

When I agreed to become the first Negro in organized baseball, I also didn't realize that distinction would get me into so many public arguments and controversies. Ever since I've been with the Dodgers, I have been in the middle of all kinds of beefs on the sports pages. Rachel says it's my own fault. She says I'm too willing to sound off with an opinion when a sportswriter is looking for a story, and she's probably right. It's hard for me to say, "No comment."

A couple of years ago, on the television forum *Youth Wants to Know*, a high-school girl asked if I thought the Yankees were prejudiced against the hiring of Negro ballplayers. I could have ducked that question, but if I had ducked it I wouldn't have been able to live with myself. I gave the girl a straight answer. I told her that I knew from playing against them in the World Series that there was no racial prejudice whatsoever among the Yankee players. "But you asked me if I think that the Yankee management is prejudiced," I added. "The only answer I can give you to that question is yes."

When the Yankees complained, Ford Frick, commissioner of baseball, summoned me to his office. A lot of people assumed that he reprimanded me, but all he said was, "Always be sure of one thing. When you believe you're right and you come out swinging, make sure you're swinging a heavy bat and not a fungo." And this seems to me to be my way on controversial subjects.

I was even dragged into the controversy that came up recently when the Yankees announced that they had scheduled a spring exhibition game in Birmingham, Ala. This means that the Yankees will not be able to use their Negro catcher, Elston Howard, up for tryout from the International League, where he was voted the most valuable player last season. The city government in Birmingham just revived an old law against mixed sports competition, not in effect last spring when major-league teams with Negroes played there. One of the sports columnists who criticized the Yankees for scheduling a game in Birmingham was Red Smith of the New York *Herald-Tribune*. Smith said that I had been guilty of making the same compromise in Birmingham two years ago when I withdrew white players from a game that my barnstorming team played against a Negro club. Apparently, he didn't know the situation that existed in Birmingham when my team appeared there. A ban against mixed competition was in effect and a group of Birmingham citizens were battling to get it removed. They asked me not to disobey the law—the disturbance I would stir up would hurt their cause.

"If you don't upset the apple cart right now," they told me, "we'll be able to get rid of this Jim Crow ordinance next year."

Sure enough, the following year there was interracial sports competition in Birmingham. But last fall, the issue came up again, and Jim Crow was brought back in triumph. If I had insisted on using white players against the Negro team, however, I believe that I would have done more harm than good.

But despite the hot water I've gotten into since that first day I sat in Mr. Rickey's office, I wouldn't trade these last eight years with the Dodgers for anything in this whole world. . . .

# A FAMILY NAMED ROBINSON

## J. K. POLLACK

*J*ackie Robinson met Rachel Isum when they were students *at UCLA. They married in February 1946. Two weeks later they headed off together to Florida to launch "baseball's great experiment." Throughout Jackie's career and his life, Rachel remained an essential component of his success. In 1955, when J. K. Pollack described their lives in* Parent's *magazine, they had three children, Jackie, Jr., Sharon, and David, and lived on a beautiful eight-acre property, dotted with lakes and trees, in suburban Connecticut. Pollack's article, written shortly after the United States Supreme Court's 1954* Brown v. *Board of* Education *decision declaring school segregation illegal, reveals both the persistence of discrimination in American society and the hopes for change symbolized by the Robinson story, both on and off the field.*

*Although "A Family Named Robinson" accurately depicts the Robinsons as they lived in 1955, it is misleading in several respects. Rachel Robinson, portrayed here as the quintessential 1950s housewife and mother, would soon enroll in the psychiatric nursing program at New York University. After earning her*

*master's degree in 1957, she carved out a successful career of
her own, teaching in the Yale School of Nursing. And the
tragedies that would befall Jackie Jr. (see "The Lion at Dusk")
place a less sanguine slant on the burdens of growing up the son
of a black celebrity in a predominantly white environment.*

● ● ● ● ● ● ●

Eight-year-old Jackie Robinson, Jr., is continually being
asked by well-meaning but thoughtless adults, "Do you want to be
a Brooklyn baseball player like your father when you grow up?"

Like the sons of all famous men, young Jackie would rather
lead his own life. And that is what he is doing—happily and
healthily in a community predominantly white, but American
enough to make the Robinsons feel at home.

Last month—with the U.S. Supreme Court decisions out-
lawing racial segregation in public schools ringing throughout the
land—Jackie matter-of-factly entered the fourth grade of his Stamford, Connecticut, public school. The only Negro child in his class,
Jackie gets along wonderfully with everybody.

That isn't surprising. The youngster comes from a happy,
mentally healthy family. Jackie, his five-year-old sister Sharon, and
three-year-old brother David are being reared in an atmosphere of
love, lofty ideals and mutual respect for the dignity of man by their
wise, warm-hearted parents, John and Rachel Robinson.

The Robinsons, who have lived in New York and California,
Montreal and Florida, recently moved to their new, modern "dream
house" in suburban Stamford where this reporter visited them.

But as a Connecticut neighbor of theirs, I am ashamed to say
that it wasn't easy for the Robinsons to get settled in their present
home—no more than it was for the 36-year-old head of their
household to be the first Negro to break into major league baseball back in 1946.

Two years ago when their family became larger and the
schools in their mixed white-Negro New York neighborhood
grew even more crowded, the Robinsons began looking for a
country home in Westchester County or Southern Connecticut.
There were plenty of listings in their price bracket but the real

estate brokers and property owners politely demurred, "You wouldn't be happy here." None of these genteel people ever used the ugly word "discrimination."

Some of them even righteously rationalized, "Understand it isn't *me*. It's my neighbors who are worried about their property values depreciating."

Even some Negroes objected. "All of us can't escape into the white society of Connecticut like you have," one bitterly wrote them.

Jackie and Rachel Robinson swallowed hard but were no less determined. They had both trail-blazed before in winning color-line battles: Jackie, flamboyantly on the baseball diamond; and Rachel, a soft-spoken registered nurse, quietly in the medical field.

After aroused Stamford ministers of all faiths began preaching and circulating petitions against their community's refined Jim Crowism in housing, it wasn't long before the Robinsons were having their house built. While waiting for it to be completed, they lived in the home of Stamford friends, publisher and Mrs. Richard Simon.

"I thought we would fit into the community fine," accurately predicted Rachel Robinson. "Naturally, I didn't expect we'd be welcomed wholeheartedly by everybody at first but that didn't seem important."

What seemed far more important to this sensible 31-year-old mother was how her children would get along in school. . . .

"I remember when I walked into school the first day with Jackie and Sharon, everybody stared at us," recently recalled Rachel Robinson. "I felt as if I were walking down the firing line." One boy, on seeing Jackie, shouted, "Look, there's a colored kid!" But the teachers were extremely helpful in making Jackie and Sharon feel right at home.

When the school bus carried Jackie and Sharon home that first day, they were each so busy by then with their new schoolmates that brother and sister didn't know each was on the same bus until the driver stopped to let them out at their home! "Oh, Jackie, if I had known you were on the bus, I would have gone back and sat with you," exclaimed Sharon, a healthy, bubbling little girl.

Jackie, a more sensitive child who is afraid of being hurt, later remarked to his parents, "It was funny at school today. I didn't know the names of the other kids but they all knew *my* name."

"I'm the only brown child in my class," volunteered Sharon.

Though their three-year-old brother David is still unaware of the stupid skin game that so many Americans still play, Jackie and Sharon have long known about it. Jackie's introduction began when he was three and lived in a mixed neighborhood in St. Albans, Long Island. All of the children in the block played on his jungle gym. But one day a little white girl who had always played amicably with him suddenly stopped doing so when two white boys arrived.

Rachel, who happened to notice the incident from her window, said to herself, "Look, there's discrimination being practiced in our own yard!"

When her tearful son came running to her, Rachel asked, "*Why* isn't she playing nicely with you now?"

"Because I'm *different* from her," Jackie wailed.

That same year when he was three and being put to bed one night, Jackie said to his mother, "Mommy, my hands are still dirty."

Rachel explained that his hands were the same color as hers and she showed him hers to prove it.

Once Jackie deliberately lied to schoolmates telling them that he was Puerto Rican. His mother decided to give him some books to read to help him learn to respect the Negro's great contribution to this country. Since then, Jackie has read many books with interracial themes like "Henry's Back Yard," "Two on a Team" and "The Swimming Hole."

His father is this small boy's idol. On one occasion at dinner, Rachel asked Jackie to finish his salad. "Daddy's not finishing his," the boy correctly protested.

"That's when I learned how to eat salads," now laughs Jackie Robinson Sr. "Until I married Rachel, I never ate shrimps, tomatoes, in fact any vegetables except potatoes. Now I eat all of those foods. But it took my own son to help me overcome my prejudice against them."

Pausing a moment, the man who cracked baseball's 70-year-old color line, reflected, "You know, that's all prejudice is: simply a *feeling* that we have for a person or thing—it can be a good or bad feeling."

An easy-going man except on the subject of prejudice, modest Jackie Robinson has overcome plenty of it in his brief years—more, he hopes, than his children will have to face.

Today, with Negroes in major league baseball commonplace but with the Supreme Court school decision still disturbing some communities, the Jackie Robinson story provides an important lesson. This inspiring success saga again proves that there is no superior race—but superior persons in every race. . . .

Meanwhile, grown tall and sturdy, [Robinson] had become engaged to Rachel Annetta Isum, a pretty, intelligent UCLA freshman whose father was a bookbinder on the "Los Angeles Times."

A popular girl, Rachel still couldn't eat at Los Angeles' hamburger drive-ins with her white schoolmates. "We had to drive past them and go to a Chinese restaurant," she recalls.

Although she came from a comfortable middle class family, Rachel worked all through school and even nights in a wartime riveting job during her senior year. When she graduated, Rachel Isum, a straight "A" student, was voted the Florence Nightingale Award by teachers and classmates. . . .

[Robinson's] greatest help . . . was Rachel Isum, whom he married in February, 1946. "Rachel was always there with the right words and the right ideas," conceded Jackie.

During his first year in Montreal, he and Rachel lived in a French-Canadian neighborhood. "Even the younger children who had never seen Negroes didn't make us feel different," recalls Rachel. That first year she didn't miss a game despite her preference, to this day, for music, opera and theater. . . .

\* \* \*

In 1947, when the Robinsons moved to Brooklyn, Jackie was named the outstanding Rookie of the Year. "If I had one day to live over again," he recently mused with great feeling, "it would be the first day I went out to play in the Yankee Stadium. I always had doubt about that day ever coming. But when I heard the band playing 'America,' I knew that it was being played not just for the other players, but for me, too."

That same year, Jackie Jr. was born. Rachel sat in the stands talking with the other "baseball wives" about children and even the latest advice in "Parents' Magazine" to which she subscribes. In between, she would rush over to the hot dog stand to heat little Jackie's bottle.

In Brooklyn one day when the Robinson baby was nearly two years old, he locomoted himself to the white family's house next door. Saying what he had been taught to say if he was ever lost, the toddler proclaimed, "I'm Jackie Wobinson Juneyah. My Daddy plays baseball fow Bwooklyn." Then he ad-libbed something extra: "I wanna cookie!" During the Robinsons' early Brooklyn days, little Jackie believed he was Jewish because his family lived in a predominantly Jewish neighborhood.

Later, when they moved to Los Angeles and bought a lot near Laurel Canyon, outraged neighbors protested to the real estate man, "Do you want Negroes in the neighborhood?"

"Why not—if they're nice people like the Robinsons?" he replied.

Yet Jackie and Rachel strongly dislike any special privileges for themselves. For example, once when a midwestern hotel clerk treated them haughtily until he discovered who they were, the Robinsons told the manager they were leaving. "We don't want to stay here if Negroes have to be celebrities to be treated courteously."

The Robinsons agree on most things, including the rearing of their children. They have lots of fun with them. But like many mothers of young children without any regular household help, Rachel admits, "At the end of some days, I'm ready to plop in a chair."

Sibling rivalry is fortunately at a minimum in the Robinson household. Sharon and Jackie have been taught by their parents not to be jealous of their little brother David because, after all, he belongs to them both, too.

Rachel Robinson doesn't believe in spanking. Jackie has been punished by being sent to his room and deprived of family companionship. "He has a chance to think things out there," says his mother. "I rarely punish Sharon. If she feels you're angry with her, one look is enough. Sure, you have to handle each of them differently. They have entirely different personalities even though they have the same parents. You really learn a lot after the first child. The second is easier and the third is a breeze!"

Both Robinson parents realize that their big job is encouraging in their children the security and character which they developed the hard way.

Because of his famous name, Jackie Jr. presents a special problem. When he was younger, grownups tried to spoil him by invariably giving him things, hugging and even mobbing him heavy-handedly. Little Jackie recoiled from all this. Once when a magazine photographer tried to take his picture, the boy turned his back on the camera—and that was the only shot the disappointed photographer got.

The Robinsons want their children to choose their own careers. "Sure I'd like Jackie to be a baseball player," admits his father, who was voted the Most Valuable Player in the National League several years ago. "But if Jackie wants to dig ditches when he grows up, that will be all right with Rachel and me."

The Robinson children love their spacious new house. It was imaginatively built with children as well as grownups in mind. The youngsters have a large basement recreation room into which they can wheel their bikes, use their paint and chemistry sets and, of course, bring their playmates.

On several occasions when I visited the Robinsons, Jackie's schoolmates were there playing. Jackie has many playmates. "I seem to be either driving Jackie to his friends' houses or they're coming over here!" explains Rachel.

When I asked young Jackie if he liked school, he exclaimed, "Yes, because I have so many friends there."

Sharon, though, doesn't have many playmates yet because

there are few girls in the neighborhood. "She looks at little girls with such longing," sighs her mother, "that we're considering adopting a little girl to be a companion to her."

The Robinson children's social life is built right into their house. All three youngsters even have extra beds in their separate bedrooms, in case playmates stay over as some have. Rachel did her own decorating. She put a wagon wheel dresser and milking stool in Jackie's room and a large dressing table in her daughter Sharon's bedroom. Baby David's room is closest to the master bedroom. When Jackie complained that David got a better room, Rachel explained that his room was up front because he was a bigger boy who went to bed later and got up earlier than David. There are also hallway night lights for the children.

Daddy has a trophy room for his numerous baseball and Brotherhood awards and Mommy has a piano to practice on when she gets the time. The Robinsons have made many new friends in the community, but they do not rush things. Both are naturally shy. "The friends we have we know are really friends," explains Rachel simply.

Her husband's one extravagance is long-distance calls. He is so much in love with his family that he phones them continually when travelling.

Jackie Robinson Sr., who can never forget his own child-hood, is happiest when working with underprivileged youngsters of all races. When he retires from baseball, as he probably will in a year or two, he hopes to be able to help them get a good start in life. During winters, he now helps boys at the Harlem YMCA. Wholesome sports, he believes, can keep youngsters from becoming delinquent.

Children naturally love him. Once he received a letter from a nurse saying that a white boy in her hospital ward dying of polio was an impassioned Jackie Robinson fan. After a strenuous double-header game, he drove three hours to visit the child.

Last January, shortly before Brotherhood Week, he also made a cross-country tour for the National Conference of Christians and Jews. Is it any wonder that President Eisenhower once

crossed a crowded room especially to shake hands with Jackie
Robinson?

Not long ago when he was at the White House urging the
creation of a New York interracial housing project, a Southern
lawyer was then also in Washington defending the school segregation laws. Ironically, as this segregation diehard was trying to
figure out ways to set aside one of the nation's most historic judi-
cial decisions, his ten-year-old son kept pulling at his coattails,
"Let's go back to the hotel. I hear Jackie Robinson's there and I
want to get his autograph."

Back in Stamford, Connecticut, his own eight-year-old
namesake son was excitedly being dressed in a blue suit and
white shirt to recite Ogden Nash's poem "The Hippopotamus" in
his class's declamation contest. "If I come running off the bus
after school, Mommy, you'll know I won," Jackie exclaimed.

"It isn't the most important thing in the world to win,"
explained his mother. "Even if you don't win, you will have
learned a nice poem."

That afternoon young Jackie came scampering off the bus,
shouting "I won!" It was a Certificate of Declamation and it was
Jackie Robinson Jr.'s first bull's-eye in a mixed school.

His parents know only too well that the desegregation battle
is far from won, and that even Chief Justice Earl Warren's two
unanimous Supreme Court rulings will not automatically end an
educational practice which has prevailed for nearly a hundred
years in America. Integration is a slow and often painful process.

But Jackie Robinson Sr., the man who calls himself "a labo-
ratory specimen in a great change in organized baseball," also
knows that many communities are already on the way with integrated schools and that, ultimately, *all* American children will be
on the same educational basis.

"I'm definitely optimistic," he admits, "because day in and
day out I've seen the progress that has been made during the past
ten years. I sometimes feel awful sorry for people who forget that
they happen to be Americans, people who say, 'But we can't do
this.' I think that the louder these people holler, the sooner integration in the schools will come about. I also feel sorry for those
Southern office-holders who threaten they're going to do this or

that to keep out integrated schools. In my opinion these people are just hurting America because if they think they are hurting the Negro, they are very much mistaken. We Negroes have come a long way in spite of people like that. Sure, we've had to fight for every inch we've gained. But I feel sure we'll eventually reach our destination."

Quietly, his wife agrees. "Every year that I go back South, I notice some improvement. Successful integration in the schools is going to come a lot faster than many people seem to think because children don't have the prejudices of their parents."

Not long ago, Rachel Robinson overheard young Jackie playing a game in which all the "bad men" were Indians.

"How would you like to play a game where all the Negroes were bad men?" she asked him.

"Now, I notice that Indians are on *both* sides," smiles this wise mother, who taught her eight-year-old son an important lesson which many grownups have yet to learn.

# WHY I'M QUITTING
# BASEBALL

## JACKIE ROBINSON

*A*fter the 1956 season, Jackie Robinson, now thirty-seven years old, reassessed his future. After eight seasons in which he had never batted below .296, the first seven of which he had scored no fewer than ninety-nine runs, Robinson's performance had faltered in 1955 and 1956. During the Dodgers' world championship season in 1955, Robinson had played in only 105 games, and batted only .256. He had rebounded somewhat in 1956, appearing in 117 games, hitting .275, and delivering a memorable game-winning hit in the World Series against the Yankees. But Robinson no longer could perform at the top competitive level that had made him a star. His lengthy athletic career, dating back to his high school days in Pasadena, injuries he had long ago sustained as a football player, the wear and tear of the lengthy baseball seasons, and his constant battle to maintain a playing weight had all contributed to his athletic decline.

    In December 1956 he secured a contract to work as an executive for Chock Full O' Nuts, a New York fast-food restaurant chain, and decided to quit playing baseball. Even his retirement, however, would become embroiled in controversy. Robinson *had sold the rights of his retirement announcement to* Look *magazine, promising not to expose the story prematurely. Meanwhile, the Dodgers, in a move that some fans likened to Benedict Arnold's betrayal of the American revolution, announced that they had traded Robinson to the club's hated crosstown rivals, the New York Giants. When* Look *magazine finally broke the story in January 1957, baseball executives accused Robinson of acting in bad faith.*

*Robinson explained all in the* Look *magazine article that announced his departure and presented his thoughts on his past and his future.*

● ● ● ● ● ● ●

I've made my living playing baseball for the last 12 years. Now, I'm quitting the game for good. There shouldn't be any mystery about my reasons. I'm 38 years old, with a family to support. I've got to think of my future and our security. At my age, a man doesn't have much future in baseball—and very little security. It's as simple as that.

A lot of people will say I'm quitting because I was traded to the Giants last month. That isn't true. I started thinking about retiring from baseball almost four years ago and have been looking around for the kind of job I wanted ever since. When it turned up a few weeks ago, I took it.

It was just a coincidence that I found out I'd been traded only a few minutes after signing a contract with William Black, president of the Chock Full O' Nuts restaurant chain. Under the terms of the contract, I will go to work on March 4 as the company's vice-president in charge of personnel relations.

So I'm through with baseball. From now on, I'll be just another fan—a Brooklyn fan. I'm through with baseball because I know that, in a matter of time, baseball would have been through with me.

I want to explain just how it happened because some people may now feel I haven't been honest with them those past few weeks when they've asked me about my plans. I've always played fair with my newspaper friends, and I think they'll understand why this was one time I couldn't give them the whole story as soon as I knew it.

I was 34 when I began seriously thinking about my future. I'd been playing with the Dodgers for seven years and I was at my peak. But at 34, you can start to go any day in this game. After you've reached your peak, there's no sentiment in baseball. You start slipping, and pretty soon they're moving you around like a used car. You have no control over what happens to you. I didn't want that.

So I asked Martin Stone, who is just about the best friend I have, to keep his eyes open for the kind of job that would enable me to get out of baseball and into a career with a future. That was three years ago. Early last month, Mr. Black got in touch with me to say he would like me to go to work for him.

As he outlined the job, it sounded like just the sort of thing I'd been waiting for. The company has more than 1,000 employees in the New York area, and I would be in charge of ironing out their problems and keeping personnel turnover at a minimum. I've always enjoyed working with people, and this seemed like both an opportunity and a challenge. After talking it over with my wife, Rae, I told Marty to go ahead and draw up a contract with Mr. Black.

I might add that Rae didn't try to influence me one way or the other. She wanted this to be my decision. I think she'll miss both the knocks and glory of these last few years—they've been so much a part of our life. But she also feels I should do what I think is right for us.

Marty and Mr. Black got together on Monday, December 10 and we agreed to sign the contract on Wednesday. Meanwhile, I tried to call Buzzy Bavasi, the Dodgers' general manager, to tell him that I might not be playing next year and therefore to be sure to hold on to Randy Jackson. But he was in Chicago and I was told to call him in New York on Wednesday.

The next evening—Tuesday—Red Patterson, a Dodger official, called me at my home in Stamford, Conn., to say Bavasi wanted to see me in New York at 11 o'clock in the morning. I had an appointment over at *Look* at that time, so I said I would phone him instead.

The next morning, at breakfast, I told my kids for the first time what I was going to do. Jackie, who is 10, burst into tears: I'd more or less expected that. But Sharon, my six-year-old, was pleased because I explained that I wouldn't be away from home so much any more. David, the youngest, didn't have an opinion, but he decided that if Jackie was crying, he'd better cry too.

I went into New York and called Bavasi. He was out. When I finally reached him, at 3 o'clock, he said he wanted to see me at home that evening. He wouldn't tell me what it was about. I said I had a guest at home, so finally he agreed to call me.

At 5 o'clock, I went over to Mr. Black's office at 425 Lexington Avenue and signed a two-year contract with an option to renew. Then, I called Bavasi. All he wanted to tell me was that I'd been traded to the Giants.

I remember I was smiling when I put down the receiver. I'd heard rumors of such a deal—along with a lot of other rumors—but it still came as a surprise. The reason I was smiling is that his announcement dispelled any lingering doubts I might have had about quitting baseball when I did—a half hour before.

I had just been able to avoid what I dreaded most in baseball—the moment when they would start moving me around. The feeling of insecurity that had been in the back of my mind was gone. I'd gotten rid of it that very afternoon.

Later in the evening, Horace Stoneham, the president of the Giants, phoned to ask me how I felt about it. I had to tell him that I'd be glad to play with the Giants—*if* I decided to play at all. I said I had some thinking to do and would give him a definite answer in a few weeks. I couldn't tell him that I was through with baseball forever because I'd agreed long ago to write this story—when the time came—exclusively for *Look*. As a matter of fact, I was working on this story when Mr. Stoneham called.

That's how my ten years with the Dodgers ended. It all happened in one day—and it turned out just right.

I'm glad I quit baseball before I was traded, and I bet I'm not the only one. I'm sure the true Brooklyn fans—the ones I really care about—will be tickled to death that they'll never have to see me playing for another club.

And I'm glad my last season with the Dodgers was a good

one and that I had a good Series. Maybe I have another good season or two in me—but at 38, you never know. I'm glad I ended strong.

There are lots of things I'll miss. I love baseball, and I'll miss playing the game. Every inning is a new adventure in baseball. I'll miss that kind of fun. I'll even miss my rhubarbs with the umpires.

I'll miss some of the players I've known—but I'll miss the game more. You play baseball for pleasure and for the money—not to make new friends.

I don't regret any part of these last 10 years. There's no reason why I should. Because of baseball, I met a man like Branch Rickey and was given the opportunity to break the major-league color line. Because of baseball, I was able to speak on behalf of Negro Americans before the House Un-American Activities Committee and rebuke Paul Robeson for saying most of us Negroes would not fight for our country in a war against Russia. Because of baseball, I made a friend like Marty Stone and got the kind of job I'm stepping into now.

Baseball has been awfully good to me.

There are memories of these ten years I'll cherish all my life: opening day in Jersey City in 1946; the catch I made in 1951 that kept us from losing the pennant that day; the final out in the 1955 Series that made us World Champions; and the time, during my first hard year with the Dodgers, when I was standing on first base beside Hank Greenberg of the Pirates. He suddenly turned to me and said, "A lot of people are pulling for you to make good. Don't ever forget it." I never have.

There are a few things I'd like to forget, like the insults from other dugouts that first year, and all the times I blew my top when I shouldn't have. I remember that after being spiked several times at St. Louis, I threatened to do the same to Stan Musial. I've always been sorry for that, because what was going on was not Stan's fault. But most of the irritations of those days I've forgotten. I've never taken my baseball home with me.

Today, I'm happier than I've ever been. I know I'll miss the excitement of baseball, but I'm looking forward to new kinds of satisfaction. I'll be able to spend more time with my family. My kids and I will get to know each other better. Jackie and Sharon and David will have a real father they can play with and talk to in the evening and every week end. They won't have to look for him on TV.

Maybe my sons will want to play ball, as I have, when they grow up. I'd love it if they do. But I'll see to it that they get a college education first and meet the kind of people who can help them later. That way, they won't have to worry about getting a good job when they quit playing.

Just now Jackie still feels badly about my quitting the game. It's tough for a ten-year-old to have his dad suddenly turn from a ballplayer into a commuter. I guess it will be quite a change for me too. But someday Jackie will realize that the old man quit baseball just in time.

# HALL OF FAMER
# STILL ON CLOUD 9

## SAM LACY

*I*n 1962, five years after his retirement, Jackie Robinson won
election to Baseball's Hall of Fame in his first year of eligi-
bility for the honor. Sam Lacy of the Baltimore Afro-
American, who had covered the Robinson story since its
inception, was on hand to describe the induction ceremonies.
Like Wendell Smith, Sam Lacy is one of the forgotten giants of
American sportswriting. Lacy began his sportswriting career
with the Washington Tribune, a black weekly, in 1930. After a
stint at the Chicago Defender, Lacy joined the staff of the Afro-
American in 1944 where he served as sports reporter, editor, and
columnist. More than fifty years later, and now in his nineties,
Lacy still turns out a weekly column for that newspaper, advocating racial equality and exposing hypocrisy as he has always
done. In this 1962 report, Lacy captures the glory, pride, and
irony of Jackie Robinson's acceptance into baseball's Valhalla.

● ● ● ● ● ● ●

Baseball ushered Jackie Robinson into immortality Monday morning, and by so doing added a touch of realism to its Hall of Fame.

The former star of the Brooklyn Dodgers was inducted along with ex-Cleveland pitcher Bob Feller, former manager Bill McKechnie and oldtime outfielder Edd Roush, bringing to 90 the total number of one time stars accorded the national pasttime's higest honor.

Because they are done in bronze, the busts of none of the other 89 immortals enshrined here can be as lifelike as that of the first colored man to win a pedestal in the famed museum.

Not since 1936, when Ty Cobb, Babe Ruth, Hans Wagner and Walter Johnson became the Hall's initial honorees has the induction ceremony attracted such wide attention.

This tiny hamlet, situated between Albany and Rochester and pinpointed only on the most detailed maps of New York State, is accessible to neither train nor plane. And only two bus arrivals daily invade the quiet life of its inhabitants.

Yet thousands of persons converged on Cooperstown Sunday night, taxing its limited housing facilities to the utmost, so as to be on hand for the 10:30 a.m. ceremony.

The family of George Brown, a retired letter carrier, slept in the car in which father, mother and three children drove down from Boston Sunday evening.

"I was at Braves Field when Jackie played his first game there in 1947," Brown told the AFRO. "I was there when Larry Doby and Satchel Paige came in for the 1948 World series with Cleveland. And Alice (Mrs. Brown) and I used to go to Nashua (New Hampshire) and Pawtucket (Rhode Island) on weekends to watch (Roy) Campanella and (Don) Newcombe play before they were brought up.

"Wheelchair and crutches couldn't have stopped this old mailman from being here today," he beamed.

Of greater importance to Jackie, however, was the fact that the huge audience included the three persons he said "did the most in helping me attain this honor."

Watching ceremonies, commemorating the event, were Jackie's mother, Mrs. Mallie Robinson; his wife, Rachel; and Branch Rickey, the man who, as general manager of the Dodgers, broke baseball's color line by signing him in 1945.

In the 70-odd years of Branch Rickey there have been many thrills—too many to sift through to find his biggest.

But the induction of Jackie Robinson into baseball's Hall of Fame here Monday morning gave the kindly old man his "Greatest satisfaction."

"Robinson himself gave me many thrills," said Rickey upon renewing an old friendship. "But the term 'thrill' is too much of a generalization.

"In my time I've been thrilled by a youngster throwing a ball or stealing a base; by a minister's sermon; by a well-written book.

"This ritual today is of another category. Witnessing this final acknowledgment of the success of a wonderful experiment is highly satisfying.

"Even the six pennants for which some have said I was responsible (St. Louis in 1946, Brooklyn in 1947–49–52–53, and Pittsburgh in 1960) failed to arouse the satisfaction I get from this experience here.

"Jackie's enshrinement is perhaps the greatest satisfaction I shall derive from a life time of baseball." . . .

"This could not have happened," Robinson told the hushed crowd, "without the guidance and advice of Mr. Rickey, my mother and my wife."

Continuing in a voice that betrayed an inward battle to hold back the tears, Robinson declared:

"I have been on 'Cloud Nine' since learning of the election last winter, and I don't think I'll ever come down."

Smiling broadly as the crowd applauded was 15-year-old Jackie Jr. On either side were the Robinsons' other two children, Sharon, aged 13, and David 10.

So it was here Monday as the ivy-covered shrine witnessed a baseball drama as ironic as it was touching.

One of the more vocal figures at the time Robinson was

signed by Rickey was Feller, the ace of a formidable Cleveland pitching staff.

He unhesitatingly predicted that Jackie would be unable to make the major leagues because of "too many batting flaws."

According to the Tribe right-hander, Robinson couldn't even make the league, not to mention Hall of Fame.

On Monday, they mounted the museum's four steps to immortality together.

# ON BEING BLACK
# AMONG THE REPUBLICANS

## JACKIE ROBINSON AS TOLD TO ALFRED DUCKETT

*I*n 1960 Jackie Robinson shocked his friends and other civil rights activists when he supported Richard Nixon for president over John F. Kennedy. Since the 1930s African-Americans, who had previously given overwhelming electoral support to the "party of Lincoln," had rallied to the Democratic banner. Most saw the Democrats as more sympathetic to the cause of integration and civil rights. Robinson, however, who had hoped that Senator Hubert Humphrey would win the Democratic nomination, joined the Nixon campaign. Furthermore, Robinson remained in the Republican fold after 1960, forging a close alliance with New York Governor Nelson Rockefeller, the leader of that party's moderate wing.

Robinson's Republicanism, although widely questioned and criticized, had firm roots. Robinson, despite his militance on civil rights issues, had conservative instincts. He believed that the solution to the nation's racial problems lay in the economic realm and that without an expansion of black business enterprise lasting gains for African-Americans would be limited. Furthermore, he feared that if blacks remained a presence in only one political *party, they would be taken for granted and their influence muted. If, as even Robinson admitted, his faith in Nixon had been misplaced, history has validated his fundamental concerns.*

*In the following excerpt, from* I Never Had It Made, *his 1972 autobiography, Robinson forthrightly explains the rationale for his 1960 decision, offers vivid portraits of Nixon, Kennedy, and Rockefeller, explains his political and economic philosophies, and expresses his shock at the conservative takeover of the 1964 Republic convention.*

● ● ● ● ● ● ●

I do not consider my decision to back Richard Nixon over John F. Kennedy for the Presidency in 1960 one of my finer ones. It was a sincere one, however, at the time.

The Richard Nixon I met back in 1960 bore no resemblance to the Richard Nixon as President. As Vice President and as Presiding Officer of the Senate he had a fairly good track record on civil rights. When I first met him, he had just returned from a trip around the world, and he came back saying that America would lose the confidence and trust of the darker nations if she didn't clear her own backyard of racial prejudice. Mr. Nixon made these statements for the television cameras and other media for all the world to hear.

Richard Nixon is capable of deep personal goodwill and grace in one-to-one relationships and particularly if he believes you can be useful to his goals. His instincts are flawless when he bends himself to win you for his cause. He can meet you today, be introduced, learn through casual conversation that you have a three-year-old daughter with the mumps and—three months later—approach you, call you by your first name, and ask about the state of health of your little girl—the one who had the mumps. This man has the most fantastic photographic memory for newsmen, politicians, or other humans useful to the art of vote getting, and he has always had a superb briefing staff. Whatever you think of the man personally, he is a consummate political animal.

I met the Vice President and several others, including

Senator Hugh Scott, in his office in the White House following the 1960 primary elections of both parties. My trip to see him had resulted from some spirited discussions I had with friends, some of whom were for Nixon and others who were for Senator John Kennedy. I had found that there was a great deal of suspicion in the black community about Nixon, primarily because so many black people were disenchanted with the Eisenhower Administration. They felt that Mr. Eisenhower had a nice grin and little or no concern for rapport with blacks. I had campaigned for Senator Hubert Humphrey in the Democratic primaries because I had a strong admiration for his civil rights background as mayor of Minneapolis and as a Senator. I had heard that he was constantly being warned that his outspoken comments on civil rights would curtail his political progress. I had heard him publicly vow that he was pledged to be the living example of a man who would rather be right morally than achieve the Presidency. But since Mr. Humphrey had not been able to defeat Senator Kennedy in the primaries, I found myself faced with a choice between Nixon and Kennedy. Frankly, I didn't think it was much of a choice but I was impressed with the Nixon record on rights, and when I sat with him in his office in Washington, he certainly said all the right things.

There was one thing that bothered me during that talk, however. The telephone rang on his desk and I heard him telling, I suppose, his secretary, "No, well I can't do that. I'm tired of pulling his chestnuts out of the fire. He'll have to work his own way out of this one."

When he hung up, he turned and smiled at us confiding that he had just been talking about the President. I couldn't help feeling that he was trying to impress me with the fact that he was really very different from his boss, the President. It sounded as if the Vice President wanted me to disassociate him from Eisenhower since he knew that blacks, in the main, didn't like Ike. It had the feel of a cheap trick. After all, even if it were true that Nixon held this view of the President, it didn't seem respectful that he would let me, whom he didn't know well, in on the secret.

The same day, after leaving the White House, I went to a private home in Washington to talk with Senator Kennedy.

Chester Bowles, the former governor of Connecticut and a man I highly respect, had arranged this meeting, hoping I could be persuaded to campaign for Mr. Kennedy.

I found Mr. Kennedy a courteous man, obviously striving to please, but, just as obviously, uncomfortable as he sought to get a conversation going with me. It is remarkable how seemingly minor factors can influence a decision. My very first reaction to the Senator was one of doubt because he couldn't or wouldn't look me straight in the eye. Every time he answered a question or made a statement, he would avoid looking at me and look directly at Governor Bowles, as though he were seeking strength. My mother had taught me to be wary of anyone who talked to you with head bowed or shifty eyes. My second reaction, much more substantial, was that this was a man who had served in the Senate and wanted to be President but who knew little or nothing about black problems and sensibilities. He himself admitted a lack of any depth of understanding about black people. When I said politely that I didn't see anything too encouraging in his Senate record, his manner indicated he was willing and anxious to learn, and I suppose I was being invited to be one of his teachers. Although I appreciated his truthfulness in the matter, I was appalled that he could be so ignorant of our situation and be bidding for the highest office in the land. I was certain Mr. Kennedy was well-versed in foreign affairs, farm problems, urban crises, and so on. Why was he so uneducated about the number-one domestic issue of our time? I knew also that he had a very bleak record on civil rights. It was said that during some of the most vital roll calls on this issue, he had often been missing.

My meeting with the Senator had almost ground to a standstill when my instinct told me what was coming next. How much would it take to get me on board the bandwagon?

"Look, Senator," I said, "I don't want any of your money. I'm just interested in helping the candidate who I think will be best for the black American because I am convinced that the black struggle and its solution are fundamental to the struggle to make America what it is supposed to be." The meeting ended on that embarrassing note.

I came away feeling I could not support John Kennedy. I did

write him a note advising him to look people in the eye. I was amused subsequently when a black friend of mine, Frank Montero, who visited the Senator said that Mr. Kennedy didn't take his eyes off him for a minute.

I ended up campaigning for Nixon despite my reservations. Whatever kind of rally we had—even when they were in all-white communities, the Vice President insisted on spotlighting me as one of his supporters. I had a staff and we set up rallies that did not include Nixon. When rallies were held in black communities, we drew such large crowds that the Democrats began sending one of their most potent political stars—Congressman Adam Clayton Powell—to conduct rallies before or after our rallies.

In political appearances, I have never tried to make what is formally accepted as a speech. I find it much more effective to talk to the people and express simply exactly how I feel. Sometimes some of the statements I made were embarrassing to the candidate I was supporting. For instance, I made the point that I was not beholden to any political party, that I was black first, and that, while I believed the candidate I was backing was sincere, if I discovered he wasn't after he got in, I'd be right back to give him hell.

I began to have serious doubts about Nixon when two incidents occurred. In the first, Nixon spoke up, and in the second, he remained silent. Henry Cabot Lodge, the candidate for Vice President on the Nixon ticket, created headlines with a statement that he believed Mr. Nixon, if elected, would name a black man to his Cabinet. The press pursued Mr. Nixon for comment on Mr. Lodge's speculation, and after evading the issue as best he could, Mr. Nixon allowed an official statement to be made that Mr. Lodge was speaking for himself. This did not sit well with me. The second incident involved Mr. Nixon's refusal to speak out in behalf of Dr. Martin Luther King, Jr., who, during the campaign, was confined in a full-security prison in Georgia as the result of a minor motor vehicle infraction. John Kennedy and his campaign-manager brother, Robert, picked up this one and ran with it. The Senator telephoned Mrs. Martin Luther King, Jr., in Atlanta to express his concern, and Bobby Kennedy applied pressure, influence, and political muscle to bring about Dr. King's release. Dr. Martin King,

Sr., trumpeted from his pulpit that he was going to gather up a bag of black votes and deliver them to Senator Kennedy to demonstrate his gratitude. I was in the behind-the-scene struggle to persuade Dick Nixon to express his concern for Dr. King, but apparently his most trusted advisers were counseling him not to rock the racial boat. Add to this the fact that Mr. Nixon refused to campaign in Harlem as his opponent did, and it is easy to understand why blacks overwhelmingly voted for Kennedy.

Several times during the Nixon campaign, I was on the verge of quitting and denouncing the Vice President. Rachel did not agree with my support of Nixon. However, she did not press me to quit until he failed to assist Dr. King. Then she and friends urged me to reconsider my stance. Mail and phone calls were coming in. People couldn't understand how I could continue to go along with the program. I kept my silence—certainly not for money. I wasn't getting paid a dime except for expenses and, in fact, never recovered some of my own out-of-pocket expenses. Furthermore, I wasn't staying in because I wanted a job from Nixon if he got elected.

It's hard to explain why I stuck, disillusioned as I was. It has something to do with stubbornness about continuing to want to believe in people even when everything indicates they are no longer worthy of support. It has something to do with the reason I went into politics in the first place and why I worked for the NAACP.

My motives were both selfish and unselfish. I wanted—and still desire—a better world, a bigger break, a fairer chance for my family. I have been very fortunate personally, but my children might not be as fortunate as their father. I don't want them to have to pay the dues I've paid, to experience the tensions and trials I have undergone. Rachel tried to understand, I'm sure, but I sensed puzzlement. I clung to the hope that Nixon would follow through on the things he had indicated were important to him in that first meeting after the pressures of the campaign were over. It was not only my own family I was concerned about but all black families and especially other black children growing into maturity. I admit that the Kennedy ticket had begun to look much more attractive. But I have always felt that blacks must be represented in both parties. I was fighting a last-ditch battle to keep the Republicans from becoming completely white. Nixon lost his campaign, and four years later I lost my battle when Goldwater was nominated.

My first meeting with Nelson Rockefeller occurred in 1962 during a public event at which we were both speakers. The Nelson Rockefeller personal charm and charisma had now become legendary. It is almost impossible not to like the man. He gives two distinct impressions: that he is sincere in whatever he is saying and that, in spite of his fantastic schedule, power, and influence—at that specific moment of your contact—he has shut everything else out and is focusing his complete and concentrated attention on you.

While I admired his down-to-earth manner and outgoing ways instantly, I was anything but overwhelmed at our initial meeting. I am aware that the enormously wealthy have time to spread charm as they like. They have their worries, but survival is not one of them, as it is with us. I wasn't about to be taken in instantly by the Nelson Rockefeller charm. After all, Richard Nixon had turned the charm on me too (although his is a bit brittle compared with Rockefeller's) and look how that had turned out.

I knew that Rockefeller's family had given enormous sums to black education and other philanthropic causes for black people and that at that time (nearly twenty years ago) a significant number of black college presidents, black professionals, and a significant number of leaders of national stature had received a college education, financed by Rockefeller gifts. While I have no need to detract from the contributions of the family to black education, I felt it certainly must be weighed in terms of what went into the amassing of one of the world's greatest fortunes.

As for Nelson Rockefeller himself, I knew little or nothing about his politics. As far as I was concerned, he was just another rich guy with politics as a toy. Our first chat had nothing to do with politics. In fact, the governor took advantage of the occasion to tell me about a private problem. Since I was an officer of the Chock Full O'Nuts Restaurant chain at that time, he thought I might be able to help him. It seemed the Rockefeller family was unhappy about one of our advertising jingles which assured the public that our coffee was as good as any "Rockefeller's money can buy." Representations about the family's feeling in the matter had been made through legal and diplomatic channels, but the offensive jingle was still being aired on radio and television commercials. I promised to mention the matter to Bill Black, Chock's president. I was surprised at Mr. Black's reaction. When I reported the Rockefeller concern, he snapped, "Good! Let them sue. We can use the publicity."

As far as I was concerned, that was the end of that. As far as I knew, I'd probably never be in contact with the governor again. However, I began to change my mind about Rockefeller when I learned the extent of his support for a man I admired deeply, Martin Luther King.

When student sit-ins began in the South and many so-called liberals criticized them, Governor Rockefeller told the press that he believed the protesting youngsters were morally justified. I also learned that, unlike Richard Nixon who failed to speak out about the Georgia jailing of Dr. King, the governor had promptly wired the President asking for his protection.

I also learned of some of the governor's unpublicized actions. Before Rockefeller became governor, the world was stunned by the attempted assassination of Dr. King by a black woman in a Harlem department store. Rushed to Harlem Hospital, Dr. King who had been wounded by a letter opener plunged into a spot just below the tip of his aorta immediately was put under the care of a team of crack surgeons headed by Dr. Louis Wright. The newspapers gave intensive publicity to the fact that the then-Governor Harriman had sped to the hospital escorted by police convoy with shrieking sirens. Harriman ordered every available facility utilized to save Dr. King. Then he stayed at the hospital for several hours, keeping vigil and awaiting word of the civil rights leader's condition. Governor Harriman deservedly got credit for his concern about a beloved black leader. But it was Nelson Rockefeller who quietly issued orders to have the hospital bill sent to him.

I learned that the governor had made frequent gifts to Dr.

King's Southern Christian Leadership Conference. I was on the scene a few hours after hate-crazed bigots burned Georgia churches to the ground. Dr. King asked me to head a national fund-raising drive to restore the churches. Two of the first substantial donations were made by my then-boss Mr. William Black and by Governor Rockefeller. We did rebuild those churches.

Yet with all his goodwill gestures and philanthropies, there was one fact which bothered me deeply about the Rockefeller Administration in 1962. Although New York has, for many years, enjoyed a reputation as a liberal state, the higher echelons of the state government were all white. There were no blacks at top-level, policy-making positions. There was not even one black man or woman who had a direct line to the governor and who could alert him to the concerns and grievances of black people. I wondered if Nelson Rockefeller's generosity to black causes was a compartmentalized activity of his private life, and I was sufficiently curious to write him a letter.

My letter to the governor was a harshly honest letter. I said I felt no self-respecting black man could respect an administration that had no blacks in significant jobs. Governor Rockefeller met my honesty head on. He telephoned me personally and told me how much he appreciated my truthfulness. He admitted that things were not as they should be for blacks in state government and that he wanted to take steps to correct this; he suggested we meet and talk things over within the next few days.

In the course of that telephone call, I bluntly said, "If you don't want to hear the down-to-earth truth about how you are thought of in the black community, let's just forget about it."

He assured me that he wanted and needed unbiased advice. The meeting, unadvertised in the press and unreported after it took place, was held in a private room at the top of Radio City Music Hall. About a dozen to fifteen people whom I had invited attended. For some three hours we told the governor our grievances about the failure of his administration to include blacks in the political and government action. The people there didn't hesitate to recite harsh facts. He was aware of some of the facts we gave him; other facts seemed to shock him. He accepted our criticism, our recommendations for change, and he acted to bring about reforms. He did not bring any apologists or token black leaders into the meeting to justify himself. He brought an open mind and someone to take notes.

Within a few months after that meeting, the governor had implemented virtually all the recommendations that the *ad hoc* committee had made. Out of that one meeting came some sweeping and drastic changes, some unprecedented appointments of blacks to high positions, ensuring influence by blacks in the governor's day-to-day policy decisions. Some of the governor's top-level people were very unhappy about these changes.

In 1964 Governor Rockefeller asked me to become one of six deputy national directors of his campaign. I had spent seven years at Chock Full O'Nuts. I decided to resign from my job rather than ask for leave. The knowledge I had acquired about the business world, I considered invaluable. I had been criticized by some of my fellow officers in the company who genuinely felt I took the part of the employees too often, that I was too soft on them. Even so I had been given generous raises and benefits, allowed to purchase a healthy bundle of stock, and been elected to the board. I was becoming restless; I wanted to involve myself in politics as a means of helping black people and I wanted my own business enterprises. I had been increasingly convinced of the need for blacks to become more integrated into the main-stream of the economy. I was not thinking merely of job integra-tion. A statement Malcolm X made was most impressive. Referring to some college students who were fighting to be served in Jim Crow restaurants, Malcolm said he wanted not only the cup of coffee but also the cup and saucer, the counter, the store, and the land on which the restaurant stood.

I believed blacks ought to become producers, manufacturers, developers, and creators of businesses, providers of jobs. For too long we had been spending much too much money on liquor while we owned too few liquor stores and were not even manu-facturing it. If you found a black man making shoes or candy or ice cream, he was a rarity. We talked about not having capital, but we needed to learn to take a chance, to be daring, to pool capital, to organize our buying power so that the millions we spent did not leave our communities to be stacked up in downtown banks.

In addition to the economic security we could build with green power, we could use economic means to reinforce black power. How much more effective our demands for a piece of the action would be if we were negotiating from the strength of our own self-reliance rather than stating our case in the role of a beggar or someone crying out for charity. We live in a materialistic society in which money doesn't only talk—it screams. I could not forget that some of the very ballplayers who swore the most fervently that they wouldn't play with me because I was black were the first to begin helping me, giving me tips and advice, as soon as they became aware that I could be helpful to them in winning the few thousand more dollars players receive as World Series champs. The most prejudiced of the club owners were not as upset about the game being contaminated by black players as they were by fearing that integration would hurt them in their pocketbooks. Once they found out that more—not fewer—customers, black and white, were coming through those turnstiles, their prejudices were suppressed.

When Governor Rockefeller invited me on board his campaign ship, I had no idea of any long-term relationship in politics. I saw this as a sign that now was the time for me to enter into a new world of political involvement with a man I respected. At the same time I could be free to pursue some business endeavors that had been proposed to me. I had been approached about becoming a key organizer in a projected, new insurance company, an integrated firm that, I hoped, could be a force in correcting some of the unjust practices of some insurance firms that treat blacks unfairly. At this time the group organizing a new bank in Harlem—Freedom National—had asked me to help put it together and to become chairman of the board, and there were other business ventures in which I felt I might be able to play a vital role. When I submitted my resignation to Bill Black, he understood my aspirations. He didn't want me to leave, and he was genuinely concerned as to whether I was making the wisest move. He tried to persuade me to stay. I appreciated his attitude, but my mind was made up. I joined the Rockefeller campaign headquarters.

One of the first things that became clear to me was that I had not been called on to be the black adviser to the campaign. Often white politicians secure the services of a black man and slot him only for appearances and activities within the black community. Sometimes they do this to avoid letting whites know that they are making a strong pitch for black support. During the Rockefeller campaign I met with groups and made appearances before audiences which were sometimes integrated, sometimes predominantly black, and other times mainly white. On several occasions, when the governor came into town for a meeting with politicians or community people, I would accompany him. At some of the larger meetings, I would be asked to introduce the governor.

I was not as sold on the Republican party as I was on the governor. Every chance I got, while I was campaigning, I said plainly what I thought of the right-wing Republicans and the harm they were doing. I felt the GOP was a minority party in terms of numbers of registered voters and could not win unless they updated their social philosophy and sponsored candidates and principles to attract the young, the black, and the independent voter. I said this often from public, and frequently Republican, platforms. By and large Republicans had ignored blacks and sometimes handpicked a few servile leaders in the black community to be their token "niggers." How would I sound trying to go all out to sell Republicans to black people? They're not buying. They know better.

I admit freely that I think, live, and breathe black first and foremost. That is one of the reasons I was so committed to the governor and so opposed to Senator Barry Goldwater. Early in 1964 I wrote a *Speaking Out* piece for *The Saturday Evening Post*. A Barry Goldwater victory would insure that the GOP would become completely the white man's party. What happened at San Francisco when Senator Goldwater became the Republican standard-bearer confirmed my prediction.

I wasn't altogether caught off guard by the victory of the reactionary forces in the Republican party, but I was appalled by the tactics they used to stifle their liberal opposition. I was a special delegate to the convention through an arrangement made by the Rockefeller office. That convention was one of the most unforgettable and frightening experiences of my life. The hatred I saw was unique to me because it was hatred directed against a white man. It embodied a revulsion for all he stood for, including his enlightened attitude toward black people.

A new breed of Republicans had taken over the GOP. As I watched this steamroller operation in San Francisco, I had a better understanding of how it must have felt to be a Jew in Hitler's Germany.

The same high-handed methods had been there.

The same belief in the superiority of one religious or racial group over another was here. Liberals who fought so hard and so vainly were afraid not only of what would happen to the GOP but what would happen to America. The Goldwaterites were afraid—afraid not to hew strictly to the line they had been spoon-fed, afraid to listen to logic and reason if it was not in their script.

I will never forget the fantastic scene of Governor Rockefeller's ordeal as he endured what must have been three minutes of hysterical abuse and booing which interrupted his fighting statement which the convention managers had managed to delay until the wee hours of the morning. Since the telecast was coming from the West Coast, that meant that many people in other sections of the country, because of the time differential, would be in their beds. I don't think he has ever stood taller than that night when he refused to be silenced until he had had his say.

It was a terrible hour for the relatively few black delegates who were present. Distinguished in their communities, identified with the cause of Republicanism, an extremely unpopular cause among blacks, they had been served notice that the party they had fought for considered them just another bunch of "niggers." They had no real standing in the convention, no clout. They were unimportant and ignored. One bigot from one of the Deep South states actually threw acid on a black delegate's suit jacket and burned it. Another one, from the Alabama delegation where I was standing at the time of the Rockefeller speech, turned on me menacingly while I was shouting "C'mon Rocky" as the governor stood his ground. He started up in his seat as if to come after me. His wife grabbed his arm and pulled him back.

"Turn him loose, lady, turn him loose," I shouted.

I was ready for him, I wanted him badly, but luckily for him he obeyed his wife.

# AN EXCHANGE
# OF LETTERS

## JACKIE ROBINSON AND MALCOLM X

*I*t was perhaps inevitable that Jackie Robinson, who symbolized the dream of integration, would have clashed with Malcolm X, the most strident and eloquent of the voices
challenging the civil rights consensus during the early 1960s.
As a spokesperson for Elijah Muhammed's Nation of Islam, Malcolm X preached a doctrine of racial separation and questioned
the wisdom and tactics of mainstream black leaders.

The confrontation between Robinson and Malcolm X took
place on the front pages of the New York Amsterdam News, *the
nation's foremost African-American newspaper. In March 1962
Robinson wrote an open letter to Congressman Adam Clayton
Powell, the Harlem representative then facing charges of corruption in the courts and in Congress. Robinson criticized Powell for
his recent alliance with Malcolm X and the Black Muslims and
for hiding behind a false defense of racism when charged with
corruption. Eight months later, Malcolm responded with a vitri-
olic attack against Robinson, charging him with being the creature of his "White Boss(es)." Never one to shy away from a fight,*

*Robinson launched his own broadside against Malcolm and the Black Muslims.*

*This exchange, reproduced here, captures both the substance and the tenor of debates in the black community in the 1960s. It occurred at a critical turning point in Malcolm X's life. Between the publication of the two letters, Black Muslim leader Elijah Muhammed censured Malcolm X for comments he made following President Kennedy's assassination and forbade him from making further public statements. Within a short time, Malcolm withdrew from the Nation of Islam and began to reassess its teachings. Ironically, his death in 1965 came not at the hands of whites—as he predicted in his letter to Robinson—but from assassins aligned with his former Black Muslim allies.*

● ● ● ● ● ● ●

## Jackie Robinson Writes Letter to "A Friend"
(*New York Amsterdam News*, March 30, 1963)

Most columnists who write open letters to public personalities don't really want an answer.

Let me state, at the beginning, that I would appreciate an answer from the person to whom I am directing this open letter and, if it is forthcoming, I will carry every line in this space, regardless of what it says.

Most people who use the word "friend" use it loosely. I don't. But when I believe a friend is in the wrong, I feel I have the right to tell him so and if the wrong I think he committed was a public act or utterance, then I feel I have the right to tell him so publicly.

This letter is for you—Congressman Adam Clayton Powell, Jr.

I write it because it is my sincere belief that you have grievously set back the cause of the Negro, let your race down and failed miserably in the role which our people justly expect you to play as an important national leader of the Negro in this nation.

I refer to your vicious attacks upon the National Association for the Advancement of Colored People, your intemperate and ill-advised suggestion that the Negro people boycott the NAACP because of the participations in its affairs of white people and your rallying call to the Negro people to support Malcolm X and the Black Muslims.

You know, Adam, that the NAACP, whatever shortcomings it may have, has been and still is the greatest organization working in behalf of all those principles of freedom and human dignity for the black man in America which was ever put together in this nation.

### Dedicated Job

You also know that people like the Spingarns and Kivic Kaplan have done a dedicated job and organized more moral and financial support for this cause than any ten Negroes, including yourself.

You know also, in spite of the fact that you and I share deep respect for Minister Malcolm X as an individual, that the way pointed by the Black Muslims is not the true way to the solution of the Negro problem. For you are aware—and you have preached for many years—that the answer for the Negro is to be found, not in segregation or in separation, but by his insistence upon moving into his rightful place—the same place as that of any other American—within our society.

I can only conclude, Adam, that this latest tantrum of yours stems from the fact that you are infuriated because Roy Wilkins and the Board of the NAACP did not rush to your defense in your recent battle with your fellow Congressmen. You set up the usual crybaby yell that you were being persecuted because you are a black man when it was pretty obvious that you had placed yourself in a vulnerable position to be condemned by many people with many different motives.

The Negro people are growing up, Adam, and I do not believe they are sympathetic any longer to the business of supporting anything anyone does—wrong or right—simply because he belongs to the race.

Whatever you may believe, Adam, I write this letter more in sadness than in anger. I, like many others, have been troubled by what has seemed to be your growing insensitivity to the cause of our people and your seemingly increasing disregard for your responsibilities to the job you have been sent to Washington to do.

Like many others, I have hesitated to say this because you have done a magnificent job in years gone by and because I did not want to give ammunition to those enemies of yours who have been the enemies of the Negro people.

The people who were your enemies and ours—the segregationists—are probably thinking very highly of you right now although they probably have contempt even for an enemy who would desert his own cause. At any rate, you have played right into their hands. They want nothing better than to hurt the NAACP and you have volunteered to give that aim a tremendous boost.

Recently, on the campus of Howard University, I received a tongue-lashing from a student who demanded to know how I could balance my belief and personal principles with my consistent defense of "a demagogue like Adam Powell." I replied that I too felt you had been derelict in your duties on many occasions, but that I did not wish to help our common enemies.

As I close this letter, Adam, I must confess with a deep sense of sadness, that I no longer know who your enemies really are.

## Malcolm X's Letter
### (*New York Amsterdam News*, November 30, 1963)

Dear Good Friend, Jackie Roosevelt Robinson:

You became a great baseball player after your White Boss (Mr. Rickey) lifted you to the Major Leagues. You proved that your White Boss had chosen the "right" Negro by getting plenty of hits, stealing plenty of bases, winning many games and bringing much money through the gates and into the pockets of your White Boss.

In those days I was one of your many ardent fans; your speed and shifty base running used to hold me spellbound . . . and, according to the attack you leveled against me and Congressman Powell in your recent column, I must confess that even today you still display the same old "speed," the same "cunning," and "shiftiness,". . . and you are still trying to win "The Big Game" for your White Boss.

Shortly after the White Man lifted you from poverty and obscurity to the Major Leagues, Paul Robeson was condemning America for her injustices against American Negroes. Mr. Robeson questioned the intelligence of Negroes fighting to defend a country that treated them with such open contempt and bestial brutality.

### Robeson's Stand

Robeson's brilliant stand in behalf of our people left the guilty American whites speechless: they had no defense.

They sought desperately to find another Negro who would be dumb enough to champion their bankrupt "white" cause against Paul Robeson.

It was you who let yourself be used by the whites even in those days against your own kind. You let them sic you on Paul Robeson.

You let them use you to destroy Paul Robeson. You let your White Boss send you before a congressional hearing in Washington, D.C., (the capitol of Segregationville) to dispute and condemn Paul Robeson, because he had these guilty American whites frightened silly.

Your White Boss sent you to Washington to assure all the worried white folks that Negroes were still thankful to the Great White Father for bringing us to America, that Negroes were grateful to America (despite our not being treated as full citizens), and that Negroes would still lay down our lives to defend this white country (though this same white government wasn't ready nor willing to defend Negroes) . . . even in those days, Jackie!

### Jackie's Column

In this same recent column you also accused me and Dr. Powell of misleading our people. Aren't you the same ex-baseball player who tried to "MISLEAD" Negroes into Nixon's camp during the last presidential election?

Evidently you were the only Negro who voted for Nixon, because according to the polls taken afterward, very few Negroes were dumb enough to follow your "MISLEAD."

Today you confess to our people that you now think Nixon would have been the wrong man. Aren't you also confessing that if Negroes had been dumb enough to follow you three years ago that you would have been guilty of MISLEADING them?

### Rockefeller

You never give up. You are now trying to lead Negroes into Nelson Rockefeller's political camp. If you admit that you were wrong about Richard Nixon three years ago, how are we to be sure that you've become so politically mature in the meantime to be right in your choice today? Your "shiftiness" is confusing and very misleading.

We hear that you are about to be appointed Boxing Commissioner of New York State by Governor Nelson Rockefeller. Does this have any bearing on your efforts to get Negroes into Rockefeller's camp? Just who are you playing ball for today, good Friend?

Our people followed you on the football field and the baseball field, but we are cautious and doubtful about your shifty position in this political field.

When Mr. Rickey picked you up from obscurity and made you a Big Leaguer, you never let Mr. Rickey down; and since Mr. Black has given you a well-paying position with Chock-Full-O-Nuts, you have never let Mr. Black down ... and now with Nelson Rockefeller promising to make you the Boxing Commissioner of New York State, we know that you can't afford to let Ole Rocky down.

You have never shown appreciation for the support given you by the Negro masses, but you have a record of being very faithful to your White Benefactors. Perhaps, if Nixon had not been such a relatively poorer man, he too would have fared much better with your support.

Your column also accused me of attacking Dr. Ralph Bunche. This is untrue. I have never attacked Ralph Bunche. No Muslims ever initiates an attack on anyone. Dr. Bunche had attacked the Muslims in general and me in particular from a college campus in the state of Mississippi, and his venemous poison was carried by all the major networks. My reply to Dr.

Bunche's unwarranted attack was made strictly in self-defense (as is this present letter an answer to your unjust attack).

If Dr. Bunche's UN position is supposed to confine him to matters "above and beyond" America's race problems, whenever he does escape the confines of UN protocol, why does he always attack our Muslim religious group? This is the third time he has attacked our religion. Is he anti-Islam?

## Mississippi

Since he was in Mississippi while making his recent speech, he would have shown more intelligence had he directed his full attention toward the whites in that area who are bombing Negro churches and murdering innocent little Negro girls.

Why waste precious time and energy on us? Muslims don't bomb churches. Muslims didn't shoot Medgar Evers in the back. Muslims have never lynched anyone.

Dr. Bunche should realize he can't fight an effective battle on two different fronts at the same time. He can't fight the Muslims, and at the same time be effective against the lynchers of Negroes.

But Dr. Bunche seems more anxious to discredit and destroy the Muslim religious group than he does the white lynchers of Negroes. Whenever I read the speeches he makes for American consumption, I often wonder if his script-writer isn't some anti-Muslim Israeli?

You also quoted the comedian, Dick Gregory, whose scriptwriter has him saying that most Negroes never knew the Muslims existed until the white man put the Muslims on Television. I must confess that this is part-true.

The Muslims have been in the Negro Community for a long time, but Negroes such as yourself, who regard yourselves as Negro "leaders" never know what is going on in the Negro Community until the white man tells you.

You stay as far away from the Negro Community as you can get, and you never take an interest in anything in the Negro Community until the white man himself takes an interest in it. You, yourself would never shake my hand until you saw some of your white friends shaking it.

Negro "leaders" never knew Muslims existed until the white man discovered them, and right today most of these same Negro "leaders" know about Muslims only what the white man has told them.

### Medgar Evers

Finally, good Friend Jackie: you attacked me for not attending the funeral of Medgar Evers who was murdered in Mississippi. When I go to a Mississippi funeral it won't be to attend the funeral of a black man!

And you Negro "leaders," whose bread and butter depend on your ability to make your white boss think you have all these Negroes "under control," better be thankful that I wasn't in Mississippi after Medgar Evers was murdered, nor in Birmingham after the murder of those four innocent little Negro girls.

If my integrity or sincerity is to be measured in your eyesight by my attendance at funerals of Negroes who have been murdered by whites, if you should ever meet with such misfortune I promise to attend your funeral, and then perhaps you will be able to see me in a different light?

If you should ever become as militant in behalf of our oppressed people as Medgar Evers was, the same whites whom you now take to be your friends will be the first to put the bullet or the dagger in your back, just as they put it in the back of Medgar Evers . . .

And I sincerely fear, good Friend Jackie, that if the whites do murder you, you are still gullible enough to die thinking they are still your white friends, and that the dagger in your back is only an accident!

Whereas if whites were to murder me for the religious philosophy that I represent and stand for, I would die KNOWING that it was at the hands of OPEN ENEMIES OF TRUTH AND JUSTICE!

# Jackie Robinson Again Writes to Malcolm X
## (*New York Amsterdam News*, December 14, 1963)

Dear Malcolm: Frankly, your front-page letter to me in THE NEW YORK AMSTERDAM NEWS is one of the things I shall cherish. Coming from you, an attack is a tribute. I am also honored to have been placed in the distinguished company of Dr. Ralph Bunche whom you have also attacked.

I am proud of my associations with the men you choose to call my "white bosses"—Mr. Branch Rickey, my boss at Chock Full O' Nuts, Mr. William Black, and Governor Nelson Rockefeller. I am also proud that so many others whom you would undoubtedly label as "white bosses," marched with us to Washington and have been and are now working with our leaders to help achieve equality here in America.

I will not dignify your attempted slur against my appearance before the House Un-American Activities Committee some years back. All I can say is that if I were called upon to defend my country today, I would gladly do so. Nor do I hide behind any coat-tails as you do when caught in one of your numerous outlandish statements. Your usual "out" is to duck responsibility by stating: "The Honorable Elijah Muhammed says . . ."

Personally, I reject your racist views. I reject your dream of a separate state. I believe that many Americans, black and white, are committed to fight for those freedoms for which Medgar Evers, William Moore, the Birmingham children and President John F. Kennedy died.

Those of us who are so committed have no intention of supporting the idea of a separate black state where the Honorable Muhammed can be the ruler and you, his immediate successor—and all because you, Malcolm, hate white people. Too many of our young people have gone to jail and too many millions of dollars have been invested in our fight for equality for us to pay serious heed to your advice. Whether you like this country or not is of little concern to me. America is not perfect, by a long shot, but I happen to like it here and will do all I can to help make it the kind of place where my children and theirs can live in dignity.

As for Governor Rockefeller, I sincerely hope that whatever

contribution I can make to his campaign for nomination and election will be meaningful. I don't know where you went to school, Malcolm. If you attended virtually any Negro college, I venture to say that a Rockefeller helped make your education possible. Neither do I apologize for my support of Mr. Nixon.

If conditions were the same today as they were in 1960, I would still support him. I do not do things to please "white bosses" or "black agitators" unless they are the things which please me. I respect Governor Rockefeller's leadership of the present and what his family has meant to us in the past. I fully intend to do all I can to aid him.

The fact that I am supporting him does not mean you should. Rest assured, I am not doing so in the hope that you will come aboard.

You say I have never shown my appreciation to the Negro masses. I assume that is why NAACP branches all over the country constantly invite me to address them. I guess this is the reason the NAACP gave me its highest award, the Spingarn Medal and why Dr. Martin King has consistently invited me to participate in the Southern Freedom Fight and invited me to co-chair with him the drive to raise funds to re-build the burned churches in Georgia. By the way, Malcolm, I don't remember our receiving your contribution.

Negroes are not fooled by your vicious theories that they are dying for freedom to please the white man. Negroes are fighting for freedom and rejecting your racism because we feel our stake in America is worth fighting for. Whom do you think you are kidding, Malcolm, when you say that Negro leaders ought to be "thankful" that you were not personally present in Birmingham or Mississippi after racial atrocities had been committed there? The inference seems to be that you would have played some dramatic, avenging role. I don't think you would have.

I think you would have done exactly what you did after your own Muslim brothers were shot and killed in Los Angeles. You left it to the law to take its course.

You mouth a big and bitter battle, Malcolm, but it is noticeable that your militancy is mainly expressed in Harlem where it is safe.

I have always contended for your right—as for that of every American—to say and think and believe what you choose. I just happen to believe you are supporting and advocating policies which could not possibly interest the masses. Thank God for our Dr. Bunche, our Roy Wilkins, our Dr. King and Mr. Randolph. I am also grateful for those people you consider "white bosses."

I am glad that I have been able to come through for the people at whom you sneer. I am glad that Negroes spent so many millions for paid admissions to baseball. I am glad that we have sold an awful lot of Chock Full O' Nuts Coffee. I am hopeful that we will be able to help get a great many votes for Governor Rockefeller.

I shall always be happy to associate myself with decent Americans of either race who believe in justice for all. I hate to think of where we would be if we followed your leadership. Strictly in my personal opinion, it is a sick leadership which should rightfully be rejected by the vast majority of Americans.

# "Lady, that's Jackie Robinson!"

## NAN BIRMINGHAM

*O*ne rarely has the opportunity to see the more human
side of public figures. A chance meeting on an airplane
in the late 1960s allowed writer Nan Birmingham to
experience a Jackie Robinson, at once smaller and
simultaneously grander, than the one that most of us know.

● ● ● ● ● ● ●

I was bone tired by 2 AM, when I boarded the plane for home
after criss-crossing six southern states in five days on the lecture
circuit. Gradually, I became aware that passengers shuffling with
fatigue along the aisle perked up when they passed the man
seated next to me.

"I should be asleep at home by now," he said quietly. "I only
flew south for dinner." "Dinner?" I asked, searching for clues to
his identity. "I was the speaker at the National Conference of
Christians and Jews," he explained. I wrestled with famous
names and came up empty.

Before dawn the PA announced that Kennedy was again

socked in. We were to land in Newark and be bused to JFK. My seatmate gave in to annoyance. "I still have to drive to Connecticut."

"Do you take the thruway?" I asked. "I live in Westchester just off the thruway. You wouldn't have to stop. Just slow down. I'll jump."

"You wouldn't have to do that," he said with a smile.

When he left his seat briefly the man across the aisle whispered, "What a great guy is giving you a ride."

"Yes," I agreed knowingly. Then I chanced, "He is Elston Howard, isn't he?"

"Elston Howard?" the fellow bellowed. "Lady, *that's* Jackie Robinson!" he added in utter amazement.

Jackie Robinson refastened his seatbelt. I wanted him to know I knew and exploded enthusiastically. "My sister, Marion, was at UCLA when you played for the Bruins."

"Really," he said calmly. "That was some time ago. I'm Jackie Robinson, and what is your name?"

When the bus pulled up at Kennedy on that gray morning, Jackie Robinson stood up in front and shouted, "If anyone needs a ride to Westchester or Connecticut, I'm driving up the New England Thruway."

A young soldier spoke up, "Sir, I'm going to Waterbury."

"Come along," said Robinson.

As the soldier and I waited for Robinson to come with his car I said with a certain know-it-all smugness, "Young man, are you aware of just *who* is giving us a ride?"

"Man, am I!" He beamed. "I can't wait to tell my mama. She's in the hospital. This is going to make her feel real good."

The morning light and exhaustion stripped away pretense, and we spoke candidly about our families and children as the car nosed north. "It's funny," Robinson said with a touch of sadness, "you think you're doing things right and it all goes wrong. One of my kids has a knack for trouble. I don't know why. He's going to be all right. I know that. But he's rebelled against everything my wife and I have stood for."

"Mr. Robinson," I ventured, "were't you a rebel? A rebel with a cause?"

"No," he said. "I just wanted to play ball."

Home, finally. Jackie Robinson carried my suitcase to the door and wished me well. He motioned to the soldier to move up front, and both waved goodbye as the car edged out of sight.

Sitting with a cup of coffee I wondered how to explain to my kids who this hero was; how to explain the brouhaha 40 years ago over a black man playing in the major leagues. Then I thought about the courage it took for that young man to walk into that stadium and face a hostile crowd—alone. I'll tell my children about that man.

# THE LION AT DUSK

## ROGER KAHN

*M*any people consider Roger Kahn's The Boys of Summer *the best baseball book ever written. What elevates Kahn's work from other baseball books is that it is not really about baseball, but about life: coming of age, growing older, fathers and sons, and coping with death and disappointment.* The Boys of Summer *chronicles Kahn's years growing up in Brooklyn and his two-year stint as a sportswriter covering the legendary Dodgers team of the 1950s. In an inspired twist, Kahn revisited these "boys of summer" as men in the autumn of their years and described their fates once their playing careers had ended.*

*Although he is only one of many people portrayed in Kahn's work, Robinson and the integration saga dominate* The Boys of Summer *as he dominated the Brooklyn Dodgers. His life, like those of many of his former teammates, had been marked by tragedy. Jackie, Jr., was dead at age twenty-four. The youth who had charmed observers in the 1950s had been wounded in Vietnam, succumbed to heroin addiction, and been arrested for felony crimes. Then at the moment of his seeming triumph over these demons, a late-night car crash had taken his life. Robinson himself, although barely past fifty, had snow-white hair, diabetes, a heart condition, and was nearly blind. Of all of the words written about Jackie Robinson, none have captured the essence of the man and his life quite so well as Kahn's poignant portrait.*

● ● ● ● ● ● ●

Of all the Dodgers, none seemed as able as Jackie Robinson to trample down the thorns of life. Indeed, the thornbush became his natural environment. But here, on the night of March 6, 1968, not a dozen years after his last World Series, Robinson stood among television reporters, a bent, gray man, answering questions in a whisper, and drawing shallow breaths, because a longer breath might feed a sob.

Jackie Robinson, Jr., no more the large-eyed imp, had been arrested in a one-night-cheap hotel. The police of Stamford, Connecticut, charged him with possessing a tobacco pouch filled with marijuana, a .22 caliber revolver and several packets of heroin which he may have wished to sell. Outside a suburban courthouse, television reporters, who had never seen the father play baseball, called hard questions with extravagant courtesy.

"Sir, are you going to stick by your son?"

"We will, but we'll have to take the consequences."

"Were you aware that he had certain problems, Mr. Robinson?"

"He quit high school. He joined the Army. He fought in Vietnam and he was wounded. We lost him somewhere. I've had more effect on other people's kids than on my own."

"How do you feel about *that*, sir?"

The gray-haired black man, Jackie Robinson, shook his head. "I couldn't have had an *important* effect on anybody's child if this happened to my own."

I turned away and Jack answered another question at length, as if in relief, as if in penance. He had not faded from public sight like most of the others. Even Robinson's declining baseball years crackled with controversy. During Walter Alston's first spring as manager, he said in Vero Beach, "Every man on this ball club

will have to fight for his job." Some veterans laughed. Duke
Snider did not expect to spend the season of 1954 on the bench.
Pee Wee Reese was offended. Jackie Robinson spoke out. "I
don't know what the hell that man is trying to do. Upset us all?"
That year a strong, mismanaged, discontented Dodger team fin-
ished second.

In succeeding seasons the Dodgers won two pennants, but
for Robinson the old spirit was vanished. He felt out of things, he
said. This manager was hostile. This front office did not provide
support. Then, after the 1956 season, Walter O'Malley traded
him to the Giants. "We hate to lose Jackie," O'Malley said, "but
it is necessary for the good of the team."

To find similar cynicism, you had to go clear back to 1935
when the Yankees dumped Babe Ruth on the old Boston Braves.
But then the star was being sent to another league. Robinson, the
embodiment of the loud, brave, contentious Dodgers, was being
assigned to his team's great adversary. . . .

He telephoned two seasons after his retirement and asked if
I'd talk to him about a biography he was preparing, helped by
Carl Rowan, the black journalist. We lunched in Janssen's, a
restaurant on Lexington Avenue, and Robinson immediately told
me how difficult it was to be a writer. "First I picked the wrong
collaborators," he said, and mentioned two white newspapermen.
"I tell one of them something for the book. He tapes me and two
days later uses it for a column. Now I'm squared away on that,
but I've got other problems. Campy. I told you there was a little
Tom in him. Suppose I go into that. I'm hitting a cripple."

"Write the damn thing the way you feel it," I said.

"And then there's a point about women. When I was at
UCLA, more white women wanted to go to bed with me than I
wanted to go to bed with white women."

"Congratulations."

"Everybody thinks it's all the other way. All the black guys
are panting to get into bed with white women. Well, a lot of white
guys are just dying to get hold of black women. I'm not kidding.
I've seen it. And, for me, with white girls, like I said, I didn't
have to make much of a move."

"You've *got* to write that. A chapter. Write it goddamn tough."

"I don't know," Robinson said.

"Pliss," said a short, elderly man, bending so that his bald head dropped between us. "Be a good boy and give your autograph."

"What?" Robinson's tenor clanged through the restaurant. The man started. "I said, could I have your autograph?"

"That isn't what you said." Robinson's voice drew eyes toward our table. The man was frightened. "Who's this for?" Robinson shouted.

"My grandson."

"All right. I'll give you the autograph to your grandson, but not because I'm a boy." Robinson scribbled on the menu. The man took it and hurried away.

"You're a fierce bastard," I said.

"He won't call a black man 'boy' again," said Robinson. . . .

This was the man Branch Rickey hired, proud, as his mother had wanted him to be, fierce in his own nature, scarred because white America wounds its fierce proud blacks. I once asked Rickey if he was surprised by the full measure of Robinson's success and I heard him laugh deep in his chest. "Adventure. Adventure. The man is all adventure. I only wish I could have signed him five years sooner."

As surely as Robinson's genius at the game transcends his autobiography, it also transcends record books. In two seasons, 1962 and 1965, Maury Wills stole more bases than Robinson did in all of a ten-year career. Ted Williams' lifetime batting average, .344, is two points higher than Robinson's best for any season. Robinson never hit twenty home runs in a year, never batted in 125 runs. Stan Musial consistently scored more often. Having said those things, one has not said much because troops of people who were there believe that in his prime Jackie Robinson was a better ball player than any of the others. "Ya want a guy that comes to play," suggests Leo Durocher, whose personal relationship with Robinson was spiky. "This guy didn't just come to play. He come to beat ya. He come to stuff the goddamn bat right up your ass."

He moved onto the field with a pigeon-toed shuffle, Number 42 on his back. Reese wore 1. Billy Cox wore 3. Duke Snider wore 4. Carl Furillo wore 6. Dressen wore 7. Shuba wore 8. Robinson wore 42. The black man had to begin in double figures. So he remained.

After 1948 he had too much belly, and toward the end fat rolled up behind his neck. But how this lion sprang. Like a few, very few athletes, Babe Ruth, Jim Brown, Robinson did not merely play at center stage. He *was* center stage; and wherever he walked, center stage moved with him.

When the Dodgers needed a run and had men at first and second, it was Robinson who came to bat. Would he slap a line drive to right? Would he slug the ball to left? Or would he roll a bunt? From the stands at Ebbets Field, close to home plate, the questions rose into a din. The pitcher saw Robinson. He heard the stands. He bit his lip.

At times when the team lagged, Robinson found his way to first. Balancing evenly on the balls of both feet, he took an enormous lead. The pitcher glared. Robinson stared back. There was no action, only two men throwing hard looks. But time suspended. The cry in the grandstands rose. And Robinson hopped a half yard farther from first. The pitcher stepped off the mound, calling time-out, and when the game resumed, he walked the hitter.

Breaking, Robinson reached full speed in three strides. The pigeon-toed walk yielded to a run of graceful power. He could steal home, or advance two bases on someone else's bunt, and at the time of decision, when he slid, the big dark body became a bird in flight. Then, safe, he rose slowly, often limping, and made his pigeon-toed way to the dugout.

Once Russ Meyer, a short-tempered righthander, pitched a fine game against the Dodgers. The score going into the eighth inning was 2 to 2, and it was an achievement to check the Brooklyn hitters in Ebbets Field. Then, somehow, Robinson reached third base. He took a long lead, threatening to steal home, and the Phillies, using a set play, caught him fifteen feet off base. A rundown developed. This is the major league version of a game children call getting into a pickle. The runner is surrounded by fielders who throw the ball back and forth, gradually closing the gap. Since a ball travels four times faster than a man's best running speed, it is only a question of time before the gap closes and the runner is tagged. Except for Robinson. The rundown was his greatest play. Robinson could start so fast and stop so short that he could elude anyone in baseball, and he could feint a start and feint a stop as well.

All the Phillies rushed to the third-base line, a shortstop named Granny Hamner and a second baseman called Mike Goliat and the first baseman, Eddie Waitkus. The third baseman, Puddin' Head Jones, and the catcher, Andy Seminick, were already there. Meyer himself joined. Among the gray uniforms Robinson in white lunged, and sprinted and leaped and stopped. The Phils threw the ball back and forth, but Robinson anticipated their throws, and after forty seconds, and six throws, the gap had not closed. Then, a throw toward third went wild and Robinson made his final victorious run at home plate. Meyer dropped to his knees and threw both arms around Robinson's stout legs. Robinson bounced a hip against Meyer's head and came home running backward, saying "What the hell are you trying to do?"

"Under the stands, Robinson," Meyer said.

"Right now," Robinson roared.

Police beat them to the proposed ring. Robinson not only won games; he won and infuriated the losers.

In Ebbets Field one spring day in 1955 Sal Maglie was humiliating the Brooklyn hitters. Not Cox or Robinson, but most of the others were clearly alarmed by Maglie's highest skill. He threw at hitters, as he said, "whenever they didn't expect it. That way I had them looking to duck all the time." The fast pitch at the chin or temple is frightening but not truly dangerous as long as the batter sees the ball. He has only to move his head a few inches to safety.

On this particular afternoon, Maglie threw a fast pitch behind Robinson's shoulders, and that *is* truly dangerous, a killer pitch. As a batter strides, and one strides automatically, he loses height. A normal defensive reflex is to fall backward. When a pitch is shoulder-high behind a man, he ducks directly into the baseball.

I can see Maglie, saturnine in the brightness of May, winding up and throwing. Robinson started to duck and then, with those extraordinary reflexes, hunched his shoulders and froze. The ball sailed wild behind him. He must have felt the wind. He held the hunched posture and gazed at Maglie, who began fidgeting on the mound.

A few innings later, as Maglie continued to overwhelm the Brooklyn hitters, Pee Wee Reese said, "Jack, you got to do something."

"Yeah," Robinson said.

The bat boy overheard the whispered conversation, and just before Jack stepped in to hit, he said in a voice of anxiety, "Don't you do it. Let one of the others do it. You do enough."

Robinson took his stance, bat high. He felt a certain relief. Let somebody else do it, for a change.

"Come on, Jack." Reese's voice carried from the dugout. "We're counting on you."

Robinson took a deep breath. Somebody else? What somebody else? Hodges? Snider? Damn, there *wasn't* anybody else.

The bunt carried accurately toward first baseman Whitey Lockman, who scooped the ball and looked to throw. That is the play. Bunt and make the pitcher cover first. Then run him down. But Maglie lingered in the safety of the mound. He would not move, and a second baseman named Davey Williams took his place. Lockman's throw reached Williams at first base. Then Robinson struck. A knee crashed into Williams' lower spine and Williams spun into the air, twisting grotesquely, and when he fell he lay in an awkward sprawl, as people do when they are seriously injured.

He was carried from the field. Two innings after that, Alvin Dark, the Giant captain, lined a two-base hit to left field. Dark did not stop at second. Instead, he continued full speed toward third base and Jackie Robinson. The throw had him beaten. Robinson put the ball into his bare right hand and decided to tag Dark between the eyes.

As Dark began to slide, Robinson faked to his right. Dark followed his fake. Robinson stepped aside and slammed the ball at Dark's brow. To his amazement, it bounced free. He had not gotten a secure grip. Dark, avenging Davey Williams, substituting for Sal Maglie, was safe at third.

Both men dusted their uniforms. Lockman was batting. Staring toward home, Robinson said through rigid lips, "This isn't the end. There'll be another day." But when the game was over, Dark asked a reporter to carry a message into the Brooklyn clubhouse. "Tell him we're even," the Giant captain said. "Tell him I don't want another day."

The next afternoon I stood in the Giant clubhouse, watching a trainer rub Dark's shoulders. Alvin had straight black hair and deep-set eyes that seemed to squint, the kind of face, Leonard Koppett said, that belonged on a Confederate cavalry captain.

"What do ya thinka Robinson?" Dark said softly, as the trainer bent over him.

"A lot. I think a lot of Robinson."

"I don't know how you can say that," Dark said. "Do you know what he is?" He sought a metaphor to stir me. "Don't you understand?" Dark cried. "He's a *Hitler*." ("And Maglie is Mussolini," I thought.) "Anybody can do something like that to Davey is a Hitler," Dark said.

He paused in thought. "Ah know ahm right," Dark said. "A little higher, Doc." Watching the deep-set angry eyes, I could not forget that when combat reached close quarters, it was the Southerner not the black who had backed off.

After baseball, the executive saddle was something Robinson bore to earn a living. He moved from Chock Full O'Nuts to an insurance company to a food franchising business. Politics was his passion. He supported Nixon for President in 1960, when Kennedy won, and he endorsed Rockefeller for the Republican candidacy in 1964, when Barry Goldwater stormed the San Francisco convention. We met from time to time and chatted.

"I wanted to be fair about things," he said, "so I went to see both Kennedy and Nixon. Now, Nixon seemed to understand a little bit of what had to be done. John Kennedy said, 'Mr. Robinson, I don't know much about the problems of colored people since I come from New England.' I figured, the hell with that. Any man in Congress for fifteen years ought to make it his business to know colored people."

"Credibility is the question."

"Well, I trust Nixon on this point."

"All right," I said. "Even if your analysis is right as far as it goes, civil rights isn't the only question. There are a dozen other issues."

"Sure," Robinson said, "and there are pressure groups working on all of them. I'm a pressure group for civil rights."

Goldwater's capture of the candidacy shook him. He recognized the nature of the campaign, Goldwater playing to conservative whites, Lyndon Johnson courting liberals and blacks, and said that we could well have a white man's party and a black man's party in America. "It would make everything I worked for meaningless," he said, "if baseball is integrated but the political parties are segregated." In Nelson Rockefeller he saw a great dark hope. He might have been appointed to the cabinet if Rockefeller had been elected President, but Robinson's political career, unlike his baseball life, trails off into disappointments and conditional sentences.

He came walking pigeon-toed through the doors of the Sea Host, a food franchising company, at 12:30, suddenly and astonishingly handsome. Under a broad brow, the fine features were set in a well-proportioned face. What was most remarkable was the skin. It shone, unsullied ebony. I should expect that Shaka, the chieftain who built the Zulu warrior nation, had that coloring, imperial black. Robinson's hair had gone pure white, and the contrast of skin and hair make a dramatic balance.

"You look better than when you played," I said.

"Lost weight," Robinson said. We walked to Morgen's East, a restaurant off Madison Avenue, which Robinson finds convenient. A few heads turned when we entered, but no one bothered him. "I lost weight on doctor's orders," he said. "I have diabetes, high blood pressure, and I've had a heart attack." He grinned. "That's because I never drink and I don't smoke."

"Bad heart attack?"

"Bad enough. I was at a dinner. It started out like indigestion, only worse. I had three weeks on my back." He looked at the menu and ordered a salad and said, "Low cholesterol."

"I don't know how to ask you about your boy."

"You just did."

"And the arrest."

"Two arrests, one in March and one in August. The second time the court ruled that he was a narcotics-dependent person. I can talk about Jackie. Rachel and I have been able to piece things together. He's a bright boy and a good athlete. If he'd worked, I think he could have become a major leaguer."

"Would you have liked that?"

"Yes," Robinson said, "I would have liked that. But he's an independent kid, and look where he was. You know Rachel has a master's degree. She teaches at Yale. So there was the culture stuff. He felt blocked there. And he was Jackie Robinson Junior so he felt that he was blocked in sports. He wanted to be something; he wanted to be great at *something*. So he decided, when he was pretty young, that he was going to be a great crook. There are some Mafia people around Stamford. It began with smoking pot. And after a while, it turned out, he knew about Mafia contracts, about murdering people. Then he went off to the war. He was wounded. He learned how to kill. When he came back, he couldn't handle anything himself. Heroin. When he was picked up, with some other kids who possessed marijuana, he started fighting the police.

"It could have been jail, but the sentence was suspended with the understanding that he'd go into treatment to cure himself of addiction. There's a place called Daytop, in Seymour, Connecticut, where rehabilitation is done by former addicts. That's where he decided to go.

"When he went in, a psychiatrist talked to Rachel and me for a long time. They wanted to explain what was going to happen so we could deal with it. The psychiatrist said that in the cure Jackie would have to confront himself and that one of the patterns is that the addict runs home to his parents. It seems to happen.

"Now, he told us, the important thing was that when Jack came home, we shouldn't let him in. He had to confront himself and this thing on his own. If we let him in, then all the Daytop work could be undone. Jackie might see it as something he could quit when the going got tough. So there we are, Rachel and me, and there is the psychiatrist saying when your own son comes to the door begging for help, you must not under any circumstances let him in.

"And I nodded and I didn't look at Rachel, because I knew if I looked at her and she looked at me, she'd start to cry."

"How could your son have been involved with dope and crime without you or Rachel suspecting?"

"I told you that he wanted to be a great criminal. I didn't tell you what he really was."

"What was he?"

"A great liar," Robinson said.

We sat silent. Robinson continued to eat slowly. "You see any of the old writers?" I said. "Dick Young?"

"I respected Dick as a good writer. We disagreed, but I give him that. A lot of writers were as uninformed as fans. What did they know how it was? What did they know how it felt to win, to lose? And they expected me to be grateful for what they wrote. Once a writer came up and said I better start saying thank you if I wanted to be Most Valuable Player. I said if I have to thank *you* to win MVP, I don't want the fucking thing. And I didn't thank him, and I won it.

"I was a great thing for those guys. They could sell magazine stories about me. That was the difference between hamburger and steak." He picked at his salad.

"How do you do with the young militants?"

"A while ago in Harlem these kids started threatening me. The Governor asked me to speak for the new state office thing and it got rough."

Nelson Rockefeller had sponsored a high-rise state building at Seventh Avenue and 125th Street, the core of Harlem. The plan would encourage integration, Rockefeller said. But ever baronial, he neglected to bring local black leaders to planning conferences. The initial leveling was messy. People had to be dispossessed. To certain blacks, the whole scheme reeked of colonialism. One night, thirty militants advanced with pup tents and occupied the site. Without neighborhood support for his benign intention, Rockefeller turned to Robinson.

"When I went there to talk," Robinson said, "the kids were angry. A detective with me said I better watch it, but I've been in that scene before, with angry kids. They see me in a suit and tie and they look at my white hair and they're too young to remember what I did, or they don't care. I began to talk and some shouted 'Oreo.' You know. The cookie that's black outside and white underneath.

"When I get with militant kids, I can handle myself. I curse." Robinson smiled to himself. "All of a sudden this gray-haired man in a suit and tie is calling them mothers. Well, you know."

He repeated some of the speech he had made. " 'Maybe this isn't the best thing in the world, but it's something. It's a chance. And if you block it, then that's it. You've lost, not Governor Rockefeller. Nobody's gonna try and build here again. And it'll be over. Nobody'll invest and nobody'll want to come here and nothing will happen except the neighborhood'll get worse. You bastards are wrong to turn against this thing.'

"There was this white man, sixty years old, maybe five feet five, walking down the street and a couple of the young militants went up behind him and knocked him flat. I went over and helped him up. That's when they really started with the 'Oreo.'

"The gang was tough. The police didn't want to get involved. That old man could have been murdered. They said he was an accountant at Blumstein's and they don't like Blumstein's." It is the principal department store on 125th Street, free with credit, persistent with demands for payment, the very cliché of the usurious, exploitive, Jewish white.

"The militants," Robinson said, "just want to burn. And maybe white society will have to burn, but they are hitting the wrong targets all the time, like an old man."

"Or you?"

"Or me."

He does not want society to burn. Burn America and you burn the achievements of Jackie Robinson. After ruinous, anarchic blaze, who will remember the brave, fatherless boyhood, the fight for an inch of Army justice, the courage in baseball, the leadership and the triumph, of a free man who walked with swift and certain strides?

It was a cold day. After lunch the wind, biting up Fifty-third Street, bothered him. He walked deliberately, and it shocked me in the street to realize that I was slowing my own pace so as not to walk too quickly for Jackie Robinson.

The noontime of the American Dream glows briefly. One is continuously being persuaded to purchase washing machines and dryers, spare television sets and youth furniture, to add a room or to move into a larger home, and then when the hardest payments have been met, and the large family is suitably housed, the children begin making their way into dormitories and shared single rooms, the world beyond the hearth.

The children were all gone from the big stone house in Stamford, which the Robinsons built in mid-1954. Jack Junior was fighting for stability, and doing well. He had stopped using heroin and joined the staff of Daytop; he talked of wanting to run a community center in a ghetto. Sharon, born in 1950, married young, was living in Washington, D.C. After a good career at Mount Hermon Prep, David has gone clear across the country to Stanford. "But we're busy, you can be sure," Mrs. Robinson said on an afternoon when Jack asked my wife and me to visit. "We're both quite occupied."

In at least one sense, the years had treated Rachel Isum Robinson kindly. She remained a handsome woman, with soft, unlined skin. Escorting guests into the living room, she bore herself elegantly, and there was a warmth to her manner, and the two, elegance and warmth, blended into graciousness.

"Won't you sit down? Can I fix drinks?" An ebony piano stood at one side of the spacious room, which was carpeted and high-ceilinged. A window wall overlooked a bright lawn, sloping toward water, the Stamford reservoir. Opposite, gray stone arched above the fireplace. One had to look closely to notice a pride of the mason's craft; no visible mortar interrupted the flow of stone. "The builder," Rachel said, "was marvelous. He meant this place to be a monument; of course, we have never been sure whether for us or for him."

She climbed two carpeted stairs into a dining alcove and returned with drinks in mugs of heavy glass. She sipped at a martini. "One thing about my background in California was that I was brought up to be as ladylike as possible. I was taught not to be aggressive. And then, marrying Jack I was in the middle of a struggle where—well, without aggressive behavior it would have failed. There was an aggressiveness to Jack's whole career in baseball. It was a kind of objection to the white society."

"A very mild objection." Treading softly, on the balls of his feet, Robinson entered his living room. He found an easy chair and reclined into a graceful slouch. He wore dark slacks and a blue knit shirt with sleeves that ended in mid-bicep. "Go on, go on," he said in a soft voice.

"How did you find spring training in the South?"

"Humiliating," Rachel said. Jack half-closed his eyes. "One of the many mistakes we made with Jackie," Rachel said, "was trying to shield him from the way the South was. When we just had little Jack, we lived in the barracks at Vero Beach, like some other families, but we were limited to camp, which made us different. The white wives were always going on shopping trips to Vero Beach. Black people weren't welcome to shop there. The hairdresser said he couldn't work with black women's hair. Well, one day I found a black hairdresser, and telephoned Vero Beach for a taxi. I was standing with little Jack when the driver pulled up. I started in, but he said wait, he wouldn't take us. I'd have to call the colored cab.

"The colored *cab*! It was a big, ugly bus. I got in with Jackie, and the driver had to swing around near the swimming pool where all the white wives sat with their children. I shrank in my seat. I didn't want anybody to see me. But just as we were turning little Jack stuck his head out of a window and called, 'Good-bye, good-bye.' All the white wives looked up and saw me in this awful bus, the colored taxi, we had to ride in.

"After I was done at the hairdresser I decided instead of the bus I'd walk back the five miles. It was slow going with little Jackie. He couldn't make it all the way. And then that colored taxi came by again, only this time it was full. It was bringing the help to serve the evening meal. The driver stopped and Jackie and

I got on again. I hated to, but that was the only way we could get back to camp.

"Another time the Dodgers were playing in West Palm Beach and I took Jackie and when we got there they wouldn't let us through the turnstile. No colored, the man said. Go around to the outfield. The colored *entrance*, they called it, was where they'd taken some boards out of the outfield fence. You had to climb over boards. Skirts were long then. I remember holding little Jack's hand and helping him through.

"I never discussed any of these humiliations. I tried to pretend they weren't there. And young Jack never discussed them with me. But he must have noticed. He had to notice, don't you think?"

"He noticed," Robinson said.

"My husband underplays things," Rachel said. "That's his style. Don't let him fool you. What he came up against, and what we all came up against, was very, very rough."

Robinson's eyes remained half closed.

"He was explosive on the field," Rachel said, "and reporters used to ask if he was explosive at home. Of course he wasn't. No matter what he'd been called, or how sarcastic or bigoted others had been to him, he never took it out on any of us.

"After we moved up here," Rachel said, "there was one clue to when he was upset, when things had gone particularly badly. He'd go out on the lawn with a bucket of golf balls and take his driver and one after another hit those golf balls into the water."

Robinson sat up. His eyes grew merry. "The golf balls were white," he said.

"We wanted this house," Rachel said. "We lived in St. Albans, a mixed neighborhood in Queens, but we wanted something more and we began to look, and there were more humiliations, although, by this time, it was almost the mid-fifties. We answered ads for some places around Greenwich. When the brokers saw us, the houses turned out to be just sold or no longer on the market, phrases like that. The brokers said they themselves didn't object. It was always other people. The Bridgeport *Herald* got wind of the trouble and wrote it up and then a committee was formed in Stamford with ministers and Andrea Simon, the wife of

Dick Simon of Simon and Schuster. They asked what we wanted. We said view, privacy, water. They lined up a broker with six places. The first five houses were all bad for different reasons. Then we saw this site. It had"—Rachel smiled—"view, privacy, water.

"But we weren't done with it. We had to find a builder, and some banks up here were dead set against us."

Robinson had reclined again. "We lower real estate values," he said.

"The banks had power over the builders," Rachel said. "They could stop credit. But finally we found one builder, Ben Gunner, a bank operated by two Jewish brothers, and they'd take the chance. Ben Gunner and I used to sit out and watch the water and talk and one day I told him I'd always wanted a fireplace for the bedroom. To surprise me, he built one. Then Ben thought children should have a secret staircase. He put one in, and a firemen's pole for Jackie to slide down and so many extra things, for which he didn't charge, he may have gone broke building this house for us. Nothing shakes it."

"And in this neighborhood," Robinson said, "real estate values go up every year."

"I'll get strawberries and cream," Rachel said. "Would everybody like strawberries and cream?"

The unshakable house was a pivot to their lives. Rachel enrolled at NYU and in 1957 took a master's degree in psychiatric nursing. From Stamford she commutes to New Haven, where she is assistant professor of psychiatric nursing at Yale's graduate nursing school. Jack commutes the other way.

Over strawberries, he said, "The baseball years seem very long ago. When I quit, I went into the NAACP, and the conservatives found me hard to take. They were men of eighty. Their attitude was: don't rock the boat. Today militants find me hard to take. Their attitude is: burn everything. But I haven't changed much. The times have changed around me. Now we're coming to the black-black confrontation, extreme against moderate. After that the rough one, black and white. Blacks aren't scared any more. If the Klan walked into a black neighborhood now, the people would rip the sheets right off them.

"Only the President of the United States can cool things, if anything or anybody can, and we have a President who surrounds himself with Mitchell and Agnew. Why the hell didn't he make Mitchell Secretary of State?"

"World War III."

Robinson grinned slightly. "Well, anyway, you see, the baseball years and the baseball experience not only seem long ago, they were long ago."

"But you're more proud of it than anything."

"Sure. No pitcher ever made me back up. *No one.* And they all tried. Near the end Sam Jones—you remember him with that big sidearm stuff—brushed me and I got up and hit the hell out of his curve."

"I'm not proud just that he performed with excellence on the field," Rachel said. "I'm proud that as a man he had integrity and strength." She paused. "Remember, don't let him fool you. When I hear him talk about it to others, it always seems less devastating than it was."

It grew late. The time was dusk. Near the door he showed me a box of candy. "I used to buy chocolates for Rachel when we were courting," he said.

"It's been nice talking again, hasn't it?" Rachel said.

"I'll try not to hit nerves writing about Jack Junior."

"Oh," Rachel said. "Don't concern yourself. Every nerve has been hit already." Then, "How are the other wives you've seen?"

"Well, Betty Erskine has her hands full with their boy. Dottie Reese seems to be bowling a lot."

"See," Rachel said to Jack. "What would you rather have me doing, bowling or working? A working wife isn't the worst thing."

He grinned a private grin and they exchanged soft looks as men and women do when there is love and respect and vintage between them.

*     *     *

We visited again, late in a cool wet May, this time by day and with our children. He had more questions now than before. How was Carl Erskine? He had enjoyed playing on the same team with him. Labine? Had Preacher really put on weight?

Rachel was away, and "Jackie got himself in a scrape last night in New Haven," Robinson said. "He's in bad neighbor-hoods working with addicts and it caught up with him. Someone hit him with a board and split his forehead. They woke me, New Haven Hospital, at 6 A.M. I've got to drive there and pick him up a little later." Then Robinson was talking to my children, who warmed to this large gentle man.

When Robinson found the older boy wanted to become an architect, he showed him something of how the house was built. My younger son wanted to fish. Robinson found him a pole and baited the hook and pointed out a rock. "That's the best place to fish from." He was playing peekaboo with my three-year-old daughter when the time came for him to leave. "You and the chil-dren stay," he pleaded. "I wish Rachel could see them playing. That's what this house was built for, children."

We meant to drive off before father and injured son returned, but the children delayed us and we had just reached the station wagon when they drove up to the house. Jack Junior stepped out of his father's car slowly and turned so that his back was toward us. "Say hello," Jackie said. "It's all right." The young man had a strong straight body. He turned. He wore a beard. Bandages covered the forehead.

He started unsteadily toward the house, resting on his father's arm. I called, "My wife can drive our kids home, Jack. Let me give you a hand."

Robinson put an arm around Jack Junior, and said softly, tender as Stephen Kumalo, the umfundisi, "No. Thank you. It's all right. I can take care of my son."

The death facts may be stated simply. On June 17, 1971, at about 2:30 A.M., Jackie Robinson, Jr., twenty-four, was found dead in the wreck of a yellow MG. He had driven off the Merritt Parkway at such high speed that the car, which belonged to his brother David, demolished four wooden guard posts. One door came to rest 117 feet distant from the chassis, which looked like a toy car, bent double by the hammer of a petulant child. Police theorized that death was instantaneous. The coroner fixed the cause as a broken neck. David Robinson identified the car and his brother's body. Jackie broke the news to Rachel.

People at Daytop believe that young Jackie fell asleep behind the wheel. He had been organizing a benefit jazz festival, which was indeed held, but as a memorial. "Jackie was putting in very long hours," says Jimmy DeJohn of Daytop. "He just must have got exhausted."

The body lay in an open coffin, among floral wreaths. The family had chosen Antioch Baptist church in Brooklyn for the funeral, and June 21, the day of the services, broke with oppressive heat. Mourners crowded the church and sat beating fans.

*"In Memoriam,"* said the program. *"Jack Roosevelt Robinson, Jr., 1946–1971."* I looked up. An open coffin downs hard and when we heard my wife gasp, Al Silverman, the editor of *Sport*, and I made heavy funeral gossip. There was Hugh Morrow from Nelson Rockefeller's office. There was Don Newcombe. There was Monte Irvin, the glorious old Giant outfielder. But the coffin was open. No chattering could obscure that for long and I looked at the leonine head of the young man newly dead. His beard was trimmed. For an instant I allowed myself to think of what lay locked within the skull, Gibran and Herbie Mann and the old colored taxi at Vero Beach and night patrols near Pleiku and the narcosis of heroin and the shock of withdrawal and a father's tender voice. And then I would not let myself think like that any more.

The family was escorted to their pew at 1:15. Rachel was clinging to another of her children. Two men had to help Jack walk. He was crying very softly for his son, his head down, so that the tears coursed only a little way before falling to the floor.

A small chorus from Daytop sang "Bridge over Troubled Water" and "Swing Low, Sweet Chariot." A solo flutist played "We Shall Overcome." One is prepared for music at funerals, but then something happened that surprised everyone: Monte Irvin, Hugh Morrow, the people of the parish, who had known the Robinsons twenty-five years ago as neighbors. David Robinson, who was nineteen, walked to the pulpit and read a eulogy. David had written it in a single afternoon and while riding to church that morning had asked his father if he could speak it.

"If you want to," Jackie Robinson said.

"He climbed high on the cliffs above the sea," David called in a resonant tenor, "and stripped bare his shoulders and raised his arms to the water, crying, 'I am a man. Give me my freedom so that I might dance naked in the moonlight and laugh with the stars and roll in the grass and drink the warmth of the sun. Give me my freedom so I might fly.' But the armies of the sea continued to war with the wind and the wind raced through the giants of stones and mocked his cries, and the man fell to his knees and wept."

David wore a dashiki. He had finished his freshman year at Stanford. Soon he would travel through Africa. Jackie Junior had intended to buy the yellow MG and help David to a stake.

"He rose," David's voice called from the pulpit, "and journeyed down the mountain to the valley and came upon a village. When the people saw him, they scorned him for his naked shoulders and wild eyes and again he cried, 'I am a man. I seek the means of freedom.'

"The people laughed, saying, 'We see no chains on your arms. Go. You are free.' And they called him mad and drove him from their village. . . ." The man walked on, "eyes red as a gladiator's sword," until he came to a stream where he saw an image, face sunken in hunger, "skin drawn tight around the body.

"He stood fixed on the water's edge and began to weep, not from sorrow but from joy, for he saw beauty in the water. He removed his clothing and stood naked before the world and rose to his full height and smiled and moved to meet the figure in the water and the stream made love to his body and the majesty of his voice was heard above the roar of the sea and the howl of the wind, *and he was free*."

David hurried from the pulpit. His mother rose to embrace him. Sobs rang through the old church; it was five minutes before formal worship resumed. But even as our small group drove back to New York, wondering how to make memorial, we had seen Jackie Robinson after the services, white-haired, dry-eyed and sure, as when he doubled home two runs, walking among street people outside the church, talking perhaps of the hell of heroin, touching or being touched by children, and we thought how proud his first-born son would have been, not of the ball player but of the man, had he lived, if only the insanity of the present had given him a chance.

# THOUSANDS MOURN JACKIE ROBINSON

## New York Amsterdam News
### (November 4, 1972)

*O*n October 15, 1972, major league baseball commemo-rated the twenty-fifth anniversary of Jackie Robinson's rookie season. Robinson, who had boycotted baseball events for many years to protest its poor record on minority hiring, consented to throw out the first pitch before the second World Series game between the Cincinnati Reds and the Oakland A's. His evident physical deterioration shocked those who saw him. Nonetheless, he retained his combative spirit. Speaking before a national television audience, Robinson chastised baseball management. While he was pleased to be at the ceremony, he proclaimed, "I will be more pleased the day I can look over at the third base line and see a black man as manager."

Nine days later, a fatal heart attack felled Robinson at the age of fifty-three. The Robinson family selected Reverend Jesse Jackson, then a thirty-one-year-old minister and civil rights leader, to deliver the eulogy at Robinson's funeral in Harlem. The following article from the New York Amsterdam News describes

*the scene at Robinson's funeral and Jackson's inspirational
farewell to an American hero.*

● ● ● ● ● ● ●

Americans of varied races, creeds, ages and status, paid their
last respects to Jackie Robinson, Friday, as the farewell service
for the fallen hero was held at the Riverside Church, 122nd St.
and Riverside Drive.

His historic achievements had not merely placed him in the
Hall of Fame but more than anything else before the civil rights
decade, had moved America forward toward the practice of
democracy.

So, insulated by sorrow from the polarization separating
their groups beyond the granite walls of the Gothic church, some
3000 persons fused together into an all-American potpourri in
tribute to the man who had captured the hearts of millions from
the baseball diamond.

"Today we must balance the tears of sorrow with tears of
joy," said the Rev. Jesse Jackson, founder and president of
PUSH—People United To Save Humanity. He had come from
Chicago to preach at the funeral.

There were tears indeed. Tears as the mourners passed the
open coffin before the service began; tears as Rev. Jackson and
Rev. Wyatt Tee Walker led some family members to a last look
and shrill cries rang out from the group.

Tears, too, as the congregation stood and turned while the
Rev. Ernest T. Campbell led the widow in the processional, to the
front seat, while he chanted "I am the resurrection and the life,
says the Lord . . ."

"When Jackie took the field," Rev. Jackson said, "something
reminded us of our birthright to be free.

"He didn't integrate baseball for himself. He infiltrated it for
all of us. His body was a temple of God, but his mind found no
peace in wickedness. His powerful arms lifted not only bats but
barriers," Jackson said. So "let us mix the bitter with the sweet."

A man of courage and strength, Jackie had met insults and

suffered in silence so as to have the chance to open opportunities for the Black man in the sports arena.

Yet, said Jackson, "Jackie was neither a puppet of God nor one of other men. Progress does not roll in on the wheels of inevitability. In order for an ideal to become a reality, there must be a person, a personality to translate it.

"He had options. He didn't have to do what he did. History calls on all of us to do something, but we are not always at home. He said 'yes' in 1947 when he wanted to say 'no.' He could not hold out for himself. He had to hold up for us."

And in saying "yes" Jackie became "a co-partner of God." Like a doctor "immunized by God from catching the diseases he fought" Jackie fought "for Blacks to get hope and whites concern."

"The universe is dependent on person and personality to transport deliverance," Jackson said. "Jackie Robinson was a balm in Gilead in America, in Ebbets Field. Hebrews needed a Moses. Indians needed a Gandhi. Science needed a Louis Pasteur . . . We needed a Jackie Robinson."

He said "yes" in 1947 and "pride in the Black community welled up when he took the field. He reminded us of our birthright to be free. He created ripples of possibility" which "seven years later the Supreme Court decision confirmed."

"For a fleeting moment," Jackson stated, "America tried democracy and it worked. For a fleeting moment, America became one nation under God. This man turned the stumbling block into a stepping stone."

Like life-giving "oxygen," Jackie "infiltrated baseball for us"; thought he could "bring justice into business but quit because he found no peace in wickedness." He was "an instrument of peace," "marched in Birmingham, Alabama," "castigated" the power structure.

He accepted the honor of Baseball Hall of Fame and no higher monument can be named for him than by "naming Blacks as managers. Anything else would be a form of idolatry," said Jackson.

Like the graves of those who had gone before, Jackie's would bear his birth date and his death date: 1919–1972. "We can't determine our birth date," Rev. Jackson said. "We seldom know our death date. But on that dash," between those two dates, "is where we live."

"And for everyone, there is a dash of possibility, to choose the high road or the low road; to make things better or to make things worse. On that dash, he snapped the barbed wire of prejudice," Jackson stated, he brought the "gift of new expectations on that dash."

"His feet danced on the base-paths," Jackson went on. "But it was more than a game." And a woman's voice said, "Yes, it was."

"Jackie began playing a chess game. He was the Black knight and he check-mated bigotry." "Yes, sir, all right, go ahead," the voice replied.

"In his last dash, Jackie stole home and Jackie is safe," the preacher said. "His enemies can rest assured of that." "Yes they can," she rejoined.

And Jackson ended: "Call me nigger, call me black boy. I don't care. I told Jesus it will be all right if I change my name.

"No grave can hold this body down because it belongs to the ages; and all of us are better off because the man with that body, the man with that soul and mission, passed this way."

Then Roberta Flack sang the traditional Negro spiritual, "I told Jesus it will be all right if I change my name." Rev. Campbell gave the benediction with the words "Go forth to your God in peace"; and the journey to Jackie Robinson's last resting place in Brooklyn's Cypress Hills cemetery began.

# APPENDIX
# JACKIE ROBINSON'S BASEBALL CAREER

**Jack Roosevelt "Jackie" Robinson. Born January 31, 1919, at Cairo, GA. Died October 24, 1972, in Stamford, CT. 5'11 ¹/₂", 195 lbs. BR TR**

| Year | Club | League | Pos | G | AB | R | H | 2B | 3B | HR | RBI | SB | BA |
|------|------|--------|-----|---|----|----|----|----|----|----|-----|----|----|
| 1945 | Kansas City | NAL | SS | 47 | 163 | 36 | 63 | 14 | 4 | 5 | 23 | 13 | .387 |
| 1946 | Montreal | INT | 2B | 124 | 444 | 113 | 155 | 25 | 8 | 3 | 66 | 40 | .349 |
| 1947 | Brooklyn | NL | 1B | 151 | 590 | 125 | 175 | 31 | 5 | 12 | 48 | 29 | .297 |
| 1948 | Brooklyn | NL | 2B 1B 3B | 147 | 574 | 108 | 170 | 38 | 8 | 12 | 85 | 22 | .296 |
| 1949 | Brooklyn | NL | 2B | 156 | 593 | 122 | 203 | 38 | 12 | 16 | 124 | 37 | .342 |
| 1950 | Brooklyn | NL | 2B | 144 | 518 | 99 | 170 | 39 | 4 | 14 | 81 | 12 | .328 |
| 1951 | Brooklyn | NL | 2B | 153 | 548 | 106 | 185 | 33 | 7 | 19 | 88 | 25 | .338 |
| 1952 | Brooklyn | NL | 2B | 149 | 510 | 104 | 157 | 17 | 3 | 19 | 75 | 24 | .308 |
| 1953 | Brooklyn | NL | INF OF | 136 | 484 | 109 | 159 | 34 | 7 | 12 | 95 | 17 | .329 |
| 1954 | Brooklyn | NL | INF OF | 124 | 386 | 62 | 120 | 22 | 4 | 15 | 59 | 7 | .311 |
| 1955 | Brooklyn | NL | INF OF | 105 | 317 | 51 | 81 | 6 | 2 | 8 | 36 | 12 | .256 |
| 1956 | Brooklyn | NL | INF OF | 117 | 357 | 61 | 98 | 15 | 2 | 10 | 43 | 12 | .275 |

Major League Totals · 1553 · 5484 · 1096 · 1736 · 312 · 66 · 145 · 823 · 250 · .317

## WORLD SERIES RECORD

| Year | Club | League | Pos | G | AB | R | H | 2B | 3B | HR | RBI | BA |
|------|------|--------|-----|---|----|---|---|----|----|----|-----|----|
| 1947 | Brooklyn | Nat. | 1B | 7 | 27 | 3 | 7 | 2 | 0 | 0 | 3 | .259 |
| 1949 | Brooklyn | Nat. | 2B | 5 | 16 | 2 | 3 | 1 | 0 | 0 | 2 | .188 |
| 1952 | Brooklyn | Nat. | 2B | 7 | 23 | 4 | 4 | 0 | 0 | 1 | 2 | .174 |
| 1953 | Brooklyn | Nat. | OF | 6 | 25 | 3 | 8 | 2 | 0 | 0 | 2 | .320 |
| 1955 | Brooklyn | Nat. | 3B | 6 | 22 | 5 | 4 | 1 | 1 | 0 | 1 | .182 |
| 1956 | Brooklyn | Nat. | 3B | 7 | 24 | 5 | 6 | 1 | 0 | 1 | 2 | .250 |

World Series Totals · 38 · 137 · 22 · 32 · 7 · 1 · 2 · 12 · .234

Led National League in stolen bases (39) 1947 and (37) 1949; hit for cycle (first game) August 29, 1948; led second basemen in double plays 1949 through 1952.

World Series Records—Tied record for assists by second baseman in one inning (3); seventh inning, October 8, 1949; tied for mark by getting four bases on balls in a game October 5, 1952. One of 12 players to steal home in a World Series game, accomplishing feat in first game, eighth inning, September 28, 1955.

Named by THE SPORTING NEWS as Rookie of the Year, 1947.

Named as second baseman on THE SPORTING NEWS All-Star Major League Teams, 1949-50-51-52.

Named Most Valuable Player, National League, 1949.

Named to Hall of Fame, 1962.

(This constitutes an extension of the copyright page.)